PRAISE FOR *ORANGES FOR MAGELLAN*

"Reading *Oranges for Magellan* was a wild experience for me. This is Los Angeles in the early 1980s, and author Richard Martin animates that city with often exaggerated details that make the book come alive. The main characters—flagpole sitter Joe, his wife Clover, and son Nate—are flawed to the bone, but that's their beauty, their depth. They lie, they tell the truth, they suffer behind their masks. There's as much humor as sorrow in this story—in the dialogue, the relationships, the outrageous events—and most of the time the two are merged. As I was reading I had no idea what was going to happen next or how the book would end. The writing is as visual as watching a film, and I loved every minute of it."

– Olivia Dresher, author of *A Silence of Words* and editor of *In Pieces: An Anthology of Fragmentary Writing*

"Not many storytellers would have the courage or imagination to attempt a novel about a failed flagpole sitter, and even fewer would have the chops to bring it off. But I now know there is at least one such writer, and his name is Richard Martin. His *Oranges for Magellan* is a madly lyrical romp of a tale, told with great authority and populated with characters you won't easily forget, especially the self-doubting but big-hearted flagpole sitter himself, a reluctant hero you'll want to hang with until the tender and redemptive end. Highly recommended!"

– Jim Nichols, author of *Blue Summer*, winner of the 2021 Maine Book Award for Fiction

"In his wonderful debut novel, *Oranges for Magellan*, Richard Martin has created a marvelously comic yet profound quest tale for our times. The hero is Joseph Galileo Magellan, a burnt-out substitute teacher who journeys no farther than to the top of an orange flagpole in an attempt to break the world's record for flagpole sitting. As in all quest stories, there are helpers and tricksters, temptations and obstacles, including the interior ones of self-doubt and guilt. The novel shimmers with vivid images, brilliant allusions, and a free-flowing play of thought, emotion, and paradoxical action within inaction. Thought-provoking and hilarious, intelligent and moving, *Oranges for Magellan* will speak deeply to anyone who has ever felt driven to do something difficult, however absurd or seemingly impossible. To anyone who tries, fails, and tries again. And to those who accommodate a loved one's passionate pursuit. In short, it speaks to our humanity. I loved every page."

– Joanna Higgins, author of *A Soldier's Book, A Novel of the Civil War; Dead Center,* and other novels.

"*Oranges for Magellan* tickles and enchants from page one, an underdog tale doubling as a rollicking safari into the human heart and its mysteries. From a lively corner of crumbling Reagan-era Los Angeles, Richard Martin's diverse cast of lovably flawed misfits explores the weirdest corners of our universal experience, asking: Are we crazy to love who we love, to need what we need? The world needs Martin's voice—wise and funny, determinedly unjaded, a scalpel paring away the unnecessary to reveal all that's sacred and marvelous in the humblest endeavors."

– Brendan McKennedy, former fiction editor at *Greensboro Review*

ORANGES FOR MAGELLAN

Richard Martin

Regal House Publishing

Published by
Regal House Publishing, LLC
Raleigh, NC 27612
All rights reserved

ISBN -13 (paperback): 9781646032686
ISBN -13 (epub): 9781646032693
Library of Congress Control Number: 2021950593

Cover images © by C.B. Royal

Credits for fictional works quoted that are within public domain:
Anonymous, *The Cloud of Unknowing* (John M. Watkins, 1922).
F. Scott Fitzgerald, *The Great Gatsby* (Charles Scribner's Sons, 1925).
Henry James, *The Portrait of A Lady* (Macmillan, 1881).
Franz Kafka, *The Castle* (Kurt Wolff, 1926).
Alfred, Lord Tennyson, "Saint Simeon Stylites," in *Poems* (Edward Moxon, 1842).

Regal House Publishing, LLC
https://regalhousepublishing.com

The following is a work of fiction created by the author. All names, individuals, characters, places, items, brands, events, etc. were either the product of the author or were used fictitiously. Any name, place, event, person, brand, or item, current or past, is entirely coincidental.

Printed in the United States of America

to Paris

PART I

"The earth is round, like an orange."

—Gabriel García Márquez, *One Hundred Years of Solitude*

1

JOE

I cracked the New Freedom's double doors and we Magellans slipped inside. The doors latched behind us like a nail gun. Half the crowd turned and scowled. Dr. Malcolm Kerridge, busy at the podium with one of his wretched graduates, paused to greet me. "Joe! Welcome! Ladies and gentlemen—Joe Magellan, late as always!"

I waved to the sullen mob. Kerridge resumed his business onstage.

"Good Lord, that sign," Clover whispered.

High above the two men an enormous purple banner with gold letters proclaimed:

DR. MALCOLM KERRIDGE'S
OUT, DAMN OBSESSION!
SEMINAR GRADUATION NIGHT

I pointed Clover and Nate to two empty seats. "I have to sit up front."

Clover kissed me, then wiped my mouth with her thumb. "Remember what happened when Raskolnikov got everything off his chest. He had a revelation."

"And then they hung him," I said.

"Shh!" from the crowd.

I looked in Clover's eyes. So moved was she by what was taking place, by what I was doing for her. For myself, yes, and for Nate, but primarily for her. All she wanted was the normal life. Was that so terrible? After everything she'd endured—drinking, the accident, the year in Frontera, bearing and raising Nate—I go and inflict these dreadful years of obsession upon her.

I tottered down the aisle. Kerridge and Jerry, Jerry the debaucher, watched a video loop on a giant monitor: Jerry running down an alley chased by three furious women, one in a wedding dress, one in a sweatsuit, one wielding a garden rake.

I searched for my seat among the other graduates, half of whom already clutched red-beribboned sheaves of parchment. One young woman, Carmen, a pathological liar, gave my hand a particular squeeze. I could have used an innocent flirtation during those twelve tortuous weekends, but that woman had disaster scrawled on her from head to foot.

The other male graduates sat spiffed out in tuxedos. I was a clown in green corduroy, my only suit. A goodly chunk of us had agreed beforehand to forego tuxes, to demonstrate our liberation from both Kerridge and our obsessions, but push came to shove and I stood alone in defiance.

I found my seat and namecard:

Joseph Magellan,
Ex-Flagpole-Sitter

When my turn came I would march across that stage like I owned it, grab my diploma, swallow failure like a handful of stinkbugs, and to hell with the whole damn thing.

The video froze and the philanderer slumped at the podium.

"Jerry," Dr. Kerridge said. "Look at me. No more tears of shame. You are cured, my friend."

"I couldn't have done it without you, Dr. Kerridge."

Kerridge handed Jerry his diploma and enfolded him in a solemn embrace. The audience cheered and the band jauntied into "Did You Ever Have to Make Up Your Mind?" Jerry made his way offstage, eyeing the audience for his next quest, if you asked me.

Each weekend Kerridge had assaulted our fixations from a different angle, a different school, from group Freudian therapy to Erhard to Esalen to behavior mod to Lifespring to Primal Scream to God knew what, Amway. I didn't care if his buffet onslaught was genius or scam. It might not have worked on Jerry, but it had worked on me because I was sick unto death of both my obsession and my failure to fulfill it.

Kerridge leaned into the mic: *"Betsy...Abigail...Gilden."* The crowd roared as Betsy, a plain, sprightly woman in her 20s, sporting a basic training haircut, leapt out of her front row seat and bounded to the podium.

"Thank you, Dr. Kerridge," Betsy said, "and good evening to my fellow co-ex-obsessives and our friends and families who have always known us so much better than we could ever know our own obsessed selves."

Clover shouted, "Amen!" Cold sweat broke on my scalp, feet, and scrotum.

On the video screen an astoundingly long-haired Betsy appeared, nude as Eve, in a vacant public park, cavorting with her back to the camera, laughing over her shoulder, haughty then shy in alternating glances, her nakedness covered only by a magnificent blonde mane which sashayed down like sunlight within inches of the bright green grass. The audience oohed and ahhed as Betsy frolicked behind that luxurious hair, behind a tree, behind a sheer scarf, now coy, now shocked at her own coyness, spinning amidst the bounty of her splendid locks. As the video ended, Betsy stepped back to the mic and asked forlornly, "Is that an obsession, or what?"

"Oh yes!" Nate hollered from the back.

"It all started," Betsy said, "when I was a little girl and I saw my first Breck commercial. The way the light played on the lady's glorious hair. And the way the handsome man watched, enchanted. By the time I was twenty, I *was* my hair. Oh, it captivated boys and men all right—but as soon as I had one, I wanted another. It wasn't the men themselves, but the look on their faces as they lost themselves in my hair. I was like a black widow with golden hair. In the end, a small nation could have armed itself with what I spent on my pride and—" Betsy dreamily touched her cropped head; her hand jumped as if brushing a live wire. She glanced at Kerridge. "But now I'm cured. Thank you, my dear Doctor. I love you. You and your blessèd 'Out, Damn Obsession!' Seminar."

Kerridge gave Betsy her diploma and a hug, the crowd erupted happily, the band played "Hair," and Betsy sprang down the steps waving and grinning.

Kerridge stepped to the mic: "*Joseph...Galileo...Magellan.*"

Of my own free will, I locomoted to the podium to stick my head into Kerridge's spiritual guillotine. Through the glare of the spotlight, the auditorium appeared packed with hungry ghouls. "Hi," I muttered, too near the mic, "I'm Joe Magellan, a flagpole—" and feedback shriek blitzed the room. I backed away and tried again. "I'm a flagpole-sitter."

"*Was*," Kerridge corrected. He snapped his fingers.

On the giant screen appeared a silent, grainy, color home movie of a brown-haired boy on a slab of plywood perched precariously in an orange tree laden with radiant fruit.

I peered at the back row. "Where'd you find that?" Clover poked through her purse; Nate stared slack-jawed at the screen.

My blood stirred at the old film, at young me in that miserable tree, lobbing oranges at the camera.

"My mother's filming this," I said. "Way back when. That's the grove across from our duplex in West Covina. We moved there when my father died. Oranges far as you could see. I rigged up that ramshackle gizmo at the top. Wired it to the branches. Sawed a hole in the middle to climb through. It was like a raft ready to go over the falls. God knows how it stayed up. Took up peanut butter and jelly sandwiches after school. Hid from church up there. Read like a fiend. Twain, Fredric Brown, *Humbug*, Salinger. *Alfred Hitchcock's Mystery Magazine,* Kerouac, Harold Robbins, D.T. Suzuki, everything. I watched the world float by below. Up there you forget where you are."

"Let's not forget where we are up here," Kerridge said.

I looked through the audience into the past. "I was so happy up there, first time I went up. I ate so many oranges I vomited, right over the edge."

"Charming," Kerridge said.

"Never ate another orange."

The film ran out. The blinding screen snapped me back. I addressed my fellow obsessives in the front rows: "You know what I'm talking about. That wild drive inside. It *summons* you. 'Get up here and sit. Don't ask why.' You resist, you fight it, you beat it down—it comes back wilder than ever."

Kerridge smacked his hand with my diploma.

"I made eleven days on a flagpole in Bend. Nine in Durango. Not much? Try it sometime." I returned Kerridge's glare. "And a *flagpole* is *not* a *penis*." The crowd rustled like a thousand petticoats. "There's no mumbo-jumbo up there. Malcolm doesn't want to hear this, but truth is a mystery. The beautiful, inexplicable truth, ladies and gentlemen."

Kerridge tapped his watch.

"I didn't go up because I hated people. I didn't go up because I was an only child. And it wasn't the war. I was only over there two weeks. They stuck me up a tree with a sniper and a spotter. The spotter's apprentice, that was me. First time up. We're in a small blind, high in a hickory tree. Nothing's happening, so I pull *Crime and Punishment* out of my pack, get a little reading in, and Dostoevsky flies out of my hands like a crazy bird. Some son-of-a-bitch took a shot at us. Never heard a sound. Blood's pouring down my face. I wasn't hit, it was a *nosebleed*. From the heat, homesickness, terror. I kept them going, tried to get a medical out, shoved a bullet up my nose, scraped it around. They transferred me to peaceful, snowy Germany. Good for nosebleeds. Eighteen months later, I'm back in the USA, a free man. And then it happened and my life changed."

Clover whispered to Nate.

"I read a story in the paper about this old bum named Shipwreck Blake." Clover slumped. "He was a flagpole-sitter," I said, "just down from a pole in Saint Cloud, Minnesota, with the *modern world record*. The pieces of the puzzle fell into place—the orange trees, the jungle blind, now this. I had a hero, a calling: I was a flagpole-sitter. Then Shipwreck my so-called hero drives me off every last damn pole!"

Kerridge grabbed for the mic. I shouldered him aside.

"But now I'm *cured*. Hip, hip, hooray!"

I grabbed the diploma from Kerridge, stomped off the stage and steamed up the aisle.

"Joe Magellan," Kerridge growled into the mic, "living proof my methods work on anybody. Joe, nice suit!" He pointed at the band and it broke into "Sittin' on the Dock of the Bay."

I bashed through the doors and strode across the lot, tearing off my tie and nitwit corduroy coat as Clover and Nate scurried to keep up.

"I never heard barely any of that stuff," Nate said. "Beautiful, splick-able truth hurts, man. Hey, Mom, next to some dork with three wifes, Dad's thing is peanuts."

"I'll peanuts you," said Clover.

I yanked open the Bug's door.

"Yihhhh!" Nate squealed.

An old Black hobo in the backseat, in a bandana hat and layers of rags, exploded awake and leapt out, taking eerily spry flight across the lot.

"Catch him, Dad!"

"Don't you dare!" Clover grabbed my arm.

I looked the backseat over. "Jesus Christ." I sniffed the air. "*Cologne?*"

"Didn't we lock it? Let's just go. I'll disinfect tomorrow. Oh, my God."

I stuffed the diploma under the seat and we tore out of the lot. In my imagination I turned the car around, plowed through the double-doors, jumped out, stormed the stage and jammed that diploma down Kerridge's throat, red ribbon and all.

"A homeless guy was in our car," said Nate, looking at the seat beside him. "A homeless guy, right here."

2

CLOVER

Joe turned away, rose from the bed, entered the bathroom, got the shower going. I lay there, exhausted, frustrated, worried, touching myself.

"Clover!"

I got up. Steam filled the bathroom. "What?"

He held the soap out. "What is this?"

"Soap. Oat soap."

"*Oats?* It's got no suds. Where's my Ivory?"

"With all the excitement, I didn't get to the store."

"You couldn't wash a *hamster* with this."

I stepped into the shower. "Jesus, it's scalding!" I turned the hot down.

"What genius dreamed up oat soap? Why not a bar of *wood?*"

I took it, worked up a lather, turned him and washed his back.

"Harder. Use the washrag."

Tenderly, with my bare hands, I washed his back. He braced against the stall, resisting my mercy, resisting his own body. It felt like wings in there straining to burst forth. I knew why he'd kept going up. I knew a rottenness was afoot in the world. Plenty to rage about and weep and gnash and climb flagpoles over. I knew the temptation to despair, to believe in nothing. I could have gone either way inside, but I patchworked my own God in there, trudged toward the light, served my nine months, walked out vowing to make up for what I'd done, to help somebody. When I heard him at that poetry reading I knew he was the one—his natural male existentialism, that alienation, lostness, literally no sense of direction, his whole dire outlook, the perfect somebody to help, yes, to love—and though it had been one aimless, sloppy, self-sacrificing mess of a marriage, here we were thirteen years later, on the verge, at last, of a blessedly ordinary life. He'd done it, by God, given it up, and I knew the cost. His obsession was gone, but it itched still, a ghost limb. That gangrenous protuberance had been killing him dead, killing all of us, and I hated it with a passion, but he missed it a little some yet, longed against his will, and I understood, I felt it, those angry furled wings, I understood.

I turned him and washed his chest. He bowed his head. I put my arms around him, held him tight, and he responded. Kissing, stepping out, drying each other haphazardly, we lunged to bed, and the day in the future called to me on which we would look back at the flagpole years and smile fondly, maybe even laugh, far from the anguish of this night, and free.

3

JOE

The next morning we cruised along in the slow lane of the Golden State Freeway in our orange Bug.

"Couldn't we stop and get another Walkman somewhere?" said Nate.

"You shouldn't have lost it," I said.

"I didn't lose it, I just couldn't find it."

Clover said, "Play the license game."

"They're going too fast. We're sitting here like a turtle."

"Pal, relax. Think about things."

"What things?"

"Life."

"What about it?"

"What it means."

"Hasn't nobody found out?"

"Anybody," said Clover.

"That's the point," I said, "find out for yourself."

"Aren't I suppose to just enjoy my childhood?"

"Who told you that?" I said.

Clover kneaded my chest muscles. I breathed in the peach scent of her hand lotion. "Are you excited at all?" she said. "About applying to schools?"

Excited about force-feeding *Pilgrim's Progress* to those juvenile delinquents for the next twenty years?

"You were born to teach. Your father was a teacher and you're his son. You have no *idea* what you can do. You could inspire a generation. I know you better than you know yourself, like that woman with the hair said. What a gorgeous head of hair she has. Had. What would you think if I had hair like that?"

"I love your hair the way it is."

She tousled her short red cut. "Maybe I'll let it grow."

"It'll grow faster than we're going right now," Nate said.

"You need to get off substitute status," Clover said. "Implement your own technique."

I laughed. "What own technique?"

"You'd come up with one if we stayed put somewhere. You already have a style, a flair. You just need to wrap it around a solid frame. When we met, you talked about books like they were magic spells. You had me eating out of your hand. You could have those kids eating out of your hand. Like D. H. Lawrence with his crazy passion—" (I was no particular fan of the flamboyant Lawrence) "—and Poe with the dead man's heart pounding away—" (If I had to teach "Tell-Tale Heart" one more time I'd stuff my *own* body in the floor) "—and don't forget Nate's namesake" (mercifully, I had never had to teach the great Hawthorne to those quacking hoodlums).

"Nathaniel Hawthorne sucks," Nate muttered.

"Watch it, pal."

"You have a wonderful name," Clover said.

"Yeah, if I was a sissy in short pants and a bowtie. I'm changing my name the day I turn eighteen. When I'm eighteen, I'll do whatever I want."

"Until that happy day," Clover said, then to me: "If you wanted to, you could turn them all into poets and novelists overnight. We just need to land you a permanent position at a fine school."

"With strong cages."

"That's the spirit."

Teaching was purgatory. A mere substitute, I had no time to connect with the students. We were mutually suspicious. I never got comfortable enough to shine. They honed in like anxiety-seeking missiles. Their wolf ears perked at each catch in my voice, wolf eyes dilated at every twitch of my mouth, leap of blood in my throat. Then I'd overcompensate with a prowling aggressiveness, assigning, for example, absurd classroom essays, such as one on the origin of the feud between the Shepherdsons and the Grangerfords in *Huckleberry Finn*, when Twain's very point was that there was no origin to the feud at all. It was no adventure in learning; it was trench warfare. The quixotic passion that drove me to teach had been ground up and the even more absurd dream of flagpole-sitting grew from the ruins, like a cuckoo taking over the nest and beaking the legitimate baby out to die. In ten years I had substituted at seven different high schools, working long enough to save the minimum to see us through another flagpole flop.

"Has anybody died from being bored to death?" said Nate.

"Would you like to be the first?" Clover said. "Enjoy the scenery."

The boy peered out at the train of gray shrubbery passing. "Those bushes look like rubber."

Clover looked at me, then away. "I've been thinking about painting again."

"Good. That's wonderful. You should."

"I miss it."

"Well, you're an excellent artist. I love your paintings."

"Which one's your favorite?"

"Which painting? You have a lot."

"No favorite leaps to mind?"

I picked the first one I could think of. "The one with the balloons? *Red Balloons?*"

"*Red Balloons? Faces in a Crowd*, you mean?"

"*Faces in a Crowd*, yeah. I love that one."

"*Red Balloons?*"

"I got the name wrong. I haven't seen it in a while."

Nate hung his head like a dog between the seats. "Could I listen to the radio?"

"No," said Clover through her teeth.

"Like one song?"

"Please keep asking," said Clover, with tender menace.

Nate slumped back and a moment later: "Holy *shit*."

"*What* did you say?" said Clover.

The boy was looking out the rear window. "Yeah, but this Black guy in a Davy Crockett hat behind that sign looked just like that homeless guy in our car last night."

"All Black people and homeless people do not look the same. Turn around, sit down, and don't say holy anything. Here, I thought you could live without this contraption for a few hours, but apparently not." She pulled his Walkman from her purse and tossed it in the back seat.

"Are you kidding me!" Nate said. "You hid it! Low blow! Oh, Mom, low blow! Why'd you bring it if you thought I could live without it?"

"Oh, you want me to not have brought it?"

"No, I want you to not of hid it." He turned it on and began nodding and making phony cool faces as that stupid piña colada song leaked into the car. I turned on the radio to drown it out. Van Morrison's loping "Higher Than the World" came on. I sang along.

"Jeez, could you turn that down?" Nate said. "I can barely hear this."

"Red balloons," Clover expelled over the music. She looked sad as hell.

I turned Van down. "Honey."

"The red is *supposed* to represent people's self-consciousness. And the faces with no features show how people lose their identities in a crowd."

"That's why I love it. It's beautiful and tragic all at once. "

"Boy, I really feel like painting up a storm now."

The morning was clear and dry and the 5 ran north smooth as an arrow, but I held the wheel as if plowing a four-masted schooner through a monsoon. I was back on that graduation stage again, humiliated, furious: You don't graduate from yourself. You can't. You cannot.

"I hope you do start painting again," I said. "Be nice to have *somebody* following their heart around here."

I turned the radio back up; she turned it off and stared at me. "Let's say the prayer. Come on. Nate! Take those off! Prayer!"

"We said it before we left!" Nate said.

"It's free," Clover said, "we can say it as many times as we want."

Clover's religious ardor, dormant since her release from Frontera, had revived the day I enrolled in Kerridge's seminar. Since then she had nudged Nate and me into the Lord's Prayer at moments she deemed needful.

"I'm driving," I said.

Clover stared ahead. She said, "Despair is the only unforgivable sin against the Holy Spirit," and nodded.

"What?" I said. She took obvious pleasure in repeating the dark saying. "Who says?"

"The Bible."

I took a Bible as Literature course once. "I don't remember that."

"Oh, you don't remember it, it must not be in there."

I played it over in my head. "What's it mean exactly?"

"Figure it out, English teacher."

"Why'd you bring it up?"

"I can't imagine."

My life was not perfect, but even if it were, consider the world—the starving, raving, homeless, war-torn, heartbroken, puking, tortured, sleepwalking, screaming, pisspants world—how could any sentient being *not* despair? Human existence was tailor-made for despair, one pile-up of wrecked dreams after another, with respites of sweeping up the glass and hosing off the pavement. How, in such a world, could even the happiest creature be free from despair?

Clover turned the radio up. The news was on.

"The nation welcomes a new president and the hostages are in Germany celebrating freedom," the newsguy said.

"Wonderful!" Clover said.

"Yippee!" said Nate.

"Something fishy about that whole thing," I said.

"Instead of painting," Clover said, turning the news down, "I should go finish my degree in abnormal psychology so I can understand you."

"They struck some dirty deal to release them the second Ronnie got sworn in."

"What do you want them to do," Nate said, "go back and be hostages again?"

Clover said, "Oh, would I love to pursue some big, fancy, heart-following compulsion while somebody took care of my responsibilities back on earth. Like raising a ten-year-old child."

"Uh," Nate said, "I can hear you."

"Put that Walkman on," Clover said.

I managed to bite my tongue long enough for her to flip the radio dial and blast the poor dead John Lennon's "Starting Over" through the car, a hopeful, stirring, happy song which at that moment felt like clowns with tiger fingernails clawing at my future.

4

JOE

We puttered into the almost empty parking lot. A street-sweeper sailed over the asphalt like a barge, its captain hanging out the window, steering with one hand.

At a picnic table outside the entrance, we partook of one of Clover's tasty surprises—cold scrambled-egg-tomato-mustard-cilantro sandwiches. Afterward, Nate and Clover broke into a spontaneous game of tag, squealing around the tables.

What heartache I'd heaped upon this playful boy and this kind-souled woman. What a sadsack excuse for a father and husband I'd been. My flagpole-sitting was a selfishness of demonic proportions. The wasted years prowled my mind like wolves. But I had been liberated from that delirious vanity. In the morning sunlight sifting down, I was awakening from years of hibernation, waking to another chance.

I leaned back and gazed at a huddle of mighty chestnut trees on the fringe of the zoo. One appeared to be swaying more than the others, more than the graceful morning breeze might explain. I squinted—the sun burned behind the tree—and beheld a dark shape, an animal, an ape of some sort, which stuck its head from the foliage. The beast appeared to beckon with its dark paw, then sank back in the roiling chestnut grove.

"Dad!" Nate called. "They're opening up!"

❧

Stopping at the hippopotamus exhibit, we leaned over a railing polished by a million filthy hands and peered into the turbid water.

"Hey, hippo!" Nate said. "Make that fat old guy come up, Dad."

"Let him be."

"We paid to see him."

"I paid. Let him be."

The hippo exploded from the murk, emitted a single primordial groan, then disappeared again like a DeSoto into the swamp.

"Good Lord," Clover said.

"Come back up!" Nate hollered. "That was like two seconds."

"How'd you like it," I said, "if a bunch of hippopotamuses stole you from your home and dropped you in Africa with other hippos gawking and hollering at you?"

"Huh? Well, he shouldn'ta got caught. What a gyp."

"Don't say 'gyp,'" Clover said.

"Why not?"

"It's a derogatory term for a gypsy."

"How am I supposed to know that?"

"You know it now."

"But I said it to a hippopotamus."

Clover must have seen me gazing into the muck and shaking my head; she grabbed Nate's hand and pulled him down Buffalo Lane. The hippo poked its majestic head out of the bog, peered at me with understanding, flared its immense nostrils, and sank back into the gloom.

When she saw me coming, Clover pulled Nate from the buffalo exhibit and off to the camels and giraffes. She was giving everybody a little breathing room and I loved her for it.

Two mangy beasts sprawled in the dust of a pen. "Great American buffalo," I said. "Stand. Can you stand?" The apathetic beasts failed to stir, but for currents of muscular twitches where horseflies gnawed their flanks. "Arise," I whispered. One turned its massive face to me and blinked like a child, lost.

I joined Clover and Nate in front of the spider monkey cage. A dozen of the little simians cavorted for a growing crowd. One maniacal imp performed flips and twists and shrieked for the pleasure of the gathering. Clover smiled at a Japanese gentleman next to her. "I know what the animal lib folks say," she said, "but tell me that little guy isn't having the time of his life."

The gentleman nodded eagerly, tore off the end of his hot dog and started to pitch it at the star monkey. "Oops," Clover said, pointing at a sign:

DO <u>NOT</u> FEED ANIMALS!

THANK YOU!

The gentleman dropped the meat on the ground, Nate grabbed it and flipped it right over the sign, the monkey caught it, smelled it, made a face, and threw it back out, hitting me right in the forehead. The crowd went mad. The monkey went mad. I gripped the railing as if on a tossing sea. Nate slipped into the mob.

"You found a friend," Clover said. She wiped my face with a Kleenex. "Nate's hungry. All I have is hundreds." She helped herself to my wallet.

I entered a glass-enclosed exhibit that appeared vacant but for a wall of man-sized foliage. Turning to leave I spotted Clover at a snack stand thirty yards away, going through my wallet. There was nothing in there she shouldn't see. One benefit of faithfulness was having no tracks to hide. She pulled out something and unfolded it. She looked up, but didn't see me. There were two such items in there—the page from *Crime and Punishment* with the bullethole, and the old news clipping about Shipwreck. She kissed it, re-folded it, and slipped it back in—that had to be Dostoevsky, page 348. She pulled the other one out. Her eyes ran over the yellowed article, the scratchy photograph of a sun-scorched old man on a tumbledown platform on top of a flagpole that leaned Pisa-like. We both knew the article well, the date, March 31, 1968, and the headline over the photograph:

FLAGPOLE-SITTER "SHIPWRECK" BLAKE
SETS WORLD RECORD—444 DAYS

Clover looked up, didn't see me, ripped the article in two, in four, to bits, stepped over to the crocodile pond, and cast the shreds over the wall into the mire. Two crocs thrashed over and clashed for the remains. It was gone.

I went dizzy, but this was good, this was letting go, this was healing. If it didn't hurt, it wasn't letting go. Shipwreck's yellowed story sank in the swamp, along with the dream of the poles, that our normal life might now begin in earnest.

A flash of movement in the foliage startled me. A uniformed zooworker, female, had entered from the rear of the enclosure. Not seeing me, she leaned on a rake and lit a cigarette, muttering to herself. Through the leaves she looked vaguely familiar. She saw me, put her smoke out, pocketed the butt, raked the enclosure a moment, then peered at me and emerged smiling. "Joe Magellan, pole-sitter," she said.

"Oh, my God. It's-it's—" I snapped my fingers.

"Carmen."

"Carmen, yeah. The liar."

"Who, me?"

"Well, what are the odds of this?"

"Pretty good, I'd say. You knew I worked here."

Had she mentioned it at the seminar? "I did?"

"'I *did*?'"

But *Clover* had picked the zoo. Or wait a minute, *had* I suggested it? Carmen watched me, gripping the rake handle with both hands and languorously rubbing her chin over the top. I looked up the road where Clover and Nate gobbled snacks at the Giant Panda exhibit. "So, you're sneakin' a smoke, eh?"

"Gonna tell?"

"Might, might not. Don't want to burn this place down."

"Don't I?"

I watched her watching me. She was a joker, a troublemaker, a sexy polecat, and damn well knew it. All us guinea pigs got a load of one another's shadows and secrets in that seminar. Even if you had no intention of opening up to your fellow ne'er-do-wells, you ended up spilling your guts just to pass the time. This lying vixen was the most eager gut-spiller of the lot, but you couldn't believe a word she said. I shaded the truth, and was not above a little verbal coquetry, but I also knew how to take life seriously, how to give higher principles a tip of the hat, and I had no use for people who didn't. In fact, Carmen was a slightly older version of the amoral ragamuffins who packed my English classes.

"It doesn't bother you," I said, "keeping wild animals in cages?"

"Ooo, you want to let 'em out? Hey, they eat all they want, get free medical care—and they *don't* get eaten alive. They're happier than they'd be in the fucking jungle."

"So, you can read animals' minds."

"I can read *your* mind, flagpole-sitter, and let me tell you, you're about as cured as me. By the way, who talked *you* into going to that little fascist's seminar? As if I had to ask."

"Nobody talked me into anything. I did what's right for my family."

The minx laughed in my face. "You said it yourself up there—your pole-sitting is a *calling*."

"It was a fucked-up obsession. I suppose lying is a calling?"

"You bet your flagpole cheeks it is. Everybody does it, but few with such gusto."

She looked over my shoulder with exaggerated surprise. Here Clover came striding up with Nate, slipping my wallet into my back pocket. "Are we interrupting?"

"This young lady graduated with me last night," I said.

"What a remarkable coincidence. I'm Clover."

"Carmen." She curtsied with the rake.

"And you're cured of...?"

"Compulsive honesty," Carmen said. "Joe was asking me if I thought he'd ever go up on another flagpole and I told him he better not or I'd go up and drag him down by his short hairs. Well, nice to meet you, Mrs. Magellan. I feel as if I know you, Joe told us so many stories about his amazing family life. Nice running into you, Joe."

Carmen slipped into the foliage and we took our leave.

"She's a pathological liar," I said. "I mean, like, certified."

"What stories did you tell about me?" Clover said.

"What's short hairs?" asked Nate.

We sat in a corner of the snackbar, me hunkered down with my back to the wall, nursing a Cherry Coke. Clover and Nate chattered and wolfed french fries interred in ketchup. I absently gazed at a cluster of trees stirring in the distance. Was that the same grove as when we came in? I had no sense of direction.

"And that monkey with the rainbow behind," Clover said.

"Psychedelic butt," Nate said.

"What do you know about psychedelic?"

"Could I get another hot dog?"

"You'll spoil your lunch." To me she said, "Whatcha see, hon?"

I shook my head. Nate looked, too, and saw.

"Whoa."

"What *is* that?" Clover said.

Nate stood. "Hey, everybody!" He pointed. "There's a monkey in that tree! A ape! It escaped! My dad saw it first! We claim a reward! We claim free tickets forever!"

I wondered what splendid panorama the beast was drinking in from up there, and what we little human beasts down below, pointing, shouting, jumping around, looked like to that leisurely brute, so free, lucky, wild and mighty, holding to the top with one hand, way on high in the swaying tree.

5

CLOVER

Headed home from the zoo, we cruised along Western, hunting for a nice place to lunch.

"There's a McDonald's!" Nate said.

"Not on your life," I said. "We're having a sit-down, family restaurant celebration meal."

I took Joe's hand and planted a kiss in the palm, with a flick of tongue. He jumped. I felt good. Real good. That ape had been Joe's dark, selfish, flagpole-sitting past bidding him adieu, and now he was captaining us into the wildflower-bright future, beginning with a fine dining experience.

As we motored up and over a slight grade along Western, he glanced over his left shoulder and pulled a squealing U in the middle of the block.

"What are you doing!"

"Very bad driving!" Nate said. "F minus!"

Joe parked at the top of the grade in front of a seedy little diner by the name of "Charley's Spot." Olive-drab paint peeled off the front of the place like bark off a dead tree. A battered garbage can stood sentry by the front door. Inside, alone, through the foul window, a beefy fellow in a green cap stood behind the counter, blowing his nose and waving at us.

"Dad," Nate said. "Is this a prank?"

"No crowd," Joe said.

"I wonder why," I said.

"These little holes-in-the-wall have the best food," Joe said.

"Oh, look—an adult movie theater. Classy."

Nate read aloud the names on the Pussycat marquee across Western: "Playtoe's Cave. Moan-a Lisa."

"Please start the car," I said. "Tout suite."

"Come on, you guys picked the zoo. I should pick where we eat."

"You picked the zoo," I said.

"Why would I pick the zoo? I hate zoos. Isn't this *my* celebration?"

I misread his insistence. I thought his stubbornness was residue from his resentment for my role in his healing, which, if it were to proceed apace, would have to be a two-way street. "Fine," I said. "The family that gets food poisoning together…"

From the sidewalk I took in the vista of the city made possible by the prominence upon which the little dive sat. "He ought to put tables out here," I said.

We eschewed the ratty Naugahyde booths and sat at the counter, per Joe's wish, again. "Just for fun," he said.

"Fun as in not fun," Nate murmured.

The slovenly lout in a Marine cap behind the counter—Charley himself, it would turn out—took our order. I regarded his red, watery gaze with concern.

"Allergies?" I asked.

"Onions," the man said, scratching his nose with the back of his hairy wrist. As he concocted our lunch, Joe asked if I had found what I was looking for in his wallet. He must have seen me disposing of the article, or had already found it missing. What did he do, check it every hour? But I played dumb. I asked him what he meant. He said I knew what he meant. I told him why was he asking then. Then I thought twice. I wanted our post-pole life to go as smooth as possible.

"I apologize," I said. "Your wallet is private. You don't seem that upset though, which is a good sign. But I am sorry. I overstepped my bounds. If I had the chance to do it over… Well, it's gone, for better or worse."

He breathed horse-like through his nose.

Charley served us our Charleycheeseburgers and from a dented vat on the grimy stove ladled himself a big bowl of Charleychunkystew which he ate at the end of the counter. I don't think Joe touched his burger. Nate pried his open and poked suspiciously around inside. I tapped his plate. "Eat." To Charley: "He overdid the snacks at the zoo."

"Zoo," Charley grunted. "Stink, cages, crappy food, rob ya blind, screamin' animals, kids runnin' 'round. Bah." He returned to his stew.

"We saw an ape trying to escape," Nate said. "They shot it with a dart."

"Oughta had a M-16 to shoot back," Charley said.

"Not funny," I declared.

Joe pointed at Charley's cap. "Marines?"

"Yep. Nam. Da Nang." Charley shivered with a memory. "You?"

"Army. Xiang Phu."

"Action?"

"Some," Joe said. "Spotter."

"Up a tree in that goddamn jungle? Sittin' duck with them gooks scurryin' around."

"I strenuously object to 'gooks'," I said.

"Dad pushed bullets in his nose," Nate said proudly.

Charley snorted. "War makes a man do things."

Joe pointed outside with his thumb. "Where's Old Glory?"

"Over this craphole?" said Charley.

Nate spun off the stool and went to the window. "Oh oh. Mom?" I was tonguing something strange in a bite of Charleyburger. "Mom!"

"Don't yell at me in public!" I plucked a tiny gray oddment from my mouth. "Sit down."

The boy sat. "Don't say I didn't tell you."

I peered at the mysterious object, rolling it between my fingertips.

"Well," Joe said, "one hell of a flagpole."

That I heard. I spun.

"Seventy foot of German steel," Charley said.

From the sidewalk in front of Charley's Spot an ugly gray flagpole ascended past the window into the Holy-Spirit-colored Los Angeles sky. "Where did that come from? That was not there."

"Them Krauts maybe got their world wars," Charley said, "but nobody forges a solider hunk of steel. Take a nuke to budge that. Ever hear of French steel? English steel?"

I wiped my mouth and stood. "Let's go. We're gone."

"That's why he dragged us in this dump," Nate said.

"Whoa, boy," Charley said.

"You called it a craphole," said Nate.

"Pay the man, Joe," I said.

Charley's gaze swept the café like a flamethrower.

Joe drew his wallet out. "Why don't you quit?"

"Quit? I'm *Charley*. I live in the craphole apartment upstairs!"

"How many bedrooms?" Joe asked.

"What do you care? Two." Charley slopped stew in his mouth.

"I'm going to take this fork," I said, "and stick it in the top of some-body's head."

"My daughter in Duluth wants me to move in with her, but if I sold this and went up with nothin' to do, I might be sittin' there one day and—"

At which point the restauranteur inhaled a glob of stew. He tried to cough it out. Gawking at us, reddening, he grabbed the ladle from the vat and pounded himself on the back, stew sailing everywhere.

"He's choking!" Nate yelped. "Dad! The Heimlerk!"

Joe leapt over the counter, positioned himself behind Charley, and gave the flailing chef's rubbery midsection a mighty squeeze. A cube of meat shot from Charley's windpipe and landed back in the vat with a splash.

"Holy Christ!" Charley rubbed his throat as if the hangman had passed by. "I couldn't get no air. God bless you, my Nam brother. You saved my rotten life!" He grabbed Joe's hand and kissed it.

"*Pay* this poor man," I said.

Joe held out a couple bills but Charley was busy. "I lived through two wars and four divorces to go out on stew." He glared with loathing at his bowl, picked it up and hurled it crashing against the rear wall.

I grabbed Nate's hand and backed toward the door.

"Hold on," Charley said. "I'm lettin' off steam. Sit down, finish lunch. It's on the house."

"If you want my advice," I said, "move to Duluth. Better dead than a living hell. Goodbye and good luck."

"Swear to God," Charley snorted, "if somebody was to walk in here and offer me a lousy grand down for this, this—"

"Seven-fifty," Joe said.

6

The rental truck pulled to the end of the long driveway next to the stairs in back that led to the apartment over Charley's Spot. Clover climbed down and marched back up the driveway toward Western. She wore dark glasses in mourning for their stillborn normal life.

"Where you going?" called Nate.

"Long walk, short pier," Clover called back.

Joe thanked God she could still joke, that she had neither stabbed him in his sleep nor gone hunting for a lawyer. He opened the back of the truck to unload their meager belongings, half of which were boxes of books. He hurt too much to feel anything. I'm no longer *ob*sessed, he thought—I'm *po*ssessed. He had moved through the last three days pounded by the brutal and all-too-deserved silent treatment of wife and son.

Nate stood watching his father, his eyes wet, his fists at his sides.

"Don't look at me like that, pal. It'll be all right."

"No, it won't. I'm not your pal. I have to change schools again. I'll never make any friends. I hate those dumb, dumb, dumb, stupid flagpoles! I hate *you*, Dad!" He ran down the driveway after his mother.

Joe was grateful he had at least gotten "Dad" in there. Empty even of despair, Joe lifted a box of books. His knees wobbled as if the authors themselves were crammed inside. He wanted to disappear, leaving no memory of him in Clover or Nate.

In the back of a dark blue limousine parked across Western, an elderly Black gentleman in a white silk suit watched Joe carry the box toward the stairs at the end of the driveway. The old man lit a cigar and raised the window; the limo rolled down Western and away.

7

CLOVER

Joe worked his rocking chair in the darkening apartment above the café. He faced the flagpole hulking outside the window. A shadow, I watched from the hall.

"Okay, Mr. Blake," he murmured. "Mr. Champion. Be you dead or be you alive, here I—"

The floor creaked under me and his breath caught, as if an animal had happened upon him in the woods. I came in and put my hands on the back of his chair.

"Don't divorce me," he whispered.

"Oh, shut up," I whispered back.

"You could hire a hit man."

"With what?" I glared at the flagpole outside as at a rival, and commenced rocking the chair to keep from strangling him.

He gave a grateful sigh. "We're okay, though?" he said. "With the money?"

"You are really something. Would it matter if we weren't?"

Charley had been so eager to unload the place that the details were hammered out lickety-split—seller financing, promissory notes, vendor credit, all the various fiduciary whatnots. Joe hated to borrow, hated even using credit cards, but a small loan was unavoidable under the circumstances. He didn't follow money, or chose to be conveniently bewildered by it; I was on top of such matters as usual. None of his other flagpole hi-jinks had involved loans or the purchase of property. He hoped to finagle a refund from Kerridge, for the failure of the cure, and to gather unemployment from the state.

"I'll never again pretend to understand," I said.

He twisted around and kissed my hand. "I don't understand myself."

"You'd hate me if I wanted to live on a flagpole. Can you *imagine*? You think it's some big mysterious symbol in a story by some self-centered shit like Proust or Hemingway that I'm too simple to understand."

"What are you talking about, you're *twice* as smart as me, *twice* as well-read."

Through the louvered windows of the living room the night coagulated and the pole turned ghostly in the streetlight.

"I know you hate me for making you go to that toupee-wearing idiot's seminar."

"You didn't make me go. That was a toupee? I thought he dyed it."

"Every weekend you came home giddy about how you were getting to the root of the damn thing. Was that all total bullshit?"

"No, no, no, honey. I don't know about giddy, but I *wanted* to believe it. I did, I wanted to. But this is the one. I just *know* it. I *feel* it. I'm gonna paint it. I'm gonna give it a name. I'm gonna do it and be done."

"Oh, you're gonna *paint* it. You're gonna give it a *name*."

"And I'm thinking of writing up there."

I stopped rocking him. "You mean rewriting the novel again?" I winced at my barbed reference to his 999-page epic, *Holder and Biggen*, about an updated and thinly veiled Holden Caulfield and Bigger Thomas on a round-the-world sailboat trip. It had been summarily rejected by fifty publishers. "I'm sorry, it's not about the novel. I just thought this nightmare was over! And I *never* thought you'd go up in the city. I thought you had to sit in the toolies with nobody around to bug you or freak you out. Like in Durango, or—"

He touched my hand. "Don't stop, please."

I resumed rocking the chair as absently as one might hone the edge of a blade. "And Bend, with the laundromat, and Goshen, for God's sake. Now here you find a place on Western, smackdab in the middle of Los Angeles, California."

"It found me. Shipwreck has to be dead by now anyway."

"Will you stop with Shipwreck? That old bastard never did a thing to you. *You* went up, *you* got down. It was the heat, the cold, the rain. It was a headache. You thought you had appendicitis. One, you were lonely. I thought that was the whole point—to be alone! What do you think that old coot did, send juju waves from Saint Cloud? Or the grave? You don't even know what that weather-beaten bum *looks* like. Scratchy-ass photograph from a dozen years ago."

"You know, it's funny how you fed that article to the alligators, and an hour later I find this new pole."

"Are you fucking kidding? You're trying to blame this on *me*?"

"No, no, no. Clover, this is it. Every last damn thing I have is going into this one."

"Which means every last damn thing me and Nate have. Forget

about *me*—do you realize how children torture other children about something like this?'"

"Torture, come on."

"*Torture. Words.* Words *are* torture to kids. I keep so much hidden from you. You and reality aren't even in the same solar system. 'Why's your father up on a pole? Is he crazy? Is he stoned? Is he a bum? Doesn't he love you?'"

"What? Naw, naw. 'Doesn't he love you?' Kids don't talk like that."

"You don't know how kids talk. Imagine what it's like for a gentle, sweet, vulnerable, sensitive boy like Nate."

"Do it, Dad!" Nate leapt into the living room from the hallway. "Get the world record! Just do it! Just get it over with!" He fled down the hallway to his room and slammed the door.

"Oh, *God*," I said.

Joe pulled me around to sit on his lap. I failed to resist. He cradled my head. I wept, bucking like a fish on a pier. He rocked me, stroked my hair, wiped my tears with his thumb. My breathing settled and grew heavy. He started when I said, "Do you go up to get away from me?"

"Oh, Clove, no. You're kidding, right?"

"I'm so lonely when you go up."

"I know. Me, too."

"But you *leave*."

"I'm right *there*."

I gushed: "Maybe you could teach a while and save more and this is only a leftover twinge from the cure and if you waited a while it'd pass and it wouldn't be so important anymore and then it wouldn't be so bad if it didn't work out. It's so hard, Joe, when you have to get down. You're so sad. It breaks my heart. It's like you're dying. I can't stand it again." Traffic played outside like a thousand snakes in the grass. "Were you ever attracted to the girls in your classes?"

"*What?*"

"Am I a good lover?"

"Where's this coming from?"

"Tell me."

"You're the *best*. You have me climbing the walls. You know that. You push all my buttons. All my love buttons. You drive me *nuts*."

"Most men, that's the first thing they'd think of, if they had to live on a flagpole—no sex. If you did do it—you'd be gone over a year. Four-hundred and forty-five days, and nights."

"You're killin' me."

"Couldn't I come up? Conjugal visits?"

"It wouldn't be flagpole-sitting if you do whatever you want up there. You'll be so busy down here turning Charley's Spot into a nice restaurant, you'll forget all about me."

I leaned away and gave him a look.

"Well, you're the one who said make the best of a bad situation."

"I was trying to calm the big dope down."

"Just cleaning the place would do wonders. Wash that big front window, for starters. And the stove, Jesus. Buy a new pot or two. You're a wonderful cook, that part's no problem. You come up with the most offbeat, scrumptious dishes. What was that thing tonight—taco peanut soup? I'm telling you, we could transform that dump into—"

"*We?*" I sat up. "Look, don't try to make this easy. Or *fun*, for God's sake. It's neither."

"I think God wants me to do this, Clover."

I started to get up; he held me gently. "God wants you to sit on a flagpole? God is the only one who knows why I put up with you. If I took a poll of ten thousand women, I wouldn't find *one* who would take this. No *sane* woman with self-respect."

He sighed and didn't say anything and I settled down and we rocked a while. It was getting darker. I had to get close to his face to look him in the eye. "Are you gonna jerk off up there?"

"I hadn't thought about it."

"Oh, I bet. Did you jerk off on the other ones?"

"I may have."

"I'll tell you," I said, "*I'm* sure gonna. Hey—we can have phone sex."

"Can't have a phone up there. No phones in flagpole-sitting."

"How are we supposed to communicate?"

"How'd we communicate before?"

"Yelling. But that was only a few days. I don't want to scream at you for a year."

"We'll figure it out. We'll figure everything out."

"Yeah?" I nuzzled his throat. He kissed me carefully, nudged me off his lap, took me by the hand, and led me tip-toeing down the dark hallway past Nate's room where we could hear Neil Diamond crooning that everyone in the world was on their way to America, the poor fools.

8

JOE

I had to leave ten messages at Kerridge's office before he called me back.

"Money back guarantee if the cure doesn't take," I said. "It didn't take."

Kerridge snorted. "Who says?"

"Me."

"Prove it."

"I'm going up on another flagpole."

"And come down weeping in a week?"

"I want a refund."

"Joe, listen. You gave me much pleasure in our little war of wills, so I'm going to reward you with a little secret: If you ever squeeze a refund out of me, you'll be the first. And you won't be the first."

"I'll sue you."

The glee in Kerridge's laugh was perverted with contempt. "You know how many lawyers I pay to protect my money from loony braying morons like you? See you in court, Joey."

"Okay, but you ought to know something—I'm taping this call."

Silence. "Let me hear it."

It was my turn to chuckle. "I'm not gonna stop taping to play it. You think the media might be interested in a famous shrink calling his clients 'loony braying morons,' was it?"

"That's a term of endearment."

"Yeah, go with that."

"It's a felony to tape a call without the respondent's consent."

"Tsk tsk. I'd happily rot in jail knowing I'd nailed your quack hide to the barn door."

There ensued a long silence full of pleasure on my side.

"I insist on a non-disclosure agreement," Kerridge said.

"Fine. Get that refund in my hand in twenty-four hours, you'll have the agreement and the tape. If not, you'll hear it on 4RealNews."

One hour later, by special messenger, I received a cashier's check for the full refund. I immediately cashed it, signed and returned Kerridge's NDA, and included Nate's Olivia Newton-John "Xanadu" tape for Malcolm's listening pleasure.

9

JOE

While Clover scrubbed down poor old Charley's Spot prior to re-opening, I embarked on a search for a carpenter to construct a platform for the top of the flagpole. It had to be worthy of my final attempt and of the flagpole itself, which dwarfed every previous pole in height, girth, and strength. The other structures had been meager improvements on the boyhood orange tree and its sheet of plywood. The best of them was gimcrack (the one in Goshen, formerly a stand for a gigantic tire above a Goodyear store), and the rest were deathtraps. I had planned them like a bear plans a shit in the woods. The spirit moved me, the means and opportunity appeared, my precious Clover finagled the details, and up I went. They were predetermined duds. I would not make the same mistakes with this baby.

Finding a carpenter willing and able to assemble and install the desired structure sixty-plus feet above the ground—a 10x10-foot redwood platform with trapdoor, balustrade to keep me from stumbling over, some kind of ladder, and a mechanism to haul necessities up and down, while keeping the project on budget—proved difficult. The demands of such an undertaking, plus technical obstacles and liability considerations, drove off every licensed carpenter I consulted.

I happened to be complaining about my dilemma to an old Turkish fellow named Alp, the owner of Mike's Shoes & Keys, half a block down Western, where I was having copies of keys made. Alp had a minimal grasp of the English language, but he was way ahead of me.

"Lu and Duc," he grunted. At first I thought he said "loon duck," which I took as a lunch suggestion.

Lu and Duc turned out to be a Vietnamese father-and-son handyman duo highly-regarded in the neighborhood. Alp set up a meeting, with a multilingual Cambodian seamstress named Sung to interpret. I explained my needs and budget to Sung, and she rattled it off to Lu and Duc. Lu appeared to be the father, though he looked but a few years older than Duc. Father and son took one look at each other.

"Okay," Sung said.

"Great." I shook their hands and thanked them. To Sung: "Are they licensed and insured and everything?"

She conveyed my query and she and Lu and Duc entered into a heated entanglement of Asian verbiage.

"Yes," Sung said to me.

I considered asking to see the paperwork, and having a written contract drawn up, but if they balked I'd be back to square one. I wanted to get the show on the road. Lu and Duc wanted the job, were ready to go, and seemed confident they could do it while keeping to my budget. I would watch them from the start and if the work was shoddy I would simply call it off. I pulled the trigger: "Okay!"

Giddy with the deal, I almost told them I had been in their country, but I wasn't sure what side they had been on. For all I knew, one of them could have put that round through *Crime and Punishment.*

We agreed to meet again the next day to iron out the details, or so I understood.

❧

Clover and I woke to the commotion of grinding machinery outside. I leapt up, ran down the hall, and looked out the living room window upon a blinding sunrise.

Lu the father was up in an antique-looking cherry picker nimbly fastening a great steel collar around the pole at the top, while son Duc unloaded redwood lumber from a ramshackle pick-up with its rear backed up over the curb onto the sidewalk.

Pulling on my pants I ran downstairs and out on the sidewalk. I began shouting about ironing out the details. The groaning cherry picker, rattling truck, and lumber crashing drowned my protest. Clover and Nate watched from the window upstairs. For one horrifying moment I imagined that Lu and Duc—even Alp and Sung—were stooges sent by Shipwreck to sabotage me one more time.

But there the redwood lumber sat, bought, delivered, and looking good. I could not deny that the steel collar Lu had already installed— and now stood on literally jumping up and down—appeared a solid foundation to the platform.

Duc parked the empty pickup, acknowledged my presence with a single nod, as if I were an innocent passerby, and commenced his construction of the platform right there on the sidewalk.

I went upstairs and got a cup of coffee and sat with Nate to watch the work outside.

"Those guys work pretty fast," he said.

"That they do." In fact, they worked as if born to build platforms on top of flagpoles. I regarded my son. "Still hate me?"

He shrugged. "Depends."

"On what?"

"On what happens."

"Fair enough. You'll do okay in school, though, huh? The hell with what those damn kids say."

"Yeah, the hell with those damn kids." He was daring me to rebuke him for the words. I ignored the dare and for a sweet time father and son, still and silent inside, watched father and son, busy and noisy outside.

I offered to drive Nate to his new school, Orville Wright Elementary, but he insisted on taking the bus. Clover was downstairs in Charley's doing whatever she was doing. Alone upstairs, I rocked in my chair at the window and watched the action proceed down on the sidewalk.

Lu and Duc nailed a section of 10-foot redwood 2x4's together, including a portion of cross-hatch undergirding, all of which they then hoisted on the cherry picker and installed over the steel collar, three feet down from the top of the pole. That three feet of pole sticking up in the middle of the platform would reduce my already limited living space, but it gave the structure added stability. They further bolted the bottom part of the attached undergirding to both sides of the steel collar, repeated the original procedure with additional sections, leaving a square hole to one side of the pole for the trapdoor, then constructed the trapdoor itself below, hoisted it up and hinged it in place. From there they built a four-foot-high banister on all four sides, also of redwood, with various braces, buttresses, and struts, to keep me from falling off and breaking my neck instead of the record.

The speed with which they were erecting this simple but elegant structure dismayed me. I had anticipated a more extended process, allowing me to properly prepare for so grand, so ultimate an undertaking. I strode downstairs, past Clover, who was up a ladder scraping gunk off the ceiling, and on out to the sidewalk to see if I could get Lu and Duc to downshift on the project.

I urged them to take a break, have a nice long lunch, maybe mis-communicate with me a little about things for a while, all of which they effortlessly ignored, plowing ahead up there without pause.

A stout woman watching from across Western came jaywalking over with her hand out. "I'm Klara," she said, with a German accent and a bulldog grip. "I own K&K's." That was the hardware store across the street. She thrust her big European forehead at me as she spoke: "You have a permit? Thing like that fell, kill a whole family."

"Ain't gonna fall."

"Lotsa things ain't gonna fall fall." She gestured toward Lu and Duc. "They're not licensed. I won't report you. I don't walk over here. I'm glad to see that swine Charley cleared out. Him and me, we crossed swords. Called me Kraut. I'm Austrian." She peered at me. "So, the woman, she's working Charley's for you."

"My wife? Yeah. Not *for* me."

Klara pointed upward with her thumb. "What *is* that? Looks like a gallows."

I looked at it. "Nope. I'm just gonna sit up there."

"Sit up there," she said, as if that were the equivalent of "E equals MC squared."

"Sit, yeah. Live. Dwell."

I watched the unformed questions pass like clouds across her face. One made it out: "Why?"

Nobody understood, certainly not her. "It's complicated."

"Well, never catch me up there," she said, turning and jaywalking back across Western. "Good luck, hangman!"

Lastly Lu and Duc rigged up a rugged rope ladder from the bottom of the trapdoor clear down to the sidewalk. I tried to tell them that was unnecessary because I wouldn't be getting down for a long, long time and nobody else would be going up. They smiled and discussed it amongst each other. Lu asked me, "How you get up?"

"Oh yeah," I said.

They then tied a thinner rope to the lowest rung of the ladder, which could be thereby raised and looped to a bolt under the trapdoor (itself lockable from the topside), which would put the ladder thirty feet off the ground unless I had some emergency need to lower it. For added safety, they provided a sturdy harness which still had "Pacific Bell" on it and which could be securely hooked to the rope ladder. They added a separate rope and good-sized rattan basket to haul necessities up and disposables down through the trapdoor.

I understood now why these two craftsmen were so highly regarded in the neighborhood.

I climbed the ladder to test it out—it was rough, stiff and sturdy. I poked my head through the trapdoor to survey the platform. Lu and Duc began jumping up and down to demonstrate the structure's air-worthiness. They insisted I mount the platform; I declined. Their feelings appeared bruised, but I stuck to my guns. I would not set foot up there until I was ready to stay.

10

JOE

Two days later, I was completing one last bit of business—painting the flagpole orange. I had climbed to the top, then worked my way slowly down, painting from top to bottom.

Clover had predicted howls of protest from neighboring business owners and residents about the flamboyant color, but I'd been at it all morning, it was now deep in the afternoon, and not a soul had raised a peep. Klara stuck her nose out of the hardware store, slowly shook her big non-German head, withdrew, and that was that. It was proving itself to be quite the live-and-let-live neighborhood, a puzzleboard of a dozen get-along cultures and languages, and focused on trudging through one day to the next. The color of a flagpole produced not a blip on their radar of concerns.

The local population was a smorgasbord of Chinese, Chicanos, Vietnamese, Israelis, Koreans, Native Americans, Middle Easterners, Greeks, Scandinavians, whites, Blacks, at least one Austrian and one Turk, and God knew how many other nationalities, races, creeds, colors, options, variations, persuasions, permutations, and combinations. If you wanted to live in any kind of peace in the midst of such an unwieldy conglomeration, your top priority would indeed be to mind your own business, which did not include the color of your neighbor's flagpole.

That stretch of Western had seen better days. It consisted of old one- and two-story buildings housing fringe businesses many of which had to be hanging on by a thread, with many of the owners or tenants living in apartments upstairs like us. The roster of nearby stores on Western included Shangri-la Flowers & Gifts, Mike's Shoes & Keys, Happy Hobby, Sun's Donuts & Chinese Fast Food, TV Doctor, K&K's Hardware, Hakan's Ice Cream, Cool Hand Laundry, ABC Printing, World's Magazine Stand, Sharp's Barber, Playtoe's Cave, and, of course, Charley's Spot.

A store here and there had been abandoned and boarded up, like wooden teeth in some old prizefighter's mouth. That slice of Western in the middle of the city was plenty busy traffic-wise, which did not necessarily translate into business. Still, Clover had examined Charley's books, and if they hadn't been monkeyed with, that disconsolate chap had somehow been turning a modest profit. All I hoped was that Clover could keep us out of the red while I was aloft.

I applied the final brushstroke to the base of the pole and stepped back to admire my handiwork, unaware of the tall woman behind me until I bumped into her, my brush dribbling orange paint onto one of her red patent leather high heels.

"Ah, sorry, damn," I said. I knelt and tried to wipe the paint off with a grimy rag, succeeding only in smearing the paint.

"The last gentleman," she said. "Forget it. I buy 'em wholesale. Besides, I *love* orange."

I stood and took the woman in—all six feet of her. I wasn't used to staring eye to eye with a female. She was dolled up in what appeared to be a red usherette's uniform, including the little round cap atop a blonde flip. Her thin face bore too much make-up for my taste, and her bare arms and fishnetted legs may have been a tad too muscled from working out, but she was not what I would call unattractive.

"What in the daisy have we got here?" she said.

"Flagpole."

"No!"

"Where'd you come from?"

"Not far." She pointed a silver fingernail across Western at Playtoe's Cave.

"You're an usher? Ette?"

"I own the joint. I like dressing up."

"You *own* it?"

"The first of many. I'm Jinx—with an x. Jinx Goodman."

She had a long, slim hand, out of El Greco, and a sure shake.

"I'm Joe. Joe Magellan."

"Any relation to the fellow who sailed around the world?"

"No. My grandfather changed his name."

"From what?"

"Miller."

"Joe Miller. Yeah, Magellan's a step up. Why'd he pick Magellan?"

I shrugged. "He'd been in the navy."

"I'm so nosy."

"It's all right. I don't know the details. He got in some kind of trouble, wanted to start over."

"Well, good for him." She regarded the paint on her shoe, held her foot up this way and that. "Must have been scary, sailing around the world way back when. Storms, pirates, scurvy. Wonder why explorers didn't just throw a few crates of oranges in the hold."

"I doubt they knew what caused scurvy." I didn't know if they knew or not, but finishing the pole had me playful, a little show-offy. I pointed a thumb at her theater. "You know the parable of the cave?"

"Know it, love it. 'And now, I said, let me show in a figure how far our nature is enlightened or unenlightened: Behold! human beings living in an underground den, which has a mouth open towards the light, and can only see before them, being prevented by the chains from turning round their heads; and you will see, if you look, a screen which marionette players have in front of them, over which they show the puppets.'"

"Wow. Is that straight from Plato?"

"It is."

"Impressive. So, porn and philosophy meet at the crossroads."

"Everything that rises must converge. Sex is not the enemy of higher thought."

I wiped off my paintbrush. "I never said it was."

She laughed, a throaty thing. She started to say something but a bus went by, then a motorcycle, so we were eyeing each other there a moment. Attractive women got away with murder, and they knew it. My policy with enchantresses like this one: stay cool. Give them plenty of room to play, like a fish on a hook. Not that I would ever stray from Clover (except for that one nothing kiss eight, nine years earlier, which I did not instigate, hardly participated in, and was more cheek than mouth), but an infrequent little mental dalliance could spice up a dull day. Not that it was a dull day. I glanced into the café window to see if Clover was watching; she didn't seem to be.

Jinx admired the flagpole. "Well, I'll say one thing, Joe, this baby sure peps up the neighborhood. It's an instant landmark. Now—what are we gonna *do* with it?"

"I'm gonna sit up there."

"Pourquoi?"

"I'm a flagpole-sitter."

"And what might a flagpole-sitter be?"

"It's a man—or a woman, I suppose—who…has a calling…to live up on a flagpole."

"Callings are good," Jinx said. She squinted at me and smiled, her white teeth and red lips dazzling in the sun. "You're alone up there?"

"Yep."

"For how long?"

"The world record plus one. Four hundred and forty-five days."

"Whoa, Nellie. Well, God bless you. I'd go bonkers up there in about two hours. Total utter bonkers."

Out of nowhere paranoia hit me like an ink blast from a squid: Jinx was a psychological saboteur on assignment. Watching her, I asked, with false calm, "Do you happen to know a man named Shipwreck? Shipwreck Blake?"

"Shipwreck Blake," she repeated, rolling it around in her mouth. "No. Yummy name. Friend of yours?"

If she was lying, she was good. "How about Dr. Malcolm Kerridge?"

"The obsessions guy? I've *heard* of him. Why? Did I say something wrong?"

There would be plenty of time to get paranoid once I got up there. Maybe this lanky glamor-puss was exactly what she seemed—a philosopher/porn theater owner, lured by the mystery of the flagpole and the man who would climb it. She was an exotic creature, standing there all prettied up, a big perky little usherette, looking at me looking at her.

"No," I said. "I'm over-thinking again."

"I like an over-thinking man," she said, smiling sweetly, and I smiled back and, for good measure, we exchanged a trace of subliminal eye action.

"Need any help out here, sweetheart?"

I about jumped out of my skin. It was Clover, leaning in the doorway of Charley's Spot with her arms crossed. She looked like hell from cleaning the place, grease on her face, her hair sticking up everywhere.

"Voilà," I said, presenting the orange pole.

"Isn't it fabulous?" Jinx said.

I thought it would be a good idea to forget Jinx's name. "Clover, this is, uh—"

"Jinx," Jinx said. "Hi."

"Hello there."

"This is Clover, my wife. Honey, Jinx owns Playtoe's Cave."

"She does, does she?" Clover said languidly.

"Well, have fun up there, Joe," said Jinx. "I'll be rooting for you. Nice meeting you, Clover. Good riddance to Charley and welcome to the neighborhood!" She started across Western in her usherette's outfit, holding up her hand to stop traffic, which it did.

"Boy, she's a character," I said.

Clover snorted. "Jinx is a *man*, Romeo."

"*What?*" I looked across Western where Jinx busied herself inside the ticket booth.

Clover snorted again and slipped back inside. I looked with new eyes at Jinx, who waved at me from the ticket booth. I'd been down there washing her shoe. *His* shoe. Exotic creature. Subliminal eye action. I was not prejudiced against that specific type of oddball, or oddballs of any stripe—a flagpole-sitter has little wiggle room in the oddball department—but I preferred to know who I was dealing with. They ought to tell you, "Hey, I'm this kind of oddball, that kind of oddball, so don't get any big ideas."

I shook my head to dislodge the experience and shook it some more. I stepped back to behold the orange flagpole and the redwood platform, finished and complete and ready to go. Oddball or not, "fabulous" was the perfect word for this marvel now awaiting my imminent ascent.

11

Joe lit three candles and sidled under the sheet beside Clover, tearing off the blankets and kicking them to the floor. He looked in her eyes and kissed her neatly. He slid the sheet down to expose her shy breasts. The sliding cotton brought her nipples up. She ran her fingertips over the back of his head as he grazed her like a guppy.

"Will you miss me up there?" she said.

"So much I could die."

"Don't say that. Do you *have* to go?"

At the moment, brushing her nipple with his lower lip, the thought of climbing up on that flagpole in the cold darkness brought nothing but dread. He banished it, came up and kissed her again, rekindled himself. Their mouths ground like two idiots. He kissed her cheeks, her fine cheekbones, her closed wet eyes, her temples, her high forehead, her red hair ardent in the candlelight, her perfect ears, her breasts again, and down over her abdomen, the blessed little heart tattoo there with "Joe" in the middle, and nuzzled impatiently below.

She held his head, a warning. "I'm sopping. I'm gonna come in two seconds." He knew she wouldn't. He worked there until time itself began to come apart. They were thick with the dope of love. "Oh, God," Clover said. "Oh, Jesus." He stopped and came up and kissed her on the mouth. She turned her head, resisting the taste of herself in his kiss. He moved down again and held her in his mouth like a slice of canned peach. "Oh, Jesus, Joe," she said. "Oh, Jesus, oh, Joe, oh, Jesus, oh, Jesus." Three Jesuses and one Joe. She grabbed a pillow and held it over her face and screamed as if falling. He wept for her, for her coming, her voice, her love, her forgiveness. He kissed her there one last time, she jumped, and he shimmied up to cover her body with his. He kissed her slack mouth and entered her quickly, she gasped and cupped his hips and moved him in and out. "Don't leave me," she whispered. The sweetness of it was like the edge of a cliff crumbling. He went slowly but she said, "Hurry," and he drove as if to save his soul. "Baby, baby, baby, baby," Clover said. With the moan of an animal perishing, he imagined climbing the ladder, growling, up through the trapdoor and onto the platform, howling, standing above the city, alone as the first man in the world, bellowing fire and thunder at the top of his lungs.

PART II

"You do not need to leave your room.
Sit at your table and listen.
Do not even listen, simply wait.
Do not even wait; be quiet, still, and solitary.
The world will freely offer itself to you to be unmasked;
it has no choice, it will roll in ecstasy at your feet."

—Franz Kafka

12

JOE

I went up in the late afternoon, in honor of the orange tree days. Back then I would climb up when the heat lifted and watch smog-murky sunsets over the plain and simple San Gabriel Valley. Of course, back then, when night fell, I would climb down to a warm apartment and a hot cup of cocoa.

Now, thousands of afternoons later, I stood on the sidewalk beside the rope ladder, holding the cardboard Flip-A-Number sign that Nate had made for me to mark the passing days. Salmon-colored clouds sped across the deep blue sky. If I got down before that sign read 445, it would not be hot cocoa waiting but a sorrow cold as Dante's hell.

Clover and Nate—and Jinx, waving in front of Playtoe's in some kind of sailorwoman's ensemble—were the only ones of three million Angelenos paying regard to the occasion. This despite the card table laden with doughnuts and coffee that Clover had set up on the sidewalk as lure for passersby. A fourth witness appeared—an old Black man in a scruffy lime sweatsuit, lemon cap, and aviator sunglasses, who began discreetly stuffing doughnuts into his velour pockets.

Clover said to Nate and me, "Can we say the prayer?"

It felt like prelude to a hanging, but we held hands and said it. I gave Clover a quick, determined kiss, and Nate a big hug, his dear lower lip quavering.

I put one foot on the first rung of the rope ladder, saw my shadow, took a breath, and hoisted myself off the earth.

I looked up and imagined my mother in the open trapdoor, coming home from the hospital, whispering, "Daddy's gone."

On the second rung I closed my eyes, and the limo carrying me and my mother pulls up to the hole in the ground.

I opened my eyes, sweating, slipped on the third rung, caught myself, and it's my first night in Berkeley alone with the purple swirling home-sick carpet of the Shattuck Hotel.

Another rung and I'm in line at Lucky's and the radio is saying,

"President Kennedy," so like my father in looks, brains, joie de vivre, "is dead."

The next, the kid next door, Bobby Petrocelli, is asking me can he come up in the orange tree and sit on the platform, and I tell him, "No, it's mine," and Bobby died in Vietnam.

Another, I'm running after my first girlfriend Holly, "Don't leave, I'll change!"

The next, I'm hitchhiking stoned into San Francisco with the fog rolling in, alone in the wake of the summer of love, sleeping under a house, waking to find my boots and backpack stolen.

Another and I'm alone again on the night beach at San Simeon, gazing across Highway 1 at the lights of Hearst Castle high on the hill.

The next rung and I'm kissing another girlfriend Rachel goodbye and running to catch the roaring plane that would carry me to Vietnam. Another and the round is smashing into Dostoevsky.

Another, I'm naked in Big Sur, my first acid trip, blowing terrified harmonica to stave off the snakes and phantom killer hippies.

Another, my mother is dying of cancer, she didn't know who I was, I told her I loved her, she can go now, tell Daddy I love him, who are you, she said, goodbye.

The next, I'm walking into the classroom, my first day teaching, petrified in green corduroy, they're looking through me, help, help.

On the last rung all the pole failures flashed before my eyes like a speeding train, I pulled myself up through the trapdoor, tied the rope ladder to the bolt, looked down, as if through the window of a rocket ship about to carry me to Mars, faked a brave smile for my sad, bewildered family, waved farewell, and let the trapdoor slam shut.

I stood and took a look. The salmon clouds had gone and left a solitary pink vapor trail like a scar across the length of the ink-blue sky. Los Angeles with its million solemn lights coming on presented itself up to me like an immense Edward Hopper painting.

I moved along the edge, drinking it in, gripping the banister, testing its solidity. My own six feet added to the six-plus stories of the pole put me close to seven stories up, and the lay of the land augmented the disorienting visual elevation. Charley's Spot sat atop a hillock of sorts, a prominence in Western Avenue, a knoll from which the plain of the city, the urbanized desert, stretched gently away in every direction.

Already that floating sensation was coming over me, familiar from the days of the orange tree. Now, however, the entire city seemed to float under me, as if the continent had come loose from its mooring and was sliding beneath the platform. I blinked and shook my head; the illusion passed just like that. If all goes as planned, I reminded myself, I'll be up a year and three months on this slab of redwood, so I better keep my imagination, or whatever this grand distortion was, on a short leash.

One mere street to either side of Western there ran blocks upon blocks of bright green lawns in the late afternoon light, tidy lower-middle class houses with picket fences, and pastel apartment buildings extending east and west to the next big business thoroughfares in the distance, Crenshaw one way and Normandie the other. A hundred and fifty feet either way, folks were watering their flowerbeds and walking their dogs and playing with their children.

More lights bloomed across the city. Skyscrapers huddled like cacti downtown. Dusk deepened. The illuminated Hollywood sign stood, a koan against the darkening hills. A river of red and white lights ran east and west on the Santa Monica Freeway to the south, and the dying orange fuse of sunset crumbled into the black Pacific. Traffic on Western whistled like a bomb coming in. I watched a man throw a pass over a green lawn to a young boy while a woman on the porch watched and clapped.

The city began to spin around me. I knelt on the trapdoor. I leaned against the pole. I'd been up five minutes. Shipwreck's world record was laughing at me. The city spun one way and the platform the other, a raft in a wild eddy.

I tried to pray; I groaned.

I ran my eyes over the things on the platform I'd brought up beforehand, companions of a sort: an orange mummybag on a strip of foam rubber, ice-chest, chemical toilet, walkie-talkie, portable radio, votive candle and matches, harmonica, notebook and pen, earplugs, all-weather tent still packed, and Nate's tri-sectioned coat hanger-fastened Flip-A-Number sign, which I had been holding all this time unbeknownst, and which I now held to my heart.

I sat up, heart slapping from a dream about dark shapes flapping above the platform. I shook my head to free it and lay back down. Torn clouds around the moon resembled the flames of Turner's slave ship. I watched it glide and burn.

13

JOE

I finished nailing Nate's Flip-A-Number sign (reading 000) to the side of the platform as he and Clover came out to send my breakfast up in the basket.

"How'd your first night go?" she asked.

"Stupendous!"

"Look at my sign!" said Nate.

"It's a beaut," I said.

"Everybody can see it!" He read: "Oh-oh-oh."

I gobbled a stack of Clover's wondrous buttermilk-pineapple flap-jacks, then lay in the hazy sun with a cup of coffee. Traffic like bleachers of fans far, far away cheered me on. I composed a mental checklist of items I would need up there: Long johns. A fold-up chaise lounge. My rocking chair, if only, but just too big. Maybe a mini-fridge at some point instead of this ice-chest. Oh, dark glasses and suntan lotion. Few more clothes, maybe a robe for when it warmed up enough to sleep naked—I didn't want to get dressed every time I got up for something. Although who could see anything anyway, except some weirdo with binoculars. Come to think of it, I could use our little binos myself.

I closed my eyes and smiled at the sun on my face, thanked my lucky stars I was up in clement Los Angeles. I would feel a nip in winter, endure a little sunburn in summer, smog now and then. Would have to put up an umbrella or tent for rain. Hold on through a temblor or two. But I wouldn't freeze or be carried off in a tornado or hurricane.

I tuned in the tinny little portable radio to the Spink Tillfieldson talk show. A debate was raging over Reagan's rumored plan to abolish Congress. I thought about calling in, but I had no phone. I couldn't argue anyway. I got too emotional. I thought of Aldous Huxley's *Time Must Have a Stop* where the guy asked his uncle why he still raged about politics when, at his advanced age, he should have been tending his soul. Tending my soul, which being on that flagpole must have something to do with, did not include screaming at the radio all day up there. I turned it off.

Buddy, I said to myself, if you would prefer to stay sane for the next fourteen months on this tiny island in the sky, you had better make friends with the now, the eternal moment, because that's all there is up here.

Part of staying sane was dealing with that relentless moment head-on, in meditation, for example; part was distraction from its unblinking gaze. Fortunately, the view from the pole in every direction, as spectacular as a king's in a hilltop palace, would offer steadfast entertainment. There was an oasis-like, otherworldly quality to the light of Los Angeles circulating through that layered riot of images and objects and expanding and collapsing distances. When I focused on a specific highlight of the landscape—the new Bonaventure Hotel downtown, the old Wiltern Theater up the street, a palm tree on Hollywood Boulevard, or the entire San Gabriel Mountain Range—the object in question began to waver and slip, like a fresh watercolor. There would be plenty to look at up there, plenty to keep me busy, amused, diverted.

I decided to write, to ground myself. I grabbed the notebook, leaned back against the three-foot section of pole that stuck up above the platform, wrote "Hello," and began to hyperventilate staring at the page.

I grabbed my harmonica; nothing came but breathless wheezings.

I turned the radio back on. A caller was ranting: "All Congress does is lie around and doodle. You could abolish it and who'd notice? It's just what the doctor ordered. Get rid of Congress and he'll lift America onto the shining hill that God made us to sit on."

The little radio began spluttering with static. I grabbed it, tapped it against the banister a little harder than I intended, something cracked inside, and it fell silent altogether.

14

CLOVER

My only customer was a young man in a T-shirt emblazoned with Lee Harvey Oswald's bruised face and the caption "I'm just a patsy!" He was changing his mind again: "No, make it two over-real-easy."

"Done," I said, cracking the eggs onto the grill. "You into the assassination?"

"Huh?" He poked at the walkie-talkie on the counter.

"Your shirt. Oswald."

He looked down. "Oh. Some guy in a band. I got it at Goodwill."

I pointed the spatula at the shirt. "You don't know who that is?" Ignorance oozed from his empty eyes and open mouth. "Do you know who President Kennedy was?"

He poked at the walkie-talkie as he thought it over. "President of America?"

"Very good."

"What do I win, a piece of toast?"

Joe barked over the walkie-talkie, "Clover!"

"Shit!" the startled young man said.

"Over!" said Joe.

"Is that the cops?" the young man said.

I picked it up. "What do you want? I got a restaurant full of famished heathens down here." I winked and the kid made a lopsided grin.

"We making money?" Joe said.

The kid pointed. "Uh, my eggs there?"

"Somebody giving you trouble?" Joe said.

"Yeah, come down and beat him up for me, will ya?" I flipped the kid's eggs.

"This portable radio crapped out," Joe said. "Could we maybe rig up an extension cord? Maybe send the plug-in up here? Over... Clover?"

❧

Throughout the afternoon he walkie-talkied me nonstop, begging for the radio, then his dub tapes and player, the *Times*, a book, pack of cards, cereal box, binoculars, a yo-yo. All I sent was lunch, insisting I was too busy. I would burn into him, whether he stayed a day or forever, that I would never again be slave to his imbecilic medieval obsession.

Along about five I sent the radio up, and the binoculars. I connected the radio to several extensions which I ran through the louvers of the living room window, lowered it to the sidewalk, and loaded it in the basket which he then hauled up. He turned it on. "It works! Oh, thank you! You sure this is okay, honey? What are *you* gonna do for a radio?"

I stood there, gazing up. "You really take the cake."

"Well, I know you like to listen to the radio when you cook."

"I'll buy another one."

"I wonder if we could pick up a used one at the TV Doctor."

"I wonder if I could climb up there and beat you to death with that one."

A little girl about five in a Gumby blouse walked by with her mother. She looked up to see who I might be talking to. "What a big birdhouse!" she said.

"A cuckoo's nest," I said, slamming the door.

15

"Cuckoo!" the little girl called up. "Come out! It's o-clock!"

Joe looked over. He waved.

"It's a man," the girl said. As her mother led her away, she waved back, and the flutter of her little hand was as powerful as the beckon of a potentate in altering Joe's life.

A UPS man slowed and poked his head out to see why the girl was waving, and the driver behind the truck honked and looked up. Walking her dog in the crosswalk at Condon, a woman in green shaded her eyes against the sun and looked up too, and people looked up from the cars stopping for her. Drivers and pedestrians up and down Western stopped and looked up, as if a UFO were hovering over the boulevard.

Joe moved along the edges of the platform, enchanted by the faces looking up and the fingers pointing and the voices exclaiming.

Traffic backed up both ways, horns battled, pedestrians glided like iron filings to the magnet of the flagpole.

Clover emerged from the café with her mouth open.

A cop in a patrol car fifty yards down Western flipped on his banshee siren a few times, to no avail. He pulled his cruiser half onto the sidewalk. He sat and appraised the situation, the flagpole, Joe peeking over. Climbing out, he holstered his baton and made toward the pole in a stoic duckwalk.

A dozen pedestrians milled around the pole, some looking up, some studying the cop.

"Get *back*," the cop barked.

They withdrew a few clumsy resentful feet. Clover remained where she was, frowning, arms folded as if in charge.

"Ma'am?" the cop asked her.

"I own this place and that pole."

"Yeah, I heard Charley unloaded this rat nest." He squinted up at Joe, using his hat to block the lowering sun. "Hey, Tarzan! I see you up there!" Joe retreated, then peeked over again. The cop pulled out a pack of cigarettes, lit one up, and contemplated the rising smoke. He walked into the squirming traffic and started writing a ticket, or made as if, for a yellow Porsche.

"I can't move!" the young female driver protested.

"Five seconds," the cop said.

The young woman blasted her horn and bellowed at the car in front, "Move it, man! Move that pile of junk!"

The officer wended through traffic, miming writing tickets, glancing up at Joe. Before long, cars were moving with enough pace to mollify the cop. Nate barged from the café with Walkman in hand. He and Clover exchanged happy urgencies and drank in the scene. The faces of the crowd shone with a faith in the thrills that this mystery would produce. Here they were, at the very heart of it.

"That's my dad up there!"

The crowd regarded him as if he had stepped out of a television show and personally addressed them. "What's he doing?" one asked.

"Sitting!"

The cop returned. "You know who's-it up there?" he asked Clover.

"Of course I know him. That's my husband. Joe."

"Full name?"

"Why?"

"Joseph Galileo Magellan," Nate said.

"That's a mouthful." The cop stepped back for a better angle. "Joe! Come on down, partner! Party's over!"

"Officer—" Clover read his name tag. "—Merton. You don't understand. Joe is a—"

"Don't say that," Officer Merton said. "Call me pig. Shout 'police brutality!' But do *not* tell me I don't understand. That's the one thing that gets my goat. I don't understand? Can you imagine the living nightmares I've seen and heard and smelled and *touched* in twenty-five years as a cop in this God-forsaken city? Do you know my capacity for understanding the most demented and perverted examples of human behavior?" He stomped out his cigarette.

"I *meant* you don't understand he's a flagpole-sitter," Clover said. "Please don't litter."

"If I have to go up there with my bum knee, he'll wish I wasn't half so understanding. Joe! I'm counting to ten! One! Two!"

"What do you care if he's up there?" Nate said.

"Three! Because it's a public nuisance. Four! Five!"

A TV truck from 4RealNews pulled up on the sidewalk behind Merton's black-and-white and disgorged Emmy-winning reporter Pete Hoover and his cameraman.

"Oh, Jesus," Merton said.

Tanned, shirtsleeves rolled up, Hoover sprinted toward the pole, tie slapping his face, his cameraman close behind.

"Pete Hoover, Mom!" Nate said, and to the crowd, "Pete Hoover! 4RealNews!" The cameraman panned the crowd, which shouldered to and fro to get in range.

"What do we got, Tom?" Hoover asked the cop.

One of the crowd said, "Hostage situation!"

"No, it's not," Clover said. "Who said that?" Nobody said who said it.

Hoover strode down the sidewalk for a better angle on the platform. As he passed through the gathering, which parted reverently before him, two or three reached forth to touch his arms and back.

Merton prioritized the dispersal of the crowd. "Time to go home! Do you have any idea what you're looking at?" The crowd blinked. "You!" He got in the face of one big fellow in a Lakers shirt. "Go. Home."

"Well, what is this?" the fellow mumbled.

"Well, what is this?" Merton mocked. "Am I dreaming? Am I dead and gone to hell? What this is, Superman, is you disobeying a lawful order. Now break it up!" The crowd began bumping into itself, faking breaking it up. It demonstrated a determined and poignant reluctance to leave before whatever was happening happened. The repercussion for staying would be worth it. It was going to be on 4RealNews—and they were too.

Two more cops arrived, younger than Merton, and huddled with him to strategize.

Jinx, in a nurse's uniform and white heels, flounced across Western through the crawling traffic.

"Hey, Jinx," Merton called.

"You're not harassing my buddy Joe, are you, Tom?"

"You know that character?"

"Friend of mine."

"You don't say." Merton made a curious face. "Give the man some elbow room!" he barked at the crowd, which sullenly gave ground as the other cops nudged them away from the pole.

"Hi, Mrs. Magellan," Jinx said.

"Hello," Clover said.

"My my," Jinx said. "This flagpole racket is hotter than I thought."

Hoover returned in a tizzy. "He's hiding from the camera."

Jinx's mouth dropped. "Pete Hoover."

Hoover eyed Jinx's nurse ensemble. "Is he sick? Is he gonna *jump?*"

"He's a flagpole-sitter," Clover said. "He *wants* to be up there. I'm Clover, his wife."

"May I ask," said Hoover, "how one would go about getting up there?"

"One wouldn't."

"Yeah, one wouldn't, Pete," said Nate.

"I'll let you talk to him," Clover said, "if he wants to." She fetched the walkie-talkie and handed it to Hoover.

He shouted into it, "Hello! Joe! Come in! Over!"

"Who's that?" said Joe.

"Pete Hoover! Love an interview about your stunt!"

"World record attempt," Clover corrected.

"World record attempt!" Hoover said. "Love to have you on 4Real-News!"

"Come on up."

"How?"

"Flap your arms. Over and out."

"I hate this job," Hoover said to his cameraman. "Call the bird."

16

JOE

As quickly as the tumult arose, the tumult faded, an hour orchid. As night fell, an occasional passerby glanced up listlessly. Ordinary life resumed along the boulevard, but we Magellans jabbered on our walkie-talkies, reliving the hubbub with awe and hilarity.

Afterward I sprawled on the mummybag and contemplated the goodness, the sweetness of life. The baffling puzzle of my flagpole-sitting had sprung into focus. My earlier efforts had not been incomprehensible flops at all, but vital rehearsals for the triumph at hand. Nothing was wasted. Despair? Get behind me! This was no mere success, this was redemption.

Short-lived redemption, for here came the 4RealNews copter thudding on a beeline from downtown. It swooped in, its searchlight scorching my eyeballs, its thwumping pummeling my nerves. I climbed inside the mummybag, a hare hiding from a hawk.

The copter departed, I crashed, awoke in creamy moonlight, crawled to the edge of the platform, and turned the Flip-A-Number sign to 001.

"One down, Mister Blake, four hundred and forty-four to go."

Jinx emerged from Playtoe's Cave and gave me the thumbs-up. I sat on the edge, lit the candle, and took in the city twinkling in the murk below.

"Joe!" Clover squealed over the walkie-talkie. She told me Hoover had given my "quest" thirty seconds on 4RealNews, including an aerial close-up of me peeking out of the sleeping bag. We laughed and yammered, exchanged declarations of love, and signed off for the night.

It all made sense now. Suffering was the infrastructure of serenity, the tar of failure paving the highway of success. I popped open my notebook and began to write:

I stretched out on the top branch of our giant sugar maple & watched a small red plane putter through the leaves and the clouds. The Trojans were clobbering the Huskies on the portable radio on my chest. My mother would be home from Good Samaritan soon with my father, and he and I would play catch again, knock grounders around, giggle about farts, dig early Elvis together, go to his office at USC before a game at the Coliseum. My bare feet braced against the trunk and my body cradled by the limb, I felt one with the great tree that churned with an old, slow, wild intelligence.

"Joey!" my mother called. She stood at the foot of the tree, alone. I'd forgotten how high I was. Climbing down, I looked back up as if I'd forgotten something. I jumped down and she told me and I fell and beat my head against the ground. The earth was grief and the tree was grief and my head and body were grief. Grief climbed down from grief and fell to grief and pounded grief against grief.

Writing those two paragraphs left me exhausted. I hadn't said a word about the maple tree to Kerridge and the obsessions gang. I held it to myself. I gave them the orange tree, the hickory in Vietnam, but not the maple, where it all began. It would have gotten to them, especially the women, but Kerridge would have torn it apart, so I held it, kept it for myself.

Where would I be if my father hadn't died? I'd have followed his path—engineer, scientist—working on some secret government rocketry project, as he had been before he died, according to my mother, whose mind at the time was losing its tether. Would he be working on Reagan's Star Wars now? Would I? There's so much I don't know about him. And now never will. Even things I remember I wonder if I remember them right.

When he died the science door slammed shut. It hurt too much to even think about doing what he had done. Engineering, formulas, machines—dead & buried. For me, numbers would not crack the mysterious nut of life or death.

My stomach groaned. When had I eaten last? If I was going the distance, I needed to take care of myself. I found the stale doughnuts Clover had sent up and gobbled away, plucked a short white hair from one, too hungry to care.

I took a last drowsy look at the city. Western Avenue, anarchy hours before, because of me, lay in the moonlight calm as de Chirico's *Melancholy and Mystery of a Street*. A shaggy mutt emerged from between two buildings. It meandered along, sniffing every object on the way wherever. I felt held to the world by a string, like a kite, but a strong string, a good solid string, and before long I fell into the seamless sleep of a man who had completed the first day of the journey he had been born for.

I woke to a scream and reached for Clover and remembered where I was. Pulling my pants on, I looked up and down the street. Jinx was out of the ticketbooth. Another scream—a woman—from the alley north of Playtoe's.

"Call the cops!" I said, and Jinx rushed into the booth. A third scream clawed the night, fainter than the first two. "Hey, god damn it!" I yelled. "Here come the cops!" Another scream, weaker still. I popped the trapdoor, dropped the rope ladder and scurried down, hesitating on the bottom rung. If some woman ended up dead because I didn't do anything, I'd never forgive myself. Came another scream, barely audible. "Fucking shit," I said, and dropped to the ground.

Jinx popped out of the booth. "Get back up, I called the cops, they're on their way!"

I raced across Western for the alley, barefoot and shirtless, roaring with petrified courage. "I got a gun! I got a gun!"

A tall old white-headed Black man in a long black coat stepped from the alley, cradling a ghetto blaster.

I stopped in my tracks. "What the hell?"

"Where's the woman?" Jinx said, right behind me.

The man's bright gray eyes shone like ice in the night. Behind him a big dark car, lights out, sat at the end of the alley. He clicked on the blaster and a hideous scream issued from the speakers, which he cut off in the middle.

"What the *fuck*?" I said.

"This guy's not right," Jinx said. "Be careful."

An old pickup rumbled past and honked.

The old man looked me in the eye. "You're soft, Magellan," he said.

"Do you *know* him, Joe?" Jinx said.

"Hell, no, I don't know this son-of-a-bitch."

"He must have seen you on the news," Jinx said.

"The *news*," the old man sneered. Around his neck a polished black stone on a gold chain caught the streetlight.

I looked back up and winced at Nate's Flip-A-Number sign, which read 001. "You goddamn wacko nut!"

"It's only one day," the old man said. "Ain't like Redding. Eleven days, was it?" My heart lurched. "Or Ogden. Six, seven days there?"

I had divulged all that at the seminar. This old man was Kerridge's envoy, Kerridge saw me on the news, sent this clown to sabotage me. "You're a stooge from that idiot's seminar!"

"Seminar," the old man growled. "For what we got, Joe, there ain't no seminar."

Chills crawled up my scalp. "*We?*"

"Ghost of poles past," said the old man.

"No," I whispered. "No."

Jinx touched my arm. "What is this? What's happening?"

"You're not him," I said. I tried to picture the scratchy face in the photograph from the article Clover destroyed. He'd had a hat on, casting a shadow. "You're not him. He's not Black."

"He's not?" he said.

A lowrider drove by, the radio blaring Blondie.

"You are *not* Shipwreck Blake."

"Am," said the old man.

I wobbled sideways and sat down on the curb. "I don't believe this." A customer emerged from Playtoe's Cave, lit a cigarette, and stopped to watch. "What was I supposed to do? Let some woman get killed?"

"You did the right thing," said Jinx.

"Absolute right thing," said Shipwreck Blake. "I knew you would. Son, until nothin' matters but sittin', you ain't got a chance in the world."

"One day," I moaned. "One miserable day."

"Yes," Shipwreck said tenderly. "That's all you have."

"It's not fair."

"It's not," Shipwreck said. "I done it, I wished I hadn't had to."

"Well, why didn't you think of that *before?*" said Jinx.

He manifested a fat cigar and lit it with a gold lighter. The dark blue limousine put its lights on and pulled slowly out of the alley. The back door opened and Shipwreck slipped inside. He closed the door and the limo rolled away down Western.

"It's over," I said.

A siren grew from the distance.

"Go back up," Jinx said. "I'll handle the cops." I sat there. Jinx got down and yelled in my face. "Joe! Get up! Stand up!"

17

JOE

In the morning Nate's Flip-A-Number sign read 000. Drivers and pedestrians along Western, honking, waving, shouting up at me, could not have cared less what the sign said.

"See yourself on the news?" a passing brown face under a white hat called up.

"The *news*?" I sneered. "No TV! It's the pure life up here!"

To the people, all that mattered was that the man on high, Joe somebody—in the flesh, legs a-dangle over the edge—had been verified, by the television sets in their living rooms, by Pete Hoover of 4RealNews, as a man above the common run. I had stepped out, up, and they were happy for me, happy I was there.

Clover opened up Charley's. She waved her walkie-talkie.

I got mine. "Hi, sweetheart. You know what I could use? A little bullhorn. Maybe you could scrounge up a used one?"

She pointed at the Flip-A-Number. "You have a day."

I waved back at a blonde fan in a honking jeep. "Hey! How are ya!"

"Sell those burgers!" the blonde yelled.

"Thanks!" I said. "What'd she say?"

"Oh, Hoover insinuated this is a publicity stunt for the café. You forgot to flip a card. Does that have anything to do with what was going on out here last night?"

The boombox screams had failed to wake Clover, but Jinx exhorting himself "Do not look down!" had snapped her to. Through the living room window she had seen Jinx work his precarious way down the rope ladder, grab his heels, and lope back to Playtoe's Cave, watched the ladder ascend and heard the trapdoor slam.

"It wasn't whatever it looked like," I said. "Shipwreck Blake was here last night."

"You must think I have the brains of a goldfish."

I didn't like lying to her, but this early in the quest a peace based on lies was more valuable than a brouhaha based on truth. "All right," I said. "A bunch of perverts were hanging around the box office, Jinx called the police and ran over, and I dropped the ladder and he climbed up on it until they went away."

"Why didn't he stay in the box office where he'd be safe?"

"He came out when they started to go away and then they came back but he'd locked himself out."

"This is so much bullshit. Why didn't the perverts chase him up the ladder?"

"I told them I had a gun." Tell one lie, supporting lies fly like popcorn.

Clover eyed the theater. Another woman—or *a* woman—was manning the box office. Womanning. "Who else would be hanging around over there but perverts?" She sniffed. "It *was* nice of you to help him. But nobody's even supposed to go up there!"

"That's why I didn't turn a card—I don't want to lose the record because some kook climbed the ladder. Clove, come on, good God—don't tell me you're jealous of some spaced-out transvestite."

She sniffed again, meaning the crisis was over. "Bullhorn," she said. "That's all you need."

ॐ

My adoring fans have forgotten me already. My 15 seconds were fun. Time to get serious. Time to buckle down.

I need a proper desk up here. A man needs a desk.

I leaned on the banister, digging the low light on the green hills. A long shadow on the sidewalk caught my eye. It was six or seven store-lengths. I shifted from elbow to elbow and it moved. I realized—it's me. It was me trying to figure out what my shadow was.

They're holding parades for the hostages all over the country. Celebrate but don't look too far back into history. The past is hungry and will eat your patriotism alive.

The wash & dry system I have will do, but 445 days without a shower is daunting. Clover could haul me up a hose, I could soap up & blast myself off like a horse. She found a great lightweight pop-up curtain rig, kind of like they use around manholes, in which I perform my ablutions.

I don't know what a story *means*. There, I said it. Throw me out of Teacher World. That's what they want—what does it *mean*? I get lost in the story, as in the woods. What do the woods *mean*? The meaning is a primal force. The meaning the *writer* intends might not be the true meaning at all. The subconsciousness's of writer & reader are at play together, beyond reason, out of control. Those young wolves sensed I was pretending to know what a teacher is supposed to know. They watched my dread of being found out leak like blood through my white shirt.

Persian rugs for sale (one a white tiger) on a chain-link fence by a vacant lot up a block (where a company of homeless people gather with shopping carts & makeshift shelter every night & by morning are gone like ghosts).

Son's Liquor, Grand Motel, laundromat, post office with old flag, Galore Nails. Day laborers outside House & Home, leaning down to every leaving driver.

William Golding said of *Lord of the Flies*: "I felt a tremendous visional force behind the whole book." How do you teach that? How do you *learn* it? How do you *read* it? I'm going to make up my own theory. The New Theory of Literature as Unknowable.

A tiny weed with one pink flower pokes up from a crack right in the middle of the sidewalk. Hard to be a flower in the city.

I need to lose myself in teaching as I lose myself in reading. I'm asking them to lose themselves. I'll stand up there in the middle of a cloud of unknowing & declare: Nobody can tell you what this means, this story, these people, this life! Find out, decide for yourself! Crash the state of wonder! Then the parents storm the classroom: How dare you tell my kid to think for himself! He's got to get into college and feed us in our old age! Don't be so fancy! Just tell him what the damn story means!

Be happy to see Spring, sleep sans long johns.

I dare to believe I can do this. It's easier to believe the impossible might happen than it is to believe the probable is all there is. The probable is not a happy place to live.

18

CLOVER

I scooted into the booth across from Nate. He drank straight from a metal malt container.

"What kinda breakfast do you call that?"

"Malt. What do you call that?" He meant my plate of crispy fries.

I looked around the empty café. "Well, it's clean." Clean as an old washed-up dump could be. Still, it was nice sitting for a minute with my son, the morning light warm through the big window, pedestrians gliding by, traffic muffled to a hum.

"Mom?" He wiped his malt mustache. "Are you jealous of Dad?"

"Where'd that come from?"

"When you and Dad were on the walkie-talkies about that Jinx."

"Men like women to be jealous. It makes them feel important."

"Is that Jinx a male?"

"Yes."

"Why's he do that?"

"Ask him. Or actually don't."

"So you could wear anything and own a movie theater in America."

"It's a hell of a country. So, hey, what do you know, here we are again, bud. You and me."

Nate nodded. "Did you know Dad was a flagpole-sitter when you met him?"

"He wasn't. He talked about it. It didn't register. He was cute, smart, we were in love. You'd think, majoring in psychology, I might have listened. He graduated, taught a while, then there he was, up on the first one. But he got down so fast, I thought, okay, that bizarre little fling is over."

"Why didn't you go and be a psychologist?"

"Oh, things happen."

"Me."

I shook my head. "I wasn't ready." I smiled. "You're the best kid, Nate."

"I thought I was a brat."

"You're the best brat. Daddy was a brat. He still is."

His wheels were turning. "Did you know Dad's dad?"

"No. He died when Daddy was thirteen."

"Oh, yeah." He looked out the window. "Am I a wanted child?"

"Been robbing banks? Of course you're wanted."

"Why does Dad go up there again?"

"You better not think he goes up there because of *you*."

"You never think he goes up because of *you*?"

"No! Why would I? If I did, I'd climb up and wring his neck. Look, Daddy and I wanted you. No matter what weird shenanigans we get up to, we wanted you, we want you now, and we'll always want you. Okay? Kook." I reached across and brushed his cheek with my knuckles.

We sat in the booth of the sad little café, early light pooling on the Formica between us. A jetliner the size of matchsticks crossed the sky, disappearing behind the platform where our husband and father sat, chasing some fickle inner mystery.

"Your face is all white," Nate said, "like you don't have any pores on your skin. And your hair is like a real dark rose."

"Well, don't stop now."

"You look like a girl in an old photograph. Where you wonder what old-fashioned thoughts they were thinking about." He kept looking, peering now. "I wonder where you met Dad."

"You know that. You don't know that? We met at a poetry reading. I told you this. Daddy read a poem. About a boy on his birthday. It was so sweet." I looked outside. "And so stoned."

"What?"

"*Creative.*"

"Were you guys on *drugs* when you had me?"

"No. Absolutely not."

"If I have a buncha gnarly chromosomes, man."

"Your chromosomes are fine. I *meant* that his *poem* was *visionary*. Want to hear it?"

"You have it?"

I tapped my red head.

"You know it by heart?"

I nodded. "It's called 'Candles.'" I cleared my throat, closed my eyes, and recited: "One difference is, I'm taller, and growing still. I crash up through the roof and keep on going. Up here I see the whole world at once. Morning is steep as the stairs on the hundredth floor, and I'm still growing. From this high, a jogger is a pair of red scissors cutting through the park. I can see every open-mouthed face in that jetliner headed to Cairo or Baltimore. In my shadow, cattle wobble like navy beans on the hip of a poppy-covered hillside. Miles of ribbons of freeway run and tides like a Ferris wheel are turned by the sun and moon. Everything is so far away it's a secret. When it's time for bed, I reel myself back through the hole in the roof like a diver reeling his buddy down through the hull of a sunken ship, and I tuck myself in. Slowly, galaxies huddle at my window, gentle as manger-side animals. For a while, getting sleepy, I count the stars like candles, candles, candles—that novelty kind you can't blow out."

Nate had closed his eyes. "Stars *are* candles you can't blow out." He opened his eyes. "He said he's like Jesus, at the manger."

"That's what they call artistic license."

"I think it's only the moon that makes the tides come and go."

"Well, that poem was the start of something big. Namely, you."

"Did you have sex right after he said the poem?"

"Uh, no. I did introduce myself. It was pretty much love at first sight."

"Did you ever smoke marijuana together?"

"Once maybe. Maybe twice."

"Did you take LSD?"

"No. Not by the time I was pregnant."

"So, you took it before then?"

"Once, I think. If you want to know how LSD can screw up your life, ask Daddy sometime."

"Did he have a bummer?"

I looked around the deserted café. "I'm only going to tell you this because we can't watch you twenty-four hours a day, and sometime somebody's going to offer you drugs and you're going to have to decide whether to take them or not, and the answer is *not*. You dig? And here's why. He was at UCLA, he almost had his degree, and right before class one day he dropped acid, as they say."

"He dropped acid in class? Was the blackboard melting? Was the teacher melting?"

"Things melting is not all it's cracked up to be. Anyway, the acid started doing its crazy stuff right in the middle of a lecture on F. Scott Fitzgerald. He wrote a book called *The Great Gatsby*. The professor was saying what a genius Fitzgerald was, what a masterpiece *The Great Gatsby* was. This professor didn't care much for Daddy to start with, because Daddy had too many opinions, so out of the blue he asked Daddy what Egg Gatsby lived in. An Egg is what they called a spit of land that stuck out in the bay. Daddy guessed East Egg when it was West Egg, or West when it was East, and the Professor made fun of him. Remember Daddy was on this terrible, horrible, awful, dangerous drug that can make you think you can fly off the roof—so he said that Fitzgerald and Gatsby and the Professor were all...pompous...dickheads." Nate gasped. "Do you know what 'pompous' means?"

"Like...fat and phony?"

"Just phony. You can be skinny and pompous."

"And him and Gasby had a penis for their head?"

"Gatsby. I can't believe I'm telling you this. So, then, Daddy got up and walked out of the class. He couldn't feel his body. He felt like he was on fire. He refused to apologize, got thrown out of the class, got drafted and went to Vietnam. And that's what can happen if *you* ever take drugs."

Nate gazed up at the orange pole, digesting the story. "But then he got nosebleeds and went to Germany and got out and met you and you got married and had me and everything turned out happy ever after."

I cleared my throat. "He *could* have gotten killed in Vietnam or a million other horrible things."

"Yeah." The point was so weak he gave it to me. "Aren't you supposed to say your opinion in college?"

"Yes, but if he wasn't on acid, he would have said it in a much nicer fashion."

"How do you call somebody a pompoused dickhead nicer?"

"Let me put it this way: Don't take drugs or I'll kill you."

He nodded and said, mostly to himself, "Alcohol's a drug."

I heard the dirge of cell doors. Oh, Jesus—was *that* why I told him the goddamn story? I showed Nate my emptying face.

"I only meant— Mom?"

"I know. It's okay."

Pedestrians floated past the window like ghosts, like guards. I might not think of it for days, then a wire got tripped and there it was—the jealous fight at the bar, my white '63 Chevy, flash of red, a muted cry, driving home with one eye shut, the morning, cops pounding on the door, taking me out to look at my rear bumper where Bobby's red shirt sleeve hung in the screaming sun.

"I didn't mean it that way," Nate said. "Did you and Dad drink, that's all I meant."

"It's the past, Nate. It's all right. It's the ancient past."

He could see it wasn't. "I don't know what to do."

"Did I ever tell you I started painting in there?"

"Yeah. Cooking too."

Two men in work clothes entered. They sat at the counter, one older, one younger.

"Hi, boys," I said. "Menus?"

Older shook his head. "Double Charley cheeseburger, giant Charley fries."

"Ditto," Younger said, good-looking, full of himself.

"For breakfast? Lemme whip you boys up a nice Brie omelet with julienne sweet peppers."

Older said, "Whip us up two double Charley cheeseburgers and giant Charley fries."

I stared at them. "How about double *Clover* cheeseburgers and giant *Clover* fries?"

"They good as Charley's?" said Younger.

"Let's find out." I got the patties and slapped them on the grill. "Nate, school."

He grabbed his books and lunch and ran out the door, calling up, "Dad! Dad! Mom told me your poem and your bummer! I'll never take drugs!"

"So," Younger said, "you gonna be down here, what, over a year? On your lonesome?"

I stopped building the burgers and stared Younger down. "Say what you mean."

"Jeez," Younger said. "Guess we can't kid her like we kidded Charley."

"I miss that old buzzard," Older said.

"Charley's gone," I said.

As I made their lunch they quietly discussed the way things change. I dumped the fries on their plates, slapped the buns atop their burgers, and slid the plates across the counter.

Younger said, "You should change that sign out there. I mean, just a suggestion."

I turned slowly, taking in the spot in one futuramic revelation.

"Damn," Older said, his mouth full. "This is *good*."

"Mmmph," echoed Younger. "What's *in* this? You're some cook, ma'am."

"I learned in prison."

"You were in prison?" said Older. "For what? If you don't mind saying."

"I don't mind saying," I said, even though I did. At that moment the inexplicable urge came over me to own and own boldly everything I'd ever done. "I killed a man."

19

JOE

I had a big map of the solar system on the wall in my room, the planets each a different beautiful color, tipped at an angle & floating in the inkwell of space. I dreamed of sending fiery rockets into that dark unknown, rockets my dad (an aeronautical engineer) and I would design together. (My father's idol was Galileo, who gave his name to me.) My dad had dreamed of being an astronaut but he was too old now. Instead, our rockets would blast off carrying pioneers who would land on other planets, claim them for America, and build cities under domes with gigantic TV sets and glass mansions and pure dichondra front yards the size of football fields, and cars that flew and went underwater and folded up to fit in your backpack. But 13 days after my 13th birthday, my father dropped dead of a swollen heart.

Nate zoomed by and yelled up something about never taking drugs. Well, that's good, but God knows what's going on down there.

On the morning of the funeral, Reverend Jack, our suddenly family minister, knocked on my door. He had come for a man-to-man. Reverend Jack helped me with my tie. His hands smelled like a barber's. He saw Graymondo on the windowsill and petted him. He was trying to think of something to say that I was supposed to never forget. He spotted the map of the solar system. He pointed at it and I looked at the beautiful colored planets and that rich black outer space, once a wonderland, now a wound. I knew as little about God as I did about death, but I knew that Reverend Jack was about to hook the two together like a ball and chain. He knelt and squeezed my shoulder with his cologned clammy hand. "Joey," he said, "do you know why the planets are arranged around the sun like they are, without any of them crashing into one another?"

What I wanted to say was, They haven't crashed into one another *yet!* The correct answer was that God didn't want them to crash into one another, and my father was dead because God wanted him to come up to Heaven where they could smack grounders around. "Because God made it like that!" I said, and the dam burst and came fierce incomprehensible tears of rage and grief.

After the funeral I went straight to *my* room and tore *God's* solar system off *my* wall.

20

CLOVER

My purse on my lap, I sat before the coffin-like desk of Donald Spoletti, the Loan Officer of First Federal-Pacific Cal-West Savings and Loan. Behind Spoletti, a large portrait of President Reagan grinned down at me. The imminent rejection of my loan application would have been easier to swallow had Spoletti tried to hide his bemusement as he scanned said application. I wanted to flee home to Charley's Spot and drink ten malts to drown my humiliation.

"Mrs. Magellan," Spoletti began. "In the context of Reaganomics, FFPCW prides itself on being one of the most eager and creative lenders in the state when it comes to encouraging small business. But you know this already—by way of the modest loan granted you in the purchase of, eh"—he consulted my application—"'Charley's Spot.' However, to grant a second, far more substantial loan, for the 'remodeling' of said Spot, and in so neglected an area, I'm afraid we'd require more collateral than a rather ancient Volkswagen, with all due respect."

"It's in really good shape." Pitiful.

"Unfortunately, Mrs. Magellan, I must inform you that, eh…"

Standing to leave, I said, "Well, thank you for your precious time."

But Spoletti was eyeing the application, crinkling his brow. "Magellan. Where have I heard that name? Magellan."

"He was the first person to sail around the world."

Spoletti shook his head, looking at the ceiling. "No, somewhere else. Very recently."

"Well, my husband was on the news for being up on a flagpole." There, I thought—an extra nail for you to pound into the coffin.

"A *flagpole*," he said. "The flagpole-*sitter*."

"That's right, Joe Magellan, the flagpole-sitter." I waited for Spoletti to say something, and imagined my purse slamming into the side of his plump, self-satisfied yuppie head. In fact, another pompous dickhead.

"That was your *husband*. Right there in front of…Charley's Spot?"

"It was, and it is."

"He's still up there?"

"What did I just say?"

Spoletti swiveled back and forth in his chair, tapping his lips with a pen, brow wiggly, eyes fixed on my new bangs, looking clear through me into some other time and place. "Mrs. Magellan," he said, "please sit down."

I hesitated, then sat, but on the last inch of the edge of the chair. All I could think was that he was going to try to have me or Joe or both of us committed, which I trusted he had no power to do.

"May I ask how long your husband has been up on that flagpole?"

I had to think, then lied a little. "Two weeks."

"Good Lord. And he's committed to remaining up there for some time to come?"

"He certainly is. Four hundred and forty-five days."

"That's an incredible effort to publicize a new business. Even heroic, in a capitalistic sense, one might say."

"One certainly might. If my husband is anything, he is a robust hero of capitalism. He loves supply-side economics. He'll do whatever it takes to put Charley's Spot on the map. Honestly, I believe he'd die up there and burn in hell if it would make that restaurant succeed."

Spoletti blinked. "He's not, eh, *imbalanced.*"

"Oh no, no, no. He's an English teacher."

He snapped out of his chair. "Stay right there, Mrs. Magellan, will you, please?"

To hide my boiling glee, I nodded discreetly, like a bid at an auction.

And at that Donald Spoletti scurried off to the office of the President of First Federal-Pacific Cal-West, big ideas filling his little head.

21

Carmen Basilica sulked to her car in the zoo parking lot. A gleaming limousine glided beside her and politely beeped its horn. She gave its opaque windows a menacing scan and marched on. The rear window lowered to reveal the white-haired Shipwreck Blake, natty in a black silk suit. "May I offer you a ride, Miss Basilica?"

Carmen slid her hand into her purse. "Who the hell are you?"

"I'm Shipwreck Blake."

Carmen stopped. "*Joe's hero*? You're Black. Aren't you dead? Let's see some ID."

Shipwreck produced a wallet and started to pull something out, but Carmen reached in and grabbed the whole thing and began to study its contents. "Walter Shipwreck Blake," she read. "That's your legal name? You got enough credit cards, Walter?" She flipped the wallet through the window. "What do you want from me?"

"You're a friend of his," said Shipwreck.

"I wouldn't go that far."

"And he's demonstrated an interest in you."

"He's crazy about me."

"May I give you a lift? I'll make it worth your while."

She regarded the limo from end to end. "You said the magic words." Shipwreck swung the door open and Carmen jumped inside.

22

JOE

Crawling from the mummybag, I stood and stretched in the gorgeous fuchsia sunrise. I updated Nate's Flip-A-Number sign, scanned the city-hive, and grabbed my journal:

16 days. Longest ever up.

Clover finally found me a bullhorn. I said, "Arf!" through it at a cocker spaniel a gentleman was walking. He stopped & we chatted. A crowd gathered & I ended up in an argument with a film buff about W.C. Fields' nose and the origin of the term "gin blossoms"! Let me tell you, the man with the bullhorn wins the argument every time.

Thoreau only had conversations *across* Walden Pond, which was more lake than pond. It CURTAILS SMALL TALK when you have to YELL EVERY WORD AT THE TOP OF YOUR LUNGS!

Days & nights float by sweet as little towns from a slow train. I sleep like a cat, write, blink at a cloud crossing the sun, alert at the bell on the food basket coming up. I am where I am supposed to be.

The smallest closet in any mansion in those Hollywood Hills is bigger than my entire home on high, yet for me this is a dream island in the sky.

Somebody mugged somebody last night at Haste & Western. Shouts, people running, a guy squirmed on the ground. I grabbed the new binos. The running men disappeared, people came out of a bar, the guy sat up, cops & ambulance arrived. Refused to go to the hospital, meandered away. I need a phone for emergencies.

Clover sent up a flimsy chaise lounge. It'll do.

Lots more greenery than you'd think up here. Some kind of maple trees every 40-50 feet along Western. They're boasting pops of fresh lime growth. Magnolias like dark pools, cypresses tall green flames. Silvery swaying eucalyptus, jacarandas ready to break, palm trees sentries in royal fright wigs.

Quieter, too. A horn, rumbling truck, siren, motorcycle, hopped-up hot-rod, passing radios make it up, but the distance transforms most sounds into water & wind in action.

The worst facet of flagpole-sitting is flagpole-shitting. The chemical toilet

& packaging accoutrements help, thanks to the astronauts, but nothing to approach the joyous freedom of a modern crapper. The pop-up mini-booth gives me relative privacy & Clover disposes of the packaged, chemicalized waste, for which I call all God's blessings upon her.

Some cloying tune was playing behind Nate when I talked to him on the walkie. I asked him what it was. "Neil Diamond, 'Love on the Rocks.'" To think that parents moaned about Elvis. The most offensive song from the 50s was Shakespeare compared to the soul-numbing pablum oozing from the radio nowadays. One thing I remember was how much my father and I dug that early stuff together—"Don't Be Cruel," "Rock Around the Clock," "Blueberry Hill," "16 Tons," "Tutti Fruiti," "Splish-Splash," "The Green Door." And how *happy* those songs were. Even when the subject was brokenhearted, suicidal despair, they *sounded happy*.

The loneliest hour is sundown. It gets me in bed early. I sleep with a mask & earplugs. I go deep when I sleep. I sleep so good either my conscience is clean or I'm an idiot.

When I wasn't writing, I had all the time in the world to read. Books were the one thing Clover and I had plenty of. What a pleasure it would be to simply enjoy the blessed things, instead of figuring out new ways to cram them down the throats of those sullen teenage demons-in-progress.

Books unread called to me, books read long ago and forgotten waited afresh, and others which, though universally loved and praised, I had struggled to connect with but never could, I would try again. I'd devour them all, a literary banquet without cease. Doris Lessing's *The Golden Notebook*, Saul Bellow's *Herzog*, Donald Barthelme's *Sadness*, Charles Bukowski's *Post Office*, Jane Austen's *Pride and Prejudice*, Richard Wright's *Native Son*, J.D. Salinger's *Catcher in the Rye*, and F. Scott Fitzgerald's *The Great Gatsby*. Those were the first books I had Clover send up, selected according to quirks of curiosity, pleasure, perversity, and hope, in no particular order.

I slapped on sun protection against the late February overcast, laid back in my chaise, and grabbed Doris Lessing, one of Clover's faves. As I recalled, Lessing, though admirably earnest, explained everything to death in an ungainly style with no discernible sense of humor. I would now try to discover what I had surely been missing.

Alas, *The Golden Notebook* proved as painful as I'd remembered. Lessing didn't write about people who had ideas, but about ideas who had people. It's a 500-page essay in which she shoehorned big artistic and political concepts into little cardboard characters. Flipping through her clanking prose, I found her declaring that a real novel, a novel that could call itself a novel, had to have the character of philosophy.

That was the problem right there. You can't write liberated, liberating fiction with the grand piano of philosophy strapped to your back.

I flipped again and landed in her Preface. There she argued that a writer is immature who wants readers to understand his or her book in the way that he or she understands it. To the contrary, Lessing says, a book is living and powerful and gives rise to lively conversation only when it is not understood!

"Doris!" I said. "Yes! I love you!"

That insight was a dew-covered rose in a wasteland of rotting furniture. Like Lessing, I deplored the autopsy approach to a novel: "We had to carve up the frog to find its meaning."

I looked out over the city. Lessing had affirmed my New Theory of Great Literature as Unknowable. God, I loved books, even books I couldn't stand.

"Hey, explorer!" It was Clover on the walkie. "Lunch?"

"Not hungry, hon, thanks. I'm eating books. Tried to read *Golden Notebook* again. There was one good line in there, and I know you love her, but I'd rather read a Russian phone book." I advanced a few of my critical notions on the book and its author.

She muttered something about me being a "damn brave man."

"I don't know about brave, I'm only being honest."

"*What?* I said you're a damn *cave*man!"

I picked up *Herzog*. I'd read it in the army in Germany. I hated it at the time, this self-centered sad sack with not one good thing to say about life. But either *Herzog* or I had changed, because I loved it now right off the bat. How can you resist the very first line where Moses says if he is out of his mind, it is okay with him! Herzog's dervishy letter writing electrified the first page, as if I'd stepped into a river and would now be swept away.

But by the second page Moses was eating a loaf of bread a rat had burrowed through and it flooded back to me—Herzog's journey was a meander through human hell, a terrible and desolate vision. Of course I empathized with Herzog's despair, but my own journey aloft stretched long and precarious before me, and I had to watch what I fed my soul up there. Herzog's gaping anxieties, forebodings, and outright terrors would not well serve my quest. I jumped around in the book with an aching sorrow, for Herzog, for every deranged person he ran into, for myself all alone at the top of that pole for another 400 plus days, with no human accompaniment, and what was I doing up there again? A point of blackness in the middle of my brain began to open; I slammed it shut, dropped *Herzog* and grabbed, by chance, *Sadness*.

Barthelme had never done much for me, but Clover claimed his writing was "like music." I would give Donald another go. The first story was called "Critique de la Vie Quotidienne." French title—bad start. Worse, the first sentence had the guy reading the *Journal of Sensory Deprivation*, while his ex-wife read *Elle*.

I wanted nothing to do with these people. Poe said, "Wisdom hates excessive cleverness." I struggled into the second page, wanting to climb into the story and push the smug narrator around, goad him into a fight, then pummel the last shred of irony out of him. If I had to hang out with the plodding Lessing or the snide Barthelme, I would leap like a bunny into Doris's humor-impaired arms.

"Joe! Hey! Joe!"

I looked over. It was Carmen, from Kerridge's seminar, from the zoo. She stood on the sidewalk like a half-dressed popsicle, red halter-top, pink shorts, and yellow sandals.

"What the hell?" I said.

She laughed like a little burro. "I told you you're as cured as me!"

"What do you want?"

"Sixteen days!"

"What do you want?"

"Don't be so grumpy. How about a little company?"

"Kerridge sent you."

"*Kerridge*? Why would *he* send me? Lemme up! Gimme the tour!"

With the savoir-faire of a butcher, Clover stood in the doorway wiping her hands on an alarmingly stained apron.

Carmen pretended not to see her. "I'd love to, Joe! But I thought you weren't supposed to have any visitors! Well, I'll think about it, Joe! Oh, hi, Mrs. Magellan." She marched down the sidewalk like she had laid the concrete herself.

"What are you," Clover said, "a rock star with your little groupie?"

"I can't stop some numbskull from coming around here."

She looked at her fingernails. "I'll be inside."

"I'll be up here."

I watched Carmen cross Western and waltz north in her little rainbow get-up before cutting up Haste out of sight.

I closed *Sadness* and opened *Post Office*. Good ol' Bukowski—a slob, a master slob, shameless, true as a bit tongue and twice as funny. A defiant roarer in the teeth of rot and lies and death. He would have dug the mysterious pursuit of flagpole-sitting. Not to mention I'd done a part-time stint at the post office in Venice while going to UCLA.

However, I ran into trouble in the opening chapter, which featured mailman Hank having sex with a lonely woman with a "big ass" who was "a good lay." It was junior high stuff. Another woman on Hank's route wanted to know where Harold the regular mailman was, and Hank tells her Harold's dying of cancer—a lie. The woman is shocked. Hank says yeah, hands the woman her mail, all bills, and she instantly forgets about Harold and whines about the bills.

Bukowski was saying people were like that, they didn't give a damn. Maybe so, but they gave a damn about their mail carrier. He/she delivers their *mail*, and there's a fondness, a trust, an intimacy that develops between them. It was a betrayal of Bukowski's honesty and authenticity.

"And look at this." I found fifteen entire pages out of a measly total of 196 which were nothing but official warnings from the post office to Hank for showing up late, not showing up at all, driving drunk on the job, fucking customers, etc. The notices were bureaucratic mumbo-jumbo, meant to be funny but not even in the ballpark. I could hear Bukowski: "Am I gonna get away with padding my wisp of a book with these stupid goddamn fake notices?"

I dropped *Post Office* on top of *Golden Notebook*, *Herzog*, and *Sadness*. I'd gone through four books in fifteen minutes. Next was good ol' Jane Austen's *Pride and Prejudice*. Perhaps the purest writer of the lot. I lay back and prepared for a voyage of sophisticated literary delight. However, not three pages into the book Ms. Austen began to let me down, and not gently. Despite Jane's comic intentions and masterful artistry, her vain characters' slavish obsession with money, marriage, and mocking one another was nothing but irritating. Yes, her choices as a woman in that era were limited, she wrote about what she knew, etc. I was a teacher, I knew all that crap. I wanted to grab back junior high Bukowski to knock the taste of Austen's doilies, adolescent romance, and silver polish out of my mouth.

I snatched up *Native Son*. Fifteen years earlier, along with Salinger and Holden, Richard Wright and Bigger Thomas had been the inspiration for my own alleged novel. Now I looked forward to Wright's passionate rage, but was snagged by picayune annoyances on the first page, such as how such as how an alarm clock could ring in a silent room, how a *brriiing* could be a clang, and how the clang could stop any other way but abruptly.

For me, *Native Son* had been the first book that dared speak Black rage and grief, dared justify Black violence against whites, dared urge Marxism on a society where capitalism and racism walked hand in hand. Wright had opened my white-bread eyes, and yet now here I was, unable to re-enter so human and ecstatic a work because an alarm clock couldn't clang briiing! in a silent room.

"What is going *on* up here?" I said. "Is it me or is it the books?"

I breathed deep, picked up *Catcher in the Rye*, Old Reliable, and settled back for a poignant, hilarious mosey through Salingerland.

Alas, after Wright's flawed but ardent bellow of rage and redemption, Holden seemed, like the frauds in Barthelme, Austen, etc., another mere phony, an anti-phony phony, from the get-go, asking me sarcastically if I really care to hear his story. I don't, I thought, stunned. What had been the most authentic expression of the heart of a teenage boy (though written by a gentleman of letters) now struck me as shaky artifice. I read more but my perception of fake anti-artificiality would not lift. I set the book down, staving off literary seasickness.

Under a queasy, cream-of-celery-colored sky, I did some Synedochean breathing to calm the tumult within. I'd had too much sun. Setting up the umbrella, I found under the chaise the one book I hadn't ventured into yet—*The Great Gatsby*.

If every book so far had turned me off in one way or another, including those I once loved uncritically, why try *Gatsby*, which repelled me more than any other acclaimed book in the language? Perversely, I grabbed it and popped it open at random:

"It was a photograph of half a dozen young men in blazers loafing in an archway through which a host of spires were visible. There was Gatsby, looking a little, not much, younger—with a cricket bat in his hand."

Fitzgerald was every bit the artisan Austen was, but who cared about her silly elitists or his corps of delusional, spoiled brats, hangers-on, and drunken party-freaks? Yes, the book was meant to *expose* Gatsby's hollow soul, the American Nightmare, blah blah, but Fitzgerald's heart's desire was precisely a fucking cricket field with martinis all around.

At random again: "But above the grey land and the spasms of bleak dust which drift endlessly over it, you perceive, after a moment, the eyes of Doctor T. J. Eckleburg. The eyes of Doctor T. J. Eckleburg are blue and gigantic—their retinas are one yard high. They look out of no face but, instead, from a pair of enormous yellow spectacles which pass over a nonexistent nose."

I had always sneered at the farcical symbol of Doctor Eckleburg on his weathered billboard. Now it had me thinking eerily of myself on the flagpole over Los Angeles:

"But his eyes, dimmed a little by many paintless days under sun and rain, brood on over the solemn dumping ground."

My neck prickled. "How does this end again?" I said. I found out: "So we beat on, boats against the current, borne back ceaselessly into the past."

That was more like it—heavy on the metaphor, straining for gravity and scope. The book proper was followed by eighty pages of notes, emendations, appendices, and Fitzgerald's own Introduction (to an earlier reprint) which ended with: "But remember, also, young man: you are not the first person who has ever been alone and alone."

Why twice—"alone and alone"? Was Fitzgerald talking to Gatsby? Was that what Gatsby's whole fancy mess came down to—the dread of being alone?

"Joe!" And alone. "Joe!" Clover was on the walkie again. "Sixteen days!" she said. "I just realized!"

I tossed Fitzgerald aside and lay on my stomach, head over the edge. Clover wore a red and white checked dress made in Heaven to go with her pale face and red hair.

"Isn't this the longest you've ever been up, honey?" She shaded her eyes, the breeze played her dress. I wanted to get down. "You don't seem too excited."

"Bad luck to talk about it!"

She nodded. Alone and alone. What was I doing up there? What was I doing? Out of nowhere a tear fell straight from my eye and on the way down broke in a mist. Clover touched her face and looked past me at the sky.

23

JOE

Bloody coup attempt in Spain. Blurry photo of tortured Basque corpse. Madman killing Black kids in Atlanta. Americans favor big cut in food stamps. Rapes, murders, accidents.

McLuhan said reading the paper is like getting into a warm bath. A tubful of soothing horror. It numbs you with gratitude that it's not you, so you can go do your job & buy & sell crap & avoid a very unproductive mental collapse every moment of your life.

How can I not climb down & do my damnedest to stem the bloody tide? Or at least have the decency to go mad with weeping. Is this passivity simply human or a sign of losing your soul?

Dream shard: pitch black sky started splitting in places & frantic sperms of light scurried in like looters.

I'm sick of my opinions. I want to go one day with no opinions. No opinions! Starting first thing tomorrow.

I love redwood. Solid but soft. It takes a nail good, as Robert Frost might have said. It is like blood & bone, one. I'm pleased I didn't paint the platform orange, as I considered. The banister is pine, solid, two-railed, two posts per platform side, plus a fatter post at each corner, the whole contraption navel high. The trapdoor, 3 by 3, is on the west side of the three-foot section of orange pole that rises above the platform. The trapdoor opens away from the pole. Walking barefoot on the smooth sanded redwood makes me happy. It holds sunshine like a sponge. Of course, it might soak up the rain like a sponge, too, but I didn't want the wood shellacked. I'd rather it be a little damp than slip on shellack & take a very steep spill.

Clover says, Don't pray for yourself, only others. But if your hurt or need is great, then go on & pray for yourself, if only to get it out of the way. God, help me stay up here, & when I get down I'll be a happy man, a wiser man, more loving, & I'll spread my happiness & wisdom & love to my family & students & everyone I meet. Amen.

Why can I write about my father's death & not my mother's? Because my father's is mythical, my mother's bone raw real. I'm sick of the past. Can a writer be sick of the past? Maybe I'm not a writer. Had Clover send up the Holder & Biggen manuscript. Couldn't bear to look at a word of it.

Up close, one at a time, people are hard to take, but as a distant suffering immensity, they are easy to pity, embrace, love. You have to go up a mountain, flee to the desert, climb a flagpole to see the human race in all its loneliness and loss. True compassion may require leaving humanity entirely behind.

24

JOE

Necessities and conveniences congested my precious 100 square-feet. Added to the original items were the new radio, a mini-fridge, blender, protein powder and vitamins, a pile of barely skimmed *Times*, hotplate, umbrella, haircutting kit, chaise lounge, night light, rocking chair, an extra walkie-talkie for chats with passersby, warmer clothes for cooler nights and cooler clothes for warmer days, Zorro sleep mask, a small Asian floor-desk, a broom (no dustpan), a little tape recorder and my smorgasbord dubs (Van the Man, Pretenders, Eric Dolphy, Chopin, John Lee Hooker, Billie Holiday, Bach, Dylan, Jimmy Reed, Neil Young, Ahmad Jamal, Big Brother, Emmylou, Miles, John Prine, Ivory Joe Hunter, Leonard Cohen, Slim Harpo, King Brinich, Lavern Baker, Stravinski, Jimi), and a potted mini-ficus—a gift from Jinx—which fit perfectly atop the three-foot section of pole extending above the platform.

Clover and I were on our walkies.

"You sure we can afford all this?" I said.

Clover cleared her throat mysteriously. "Look at it as an investment."

"In what?"

"Honey, you've got twenty-one days. Enjoy the perks. Over and out!"

A restlessness befell me, a gnawing discontent. I lost what routine I'd gathered. Clover had sent up a fresh stack of novels, to no avail; I remained disconnected from the written word. My magnificent vista turned flat as plywood with buildings and trees and a sky painted on. The news was like claws. Every talk show conversation foamed with contempt. So familiar was I with the music on my tapes and the radio, it all blurred into one long irksome echo.

I weighed asking Clover to buy me a little TV. Would a TV disqualify me from the record? I foresaw Shipwreck getting wind of it. However, the mere thought of acquiring a TV calmed me down enough to consider meditating. Way back I'd discovered I had a bit of a gift for the ancient pursuit. From the first time I tried it, under the roadside tutelage of a fellow hitchhiking hippie in San Anselmo, it came easy. I immediately enjoyed its effects. Since then I'd cobbled together a personal method from various books and teachers. Meditation centered and settled me, and allowed me now and then a small nirvana of sorts, an experience of extraordinary clarity, simplicity, stillness, emptiness of mind and emotion.

But at the moment it was impossible. I couldn't do it. I had an itch. A bee buzzed around me. A horn honked. Impatience poked and nagged me. The sun licked me with its rough tongue. I set up the umbrella and the breezy shade was too cool. The oms felt unnatural, forced, no flow. I tried the Jesus Prayer for mercy, but got into an argument with myself over whether it was mercy which I truly wanted most. I was stuck mulling whatever secret rigmarole Clover was up to down there. I tried writing:

The university administration offered me a choice: suspension, or an abject apology to both the prof & the class. The class? I gave them the time of their lives. I would no more apologize for calling those three pompous dickheads than Antigone would have apologized to the evil king for trying to bury her brother. Suspension it was.

Waiting for a Greyhound to take me south to move back in with Uncle Wayne, I daydreamed about dying some tragic & painless death as a result of the suspension & what a lesson that would prove for everyone who had played a part. All of them huddled around the coffin, bawling buckets of remorse. But forget *enemies*—what *friends* did I have who would attend? Uncle Wayne, but he was not an expressive man, so there might be not a single tear shed.

All I remembered of the entire desperate bus ride from Berkeley to Pomona was my little goateed seatmate, an anthropologist who had been living with cannibals in a jungle in Papua New Guinea. The diminutive fellow referred to Margaret Mead as "Margie" & wore brand new red saddle shoes too big for his small feet, with no socks. Whether the little chap was an anthropologist or a magnificent liar, I was grateful that his graphic adventures in cannibalism took my mind off my own dismal life for the while.

"Were you ever afraid of getting eaten?" I asked. "Hell, yes!" said the tiny gentleman. "But I never lost my head. If you forget everything else, lad, always remember: Whatever happens, never panic."

I stopped and read it over, wincing throughout. I'd fix it later. I continued, in the now:

Is the old man still out there, lurking, watching me from his limo? Where did he get his money? What brought him out of the woodwork? On my first night up. Is it possible he sees me as a serious threat to his record? No sign of him since that repulsive, cruel, evil boombox prank.

I ought to name this thing, this pole, this apparatus of my life.

I heard a loud purring from under the pole. It sounded like a thousand-pound cat. I popped the trapdoor for a look. It was Carmen, rubbing her backside up and down the pole, purring indeed. She wore orange sunglasses, a black thong, and a pink pirate blouse, the top buttons undone, no bra. Lying on my stomach, I gazed through the trapdoor right down her blouse. She smiled up at me—with orange eyes! As the door to Clover's Spot swung open, I tried to stand, fell through the trapdoor head-first, and woke thrashing and gasping.

25

CLOVER

Joe lay on his stomach, looking down through the trapdoor like a god through the clouds of Mt. Olympus. "People like things to stay the same," he said. "We're gonna lose every damn customer."

"I highly doubt that," I said. I was on a stepladder leaning against the front exterior wall of the café. I'd hired a couple UCLA students who painted the olive drab building a bright rose, painted out "Charley's Spot" on the sign in front, which I was now replacing with "Clover's Patch" in a rich ruminative blue. They were the same sort of brazen colors I employed in the paintings that Joe hated.

He watched me on the ladder.

"Be careful on that thing. That's all I need, you falling off there and breaking your neck."

"You sweet-talker, you." I was filling in the outline of the big *C*.

"You're pretty slick with that brush." I did not remind him I was an artist. "Did you deliberately pick colors that clash with my orange?"

In fact, now they were up, the rose *was* too strong and the blue too dark, and I loved it.

"It's fine for a Diego Rivera mural," Joe said. "Kinda turbulent for a sandwich place." I ignored him. "Is everybody going to know what it means, 'patch'?"

"What else would it mean, a patch of Clover."

"Pirate, maybe?"

"A pirate store?"

"I'm just asking, is *Patch* the name of a café?"

"Is *Spot* the name of a café?"

"Hey, you know what—it makes you happy, go for it. They'll figure it out. By the way, you happen to know what day it is?"

"Uh, March 6th?"

"I have a month up."

"Oh."

"That's it?"

"I thought it was bad luck to talk about it." I dipped the brush in the can.

"By the way, how much is all this setting us back?"

"Not even half of what all your little distractions up there set us back."

"You did all the paperwork for changing the name?"

"Stop buggin' me, boy! *Sit!*" I painted and sang "Starting Over" and heard the trapdoor slam shut.

26

Joe rubbed his grizzled chin. He would shave. He grabbed his razor, Foamy, water bottle, wooden bowl, hand towel. He sat on the edge of the platform in the noonday sun and gazed into the round hand mirror that hung from a nail in the banister.

Frustrated with Clover's defiance, he remembered his dream of Carmen and strove to see himself from her perspective. He smiled and squinted, as if he were happy to see himself even though he couldn't quite figure himself out. There was a familiarity in that face that led strangers to be certain they knew him from someplace.

It was an earnest face, featuring curious coffee-bean-colored eyes. A face of ardent independence, or resistance. Watchfulness shimmered in it like moonlight off a deep lake. If you want to be my friend, this face announced, you will have to work a little bit, but the reward will be worth it.

It appeared younger than its thirty-five years. Good skin, but for a chicken pox scar under one eye. Good bones, if a little too much forehead. And there was a catch in there somewhere, a wariness hidden in those dark eyes (the right eye a quarter of a notch higher than the left), yes, a wariness lurking in that sensitive, determined, slightly tilted mouth. And a nice-sized nose, bent a creak to the right from a drunken brawl at a pizza bar in Nuremberg.

Joe thought, You keep looking at your face—bent nose, lopsided mouth, eyes offset—you become a Picasso. He noticed, in the midst of shaggy topsoil-colored locks, a single gray hair, right in the front. Was it the light? He yanked it out; it was white as a ghost. He looked and found another. His heart skipped a beat.

Well, nothing he could do about it now. He needed a trim. When the army shaved his head in basic he swore no barber would ever cut it after he got out; no barber had. That first week home he had bought a ten-piece haircut kit from Thrifty's. The cut looked a little off here and there sometimes, but it did the trick, and Clover helped with the stuff in the back. But up there, who cared?

Or, if not a wariness, something like a…*guarded*…*sorrow*?

And a sturdy chin, he added, as if some tenacity were settling through the years at the bottom of his complicated Scorpio visage.

Or if not sorrow, then a glimmer of—dare he think it—*wisdom?* There was definitely some sort of *otherness* in there, a fitful presence sliding feature to feature, a trace ahead of his perception. He began to wonder if his face were in some sense *haunted.*

Enlivened and disturbed, he peered in for the secret of those brooding eyes. It was as if all his life he'd been driving somewhere alone, and now in the mirror he made out the dark shape of a stowaway in the back seat.

He remembered climbing the ladder that first evening, and his memory of the night he spent on the beach at San Simeon. He had gazed at the lights of Hearst Castle in the high distance, and wondered if the place were haunted. In the blackness of the coast the illuminated castle floated in the night sky, blazing. He identified with the befuddled surveyor in Kafka's *The Castle*, gazing at the looming edifice, wondering who had summoned him, what he was supposed to survey, how he might get up there, and why the village was making it so absurdly difficult to get answers to his questions. "San Simeon," he said, staring at himself. And thus was the pole named. "San Simeon," he said, satisfied.

It was not a bad face, he concluded, not a bad face at all. A man's face is his castle, he thought, haunted or not. Now he would shave. He would let her revel in her flamboyant rose café, and any other tomfoolery she had up her sleeve. He squeezed a load of Foamy into his hand, smeared it over his face, and drew down the razor from the bottom of his sideburn to the corner of his jaw, smooth as a paint stroke, thinking, Everything I know about shaving, I taught myself.

PART III

"O, my sons, my sons, I, Simeon of the pillar,
by surname Stylites, among men;
I, Simeon, the watcher on the column till the end..."

—Alfred, Lord Tennyson

27

JOE

First rain up here late last night & this morning the city! Every piece of trash washed away, sidewalks & pavement like new. Cloudless sky so blue you can hear it, trees & buildings ravished by sunshine.

Got the tent up but forgot Nate's cardboard Flip-A-Number sign. Poor thing swole up like oatmeal and crumbled. Boy was devastated. Yelled at me. Good for him. Clover sent up a box of chalk and a blackboard.

Felt so good I delved into the second batch of books Clover sent up. Alas, the curse remains.

Always loved Dostoevsky's *The Idiot*, but all I saw now was how deviously manipulative sweet little Prince Myshkin was. At every turn, the author's meaty hands left sweaty prints on the plow. What was once the richest, freest style now seemed flamboyant amphetamine-driven bloviation.

Made it to page 2 of Faulkner's *Light in August*. Faulkner's oceanic vision of the South as national subconscious had turned into a swamp trudge, tangled in magnolia roots, couldn't breathe!

I didn't even make it past the first paragraph of Henry James' *The Portrait of a Lady*.

"Under certain circumstances there are few hours in life more agreeable than the hour dedicated to the ceremony known as afternoon tea. There are circumstances in which, whether you partake of the tea or not—some people of course never do—the situation is itself delightful."

Fie! If he's spoofing British fooey, he's taking far too much pleasure in it, a la Fitzgerald with the American Dream.

Tried Sherwood Anderson. In the title story from *Certain Things Last*, the guy says he's been considering writing a book for a year, and tomorrow he's going to finally start it. I was not about to read another book about anybody writing a book, or not writing a book & reflecting ironically upon his failure.

Nabokov's *Despair* commenced with a cute, smug hoax, smart-aleck post-modern trick on the reader. Narrator on first page describes his mother in detail, then says he's lying, then says lying is one of his best characteristics. Fellow says he's lying on page 2, how can you believe *anything* he says?

Unreliable narration is one thing, but I'm not reading a book that ends telling me it was a dream. In this world of lies, fiction is the one class of expression you must be able to trust.

Flaubert's *Sentimental Education*: read a few pages, remembered it, no need to go on. Moreau is patently mad, obsessed with his fevered image of the semi-idiot Madame Arnoux. Moreau is an infantile, self-centered halfwit & Madame Arnoux fulfills his quest for an unfulfillable "love," i.e., teen-like lunacy. I thank God for the grounded serenity of my relationship with Clover.

Next tried Alice Walker—*The Third Life of Grange Copeland*. Walker has a bigoted white woman drowning in an ice hole. Grange, a Black man, gives her his hand, but she refuses, choosing her racist hatred over life itself. As she goes under, she calls him "nigger" with her very last breath. Teach me about racism, I got a lot to learn, but one time a riptide caught me & I came close enough to drowning to know that if the devil himself had offered me his hand, I would have grabbed that thing & held on, just as that white bigot would have grabbed Grange's black hand and just as greedily as she would have grabbed the hand of Jesus himself.

My literary bitchiness is intensifying. I'm looking for any little reason to stop reading. Surely it will pass. I love potatoes—salad, fries, steamed, cold boiled potato sandwiches, Clover's tater enchiladas, even salted raw—but every now & then I can't stand the dull, crude, ugly, profane tuberous things. The same could be true of literature. It's never happened before, but up here, after all, special circumstances prevail.

This roadblock sent me back to the first time I realized what a story was, what it could do to you. Oddly, it was about a rocket ship. Uncle Wayne gave me a collection of science fiction to take my mind off my father's death. One story in there, "Shipshape Home" by Richard Matheson, was about a group of people who live in a tall building which they discover is a disguised alien rocket ship designed to shanghai earthlings back to the alien planet. At the moment of discovery, the rocket engines start up under the building. The people run outside to what they think is a safe distance, but the ground starts lifting up right under them—the whole entire block is an alien rocket ship taking off!

I remember laughing at the surprise & chill of it, a horrible predicament you escape, then look around & see you're still in the middle of it, with no way out. No matter how smart you were, there was always something big & powerful & unknown going on behind everything, inside everything, that could be wonderful or terrible or both. God help me if I had now somehow lost that capacity to lose myself in a story and its telling.

A man strolling down Western caught my eye. He was in the street, walking along the line of parked cars. Though he was dressed sportily, the quality of his clothes was uncertain at that distance. Was it poverty simple or millionaire casual? His scruffy hair could have been the result of a bad cut from a fellow homeless one, or chic yachtsman cool. The man was in no hurry. He had nowhere to go and nobody to see, or else everywhere to go and everybody to see and the power to make them wait. The fellow fished a chain of keys out of his pocket and dangled them as he walked. All those keys could have fit important doors, or could have been stolen. I wondered which of the cars the man would get in. As he looked through his keys, he hesitated at an old beat-up Honda, and I conceived the man's entire flop of a life, but he walked on, stopped at a shiny new Mercedes, got in, pulled out, and sped off.

I gulped the exquisite iced lemonade Clover had sent up with the books. As my taste buds rang and my head filled with the reverie of making love with her that last night on Earth, forty-one days before, someone began pounding on the café door. I looked over: a young couple peered into the café. I called down, they looked up.

"Hi!" the woman said. The man pointed at the blackboard. "Forty-one days!"

"Yep. Hey, you want to use the walkie-talkie? I have an extra one I can lower down."

The couple looked at each other. "Well, we'd like to eat," the man said. "Are you closed? The sign says 'Closed.'"

"What? No, no, no. Is she in there?"

"Somebody's banging around. There's a sheet over the window."

"*Sheet?*" I got on the walkie. "Clover! Come in!"

"What!" Clover barked.

"We got customers! Open up! Why's a *sheet* over the window?"

"Sit! Over and out."

"Clover!"

Our customers wandered off as I lay on my stomach and hung my head upside-down to see inside. A sheet, indeed, hung over the window. I had a bad feeling. I spotted Nate coming home from school.

"Nate! Come on! Hurry! Get in there and find out what she's up to! Tell her to please pick up the walkie-talkie when I call her!"

Nate knocked on the door and Clover peeked out and let him in.

28

CLOVER

"Oh shit, Mom!" Nate said.

A sledgehammer over my shoulder, I stood tall in the magnificent chaos. "It's the resurrection of our sad café, demolition phase."

The counter stools had been torn from the floor; the counter itself slumped in chunks against the walls.

"Did you tell Dad?"

"Why should I tell Dad?"

"He'll freak out!"

"Tough titties."

He walked among the shambles. "Oh, man, is he ever gonna have a bummer."

I surveyed the upheaval. "I'll have to hire somebody for a few things. I got a loan."

"Dad doesn't borrow money! Don't let no lender nor borrower be, man!"

"Nothing he can do about it. Besides bitch 'n' moan."

Nate dropped his books where he stood. "Can I wreck something?"

29

JOE

I was rumbled awake early by a big fancy white truck pulling in the driveway, with "Bernino's Fine Furnishings" on the side. Two men leapt out. I popped the trapdoor. "Hey!" One fellow glanced up and saluted impertinently. "You got the wrong place!" I said. The other guy ignored me and knocked on the café door.

Clover stepped out in her bathrobe and slippers.

"I told them they have the wrong place!" I said.

She seethed at the men out of my hearing, gesturing and jabbering. They jumped back in the truck and drove up the driveway behind the café, choosing to exit through the alley, I imagined. Clover marched up the driveway after them in her skunk slippers. I could see the truck maneuvering in the back, parking, it appeared. Not a good sign.

"What are they doing back there? Clover! What the hell are you *doing* down there? What's in that truck? What have you done?"

She turned and pointed up at me. "Why am I afraid of you? As if you could do anything about it! I'm *renovating*, Mister Flagpole-Sitter!"

"Renovating? Renovating *what*? That *dump*?"

"My *life*!"

The rear gate on the truck clattered up like the gates of hell opening.

"Oh, my God! How do you think we're paying for whatever's in there?"

"I had a nest egg." She headed for the back. "Come down and stop me!"

I paced the platform like a wild shot on a pool table. "Nest egg! Where'd she get a nest egg?" What else was she doing down there? Anxiety bucked through me like toxic waste. I gasped for air. "Oh no," I said. I had to get down.

Dreadfully familiar, this particular hysteria had assailed me sooner or later every time up. It was the many-triggered phenomenon which had been the beginning of the end of each attempt. This was no passing urge to dismount. This was a primal compulsion to get down, as powerful as the compulsion to go up, a red light screaming that catastrophe would strike if I stayed.

In the middle of my head a lion with Shipwreck's face roared: Get Down Now!

Storm clouds rolled in like freighters, black, silver, military green. I drove the pen over the desert of the page:

Please help me don't make me get down! 42 days & she doesn't care. HOW COULD SHE DO THIS TO ME!!! We're broke & she's buying high-class crap for that rathole. Which is worse, a secret nest egg or no nest egg & she's charging it? GOD HELP ME STAY UP! Keep me away from that trapdoor! I'll hate myself if I get down! I'll hate her! I'll hate everything!

Is that commotion from the monster clouds or the workers unloading fine merchandise that will put us on Poor Street?

I flashed on "The Short Happy Life of Francis Macomber." "Why didn't you poison him?" Wilson asked Mrs. Macomber. If I die right now, what would I have to show—failure after failure—as father, husband, teacher, writer, flag-pole-sitter.

A gigantic old crow tried to peck me on the fucking head! I looked right into his ghastly eyes! Now he's sitting on a phone pole looking at me. Do I have a death mark? Now he took off. I'm the Ancient Mariner!

Think of something to stay! What would Hemingway think of my quest? He'd make a snide bullfighting comment. He wouldn't last a week with nothing but his miserable nada self. How about Emily Dickinson? She'd love it. She'd envy me, from her little room, peeking through the plain cotton curtains. Clover, I hate you! Camus would drag on a cig & squint & nod. He'd understand. Sartre would harrumph and bloviate. Sylvia Plath would love it. Maybe she wouldn't've put her head in that oven if she could have come up here, gotten away from her husband, kids, life, achtung abuses. Even if the rules allowed it, Clover'd never come up, but Sylvia might have, or Emily. Emily would never hide a nest egg from me. Sylvia might. Fitzgerald would hate it up here. He'd get a tummyache. He'd find out what alone and alone was all about. Hawthorne would love it. *The Flagpole of the Seven Gables.* Thoreau, *Walden Pole.* Emerson would haul a podium up. The Brontës would love it. Shakespeare? He could dig it. "To be up or not to be up." Salinger would get it.

WHY ARE YOU DOING THIS TO ME, YOU CRUEL COLD-HEARTED RENOVAT-ING NEST-EGG-HIDING TRAITOR BITCH!

30

JOE

I tried to pry the renovation details out of Nate, but the boy was caught in the middle and I had no will to push. If Clover was cracking up, she was cracking up. If she put us in the poorhouse, that's where we'd go. If I went nuts in response, or fell off in some nightmare walkabout, amen. I couldn't do nothing about nothing. It was a desperately relaxing place to be, and sleep was the only response.

Sleep usurped my life. I succumbed to twelve hours of unconsciousness a night, plus prolonged, drooling naps throughout the day. All roads led to sleep. The sun, the moon, the flagpole, the stars, clouds, traffic, food, politics, money, marriage, the future—everything was a sedative.

Coming to, I would gaze entranced at the city and fill the journal with mad scrawlings:

On the side of a distant building through the binos: illuminated earthquake mural of an elevated freeway falling apart and a black tidal wave in the background rising out of a red sky to engulf the city.

Had a tsetse fly bitten me? I ate like a parakeet. I lost weight. I neglected to wash. Clover saw it as a show of self-pity, a passive-aggressive ploy.

She had hurtled us into bankruptcy and pounded a spike through my trust. If she had a nest egg, she hadn't loved me enough to let me know. Clinging to the betrayal might have been all that was keeping me sane. That and sleep. My earplugs and mask sank roots into my eardrums and eyeballs.

31

NATE

I got off the bus and headed towards the entrance of the school. A bunch of guys were standing around the flagpole. They watched me coming. Tommy Trabert and his big head stepped in my way. He wasn't my friend. "Where you going?" he said.

I was short for my age, but I had a lip on me like Mom said. I got that feeling where I had to say something to get my breath: "Emergency meeting, United Nations."

"The *what?*" Tommy said. "You a comedian, dipshit?"

One of Tommy's dumb friends poked him. "Don't poke me! See that flagpole, *Nathaniel?* Climb it. Like your *monkey* daddy. Oof, oof!"

When Dad first went up, a few kids said things. They did it before at other schools with other poles. I acted like I ignored it. He got down then people forgot. But he was staying up now. So if I wimped out, it would go on in on.

The other boys went, "Climb, monkey Nathaniel! Oof, oof!"

They backed me toward the flagpole. If I got mad I wouldn't be so afraid, but you have to really be mad. I tried to remember the boxing lesson Dad gave me, keep your guard, move your head, bob in weave, pay attention, breathe, turn your wrist when you do a punch, a jab, a hook, a uppercut if you were real close. It was the same boxing lesson Dad's Dad gave him. My back hit the pole.

"Climb, monkey," Tommy said real soft.

"Climb, monkey!" said the dumb sheep. That's what Dad said people were. Sheep one day, lynch mob the next. "Climb, monkey!"

"I bet you're a crazy little monkey like your crazy old man," Tommy said.

"My old man's not crazy!" I yelled in Tommy's big square face. "Mail-box head!"

Tommy's eyes got little. He poked my heart bone. "Your father's a rangtang." Poke. "Daddy Rangtang. That means your *mother*—" poke "—is *Mama* Rangtang."

I made a fist down by my side and breathed and relaxed and gave him a right uppercut with all my might. It connected perfect right under his chin. Electricity went in my hand bone and his teeth clanked and his head went up like a Pez holder. He walked backward grabbing the air. The other boys made barnyard noises. Tommy put his head down like a bull and charged me. I stepped to one side and he ran smack in the pole and folded down like a cheap deck of cards.

I stepped on his back and shimmied up the pole. I was out of reach before one of them made a grab. I stopped ten feet up and looked down. I felt like a feather. "You want climb?" I said. I shimmied up some more. I felt like Jack going up the beanstalk. My hands were sticky I guess from the sweat drying. My rubber shoes held the pole like brakes. I felt like a fly. "You want rangtang!"

Mr. Powell came running out. He was the principal. "All right, break it up!" Tommy was woozy, like one leg was shorter than the other. "Tommy, can't you stay out of trouble for *one*—" Mr. Powell was looking up at me with his mouth open. "*Nate?*"

"He started it!" Tommy cried. "I was standing here!"

"Get down off there!" Mr. Powell said. "*Now.*"

I shimmied higher.

"It was a sucker punch," Tommy said. "Right?" he asked the sheep, but they were watching me. Somebody further away yelled, "Go, Nate!" and the rest jumped in, "Go, Nate! Go, Nate! Go, Nate!"

"Shut up! Shut up!" Mr. Powell said. "Nate, if you fall off there, I'll break your neck."

"I'll fall all I want!" I said. "It's America, Mr. Powell!"

"It's America, Mr. Powell!" everybody said.

I climbed higher and kept going toward the flag—everybody yelling made my muscles stronger. Being mad helped too. I hoped I would stay mad until I got down. I climbed toward the gold ball at the top of the pole, and the yelling, like at the beach, you could barely hear it any more.

32

JOE

A persistent banging from below brought me to. I sat up, exhausted from sleep, and the day jumped at me like a white tiger. I looked over the edge at a hatted man pounding a newspaper machine in front of Cool Hand Laundry.

"Hey!" I said. The guy banged on. "Could you knock it off!" He stiffened and looked around. He was sunburned and wore big Jackie Onassis dark glasses. "Up here," I said. "How about destroying something a little farther away?"

He held up a red-and-white cane and swept it back and forth in my direction.

"Oh," I said. "Sorry."

His face was nearly as red as the tip of his cane. "What!"

"Never mind. Go ahead, break in. Knock yourself out."

"Who?" He approached the pole, probing the air with his stick like a feeler. Besides his dark glasses, he wore a too-large tan leisure suit, plaid golf cap, and a pair of yellow gloves. "Where you?" His stick hit the pole. "Ahck!"

I opened the trapdoor. "Forget it! I'm on a pole! Carry on!"

"Tota pole?"

"Resume your criminal activity."

"What doings you up?"

"Yeah," I said.

A teenager in saddle shoes slowed as she passed.

I said, "Well, to paraphrase Thoreau to Emerson, 'What doings you *down*?'"

"Roy Anderson?" said the goof.

The girl stopped, then a gay couple holding hands, then others. No challenge to the first night's mob, but a blessed diversion when I needed one most.

"What *are* you doing up there?" saddle shoes asked.

"Roy Anderson," the blind man said.

"World record," I said.

"Oh!" one of the gay fellows said. "You're the one's camping on a pole!"

"Wait a minute." I found the bullhorn and sat in the opening, my legs swinging in space. "Testing, testing." The gathering—a dozen strong now—cheered. "It's called flagpole-sitting."

"How long you been up there?" said someone.

"Forty-nine days."

Came heart-warming murmurs of awe.

"How long you gonna stay?"

"Four hundred and forty-five days."

They gasped; I laughed. What a tonic! I kicked my bare feet. A minute before I'd been a zombie waking in an alien sun. To hell with despair. Fuck bankruptcy.

"He was on TV," somebody said. "What did you do when it rained?"

"Got wet," I said. Their laughter cleaned my chakras pipe.

"What'll you do if there's an earthquake?"

"Hold on!" I said, to more laughter. If teaching were so easy. Clover had to be in there eavesdropping, conjuring a way to put the jimmy on it.

"You got TV?" asked a scroungy teenager with a skateboard under his arm.

"Nope. The pole life is the pure life."

"Radio?"

A lie about the radio would have tarnished my joy at having no TV. "Little one. I barely use it."

"You got bored up?" It was the blind man who had started it. I'd forgotten about him.

"No, sir. Never bored."

"What you do do up?"

The crowd tittered.

"Think. Read. Meditate. Write. Lots to do. Exercise. Watch the world. Be."

"Are you gonna write a book about it?" from somebody else.

"Hmmm."

"Why you up?" asked the blind man.

The crowd moaned. "World record," a woman on a bicycle said.

"Stupid," the blind one said. "You up protest peace on world? Food for starve?"

"Guinness Book of Records," said someone.

"Ignurnt," the blind man said.

"Shut up," saddle shoes said.

The blind man poked red saddle shoes' butt with his stick.

"Hey, watch where you're waving that thing, dork."

"How do you get your food and supplies?" somebody asked.

"My wife and son send it up in a basket."

"Wife son slave, you sunbath," the blind man said.

"Not at all," I said. "My wife and son are independent and have their own lives. They support my calling one hundred percent, but I would never take advantage of that."

The blind man snorted. "How you go bathroom?"

I said, "I don't think people want to hear about that, sir."

"How you go bathroom?" he repeated.

I waited for my mob to shout the imbecile down, but it waited silently. "Well, if you must know, I use a chemical toilet, like the astronauts."

"You stink. How you wash?"

"I lick myself like a cat." My crowd howled.

"You lonely up on?" the blind man asked.

"You don't have to sit on a pole to get lonely. As you may well know." Laughter. "Let's let somebody else ask a question."

"Why you *hate* blind man?" said the blind man.

"I don't hate you, champ. I don't even know you."

"Know Camus?" the blind man said.

"*Camus*, did you say?"

"Albert Camus," the blind man said, pronouncing the name in perfect French. "Tota pole man know Albert Camus?"

"Of course I know Camus. I teach literature."

"Know *Stranger*?"

"The novel? Of course I know it."

"Man from beach? Minding business. Pop! Dead. Snip snap snop."

My scalp went prickly sweat. Nate came running up the sidewalk.

"Nate! Here's my boy, Nate!" I informed the gathering, which parted to let him into the café.

"Abandon family for sunbath and mastrabatten!" the blind man barked, with a head thrust that caused his dark glasses to bob off his eyes—gray eyes which saw me see him.

"You!" I grabbed the bullhorn. "It's him! Pull that guy's hat off! It's Shipwreck Blake! He's not blind! That red crap's make-up! Grab that son-of-a-bitch!"

The crowd drew away from the unblind man who proceeded to retreat backward down the sidewalk, slashing and jabbing his stick as if it were not cane but sword.

"Grab him! Don't let him get away!" The crowd watched like goldfish as he dashed up the café driveway and down the alley. I dropped the bullhorn and grabbed the walkie. "Nate! Over! Nate!"

"Hello?" Nate said. "Over?"

"Shipwreck Blake was out here! He went down the alley toward Wilshire! He's dressed like an old blind French clown with red sauce on his face."

"Huh?"

"Oh, hell, he's long gone now."

"I got in a fight."

"What? With who? At school? Are you hurt?"

"No."

I heard a big crash in the walkie. "What was that!"

"Floor guys."

Men yelled Spanish at each other.

"Put her on," my teeth said.

"She's not here. I got in a fight! Don't you care about that?"

"Of course I do. You said you weren't hurt. Where is she?"

"I think at the bank."

"The *bank*? She left these goofballs working there with no supervision?"

Nate didn't say anything.

"Who was the other kid? Is he hurt?"

"Tommy Trabert. I uppercutted him. Like you showed me. He got a bloody nose. I guess my fist hit his chin and then his nose."

"Bloody nose, eh? Well, well. What were you fighting about?"

"You."

"*Me?*...Oh."

"Then I shimmied up the flagpole."

"You whatted what?"

"I went all the way to the top."

"You did not."

"Did."

"*How?*"

"Don't ask me. I felt like a lizard. I had a hold of the flag."

"Good God, Nate. You could've killed yourself."

"I looked down and I couldn't move. I wasn't mad anymore. The fire department had to get a ladder and pry me off."

"The fire department! Jesus Christ, Nate."

"They're gonna send you a bill."

"Well, good luck to them. Mom can go renovate the fire station."

"Mr. Powell wants to talk to you or Mom."

"The fire chief?"

"The principal. I didn't mean to do it, Dad. Something took me over. Do we have to tell Mom?"

33

JOE

Setting up the phone for the call to the principal, to grant Nate's wish to keep Clover in the dark about the fight, was quality, fun, father-son time. I directed him to my MasterCard in my wallet in my suit in the closet (I had no use for any of those where I was) and sent him to K&K for extension line and a connector. Then we rigged the phone out the louvers of the living room window down to the ground, into the basket, and up to the platform, voilà. It was good having a phone up there. Made me feel connected, even if I had no one to call or be called by.

"What are we gonna tell Mom about why we got the phone out here?" said Nate.

"She'll never know. We'll have it back down there by then."

Which started me thinking how I might finagle Clover into letting me keep it, even though technically it wasn't within flagpole-sitting parameters.

As for the call to Principal Powell, it went neither as planned nor imagined. "This is Joe Magellan," I said. "Nate Magellan's father."

"Yes," said Powell. "Thank you for calling, Mr. Magellan. I have to say, for starters—this disturbing little event was completely out of character for Nate. He's been a model student, bright, quiet. As far as we're concerned, this came out of the blue."

I winced at a son of mine being called a "model student." I heard "Stepford student."

"I guarantee it'll never happen again," I said.

"I trust not. You've raised a good boy."

"I appreciate that."

"But I'm curious, Mr. Magellan, if I may. Has Nate shown any other...peculiar behavior lately?"

"What do you mean by that?" My question was a whip and Powell heard the crack.

"Mr. Magellan, let's explore this. You take off your defensiveness hat, and I'll take off my principal's hat. Deal?"

I gnawed my tongue at this bureaucrat's presumptuosity. Think about Nate, I thought. "Deal."

"Have there been any major changes recently, around the home-stead?"

A siren went by under the pole.

"My goodness," Powell remarked.

"Well, you know where I am."

"I can't say I do."

How could he not know? "I'm the flagpole-sitter."

"You're the flagpole-sitter," Powell repeated. "You're the *flagpole*-sit-ter."

"Yes."

"*Magellan*. Of course. So *that's* why he climbed the pole. Forgive me for being a complete ignoramus, Mr. Magellan."

"Joe."

"Thank you, Joe. Call me Andy. The flagpole-sitter!"

"Nate never mentioned it?"

"Not a word. Joe, let me confess how much I admire you. I can't be-lieve I didn't put two and two together. Good Lord. Well, frankly, I don't blame Nate for one blessed second now. If I could live on a flagpole, sir… If you knew—I'm trusting you to keep this under your hat, but if you knew how—I won't say miserable, I won't say insane—what is it? Well, be a middle school principal for a while, Joe."

"I utterly understand. I've been an English sub in high school."

"Have you? Dear God. Brother, if I could join you on that pole, what a dream."

"That's kind of you to say."

"Kind has nothing to do with it. This is a matter of following a whole different drummer. This is taking the fork least traveled. Oh, what *bliss* t'would be to live on a flagpole with my stamps and my fish."

"Well, it's the life, that's for sure. Let me ask you, Andy—does this development mean that Nate might not be in quite the predicament we feared he might be in?"

Andy laughed, then turned solemn. "Sir, I wish you could have seen your son flying up that flagpole. It was *innate*. He was *propelled*. However, my wife had just been screaming in my ear about some damn thing and as a result I was unduly hard on the boy. I love her like death, but as Chaucer said… You taught English, you say?"

"Yes, I love Chaucer."

"Well, in any case, I took my frustration out on your boy. I'll call him in and apologize first thing."

Principal Andy was going to apologize to Nate.

"Of course, we can't have him going up there again," he added. "Not only could he get hurt, it would be insurance hell for the school."

"What about that, uh, fire department bill?"

He laughed. "That was a ruse to put the fear of God into Nate."

"It put the fear of God into me. And the other lad, how's he?"

"Tommy? We're dealing with him. Troublemaker, all caps. He started it. Your boy got a good whack in, for which please give him a pat-on-the-back from me. Joe, look, I have a full desk here, but at some point, if I may be so bold, and you could spare the time, I would be honored, thrilled, and overjoyed to be regaled by you at length as to what it's like to sit up there at the top of the world, in sweet solitary serenity."

"Oh, sure, absolutely, love to, yeah, any time, please do."

34

Pete Hoover, the TV reporter who had stumbled onto Joe's quest the very first day (and immediately forgot it) was about to stumble on it again.

Hoover was taping an interview with a certain Dr. Malcolm Kerridge for his weekend show *Pete's Portraits*, which he hated more than his street reporting if possible. He hated humanity in its entirety, an easier simpler approach than trying to sort the assholes from the tolerables, but being trapped in a studio with one of the more despicable of the lot was a special nightmare. While Kerridge gave a windbag response to a question about his seminar methodology that Hoover had no interest in to start with, the newsman pondered money and fame, how he had never had enough of either, whereas this natural-born swindler before him wallowed in both. Worse, Hoover's current piece of crap interview would make the quack even more rich and famous. As he watched Kerridge's flapping mouth produce vanity upon vanity, Hoover could feel the bile oozing like toxic green Jello from his liver. He idly focused on the hairpiece lounging like a flap of tar upon the conman's skull. He could not fathom how these morons could fork over hundreds of dollars for this blatant fraud to fill their empty heads with hogwash.

"…utilizing a unique and secret amalgam of techniques and systems, ancient and ultra-modern, for dynamic streamlined living, liberated forever from a plague of specters and manias."

Hoover wanted to hit this humbug over the head with a 2x4, quit his job, give his car and house away, and traipse across the country in a filthy robe with a sign that read, "Fuck You, You Stupid Deluded Motherfuckers!"

Instead, he said to Kerridge, "You must be inundated with kooks seeking a quick fix."

"Not kooks at all, Pete. Each one is a special human being with a special affliction that requires a special solution. In my last group, I cured a millionairess who talked on the telephone sixteen hours a day, a failed substitute teacher obsessed with sitting on flagpoles, a brilliant young lady who compulsively joined religions—she was up to twenty-three by the time she came to me—a woman with her hair down to the ground—"

"'Sitting on flagpoles'?"

"Oh yes. Healing that particular deranged soul was one of the proudest moments of a long and storied career. He entered my seminar in enslaved misery and left a happy man, emancipated from his ridiculous obsession."

"Is that so? Did you happen to see a little story I did, oh, gee, six, seven weeks ago? It sank like a stone, but it was about, if you can believe it—a *flagpole-sitter.*"

Kerridge blinked, then shook his head thoughtfully, but the barn was empty. "Can't say I did. Don't watch much news, too busy making it. And speaking of work—" He flashily checked his Rolex, stood, and held out his manicured hand. "It's been an unadulterated pleasure."

"It was over here on Western," Hoover said. "What was his name? Joe something. Ring a bell?"

"Nope," said the Seminar Master. "Mine was John. John Mandrake. Well, gotta run. The sick and the lame beckoneth."

35

JOE

I woke to the rude proddings of the first Santa Ana of the year. Santa Anas were vexatious winds that dropped in like in-laws on Southern California in the spring and fall. They fluctuated erratically from 10 to 40 mph, slapping the region silly for days on end. Devil's Breath was one nickname for the troublesome phenomenon. These searing winds charged in from the east, through the Cajon Pass and Palmdale. They were insolent as a cosmic drunken clown smacking you around, uprooting trees, knocking semis over, ripping roofs off buildings, and setting brush fires ahowl. They were not what a man wants to be sitting on top of a sixty-foot flagpole during.

I nibbled my french toast and gauged the wavering of the platform—only inches one way and then the other, enough to remind me of where I was and where I might suddenly be. The pole had obviously survived hundreds of Santa Anas, but none with the added mass of the platform plus accoutrements plus me. Charlie had attested to the durability of the pole, and I believed in the workmanship of Lu and Duc. I took my shirt off, rocked in my chair, drank my coffee and observed the joust of the world and the wind. A lone gull fought the force to a standstill, turned, and shot swooping the other way as if along a greased chute. Rows of palm trees staggered like dinosaurs trying to stay in line.

At times the motion of the pole grew cradle-like, soothing. In a contemplative state, I witnessed in the distance a local marvel I had heard about but never seen. In fact, I'd dismissed the reports as urban myth. Now, first spotting the creatures miles away, I thought them to be bright green balloons freed in a horizontal rush against the sky, but when they disappeared en masse into the top of a swirling palm way up near Sunset, I recalled the story of the wild parrots. The birds hid in the palm then exploded and scattered straight toward me across the distance. I feared as they came that I was violating some territorial imperative, that they were hopped up on the Santa Ana and bent on swarming me with claws flashing and beaks tearing. They passed five feet above me in a dazzling flail of green wings and red crowns—two dozen of them easy—and nestled in a eucalyptus tree over on Windsor. There they commenced to hop about and gobble leaves and make a bewildering racket of squawks and screams like a gang of high-strung cowards sounding tough. Behind them the golden statue of the horn-blowing angel over the Mormon temple on Santa Monica towered, so that the caterwauling of the wild parrots appeared to emanate from the angel's golden trumpet.

36

CLOVER

I used my fingernail to scrape the last smidge of tape from the spank-ing-new picture-window, which stopped my breathing when it appeared to quaver in a mighty gust. The arrival of the accursed Santa Anas was not auspicious for the opening of a restaurant into which I had sunk $25,000 worth of renovation.

"Finished," I whispered. "Finished and done."

In the morning light I beheld my masterpiece: Clover's Patch. The mortar and pestle of my mind and heart ground hope and foreboding into a heady paste. The Grand Opening was hours away.

Twenty-five grand had not gone nearly as far as I'd imagined, but far enough to transmogrify Charley's dump into a gleaming little café I would have been delighted to discover and tell my friends about. If I had any friends. Well, I'd have plenty soon enough.

A new Blozik exhaust system, Candemere grill, and set of Tremaine cookware sparkled in the kitchen. The Space-King 2000 Air Recreator hummed with a subliminal OM. Trees and hanging greenery from Bai-ley's evoked the gardens of Babylon. Paint as white as a pearl covered the walls once stained with smoke and stewbombs. Charley's grimy counter and cracked, greasy Naugahyde booths and stools were no more, replaced by polished Chinese pine tables with yellow candles and blue flowers. Where once scarred linoleum lay, the Lomar Cresmite flooring shone like blue marble. Adorning the bright walls were tasteful aluminum-framed prints by Bonnard, O'Keefe, and Van Gogh, while Ornette Coleman played on the Keurlitron sound system.

Nevertheless, unknowns battered me. Should I have advertised more, would anybody call for reservations, or show up, had the de-signers and workers ripped me off horribly, how high would Joe blow his top when he found out about the loan, what if I/we defaulted and lost everything, was I a good and creative enough cook to pull this off, should I have hired a cook, had I prepared enough cold food and would I be able to cook hot food fast enough, what if I poisoned somebody, would people laugh when they saw the motley menu, how much could I depend on Nate, how long could I put off hiring somebody to help, what would become of our marriage and family if Joe got down or the café failed, and were the Santa Anas an omen of doom? My qualms writhed like snakes until the phone screamed. I grabbed it, praying for the first reservation.

It was my husband, calling from his "What, me worry?" isle in the sky. Don't even bring up the multi-level hassle I had to go through to fix the mess he got us in with the phone shenanigans. I had to get another line for this place so he could keep the one he stole from me. It wasn't quite the ascetic hermitage up there he liked to think. I never bought his needing the phone suddenly one day because he thought he was having a stroke, though he never called 911, and why couldn't Nate have simply called? At some point you have to stop when you feel your brain cells turning to mush trying to understand a man like that. Plus, of course, Nate had told him I was at the bank and I didn't want Joe asking questions about that any more than he seemed to want me asking questions about the stroke and the phone, so it was a fair exchange.

"You gotta come out and look at these amazing parrots," he said. "I think you can see them from down there, they're still over here on Windsor chowing down on eucalyptus leaves."

"I have other things on my mind right now."

"I know, I know, but... Can't you hear them yowling out here?"

"I have to put the banner up." I wanted him to bitch about that so I could let him have it, but he wasn't listening, as usual.

"You know, Clover, now that we're talking, I've been feeling kind of funny lately."

"Funny how?" That was the last thing I needed right then, nurse-maiding him.

"Oh, a little...selfish or something, I guess."

"You? How could you possibly be feeling a little selfish or something?"

"I only wish I could be down there helping you."

"Well, come on down!" I sang.

"You don't think I'd love to?"

Don't push it, I told myself. "Honey, I got it covered." I began playing with the new Moonrunner Illumination System, adjusting the lights in different sections of the café with three dials hidden behind one of the abalarhuna trees. "I'm having a blast. And you should too. You've got, what, forty-six days now?"

"Fifty-four," he said flatly.

"Fifty-four! That's amazing. Are you happy? I am. I'm happy for myself, and I'm really, really, *really* happy for you."

"By the way, how's that 'nest egg' of yours holding up?"

I opened my mouth to lie again, but weighed the truth like a warm, perfectly ripe peach in my hand. I felt the mad temptation of fearlessness. He could have been a stranger calling the wrong number so little did I care about his reaction. After all, what could he do? He couldn't hurt me, any more than he could help me. He was the absolute least of my worries.

"I took out a loan," I said.

"What?"

"I. Took out. A loan."

"No, no, no, no, no, no, no."

"Yes, yes, yes, yes, yes, yes, yes."

"I don't believe you. You had a nest egg."

"No nest egg. Loan."

I pictured him closing his eyes like he does. "You lied. You lied to me."

"I lied to you. Yup."

"Oh, my God. How much?"

"Twenty-five."

"Oh. Well, that's not *that* bad. It's not *good*—twenty-five hundred on top of the first one."

"Boy, you are a babe in the Money Woods. Twenty-five *thousand.*"

"No. Oh, Jesus, no." I think he slapped the platform. "Twenty-five thousand *dollars?*"

"Yup."

"You borrowed twenty-five... Our Father Who art in Heaven! What did you borrow it *on?* Not Charley's Spot."

"*Clover's Patch!* Read the sign, man! Yes, I borrowed partly on *Clover's Patch.* And partly on *you.*"

"Me? What me?"

"Mr. Spoletti, from the bank, happens to be a big fan of your 'P.R. Genius.' He believes your efforts on behalf of the restaurant, in line with the new capital creativity of the Reagan era, is an early step in the revitalization of the Western Avenue corridor, which is already on the boards with the city and the bank and other interests, so it works out nice."

"Clover, please tell me in simple human English."

"As long as you stay up, we're safe. Basically, you're the collateral. We make the payments, you stay up, the restaurant's safe."

"That's in the contract? *I'm collateral?* How could you get a loan on *me* without me even seeing it, much less *signing* it?"

"You did sign it."

"You faked my signature! This is insane. It's evil!"

"Sue me."

"What's the interest? I want to see this loan agreement."

"Come on down, have a look."

"I'll call Spoletti myself."

"Go ahead. We'll lose the place. Honey, look, it'll be a smash hit. Believe me, you should see it. You stay up, we pay off the loan, the place flourishes, you come down with the world record, everybody's happy."

"I'm not up here for some Mad Hatter loan. I'm up here because I *want* to be, not because I *have* to be."

"I thought you said you *had* to break the record."

"Yeah, have to/*want* to, not have to/*have* to. Twenty-five thousand dollars. How much is left?"

"Not much."

"What in the name of life and death did you spend it on?"

He was bringing me down, way down. "For starters, that telephone you're talking on, and everything else up there on that well-stocked oasis of yours."

"I don't see twenty-five grand worth of crap up here."

"You should see it down here."

"Are you *drinking* again, Clover? Are you on *drugs?*"

"Shut up. How could you say such things right before my opening? What a nitwit you are! Leave me alone!" I slammed the phone down.

Meanwhile, in Washington DC, a lost soul, armed and obsessed with a movie actress he had never met, was making preparations to shoot the Leader of the Free World.

37

JOE

Up on the ladder, Clover finished draping a pale blue banner across the ruby front of the place: "GRAND OPENING! WELCOME!"

Whether her dream soared to success or went down in flames, it would be in my best interest to have encouraged her beforehand, even if only at the last second. "It looks great. Very classy."

"Thank you." She looked vulnerable, shy, like when we met. "I don't have many dishes yet."

"Well, it's the first day. You're a good cook. What do you have?"

"Oh, God. Spaghetti. Other pasta. Soup. Salads. Cold and hot sandwiches. Other stuff. You know, oddball things I've come up with through the years. Scrambled egg sandwich." She laughed like an anxious child. "A few desserts. And hamburgers and all that, of course. God, it sounds horrible."

"Naw, it sounds good." I was biting my tongue in two. Twenty-five thousand dollars for spaghetti and scrambled egg sandwiches. "Good solid vittles." Clover's Patch would be an unmitigated black hole from which no beam of light would ever emerge. "You have any help?"

"Nate?"

Nate? "Well, he'll, he'll, he'll catch on. He'll do fine."

"Oh, God, I should've hired somebody. Is it too late? What was I *thinking?*"

"Opening night, nobody expects perfection. Have fun, enjoy yourself. Breathe. Relax."

She gazed up. "Thank you." Her poor face shone with flopsweat. "I know you have strong doubts about this."

"I have no doubt whatsoever."

No doubt that the forces of the universe were lined up against her and her Patch and therefore against me and my quest. A madman would put a bullet an inch from the president's heart that afternoon, a gesture of affection for an actress he had never met. Customers would hardly have been trampling one another to get into the place even if the entire nation had *not* been watching video of the shooting over and over and over again, but the timing of the event guaranteed that the Grand Opening of Clover's Patch would be an immense heartbreaking dud.

38

Eight customers—or eight human beings—showed up, including a drunken Hungarian who claimed to be the food critic for the *Los Angeles Times*, though he barely knew enough English to order a roast beef sandwich. A charming couple who were celebrating their alleged wedding anniversary climbed out the bathroom window without paying their bill. And a homeless weightlifter offered Clover "permanent protection" in exchange for a daily plate of spaghetti. That meant a grand total of four paying customers and a take of thirty-nine dollars and fifteen cents, including tips.

Clover closed early. She and Nate sat as if in a tomb. All she could think about was how Joe would react. She yearned for reassuring comfort but foresaw a bouquet of I told you so's.

"You didn't know President Reagan was going to get shot," Nate said. She shrugged. "Everybody'll come tomorrow. Boy, that big foreign nerd that said he was a food critic!" He hoped she would laugh, or at least tell him he shouldn't call the man a foreign nerd, but she got up and began shuffling around like an old woman, putting away her unwanted food.

Through the evening caller after caller to talk radio jabbered about the Reagan shooting. Joe imagined himself the only person in the solar system who had not seen the video. The phone rang. He knew it would be a bittersweet call.

"I'm scared," Clover said.

"It's only one night, honey. These things take time. It'll get better."

"What if it doesn't?"

And just like that, Joe let the devil in: "Well, sweetheart, that's a possibility you might have considered *before* borrowing twenty-five thousand dollaroonies."

"Is that supposed to be funny? I could use some kindness right now. I said I was scared. Does it take a lot of effort for you to stop being an asshole for one minute?"

"Why couldn't you let that place be the simple greasy spoon it was born to be? Where simple, greasy people come to stuff their simple, greasy faces?"

"You're *thrilled* at this disaster, aren't you? You *want* me to fail. So you can get down from another idiotic fucking flagpole and blame it on me."

"Or you deliberately planned this disaster to *make* me get down and bail you out!"

"You actually believe that, you twisted fuck? You starry-eyed sadistic pinhead!" She slammed the phone down.

"*Damn,*" Joe said.

The urge to rub her face in it had devoured his best intentions. He hadn't even had a chance to request his immediate object of desire—a television. He *had* to see that video of the Reagan shooting. It was the one thing in the world that might take his mind off Clover's nosedive of grandeur. If he asked to borrow their little TV now she would bring the set out on the sidewalk and beat it with a skillet. He grabbed the journal:

Suddenly looms the likelihood of having to get down to clean up Clover's $25,000 mess.

And so what? Have I not proved by now, to whoever cares or matters, that I *am* capable of sitting up here for as long as I want? 54 days & nights, ladies & gentlemen. There's nothing left to prove. Fuck that record. And *she* brought up my getting down. I'll wait for her to ask.

And I am not "thrilled" at her debacle. I would have *loved* to see the place light up the town. But it was not meant to be & now we're in the red for 25 GRAND!

I'll get down & teach. Permanent, no subbing. Throw my heart & soul into it. This is all my fault, me & my fucking obsession. Sitting seriously has taught me to take teaching seriously.

I no longer believe that was Shipwreck Blake at the sidewalk Q&A. This city is thick with kooks & psychos. Even if it was, fuck him. I don't care what he thinks about anything.

Joe happened to spot Jinx in Playtoe's ticket booth. Lights played over him. "He's watching TV," Joe whispered. He called information and got the number.

"Playtoe's Cave," Jinx purred.

"Jinx, it's Joe."

"Joe!" He looked over and up. "You got a phone!"

"Yeah. Can I borrow your TV?"

"Borrow my TV? My God, you don't have a TV! I-yi-yi, you haven't seen the shooting? You won't believe it. Well, I need this one, but lemme see what I can do. Don't go anywhere."

Jinx hung up, went inside the theater, emerged with a young man in a tie in tow, shooed him off down Western, and returned to the booth with a wave Joe's way.

Jinx is all right, but if I had my druthers, Playtoe's Cave would vanish, because of Nate. The patrons over there don't hang around, they go in & come out & skulk away. Pitiful. Not that I haven't visited such an establishment once or twice myself. I'm glad I didn't sneak any porn up here. If I wanted some, I suppose I could ask Jinx. How could he turn me down, doing what he does? But what if he said no for some oddball moral reason, maybe related to Clover? Who cares, it's moot. I'll be down in

JINX'S GUY IS COMING OVER WITH A BRAND NEW TV!!!

The fellow secured the 13-inch set in the basket and Joe hoisted it up. He called Jinx to thank him. "I'll pay you back."

"My treat. I'm rich. Enjoy!"

Joe plugged the TV into the extension cord—relieved it didn't overload the Mickey Mouse electro-system—right in time for the eleven o'clock news. First thing popped up—the video. He watched, so transfixed he thought he smelled gunpowder.

He looked up. Black smoke gushed from a two-story building half a mile down Western. "Fire," Joe whispered. "Fire!" he hollered. "Clover!" He grabbed the phone and dialed 911. "Come on, come on. Yes! There's a fire." He forgot the address. "On Western, half a mile north of Charley's—Clover's—Playtoe's Cave Adult Theater Movie Place. Right, yes. Hurry!"

Joe watched black smoke mushroom into the gray sky, and flames blurting. Jinx and others emerged to watch. He called Clover. She'd been crying. "Clover! There's a—" She hung up with a bang.

Alone, he watched the flames mount, watched the video in slow-motion, heard the sirens coming, the shots, analysis, watched the trucks arrive, water blast the air, the shooting again, the valiant Secret Service man, poor Brady, Reagan jammed into the limo, machine guns up, black smoke mushrooming, limo hustling away, flames failing, smoke going gray, the video again, and the air smelling like the oven-toasted Triscuits his mother used to make when he came down from the orange tree.

39

JOE

The second day of Clover's Patch was grimmer than the first. The third was like a morgue. That ghastly loan. We puckered up for bankruptcy before, but this could be the kiss. Unless we find some idiot to take this quagmire off our hands, like Charlie found us.

Can't bear to read a novel, but waiting for Clover to beg me to come down and save her, I dipped into Camus' Notebooks. He writes about Chuang Tzu & Lucretius & some immense bird 9000 miles high looking down on a stampede of wild horses; about Van Gogh & self-forgetting & reaching for integrity beyond the boorishness of most people's lives; about the significance of his own writing & achieving grace by going beyond Christianity & caring about the damned. I thought Jesus went down to hell to comfort the damned. Did he go down there to rub it in? There had to have been some possibility of redemption for those poor bastards. Just like there's got to be some way out of this hell the Magellans have gotten themselves in.

I don't like to believe in hell, unless it's for other people, but I think you can be outside of Heaven looking in. I like the idea (Swedenborg?) that you have to let go of everything to get in—memory, ego, faith, your face, your name, your memory even? You can't smuggle one miserable grain of your self into Heaven. But if there's nothing left, then what gets in?

"Joe! Hey, Joe!" I looked over. It was Pete Hoover, the unctuous newsman from 4RealNews. His truck sat under the pole, his cameraman alongside, smoking, shaking his head. "Howdy!" Hoover said. "Remember me?"

I grabbed the bullhorn. "You said I was up as a publicity stunt for the restaurant."

"I was roundly mistaken! You've been up this whole time? Must be a month!"

"Fifty-six days."

Hoover slapped his own face. "And the record is…?"

I would likely be getting down soon without the record and thus preferred not to discuss it. "What do you care?"

Hoover stepped back and eyed the pole, the platform, me. "Are you serious about this? Are you indubitably *determined* to make that record yours?"

I was indubitably determined to climb down the second Clover begged me to, but I sensed that Pete was hatching some brainstorm that might accrue to my benefit, and may have the clout to pull it off. For example, if he managed to get me on TV again, I could express my desire for a permanent teaching position, and I'd be flooded with offers, because gifts rained down on humble Americans who appeared on TV with heartfelt needs in unusual circumstances.

I sent him down the walkie. I said, "Hell, yes, I'm determined."

"Excellent. You wouldn't happen to have a book in you, would you?"

"As a matter of fact, I have one *out* of me. It's a novel about Holden Caulfield and Bigger Thomas sailing around the world."

"You can't steal other writers' characters, my friend."

"I don't steal them. I don't even use their names, I call them Holder and Biggen. I changed them all around."

"Litigation City, amigo. Salinger's lawyers'd be on you like snakes on a hamster. Anyway, forget fiction. People don't want a bunch of fairy tales. They want facts. Think more something like, oh, *The Magnificent Adventures of Joe Magellan, American Flagpole-Sitter*. We'll work it out." Hoover's gold crowns flashed in the sun. "You have an agent?"

40

JOE

Clover hasn't opened for three days. Won't talk to me. Nate scurries off & sneaks back in the afternoon. He's under orders. I'll fix everything after *Pete's Portraits*.

Overcast. Sky like gauze. The light is silver, watery. Ahmad Jamal's "Excerpts from the Blues" playing. The trees down by Wilshire Country Club doing the hula. Yellow Piper Cub against the rice paper sky. Man in a ragged overcoat smokes & rocks foot to foot in the alcove of Glorious Cakes, Balloons & Gifts.

How I'll love taking her in my arms. She'll cry like a lost child found. Me, too. I'll amend my wrongs. *Ask*, Clover. You don't even have to beg. Just *ask*. Then I'll have no choice.

Tiny little earthquake in the middle of the night. First one up here. In-ter-est-ing. The light came on in the apartment, she peeked through the curtains, light went back out.

People got their snapping point. She could crack & torch the place for the insurance & the flames could spread up here.

I'd like to teach somewhere cool, Oregon, Washington, maybe Seattle, my birthplace. Teach only works I adore. I'd learn to teach in a way that when my students opened a book it would be like the first book they ever opened & we would enter it like Lewis & Clark entering virgin woods.

On the other hand, what if the restaurant takes off as a *result* of my inter-view with Hoover? I must build this bomb with care.

"Joe!" It was Jinx below, in a yellow meter-maid pantsuit. He crooked his thumb at the "CLOSED" sign on the café. "How is she?"

I popped the trapdoor and lowered the walkie. "I know you two don't get along—"

"It's not me, it's her," he said. "I'm fine."

"Could you get inside and see how she is?"

"Oh, Lord." He peered through the window. "Her and Nate in the back. She's got her head down. There's a candle on the table."

It sounded like an Edward Hopper painting. "Look, here's the story. The place is going under. She got this hideous loan. She won't talk to me. We had a fight. I just want to make sure she's okay. Get a read if you can. I know you're a student of human nature. I'll owe you."

41

Mother and son sat at the Chinese pine table in the rear of the moribund restaurant. Jinx rapped on the glass.

"It's a meter maid," Nate said.

"Oh no, it's that freak. Tell him I'm sick."

Clover watched as Jinx inveigled his way in and past the boy.

"We're closed," Clover called as Jinx barged over.

"Just want to say hi, see how you're doing."

"I'm fine," Clover said, "everything's fine," and wept. Jinx placed a hand on her shoulder, bringing louder weeping. The candle danced and skeleton shadows jumped around the room.

"Well, this is some party," Jinx said. Clover snorted and a snot bubble came out of her nose. Jinx dug out a tissue and sat beside her. "How are you, Nathaniel?"

"Mom's gonna declare bankruptcy," he said.

"After two lousy weeks?" Jinx said.

Clover blew her nose. "I loathe this place. I loathe every square inch of it."

Jinx looked around. "What about these gorgeous tables?"

"I'm thinking bonfire."

"Those lovely prints?"

"Puh."

"You should put your own up," Nate said.

"Yeah, change the paintings on the *Titanic*."

"You're an artist?" Jinx said.

"Ha."

"She's real good," said Nate.

Jinx picked up a piece of paper from the table and tried to read it in the candlelight.

"Oh, God," Clover said.

"That's the menu," said Nate.

"It's embarrassing," said Clover.

"It's," Jinx said, "spare."

"I was doomed from the start. I'm such a fool."

Said Jinx, softly: "Clover, may I dare to express what's in my heart?"

That Clover had let this deviant in and was having a conversation with him were symptoms of how badly she craved adult help with this disaster. As encouraging as Nate had been, he only deepened her gloom, for she was taking him down with her. She shrugged.

"First," Jinx said, "I know you don't like me." Clover opened her mouth, but Jinx held up his hand. "I understand. My way is unacceptable to you, especially as a mother. But I've made the most of a hard life. I'm doing what I need to do now in order to do what I want to do later. I have a plan, I'm marching toward it, and I don't care what anybody thinks. Second, you need help. I've needed plenty, and every time I got it, things turned around. Sometimes quickly, sometimes slowly. Third, what do you want to do?"

"Blow this place up." She dared to look at Nate, who looked back as if she were about to abandon him to the wolves. In fact, if it weren't for Nate, she would have headed for the hills and never looked back.

"Whatever you want to do," Jinx said, "you're not doing it. If you were, you'd be fighting for it, not throwing in the towel."

"Don't people ever give up on what they want to do?"

"I'm not talking about people, I'm talking about you. I've watched you. I study folks who don't like me. I love challenges, and it's a challenge to understand a person who doesn't like me. I study you and I see a tough woman. I know because I'm tough. And I know you see it in me, and that's why you don't like me. You've been around the block too. I don't know your particulars, I don't need to know your particulars."

Clover, steadied by this bracing honesty, glanced at Nate, who waited keenly. "I've been through some things," she said.

"And come out the other side. The problem is—it's not *your* Patch yet. The sign says it, but that's a sign." Jinx looked around. "This bland, pretty, yuppie, elitist, cookie-cutter eh—it ain't you."

Clover swept the place with a look like the look Charlie had swept it with. But instead of launching a stew bomb, she groaned. "I don't have the energy to get back on the horse."

"When you find the horse you're meant to ride, you'll have all the energy in the world. Again—what do you want to do?"

I want ten gin and tonics, Clover thought, and a thousand hours of mindless sleep.

42

JOE

By the time Jinx emerged, I was ready to eat my own hands. I pointed at the walkie in the basket and he grabbed it.

"What happened!" I said. "You were in there for two freaking hours."

"We had a good talk."

"Well, how is she?"

"She's fine."

"*Fine*? How could she be *fine*? What'd she say?"

Jinx shook his head. "Can't get into that. It was confidential. I'm entrusted."

"I knew it. I *knew* it! You were entrusted by *me* to find out what she was up to! So, she recruited you. Thanks, good buddy. I should've known you'd go over to the woman's side. Sorry, but that's the ugly truth."

Jinx spoke slowly, solemnly: "I can say this much, Joe: You have a wonderful wife down here. You better be nice to her. You hear me? Or else I'll climb up there and show you some ugly truth all right." He dropped the walkie in the basket and marched across Western like nobody's business.

I dreamed I was at the blackboard diagramming a three-page-long sentence from *Moby Dick* for a class of growling teenagers handcuffed to their desks and overseen by a drunken armed guard.

I woke to the rumbling of the Bernino's truck returning. It pulled into the driveway and back behind the restaurant. Over the next hour I heard what had to have been all or a major portion of whatever she had purchased being loaded back into the truck. My heart leapt throughout: she was throwing in the towel.

Said towel, however, remained unthrown in. The silent treatment resumed, as did the clampdown on Nate. I was more in the dark than ever.

As for the interview Hoover had promised, he failed to return my calls.

The platform shrank before my eyes. I had acquired so much crap up there I could barely move. The city stared at me unblinking. A crow lumbering by regarded me sideways with what looked like horror.

I turned on the TV and crawled in the mummybag. *The Mike Douglas Show* was on. Mike was interviewing Mother Teresa, who recounted a funny experience she'd had on an airplane. Then Mike interviewed Richard Pryor, who discussed his role as God in a recent movie. I fell asleep with the TV on and dreamed a Black Mother Teresa was telling jokes I couldn't hear for the noise of the helicopter she was leaning out the door of as it flew in circles above the pole.

43

"Seventy-seven, seventy-eight, seventy-nine," Shipwreck Blake counted out his hundred daily sit-ups. Slim and fit in his black underwear on the dark red carpet of his bungalow at the Chateau Marmont in Hollywood, Blake glanced sideways at the TV where Pete Hoover and Joe Magellan neared the conclusion of their interview in front of Clover's Patch.

Hoover stood before the closed restaurant, craning his neck at the orange platform against a milk-bright sky. Joe sat in the open trapdoor, swinging his bare feet like a child.

"And what are your plans *after* you set the record?" Hoover cued.

The screen filled with an upwardly close-up of the flagpole-sitter in the rectangle of the trapdoor, stroking his chin, as if he'd never thought of the question before. "Well, I'd love to land a permanent teaching position. And polish up my book on what it's like to live on a flagpole in the late twentieth century."

"Fascinating. America looks forward to that."

"Although I only have seventy days. Who knows what's going to happen? And who could blame me, a husband and father, if I was forced to get down to deal with unforeseen family crises."

Shipwreck stopped his push-ups. "Here he goes," he whispered.

"But you *are* determined to make that record yours," Hoover said.

"One hundred percent. But life deals bad cards now and again."

Hoover laughed. "Well, without that record, your book wouldn't be worth a plugged nickel."

"Oh, I don't know. More books are written about tragedies than triumphs. The most moving literature is rooted in valiant so-called failures."

"He's comin' down," Shipwreck said. "Boy's comin' down."

Hoover said, "You're a coy one, Joe. You have the city on the edge of its couch. You're toying with our heartstrings." He spoke to the camera. "Will Joe stay up and become the counterculture anti-hero of our time, or will he climb down like a beaten cur with his tail between his legs?"

"*Cur?*" Joe said.

"Cur," Shipwreck said.

The camera focused on Hoover for the wrap-up: "Thank you, Joe

Magellan, for letting us invade your private sanctuary. A special man, a special mission, and like all prophets in their own hometown, a man unappreciated by those who owe him the most, who receive from his peculiar effort a spark of something approaching, dare I suggest, *heroism*, in the tradition of Thoreau, Saint Francis, and Neil Armstrong. Thank you, Joe, for shining a unique light on this crazy wonderful thing we call modern American life. Joseph Galileo Magellan—remember that name. You're going to hear a lot more from this courageous and eccentric individual. A man who has given it all up and gone to the mountaintop. And, in a moment, we'll continue our look at 'The Last Individualists' with a profile of Dr. Malcolm Kerridge, and how the King of Obsessions Seminars let a big one get away."

Shipwreck shut the TV off. "Oh, Simeon," he said.

44

JOE

Clover was talking to me again, finally, warily. "Just a hint," I said. "I'm on your side, you know, honey."

"Said the fox to the hen."

"I don't blame you for being careful. I said some things I shouldn't have, out of excess worry and concern and love, and I regret that. I'm sorry about that."

"That's big of you."

"When you want to talk, I'll be here."

"Where else would you be?"

"Did you see my interview?"

"Some. We were working. Pete painted you as quite the mysterious hero."

"Well, if I'm a hero, you're the heroine, sending my meals up and hauling my crap away and everything."

"I don't remember you mentioning that in the interview."

"I did, but they cut it." I meant to, but I forgot. "By the way, I saw those picnic tables being delivered, so I know you're turning it into *some* kind of normal little down-home eatery." Silence. "I hope you got a hefty refund for the stuff you sent back." More silence. "At least picnic tables are real American furniture. George Washington ate off picnic tables at Valley Forge. I was thinking you must be turning it into something more fitting with the reality of the situation."

"That's what you were thinking I must be doing?"

"Goddamn it, Clover, what *are* you doing, then! This is outrageous. That place is as much mine as it is yours. What kinda damn game are you insisting on playing here?"

"Why don't you get down and see for yourself? One minute from now you could be poking around in here inspecting every square inch of whatever game I'm insisting on playing."

"Are you asking me to climb down and help you?"

She laughed. "You're the last thing I need down here. Plus, you'd blow the loan."

"I don't believe one damn word about being collateral on that loan. That's a buncha medieval bilge!"

"Well, Daddy-o, climb down and find out for yourself."

"Clover, could you have some mercy? Please? Imagine if you were up here, out of the loop. I'm worried about you, honey, is that a sin?"

"No. It's sweet. Thank you. But I don't ask what you do up there."

"What the hell *would* I do up here! And whatever it is, I didn't borrow twenty-five grand to do it! You know, I liked you a lot more when you were having a nervous breakdown. Could you put my son on, please?"

"He's busy with his homework. Oh, by the way, he got into some trouble at school a while back. Little flagpole incident. Maybe you heard about it?"

"All right, yes, I should've told you about that. That wasn't right. I'm sorry about that too."

"That's why you wanted that damn phone up there all of a sudden."

"Yes."

"No stroke, eh?"

"I confess everything, I deny nothing, I'm sorry about everything, okay? I was trying to protect your fragile state at the time, as a matter of fact. And I did take care of it. I handled that. I straightened that out."

"Yeah, the principal called the mother with an update on a fistfight and the fire department rescuing her son and she had no idea in the world what he was talking about. *And* you got Nate to lie to me too."

"It was all my idea not to tell you, don't take it out on the boy. Like you're using him to take it out on me."

"I'm doing no such thing. He's busy."

"You're crossing an evil line, Clover."

"Bullshit."

"I'm coming down."

"Yeah, sure."

"You know, Clover, you have no more idea what's going on in my head than I do in yours. You think you're crazier than me? Let's find out. I'll be right down."

"Okay, okay. Not that I believe you. Nate! Your father's on the phone. He wants to grill you about what I'm doing."

She dropped the phone on the counter. Nate picked it up.

"Hi, Dad."

"Hey, pal. Doin' homework?"

"Yeah. English."

"English? I know a little 'bout dat subjick."

"I promised Mom not to tell you what she's doing."

"I know. I understand. We don't want to upset her. But remember when we didn't want to upset her with your fight/flagpole/firetruck jam and I saved your hide?"

"Yeah, but she found out."

"Well, that wasn't my fault. So, she's changing things around down there again?"

"Dad."

"She's being unfair and mean and ridiculous, Nate. You see that, don't you, even as a kid?"

"You want me to break a promise?"

I thought about it. "No. You're right. Okay. What sort of homework you doing?"

"Writing a story."

"Magnificent. Fifth grade, you're writing stories. What's it about?"

"I just got started."

"Well, good. Starting is a fun place. Anything could happen. Can I help?"

"We're supposed to do it ourself."

"Okay, but if you need feedback." Silence. "So, did you like my interview?"

"Yeah. I liked the part about you being like a astronaut."

"Oh, good. So, look, I saw those picnic tables being delivered. I guess she's gonna start a barbecue joint, huh?"

"I can't tell you anything."

"I'm your father, Nate. Is that woman standing there coaching you? She cannot curtail your constitutional freedom of speech."

"Dad," Nate pleaded. It stung my heart but did not deter my will.

"I want to know what's happening with my family down there, Nate. Is that so terrible? Could somebody think how *I* feel up here in the dark, with no damn idea what she's doing."

The boy burst out bawling.

"Oh, damn. I'm sorry, Nate. *Damn* me. Forget it, okay? Nate? Don't cry, please, pal?" I thought: I'm getting down right now. It's demonic folly to stay up. I have to end this before all is lost. "Do you want me to get down?"

"I don't know," he blubbered.

"I miss you, pal. I miss talking, and kidding around and everything. Playing catch and everything."

"We never play catch that much."

"Yes, we do. We play as much as me and my father played. Pal, look. I love you like *crazy*. You know that, right?"

"I gotta go."

We hung up. I thought how any time you talk to somebody it could be the last. But you couldn't live like that, you couldn't look at it like that. Maybe you could, but for how long?

45

JOE

Hoover's interview produced a second flurry of attention, a Honk! here, a Hey, Pole Guy! or Galileo! there. It brought me no thrill, only revulsion. Those rubberneckers below wouldn't shed a tear if I fell off and cracked my skull. The fantasy of Clover begging me to get down had undermined my will to stay. I'd been one inch from descending with an honorable surrender in hand. I gazed at the city, its garish raiment masking the void. The thought of my life's only sweetnesses—Clover and Nate—stung me with a scorpion's fire. I rocked in my chair like the madman in Gogol. The obsession, the vampire flagpoles, had sucked the life out of every last thing.

And yet what if even one of those gawkers drew from my absurd quest a crumb of inspiration for their daily toil, of sustenance for their very soul? But what of the inspiration I've drawn from Shipwreck? LOOK WHERE IT'S GOTTEN ME!

Few days ago the city put up temporary cardboard No Parking signs on both sides of Western. Last night I found out why. I woke at 3 a.m. to the hideous grinding of a monstrous yellow vehicle creeping under the pole, hauling behind it an entire, immense, white, wooden two-story house! Like a lost parade float the spectacle crept up Western toward Hollywood. I lay gawking over the edge, watching that old whale of a house, expecting the whole wobbling, trembling entity to twist, burst & collapse in one great Daliesque cascade. But it turned up Los Feliz intact, still chugging along. Went back to sleep, dreamed that the platform & pole & everything up here was made of ice. I looked at my arm—I could see right through it—I was made of ice myself & the rising sun woke me.

☙

I received a good dozen calls from media types for additional interviews—*paid*. Not much but *paid*. Hoover warned such chats would "dilute" my "market value." The last thing I wanted to talk about was that damn record, and the pittances bandied about wouldn't've put a dent in Clover's diabolical loan. I unplugged the phone and lay in the chaise under the umbrella, scribbling, trying to meditate, groaning prayers for God knew what form of miracle, staring blindly at crap TV, nauseated at feeling sorry for myself, and sleeping. With *Joanie Loves Chachi* on, I scratched in the journal:

I got sloppy with some pancake syrup & woke in the middle of the night with something crawling on my foot & then something else & I grabbed the flashlight & found the platform thick with ants. There must have been thousands, all over me & the entire area. I imagined them detecting my fear & stinging me all at once & going into paralytic shock & dying up there. I was one second from jumping over the side before I determined there were only a dozen or so actually on me. They had caught a whiff of the syrup, marched up the pole & poured through a crack in the trapdoor.

I killed as few as I could. Shook everything out, swept them off (trying not to think of all those ants falling 70 feet), scrubbed the syrup out, poured water down the pole to drive back those still coming up & smeared a circle of soap deterrence around the top.

I felt eyes burning into the top of my head. I looked up and here was a big beady-eyed blue jay staring from the banister, three feet away. Chills champagned around my scalp. Its black eyes gobbled the sight of me. It turned sideways and tilted its head. The tip of its tailfeathers had a curl. "Curly," I said. I set a pinch of bologna on the banister. The bird hopped away, hopped back, pecked once at the substance, squawked as if poisoned, lurched into the sky, and peeled away down Western.

I watched it land on an odd black hulking shape on the roof of a building a few blocks away. It immediately took off again, disappearing behind the building. My eyes returned to the dark shape and studied it until I realized it was the burned air conditioning unit on the building that had caught fire the other night.

I began to take note of other remote objects. Turning 360 degrees, I counted one, two, three, four, five construction cranes at various distances. I felt a kinship for the men who captained those cranes, though they built buildings and I merely sat here. And they got down for lunch and went home every night to their loved ones. Through the binoculars I watched the nearest cranesman. He appeared as earnest as a surgeon as he wheeled and worked his massive contrivance. I considered how much he was making while I sat for nothing.

"The hell with Hoover," I said. We had no contract. I plugged the phone back in. I hadn't made a nickel from his interview. And not one school had contacted me. The hell with him, the hell with them. It would be something to make a few bucks off this last miserable flagpole, I thought, but it wasn't going to happen with Hoover in charge.

It was a lovely smog-free day in May. No, June. Sunlight frithered down like golddust from a blowtorch-blue sky. Jacarandas broke like immense lavender chandeliers. A breeze mussed me kindly, bringing again the enchanted aroma of bread baking. The mere thought of making a buck or two up there had slipped me back into my rightful, organic place in the city's midst. In time I would be father, husband, and teacher again, but for now I was a flagpole-sitter, the city needed a flagpole-sitter, whether it knew it or not, I was it, and I damn well deserved a little moo-la for my trouble.

The phone screamed and my heart leapt like a cat. I crossed my fingers for another media type angling for an interview. "Joe Magellan, flagpole-sitter," I answered. "I want five hundred to open my mouth."

"That's more than I ever got." It was Jinx. "Still mad at me?"

I looked over at the booth, manned now by someone else. "Where are you?"

"San Diego. Business. Hey, provocative interview with Mr. Hoover. Congratulations."

A homeless woman with a trash bag full of banging cans and bottles made her way from receptacle to receptacle up Western.

"I want to get down, Jinx."

"You do not. *Why?*"

"I already proved I can do it."

"Um, the only way you can prove you can do it is to *do* it. You can't give up the first time the devil whispers 'give up.' Flagpole-sitting is a battle of good and evil."

"Oh, come on."

A fat man with a long red scarf around his neck rushed out of a brick building and jumped in a taxi.

"Running a porno theater is a battle of good and evil. I pray every night to be forgiven for what I do, to be helped to change my life. And I will. I am. As for you, sir, don't worry, just sit."

"I'm not worried about me, I'm worried about my family."

"Your family's fine. Joe, listen—if you get down now, you'll lose everything, including, dare I say, some not small part of your soul."

I considered: I'm on a pole seven stories in the air, where I've lived for ninety days and nights. My wife and son won't tell me what they're doing to a place that carries a Rube Goldberg loan from hell which requires me to stay up on the pole. I'm talking to a transvestite named Jinx Goodman, the owner of an adult movie theater, and he's telling me the flagpole is a cosmic battleground which will lose me my soul if I throw in the towel.

"How did I get here?" I said. "There's something seriously wrong with me."

Jinx laughed heartily.

"I'm in somebody else's living nightmare."

"Naw, you're in the right living nightmare. Sitting on a flagpole? You know what a living nightmare is? It's being the gay son of Southern Baptist Nazi parents who tell you every day that you're going to burn in hell forever. It's running away at fourteen and getting gang-raped. It's getting put in a mental hospital at sixteen and drugged and elec-tro-shocked, then getting abused every whichway by three sets of foster parents. It's turning tricks and shooting smack at seventeen. It's fifty other little horror stories you don't want in your head. *That* is a living nightmare, old sport."

"Jesus, Jinx. All that happened to you?"

"No, it happened to Bob Hope. Yes, it happened to me. And do you hear me whining? Do you see me abandoning my dream? My vision? Do you see me throwing away eight years of sobriety because of one bad day? Do you see me slipping and sliding around on an oil spill of self-pity like, oh, I won't mention any names, but he's having that bad day, poor baby, and doesn't have it in him to do what he was born to do."

"Born to sit on a flagpole? That's a horrible story, Jinx, but it makes me feel even more deluded for wasting my life up here. Especially with my family staggering around down there in one helpless jam after an-other."

"Have you ever heard of Gauguin? He walked out on his family and screwed young girls in Tahiti. Compared to him, you're the family man of the year."

"Yeah, Gauguin is some standard."

"Trust me—the absolute *worst* thing you could do for Clover and Nate is to get down off that pole now. Extreme success is a-comin' 'round the mountain, for *all* concerned. Don't mention this to *one soul*, Joe Magellan, but…I'm going legit. Namely, turning Playtoe's Cave into a genuine movie theater. You might not guess it, but I love realistic stuff, like John Cassavetes and Henry Jaglom." Jinx gave a shy laugh. "Thought I was a dumb blonde, eh?"

"Not hardly. I'm the one trying to figure out my life. Or even this conversation."

"I'll simplify it. You achieving your dream is crucial to me achieving mine. Joe, you're the spark that's ignited the revitalization of the entire Western Avenue corridor."

"Wait a minute. Where have I heard that revitalization line before? Have you been talking to that nut banker of Clover's?"

"Nut banker? Mr. Spoletti is an economic visionary. I gotta go, my meeting's starting. Stay put!"

I sat in an old rowboat on a gently rocking body of black water. You could see five or ten feet in the darkness. I felt around in the boat for an oar, fearing spiders or snakes, but found a baseball bat and an old dirty orange sweater that glowed in the dark. I thought I could unravel the sweater and use it to fish with the bat, although I dreaded eating raw fish and couldn't build a fire in the boat. I tried to paddle with the bat, but which direction? Something huge behind me started rocking the boat. Its awful shape rose above me, the phone rang and I woke with a cry. "Goddamn monster!"

It was dark and I was cold. I got in the mummybag and, safe now, luxuriated in the lingering terror of the dream. I imagined using that bat on the monster. The phone kept ringing and I answered, still half in the dream.

"Joe."

"Jinx? You sound funny."

"I wake you?"

"I was in this boat and something started shaking it."

"Your conscience?"

I sat up. "Kerridge?"

"By the way, your wife is turning that place into a hippie den."

"A hippie den? What the hell's that? And how do you know anything about it?"

"Better watch out, them hippies dig that free love."

"Who is this?"

The caller said what sounded like, "Son of Salmon."

"Son of a fish?"

"S-i-m-e-o-n. Pronounced 'salmon.'"

S-i-m-e-o-n, I thought. I remembered I had named the pole San Simeon, which I had told nobody.

"You *do* know who Saint Simeon is," the caller said.

"I know *what San Simeon* is."

"Saint Simeon Stylites. 'Let this avail,'" the caller recited, "'just, dreadful, mighty God, this not all be in vain, that thrice ten years, thrice multiplied by superhuman pangs, in hungers and in thirsts, fevers and cold—"

"What *is* this?"

"—in coughs, aches, stitches, ulcerous throes, and cramps; a sign betwixt the meadow and the cloud patient on this tall pillar have I borne rain, wind, frost, heat, hail, damp, and sleet, and snow; and I hoped that ere this period closed Thou wouldst have caught me up into thy rest, denying not these weather-beaten limbs the meed of saints, the white robe and the palm.'"

"Hmm," I said. I decided this erudite kook meant no harm. Did I imagine the fans of a flagpole-sitter would be *normal*? "Sounds like Tennyson."

"Correct. 'O, my sons, my sons, I, Simeon of the pillar, by surname Stylites, among men; I, Simeon, the watcher on the column till the end, do now from my high nest of penance here proclaim that Pontius and Iscariot by my side show'd like fair seraphs.'"

Pillar? Watcher on the column? High nest of penance? Like tumblers in a lock, a series of connections fell into place. "Who is this Saint Simeon again?"

"An ancient flagpole-sitter. Pillar-sitter."

Finally, at the end of the long, dark, sleepy valley of my mind, a porchlight came on.

"Shipwreck," I whispered. "Shipwreck Blake."

"Things happen on a pole, Joe," said Shipwreck Blake, tenderly. "Mysterious things."

I strove to recover, like a fighter from an uppercut. "Is that a threat, old man?"

"Don't play brave, son. Get down now, while you can," and he was gone.

I held the phone until the dial tone began. I felt acutely watched. Seen. The sky looked like wet putty, unnaturally near. I felt I could take a stick and poke the sky and the tip of the stick would go clear through.

A dumpling formed in my throat which I fought to not swallow. I could smell the clouds, dank, salty, alive. I thought of the old article Clover had torn up, and the bullet hole in the page from *Crime and Punishment*. I was the biggest sitting duck in the world. I remembered the blind man and his "Minding business—pop! Dead. Snip, snap, snop."

If they found me shot up there, would anybody suspect Shipwreck? The only other person who had seen Blake was Jinx, and what chance would *he* have convincing anybody to investigate the old fool as my assassin? Slowly, I lay down, on my back, barely breathing, still exposed to any madman with a rifle in any tall building for, what, a mile in every direction?

How could he know what Clover was doing with the place? A *hippie den*, he said. Was she back on drugs, as I accused, as she denied? She could be setting up an opium den with army cots and hundred-year-old Chinamen, with Nate as watch-out, how would *I* know?

No, I thought, Blake's lying. You can't believe a word he says. Worse than that liar Carmen. Jesus—what if he's hanging around down there, disguised as a workman, pretending to help but up to God knew what? Think of the crap he'd already pulled. This imbecilic flagpole-sitting was *everything* to him. What *wouldn't* he do to protect that record. *His* record. I had a restless night.

46

JOE

Clover's talking. The "hippie den" turns out to be a "coffeehouse." Coffeehouse? More beatnik than hippie. Is this 1950? In any case, how did Shipwreck know? And what can I do about it?

More renovation, furniture, doodads, crap coming & going. Along the front & down the side gigantic Mexican-painted pots of cacti and flowers, round bistro-style tables on the sidewalk under the flagpole, and a green & white striped awning over the picture window, eliminating what scant view I had inside. She defiantly informed me that all her faceless paintings are hung in there.

I say: Go for it, darlin', because WHAT CAN I CAN DO ABOUT ANY OF IT! I hereby adopt STOICISM. GO & BORROW TEN MILLION DOLLARS from the GODFATHER if you like, because I AM just as COOL as a ZEN MASTER'S CHESHIRE CAT.

I stopped writing to forestall an aneurism. A white sports car raced up through the curves of the Hollywood Hills, in and out of the shadows.

Clover's plan: pass-the-hat poetry readings & acoustic music, a nook for perusing literary journals, etc. That'll get the beatniks snapping their fingers. Espresso, bagels & pastries, no hamburgers or greasy spoon vittles but a changeable set of her original mishmashes as specials of the day. I suggest she needs a permit for live music. She brushes me off: "I know what I'm doing." Okay, if you say so, but YOU KNEW WHAT YOU WERE DOING WITH THAT FANCY DAN RESTAURANT TOO!

The worse that place does, the sooner I'll have to get down & we can commence the happy, normal life that is ALL SHE EVER WANTED IN THE FIRST PLACE. Why drag this thing out? SURRENDER ALREADY, DEAR! I give it a month, only because she has a little fight in her this time, which Benedict Jinx Arnold obviously implanted.

Almost nobody even speaks English in this neighborhood, this U.N. hotbed, so who's coming to these poetry readings, unless she has 15 different translators.

Clover & Jinx chat it up now like long-lost sisters. Well, she has somebody besides Nate to talk to & if she cracks when the den flops, Jinx is sharp enough to see it coming & may let me know.

While the two of them renovate (Clover the eatery & Jinx the theater), every owner along Western, with help from the city, is out sprucing up— fresh paint, steam-cleaning sidewalks, planting flowers, replacing dead trees. You'd think Jesus was coming, but it's only that fishy "revitalization." I haven't seen the band of homeless folks lately who crashed in the vacant lot and vacant doorways. You hear "revitalization," you can bet two things: one, people with nowhere to go suddenly get goned. Two, mucky-mucks somewhere are lining their pockets backstage. This is Lost Cause Avenue & no steam-cleaning chewing gum or whiting-out of the homeless is going to change that.

Nate & I talk every day, about school, Lakers, whatnot, and…BOOKS! He's got the book bug! What a joy, what a thrill, talking to your son about literature. Huck & Tom, Holden, *To Kill a Mockingbird*. Better than catch.

Nothing's come of the interview. I don't give a damn that nobody gives a damn I'm up here. Hoover keeps saying he's "working on something big" but "can't say" what. Surrounded by big talkers. Nothing from Shipwreck since his threat/call. Jinx says nobody resembling Blake has been around. She's the only one besides me who's seen the man. His tawdry MO: pop up with some idiot stunt, crawl back into the woodwork. Should have seen through his inept bluster long ago.

For an hour in the middle of the night I watched a dry thunderless lightning storm way out over the ocean in the same spot in the corner of the black sky. Though I knew it was coming it was a shock every time.

"Magellan!"

Looked over: white guy in a fake-looking mustache, giant dark glasses, and a floppy tennis hat. It was certainly not Shipwreck.

"It's me!" the man stage-whispered. "Dr. Kerridge!"

"Malcolm? Good God, man. What are you doing? Have you got a mirror?"

"I have a TV, and I happened to see that preposterously flattering story on you."

"Oh, you liked it. Hoover did something on you, too, didn't he?"

"Did he? Joe, listen—I need to talk to you. May I come up?"

"Lemme think… No."

"I gave you a refund!"

Although the charlatan had delighted in humiliating me at his seminar, he had forced me to take pole-sitting seriously, or seriously enough to try to get it out of my system. I had squeezed that refund out of him and won the war. Looking down now upon the little exposed wizard in his uproarious get-up, I dredged up a spoonful of mercy for him. A winner's mercy, but mercy still the same. I lowered him a walkie-talkie.

"What can I do for you, Malcolm?"

"Hey, where is everybody? Your fame cooled off. How long you been up, six months?" He pretended to see the blackboard for the first time: "Only a hundred twenty-five days? And your fans abandoned you already? That's sad, sad, sad. Hey, I have a proposition. The cure looks shaky, I admit, but all you need is a booster."

"Oh, a booster, eh? What's a booster gonna run me?"

"It's on the house. I'll even throw in a stipend for your trouble. Free touch-up, plus, say, fifty bucks."

"Five hundred."

"Hey, this is a gift horse, stupid!"

"A thousand."

"Okay, five hundred. So, I go up, give you a booster, five hundred, you get down, do another interview with Hoover and say I cured you after all."

I laughed, then remembered the plan was to dismount when Clover's beatnik den tanked. "All right, what the hell."

"Excellent. How do I get up there?"

"Put it in the basket."

"Put what in the basket?"

"The five hundred."

"I'm not putting five hundred dollars in a basket. You could grab it and tell me to fuck off."

"You don't even have it. How could you know what I'd hold out for?"

"I brought a number of hundred-dollar cashier checks. First, I come up."

"And try to push me off?"

"I'm a doctor, you clodhopper. How dare you suggest such a thing?"

"It's against the rules to have anybody up here."

"What goddamn rules? What do you think this is, an Olympics sport? How can I do a touch-up from down here?"

"Say, 'Mumbo-jumbo, touch-up, alakazam,' send up the five hundred, and I'll go on TV when I get down."

Kerridge tore his tennis hat off his head and threw it at me; it went up ten feet and came back down, knocking his Audrey Hepburn sunglasses off. He then tried to climb the pole, a pitiful exertion. He stood there, panting. "Get down off there! Now! I command you! As your doctor!"

I shook my head. "Do I still get the five hundred?"

Kerridge twisted his hands around the walkie-talkie as if it were my neck, threw it in the basket, pulled his hat down and scurried away.

The curtains in the apartment swayed. "I love you, Clover," I called. It was a poor, selfish, deeply impaired love, but I would be down soon with a new love, healthy and bounteous and normal and sane as never before.

PART IV

"124 days out. Scurvy throughout the ships.
No food. Eating rats and wood."

—Ferdinand Magellan

47

JOE

What I couldn't make sense of was Clover's bizarre calm as this fresh disaster came riding on in.

A smattering of the curious wandered into the beatnik rebirth of Clover's Patch; few returned. She had hired a couple student temps, designed a more professional if still modest menu, scheduled poetry readings, yoga classes, and performance art, and promoted the place with ads in the free weeklies and posters around the neighborhood. The effort produced little but the promise of another glug, glug, glug when the beatnik ship went down.

I wondered if her serenity in the face of more inevitable failure could be a symptom of deterioration before complete collapse. A carefreeness in her voice, detached from reality, reminded me of my mother at the end, murmuring to herself about a French landscape of gardens and golden clouds that resided solely in her gnarled imaginings.

It was only a matter of time. The hipster hangout would bomb, she'd throw in the towel, and I'd do what I had to do, the only right thing—climb down and pull her chestnuts out of the fire. I would sacrifice my quest to a higher good, the family, the bedrock of American civilization, which itself held the world of nations together in longing and hope. Nobody could fault me for climbing down to, microcosmically, save the world.

On the third morning of the neo-beatnik era, Clover sent up, along with my breakfast, a copy of the *Los Angeles Times*. In red she had circled a front-page story entitled "Old Dying Western Slated for Rebirth." Said story focused on an entity known as "The Committee for the Revitalization of the Western Avenue Corridor."

"Uh-oh," I whispered.

Clover and Jinx had been throwing around the R word; now the *Times* was in on it. Said Committee included merchants up and down the avenue, including Clover, Jinx (whose soon-to-be-legit movie house, the paper reported, would be re-named Plato's Cave), and dozens more. It was a shameless puff-piece, suggesting that the Committee, via Reaganomics, aided by Spoletti's bank, among others, and the diversion of a chunk of Community Redevelopment Agency funds from downtown's Bunker Hill project, would soon resurrect dilapidated Western and create a commercial tsunami for the city as a whole.

The revamped Clover's Patch received respectable mention, while the flagpole and I received nary a peep. Wasn't I responsible for Clover getting the loan that started all this? Hadn't Jinx credited me with inspiring her and the whole revitalization deal?

However, if I were indeed dismounting soon, would I want any mention at all?

On the third hand, my getting down had been contingent on the tanking of Clover's Patch, which it now might not, if this article was any indication. My pancakes grew cold as I read and reread the story, my mouth open like an unhinged oyster.

This was no pipe dream of Clover's and Jinx's. Yes, the article was a puff-piece, but a puff-piece on the front page of the *Los Angeles Times*, and, as it turned out, it helped accomplish the impossible.

Clover's Patch perked up that very day and night, and each day and night thereafter. By the weekend, at peak hours, it was standing room only. Customers overflowed onto the sidewalk and a patio in the rear which Clover had wrought out of the parking space, cozying it up with rows of bamboo in redwood planters. In response to the surge, she had to hire a second-shift crew.

As if in a bad flying dream, I gazed down upon the merry mob, a dizzying racial, ethnic, cultural, and socioeconomic cross-section of the neighborhood and the city, all eating, drinking, chattering, reading poetry, making music, performing God-knew-what art, and living it up as if the world were coming to an end.

The poetry that reached me from below revealed exactly what I expected—the smug, the clever, and the sentimental all at once. The live music was the kind of high-pitched, doodling pop-folk-jazz that set my teeth grinding. Nevertheless, a local TV station did a spot on the "fresh cultural mix" of "the Patch," and its popularity further soared.

Plato's Cave re-opened on schedule, with a second-run showing of Woody Allen's *Stardust Memories* and John Cassavetes' *Killing of a Chinese Bookie*, a downer double-bill which had the hordes laughing and skipping across Western (in the new mid-block crosswalk with signal that the Revitalization Committee had installed overnight) right over to Clover's Patch, where they were met with coffee, French crullers, and various artistic shenanigans.

It appeared that Clover would not soon be begging me to climb down and save her chestnuts after all. The money she was raking in failed to cheer me. It had to have been going out as fast it was coming in, what with the second crew and the monstrous bamboo planters and God knew what other extravagances down there that I couldn't see. I'd been *this* close to a noble descent, but the universe, that nosy Samaritan, just had to stop and help a damsel in distress.

48

JOE

Pete Hoover slapped his leg with a roll of papers and spoke into the walkie. "What do you want out of this, amigo?"

"The record."

"Correcto!"

Clover's customers by the dozens, every color, creed, and class, young and old, female and male and in-between and beyond, streamed in and out (how did she jam them in there?) and lounged at the bistro tables out front. Sipping their espresso and smoking, they nonchalantly eavesdropped on the chat between the famous newsman and Clover's kook flagpole husband. Despite their dark glasses, crossed legs, and cigarette rings, they were finding it difficult to maintain their hipness while craning their necks to eye me in the open trapdoor. I read their ironic hipster minds like a cereal box. They didn't quite feel safe judging me as an outright nut yet, because I might turn out to be cool like them somehow, or even cooler, God forbid. I hoped Clover was charging them an arm and a leg for those toy cups of coffee and those European doo-dad do-nuts.

"And what," Hoover asked, "do you wish to obtain *from* the record?"

"I wish to obtain never having to think about the damn thing again as long as I live."

"Oops! A, uh, hound dog attitude like that won't sell no deodorant." He slapped his thigh with the papers again. "You want to be a hero, Joe?"

"Nope."

"*Exactly.* That's the rebel stand we're looking for. No true hero wants to be a hero. No true hero wants any part of that disgusting fame lying there like a slut with tits of gold."

"Well, I wouldn't kick my fair share out of bed."

"Of course you wouldn't. I also want liberation from this repulsive job I have chasing after dumpster fires, train wrecks, and goofballs."

"Goofballs like me?"

"Well, there's fake goofballs and then there's genuine goofballs. A genuine goofball is what America is all about—individualism, iconoclasm, genius, pursuing an insane dream, etc., like Columbus. Tell me Columbus wasn't a goofball. I'm putting my life on the line for you, Joe. Hell, I did that hatchet job on Kerridge because his failure is the foundation of your success. You know, Bert, the station manager, he's a member of Kerridge's cult."

"*What?*"

"Yep. He went to the seminar couple years ago, got cured of some idiot fetish, raking leaves all night at his mansion or something. So, of course, he didn't want me to touch his little guru Kerridge. I'm at the tippy-top of his shit list now. Who cares? I hate that cocksucking job."

"Well, he wouldn't *fire* you, would he?" If Hoover got the ax, I'd lose my media outlet. "You're one of the stars of that station."

"*One* of? Don't worry, partner. He's got clout, but he doesn't call the shots. Still, everybody's expendable, so you never know. Except heroes, of course. I'm a star, but no *hero*. *You're* the hero, baby—one hundred and forty-six days and countin'."

There was a time I would have cut off a toe for one hundred and forty-six days. Now I had it and it was ashes in my mouth.

Pete smacked himself in the head with the papers and glanced at the cool cats at the bistro tables. "Clover's sure reaping the fruits of your quest, eh?"

"What's that you keep flogging yourself with?"

Hoover held the papers up. "Our contract!"

"Why do I need an agent again? More free interviews?"

"You gonna handle your own commercials?"

"Commercials!" However diminishing my view of the quest, I was not about to whore it out. "I'm not doing any stinking commercials."

"Ever hear of the Xerox Star Computer?"

"No. I don't know anything about computers."

"Who cares? Mickey Mantle never ate a damn corn flake in his life. How's five thousand dollars sound?"

"Five thousand dollars!"

"Plus a free new computer that runs five grand itself. Joe. Xerox is throwing in a printer too. Five thousand clams, computer, printer. For a one-minute gig."

"Nobody's supposed to come up here."

"No sweat. They got cranes, zooms, copters."

"Five thousand. How much do you get?"

"A pittance. Ten percent. Chicken feed. But it's a start. I'm going places, and I'm taking you with me. We'll show those giggling monkeys. Lower that basket."

Taking a gander at the contract didn't mean I was going to sign it. Maybe by a miracle Hoover knew what he was doing after all. The world was so cockeyed that any energetic loudmouth could be king if he just kept plugging along. I lowered the basket.

"Oh, the saints!" Hoover pulled a book from his coat pocket and dropped it in the basket with the contract. I had asked him for info on this Simeon character so I could find out if Blake had been bullshitting me. "They got a chapter on that pillar guy in there," he said. "He's a genuine goofball. Syrian. I think we can put that fella to good use."

I hauled the basket up. The book was entitled *Saints, Saints, Saints!* The contract was inside.

49

Carmen and Shipwreck sat in a rear booth in the Roosevelt Hotel bar, empty but for them and the bartender. Carmen removed a pill bottle from her purse, knocked an orange capsule in her hand, and washed it down with her Bloody Mary.

"What was that?" said Blake.

"None your beeswax."

"Don't want you takin' a tumble up there. Long ways down."

"Get me up, I'll take over." Carmen took a drink. "What if he gets pissed, *shoves* me over, claims it's an accident? Who's gonna believe a pathological liar? Aw, who cares. I'll have that horny huckleberry eating out of my hand. So, when's this happening?"

"I'll let you know." He sipped his Sugar-Free Sprite.

Carmen mimicked a phone call. "Information, please? Is five hundred lousy bucks going to keep me on call until the twelfth of never? No?" Shipwreck pulled out his wallet and slid some cash across the table. Carmen counted it. "Mmmm," she said. She slipped it in her purse.

"Have you ever read the Bible, Carmen?"

"I've heard of it. Are you in it?"

"Do you understand the role of temptation in the spiritual development of a man?"

"Shippy, you're just another control freak, guarddoggin' what's yours. But go ahead and call bullshit pudding, fine with me." She polished off her drink and looked at her watch. "The monkeys beckon." She scooted out of the booth and stood unsteadily. She put her hands on the table and leaned toward him. "Lemme know when. I can't wait." She lurched out of the bar into the sunlight, which flooded the place a moment before the door swung shut.

50

CLOVER

The Patch was packed, all of us gathered around the TV in the corner. A re-run of *Mork and Mindy* was on with the sound down, but it was Joe we were waiting for.

As much as he disdained the whole commercial thing, I felt such pride for him—for being on TV, for gaining the status to be paid good money for his spokesman services. And I was proud of myself, too, for bringing together this rainbow of humanity to both witness his success and enjoy my own, my establishment, my Patch.

Mork and Mindy went to break. "Here he is!" I hollered. "Quiet! Quiet on the set!"

Blue sky appeared on the screen. Sitar music keened. A school of swallows flashed one way and the other. A single bright star shone like a diamond in the dark blue sky. The camera panned down to reveal a man in all black, meditating.

"Dad!" Nate barked.

Joe sat alone on what appeared to be a completely empty redwood patio. They had removed all his stuff from the platform. You couldn't even tell he was on the pole.

As the camera circled him, the sitar softened and a stentorian voice, à la Orson Welles, intoned: "In the fourteenth century, a man named Saint Simeon of Stylites lived on a pillar of stone, fifty feet in the air, for the last thirty years of his life. Simeon wore an iron collar around his neck, fastened to a short chain, to keep him from falling off. When he died, a maggot from one of his sores fell to the ground and landed at the feet of Basilicus, king of the Saracens. The king picked up the maggot and placed it on his eye and the maggot was instantly transformed into a dazzling pearl, so large and so beautiful that Basilicus left behind his entire kingdom and wandered into the desert with the pearl his sole possession."

"Ew," somebody said.

"Far out," from another.

The camera closed in on Joe's face, tanned, serene, eyes closed. A breeze fingered his roan locks. The music of the sitar ceased. Joe's eyes opened. Alarmed, he looked up at the star; it began to grow in the sky; it was hurtling right toward him.

The star struck the platform and exploded, the TV went black, then came back to show Joe sitting before the illuminated screen of a home computer. The camera drew back to reveal him high above the city, alone on the platform but for the warm and glowing machine. Then an extreme close-up of Joe's crooked mouth, which whispered, "Xerox Star."

The screen went black. Clover clicked the TV off and the place erupted with cheers.

"Wow!"

"What just happened?"

"Mochaccino on me!" Jinx shouted.

The crowd mobbed the counter and Solana and Tomi lined up cups and poured the sweet, brown, foam-topped beverage.

I could barely make sense of any of it. I retreated to a corner table and Nate joined me.

"That was something," I said.

"That was Dad." He stared at the blank TV. "Does he have sores?"

No, it was not the normal life, but with Joe making money, too, now, I daydreamed about opening Clover's Patches around town, the state, the world. I handed Nate the walkie-talkie. "Ask him."

He pushed the button. "Dad? Hello? Over."

"Hey, pal. How was it? You watch it?"

"Everybody did. It sure was something. There's a party down here for it. For you."

"Yeah, I hear. Mom like it?"

I nodded.

"Yeah. Want me to get her?"

"I really admire you guys turning that place into something special down there."

"I don't do much. Mom and Solana do the most."

"Solana?"

"It means sunshine in Spanish. She's a business student."

"She's a waitress?"

"She kind of runs it."

"Wait a minute. A business student is kind of running the place?"

"She goes to UCLA. And Tomi cooks some. She does other things, too. Natalie's the main waitress. And a couple new ones."

"Jesus Christ," Joe said. "It's all women?" I rolled my eyes. "I guess it's better than men sniffin' around. Don't know how healthy it is for you to be surrounded by nothing but females though. She doesn't make you listen to that hippie poetry, does she?"

"*You* wrote hippie poetry."

I gave Nate a thumbs-up.

"I never wrote hippie poetry. Is that what *she* said? Never mind. How'd your story go?"

"I'm still writing it."

"Must be a novel by now."

"Three pages."

"I'd love to see it. Lemme know if I can help."

"We're supposed to do it ourself. You're not gonna stay up there for thirty years, are you?"

"That's the ancient record. Nobody'll top that. That's Saint Simeon."

"Well, wash real good, okay? Don't get maggots."

51

JOE

The Star commercial is the talk of the town. *Advertising Age* is doing a cover story on it: "The Greatest Anti-Ad Ad Ever?"

The ad hasn't sold many computers, says Hoover. No foolin'. It's a glorified typewriter. There it sits in the corner, gathering dust, the eyes of rust upon it. But I'm getting more offers. Coppertone, Euphorium Flotation Tanks. "We're mulling them," says Hoover. Mull fast, I told him.

He did a follow-up report on me, slipped in another jab at Kerridge, & GOT FIRED!

The station manager had more clout than Hoover thought. The firing itself got big coverage, including my role, which generated more offers. I'm making plenty more up here than I ever did teaching. Absurd, hilarious, disgusting. But I'm not saying no. Guess I'm like Jinx with her porno movies, selling my principles for enough money to buy my principles back and have some left over.

And I was THIS CLOSE to getting down. If Clover had whispered, "Come down and help me, please," I'd've been down before she hung up. Thank you, Clove, for being stronger, more stubborn, more deluded than me.

I need books up here on birds, architecture, trees, constellations.

Tarot/palm reader wearing huge sunglasses and fanning herself, sitting in a chair beside a sandwich board outside her shop ("The Past, The Present, The Future"). Flapping awnings, blue, red, green. Balloon/cotton candy man goeth by once a day, "Fresh cotton candy! Colored he-lee-um balloons!" Top of downtown hidden in a milky daze. Sci-fi sky orange and purple, sun bouncing off a million windows, city pink. "Elbows," a pool hall, neon ball and cue. Black crows riding the crêpe end of the day.

I've been reading about Simeon in *Saints! Saints! Saints!*

"Pilgrims came to see Simeon to witness his amazing feat and bask in his spiritual light. World leaders consulted with him on religious and practical matters. The poorest of the poor, kings and queens, whores and whoremongers, people of every faith and color stood under the pole to be near his exalted presence."

And then this . . .

"At Simeon's death in 495 AD, a bluebird was seen flying from the platform and disappearing into the sky. Saint Simeon left a diary recording his thoughts, but this journal, like the bluebird, vanished after his death."

52

Sam Knight, the owner of the prestigious Westwood art gallery of the same name, read the *Times* article on the revitalization of Western Avenue, a week later caught *Stardust Memories* at Plato's Cave on the way home from the gallery (trying to get out more after an untidy divorce), and, for a look-see, joined the crowd crossing Western to Clover's Patch.

Sam found the coffeehouse quaint and energetic. The menu, an eccentric hodgepodge, brought a smile to his cosmopolitan face. Living dangerously, he tried some "honey-fried plumcakes" and a side of "potato salad de Clover with Jerusalem artichoke and mint." He was delighted by both. The featured poetry and music proved dilettantish, and he was about to make his lonesome way home when the primitivist faceless paintings adorning the walls awakened his professional eye. Informed they were the work of the coffeehouse's proprietress, he introduced himself and he and Clover, over espressos, sat at a corner table, falling easily into a prolonged conversation about art and coffee and food and life. He believed he detected signs of interest from her, delicate and momentary, in her body language, her laughter.

Thereafter, Sam stopped in for additional tête-à-têtes. Clover made no secret of her marital status, and offered no blatant complaints in that area, but how much happiness could there be in a marriage with the husband on a flagpole and the wife left alone below, a sensitive and lovely artist.

One evening Sam followed his pounding heart and dared to stay while Solana and the crew cleaned up.

Clover, however, grew distant. He feared he had misread the signals. The conversation died on the vine.

"Should I go?" he said.

She looked at him, and away, thought, and back, and shook her head. "I'm just worried about Nate. It's no fun having an eleven-year-old in summer school."

"I understand." Sam knew about this already. It seemed a small thing to him. "Is Joe upset too?"

"Ha. He doesn't even know Nate's *in* summer school."

So, Sam thought, she's telling me things she's hiding from Joe. "But it's July and the boy goes to school every day."

"He's in his own world up there. Not to mention, it's my birthday."

"Your birthday? Well, happy birthday. I wish I would have known."

"Nate forgot too. He's a kid. I didn't want to remind him, he would have told Joe, and I wanted to see if Joe would remember on his own."

Sam reached across the table and rested his hand on her arm, not too tight, not too light. She wept quietly. "Aw, Clover," he said, just right.

53

JOE

SIX MONTHS!!! ONE HUNDRED & EIGHTY DAYS!!! And not a word from Clover. Thank you, darling. Well, she's busy, God bless her.

My commercial for the *Times* is in the can & set to run in movie theaters next month. It shows me sitting up here on my chaise reading the Sunday comics. I say, "If it weren't for the *Los Angeles Times*, I don't know where I'd be!" EIGHT GRAND for THREE HOURS WORK! That's a LOT of substitutin', baby. Even commercials, viewed from the right perspective, make an effective tool in a man's search for truth.

Everyone (except my wife) wants a piece of me—commercials, interviews, autographs, a chat, a look-see, a wave, a photo op. Hoover printed up a sample card with my signature for autograph seekers:

Flagpole-Sitter Extraordinaire,
Joseph Galileo Magellan

Pete's idea was to toss the cards down to the "riff-raff." I declined. Although who would dare argue that my quest is *not* extraordinaire?

He's "rationing" my commercials. Overexposure is death, he says. He appears to be correct—my "price" goes up day by day. Man doth not live by spirituality alone.

He tells me a small but respected publisher is nibbling at *The Strange Adventures of an American Flagpole-Sitter*. Ten years slaving over *Holder & Biggen* without a nibble & I get a bite on my flagpole ravings before they're even typed up.

Couple more months of milking the golden calf, the loans'll be paid off & $$$ in the bank. I yield to the force that through the orange flagpole drives my green cash.

Teaching will be a breeze. The kids'll stare in awe as "The Flagpole-Sitter" walks in. They won't care if I have that record. They'll only want to know what it was like up here. Nobody cares about that damn record.

જી

Clover sent up a splendid pair of Felix Zelmer binoculars to replace the cheapies. I have to watch how much I let her help me.

I ate peanuts and watched a crane operator miles away doing his thing in a monstrous praying mantis machine that appeared through the FZ binos to be ten feet in front of the pole. I kept waiting for him to bark, "What are *you* lookin' at!"

I turned my scrutiny to the high-rises downtown. I focused on the Union Bank building, little people in the windows at the top scurrying around, shuffling papers, juggling numbers, dancing to the fiddler's tune.

I looked down Western and was startled by the face of a man with a beard who from his furtive expression and head movements seemed to be looking for an immediate criminal opportunity. I looked at him without the binos and he appeared to be an innocent window-shopper.

The phone rang. It was Nate. "Guess who I read a story by? Nathaniel Hawthorne."

"You *did?*"

"Yep. From your book of his stories. 'Rappaccini's Daughter.'"

Good Lord, no children's story that. "It's a good one, but kinda creepy, huh?"

"Well, poisoned plants. The stuff you wrote on the sides is pretty thought-provoking." He meant the annotations. What in the world had I written? God knew what drugs I was on at the time. "I thought you said it was horrible to write in books."

"Well, not if you *own* the books. So, Hawthorne writes kind of complicated sentences, huh?"

"I didn't understand everything. I could tell it was good. It was like getting lost in the woods at night in a bunch of vines and trees."

"That's good. I like that." Could "Rappaccini's Daughter" damage a young soul more than *Three's Company*?

"My summer school teacher goes, 'Do you know who you're named after?' and I go, 'Uh, like, yeah,' and she goes, 'He's a special writer,' so I went and got him."

"Did you say *summer* school teacher?"

"Uh-oh."

"You're in *summer* school? Why are you in *summer* school?"

"I have to."

"My son is flunking fourth grade and nobody tells me?"

"Fifth grade. It's not flunking, it's unsatisfactory. I knew you'd get mad."

"I'm not mad about the unsatisfactory, I'm mad nobody told me."

"We didn't tell Mom I got in a fight and climbed the pole and the fire department."

"What did you get unsatisfactory in?"

"English."

"English!"

"The teacher didn't like me. I think I was a smart-ass. I made up interesting answers to questions."

"Well, that's imagination. Good God, how bad could you be in English if you're reading 'Rappaccini's Daughter'?"

"I'm applying myself now."

Curly landed on the railing, hopped down on the platform, grabbed a peanut right out of the bag, hopped back on the banister, looked back at the bag, glared at me, and took off.

"If I tell you a secret," I said, "you have to promise not to tell Mom." He eagerly agreed. "After I have enough from the commercials to pay off Mom's loans, I'm getting down."

"Getting down! Off the *flagpole*?"

"Yeah! I'll help you with your homework, we'll play catch, go to the zoo, read together, Hawthorne, sports page."

"You can't get down! You'll ruin my story! Everybody knows me because my dad's the Flagpole-Sitter of Western Avenue! If you get down, I'll-I'll-I'll never talk to you again!" The boy smashed the phone into the receiver.

54

CLOVER

While Mandolotti's 6th Chorale pulsated on the soundtrack, a red Corvette convertible raced along a forest road through shadows and sunshine. The fake blonde riding shotgun fiddled with the driver's shaggy hair as the car sailed through the trees. The camera circled the car in a gut-lurching 360, then zoomed in on the driver: Joe Magellan, who else. His eyes were shut and he wore a goofy smile. His eyes opened, the music ceased, and the camera drew back, revealing Joe on the platform on his back in the mummybag, feeling around, I imagined, for the car and the missing blonde, not necessarily in that order. A basso voiceover proclaimed:

"Corvette Dreams."

The Waltons came back on and I shut the TV off. It was a good thing I'd foregone further coffeehouse viewings of his ridiculous little commercials. I hadn't even told anybody about this one. Nate and I watched it upstairs while Solana ran a reading in the Patch.

Nate said, "Wow, Corvette convertible. Who's that blonde-head woman?"

"What blonde-head woman?"

He laughed. "She wasn't even really there, Mom. He wasn't even in a *car*. They put her in with special effects."

"That doesn't make any difference, Nate. It was a male chauvinist sexist fantasy, and he should be ashamed of himself, I don't care how much they paid him."

"Will we get a free Corvette?"

"Did you hear what I said?"

He sat on the couch like a snake ready to slide down on the floor. "What would happen if Dad got down?"

"Why? Did he say something?"

"He made me promise not to tell."

"I'm making you promise to tell. Right now."

"He's gonna make a bunch of money off the commercials and then get down."

"What!" He was using the boy to prod me.

"I told him not to. I'm writing a story about him. It'll ruin it."

I put my hand on his. "We have to make sure he stays up."

"How?"

I laughed. "Cut the ladder!"

"He could come down the pole."

"Nail the trapdoor shut from underneath!"

"He could tie sheets together and go over the side."

"Build a moat underneath and fill it with crocodiles!"

"He could step on the backs of the crocodiles."

We laughed and laughed, looking out the window at the orange flagpole in the silver sky and making up crazier and crazier ways to keep him up there for as long as we wanted.

55

JOE

Clover sent up 3 new novels & the paper. Scary how much I need her. We've been through hell, remained true (but for that one tiny little passive kiss only a Puritan would count).

Read the news today, oh boy… Hinckley shot four people he never met to impress a movie star he never met & a jury found him S-A-N-E… Shameless ex-President Nixon, wearing his disgrace like a red mini-skirt with no underpants, tours Europe… Mark David Chapman, sentenced to 20 to life for killing John Lennon, reads to the judge from *Catcher in the Rye*… USSR warns U.S. about producing neutron warheads… Ching-Ching the Panda is pregnant… Voyager II discovers "mysterious sounds" from outer space.

Get down, Joe, save the world. Give away your $, march, pray, set yourself on fire.

Made it to page 7 of *Zuckerman Unbound*. Everybody recognizes the protagonist, a famous author. They praise or tease or rebuke him. Not one encounter has a scrap of authenticity to it. Everything's a prop in Roth's relentlessly self-obsessed ironic spew.

Updike's Rabbit was an early hero of mine, but I'm not feeling it for Harry no more. You're wrong, John, in *Rabbit is Rich* it's Rabbit & you yourself who have run out of gas, not "the fucking world." When I was young, Updike was like chocolate, that lyrical, cynical, detail-clogged irony. *Rabbit Is Rich*, like *Gatsby*, is a link in a long & rusty chain of books about the American Nightmare. Bang that same old tired shitty fucking drum, baby!

Thorn Birds is a best seller, a blatantly cornball epic. Clover said I would hate it. She said she hated parts of it herself, but she read the whole thing—700 pages. It starts with a little girl & her very first doll. McCullough rambles on about the doll's face, eyes, dress, hairspray, make-up, then some boys come along & tear the doll limb from limb. The scene is as earnest as a baseball bat, but more honest than the slathered ironies of Roth & Updike. I made it to page 5, two pages more than *Rabbit Is Rich*.

Can't read irony, can't read earnest, can't read shit. It's me, my head, jammed with thousands of writers' anguish, dreams, viruses of yearning, billions of words from brilliant outcasts, visionaries, born to never fit, born to smirk & weep & howl.

Nobody writes quietly enough. It may be impossible to write quietly enough. The greatest writer of the future will be the quietest writer who ever wrote.

Failure has mysterious power. Everyone fears it, nobody respects it. Look at the losing team in a big game. Look at their faces as the clock runs out. Failure is complete, nothing can salve that scald. Victory begins fading the moment it's won. The victor has no words to describe the feelings because the feelings are transient & cannot be sustained. If he has a conscience & catches the shattered eyes of the loser, the victory goes sour. The failed has one feeling—pure, sustained, impossible to mistake, easiest thing in the world to describe. He's a saint, burning at the stake. Lots of winners thanking Jesus, but no saints on the winning side.

That's how I know I have not failed at this: there is no burn. I have conquered the pole not by conquest but by no longer caring. I'm hauling in cash—money & enlightenment. Be down in short order. The hell with the record. The record means nothing.

56

JOE

The pole and platform were overgrown with orange roses, Spanish moss, apples, baby ivy, gardenias. Women's eyes admired me through the foliage, intrigued by my mystery, their lips parted, breath hot. I flew from the pole over rolling hills and a lake with an immense reflection of my face. I circled a clearing in the woods and landed on my feet. Nate was there and we laughed and threw a football around. Clover was at her easel studiously painting the scene. Too near, another woman whispered my name and touched my neck.

I opened my eyes. Carmen! Kneeling beside me!

"Jesus Christ!" I sat up and tore my earplugs out. "How'd you get up here!"

"Well, hello to you, too." She wore blinding white shorts and a purple polka-dot tube top. The trapdoor stood open, the rope ladder swaying. "How'd you get up here!"

"Magic."

"Well, get down!" I pulled my pants on and got out of the bag. "Get off here! *Now*! I'll *throw* you off!"

"Don't say that!" She sat on the platform and grabbed her head. "Why'd you say that!" She rummaged through her silver purse. "You killed my buzz. You murdered it."

"Get up!" I grabbed her by the back of her arms.

"I'll scream! You never *heard* anybody scream!"

I let her go. "Carmen, goddamn you! What do you *doing* here?"

"What is that *smell*?"

"How'd you get *up* here? What do you *want*?"

"Is it *you*? It's *you*. Lucky for you I *love* funky."

"I'll pay you to get down right now."

She fumbled with a bottle of pills in the moonlight. "I'm already paid a lot more than you got."

"Who paid you? Kerridge!"

"Water. Quick! I'll choke!"

I grabbed a bottle from the fridge and she gulped her drugs.

"I'll give you ten seconds to get down!"

"You gonna call the police? Flagpole-sitter has company, breaks rules, fails quest."

"Carmen, you're violating a sacred thing."

"Jesus, you're a breed, you two."

"Who two? *Kerridge?*"

"That gasbag? I have *some* standards."

"Wait a minute. Not Shipwreck."

"Could you sit down? You're rocking the boat."

"Shipwreck *Blake* sent you?"

"No, Shipwreck Jones."

"*Why?*"

She shrugged. "We'd do it, somebody'd get wind of it, you'd get down, he'd win. But your freak-out is turning me off big-time."

"He'd never do this. Why should I believe a word you say? You're a born liar!"

"This dexie better kick in, I'm gonna be *real* hard to handle."

"Where'd you meet him?"

"He accosted me at the zoo."

"What's he look like?"

"Old guy, Black, white hair. Dark blue limo."

"He got you up here?"

"He climbed the pole, got the trapdoor open, lowered the ladder, climbed down, I climbed up."

"Impossible. He's seventy something."

"Squeeze his biceps some time."

I listened: a thwapping helicopter in the distance, far off but headed our way. "Get in the bag! Quick!"

She did, and patted it for me to join her.

I pushed her head inside and adjusted the umbrella to block the bag from the sky. "Stay in there till the helicopter's gone. I'll give you ten dollars."

"Hundred," she mumbled.

"Twenty. Stay in there."

"I'm getting turned on!"

I leaned casually against the balustrade. The 4Real chopper circled the pole three times, hovered, then banked back into the night.

Carmen poked her head out. "I can't breathe. Boy, I feel funny."

"Shipwreck must've tipped them off."

"It feels like… Did I take fucking *Dalmanes*?"

"Okay, time to go."

Instead, she took off her top, shorts, and shoes and flipped them out of the bag.

"Whare are you doing? Put those back on!"

She lay unmoving, eyes closed, breathing slow. I knew Dalmanes were downers. How many had she taken? Could I forcibly dress her and get her down the ladder?

"Shipwreck," I whispered, "you miserable unprincipled *pimp*. How could you *do* this to me?"

My eyes passed over the curves in the sleeping bag. I'd been up there a long time.

The thought came: nobody might ever know.

Nobody might ever know? With Shipwreck and Carmen in the mix? The thought of betraying Clover sickened me. I could never hide it from her. It would be marital suicide. And if Nate found out? Unthinkable.

I continued to think.

Through the years I had provided little more than roof and food for my family, but I took much pride in one domestic achievement: my complete and utter faithfulness to Clover. Aside from that one little kiss. I had just failed at a pole attempt, the person was of age, it was a gesture from them to me of gratitude for academic assistance or inspiration far more than any sort of attraction or romance, at least that's how I saw it, when I thought about it afterwards, though we never discussed or repeated it, and the attention was balm to my rattled ego. It was barely even a kiss at all, but if Clover had had that not quite a kiss with somebody else, I couldn't imagine. If I would have been able to forgive her for it, I never would have let her forget it. She had not had the chance to forgive or forget, of course, because she never found out. That I had so easily hidden it, nearly conscience-free, proved its insignificance.

I sat in the rocking chair. Carmen stirred. One of her slim tanned arms flopped out of the bag. Even in my wildest imagination I would never do anything—she was drugged, for God's sakes—which allowed me to continue to think about it. I winced as her white hand squeezed the night air in dream. I would fall asleep in the chair and wake and she would be gone. If she tried to wake me, I would feign sleep.

My and Clover's sex life had been outstanding, thrilling, beyond compare. A+. Not as frequent as in the beginning, not as frisky, but whose was? You know what the other likes, you go there, why mess around, nothing to prove, it's simpler, why waste time, as long as both get what they want and love what they get. It had picked up in the days before I went up this time—incendiary, desperate, as if I were leaving for the front.

Carmen lay on in that cozy orange bag, snoring daintily. The fabric rose as her chest swelled with each open-mouthed Dalmane wheeze.

Then I thought, what if she's ODing! No, no, no, she took one damn downer. I knelt and poked her lanky forearm and she stirred again. All I had to do was wait till the pill wore off and then get her down before morning light.

I rocked. I hadn't touched anybody for 232 days, and nobody but me had touched me. I remembered the Tolstoy story about a monk on a mountain being visited by a drunken woman in a snowstorm. To avert temptation, the monk cut off a toe. At the sight of the bloody appendage, the woman ran screaming into the night. I, on the other hand, rather luxuriated in lust's crosshairs. My heart jumped like a jackrabbit at the black risk of it moving along the walls of my mind. I knelt and sniffed the little snoring liar's moonlit hair, her lying face like a Fabergé egg. Who wouldn't think about it? While I continued negotiating with doom, her lithe liar's heat permeated every fiber of my mummybag. I let my mind form the words: I'd love to fuck this hot little stoned evil strumpet's brains out. There, I thought, that's out of the way. But having sown the words, they rooted and sprouted and spread like kudzu. I rode the insane wickedness like a red wave. What I could do, I could sidle in there, keep my clothes on, keep my back to her, conk out for a few hours, God knew I needed sleep, it was my damn sleeping bag, and hell, Abraham Lincoln slept with some friend of his, some *guy*, and nobody thought twice about that, it was cold in the eighteenth century, and it wasn't much warmer up on that flagpole, and if Abraham Lincoln could sleep with somebody—*next* to somebody—to stave off the cold, to hold the cold at bay, why couldn't I? Was I better than Abraham Lincoln?

57

NATE

You couldn't barely move in Mom's Patch. It was chock-full from the party for her for Sam selling this no-face painting of hers for 500 dollars. Also about him hanging up her paintings in his gallery with some other woman painters. There was lots of champagne and caviar. Mom and me and Sam were sitting in a corner where you could watch everything.

"Excited?" Mom asked me. She was guzzling champagne glasses like someone was coming to take them away. I nodded. She said, "You ain't acting like it." I shrugged my shoulder. "What's your problem?" she said real loud.

Sam twitched like someone pinched him. "I believe I'll circulate," he said. He milled in the crowd.

I made a face at her glass. She said, "It's only buncha little bubbles. You couldn't get a guppie drunk on bubbles."

I said, "You said you only had a beer when you came home from Sam taking you some place."

"What taking me someplace? We had a stupid meeting to go over my paintings."

"You knocked the lamp over when you came in," I said.

"It was DARK. I was TRYING not to WAKE you. Look, buddy, I don't answer to you. I have lots of pressures. Stop trying to crap on the wonderful night. When I need a mother I'll rent one." She took a drink but kept her eyes on me, like she was daring me to back talk.

"If it's so wonderful how come you're acting so mad?"

"Because you're BUGGING me. You're throwing a bucket of party poop on the parade. You're naggy AND nosy." She tickled my ribs too hard.

"Does Dad know you like Sam?"

"Who cares what he knows? Sam is my AGENT, like Daddy has Pete. It's BUSINESS."

༄

I sat on my bed and read my story to myself:

MY DAD, JOE MAGELLAN, THE FLAG-POLE-SITTER
By Nathaniel Hawthorne Magellan

My dad Joe Magellan is a flag-pole-sitter. That means he climbs up on to a pole and lives there. There is a platform on top made out of redwood wood. He is going to brake the world record and live there 445 days without getting down onec. He goes to the bathroom in a chemcal toiliet. He has to wash good because there's magotts. I and Mom give him food to eat in a basket on a rope. There is a umbrella for rain or shine. He is in commerceals and is getting rich. Other children treat me differnt now. My mom is getting rich too. She runs a coffeehouse named Clover's Patch. We live in the apartment under the flagpole. We bought it from Charly. Jinx a man has a movie theateer across the street. It used to be dirty but now it's regular. Onec I got in a fight and decided to climb the flagpole in school.

My mom has a painting agent Sam. They go out for a beer and talk about painting till late. She ran into a lamp. She was in jail a long time ago. Sam sold her painting. He's going to hang up more paintings by her. Dad the flag-pole-sitter dosen't know any thing about any thing.

The END

58

JOE

Goddamn it, Goddamn it, Goddamn it to hell! How could I have let that little lying liar! I took the hook & I'm waiting for the yank that'll rip my guts open. Everybody's guts.

The smell of night-blooming jasmine, bittersweet, cloying, semenish.

The pop-pop-pop-pop-pop of gunfire in the middle distance.

A billboard to the east shows a car with doors that open upward like wings. I think of the flying birthday poem that brought Clover to me.

A mockingbird sings atop a phone pole. The mockingbird has 43 different trills—all stolen from other birds.

No way in hell will Clover not find out. No way in hell.

❧

The phone screamed like a buzzsaw.

"Joe. Blake here."

I jumped up. "You miserable fucking snake!" I strutted along the banister. "Where are you? Can you see me?" I made fists and gave fingers. "What am I doing right now?"

"God knows, son."

"I'm not your son! You don't scare me anymore, old man. You lost *all* my respect. Every drop." I moved around the platform like a framed man in a prison cell. "And I'm not starting over!"

"Why would you start over? 'Cause you brought a girl up there?"

"*You sent* a girl up here!"

"A gift."

"From the devil."

"You a saint?"

"I'm a *married man.*"

"You're a flagpole-sitter. So what happened with her?"

"Nothing!"

"Is that so. Then why are you blowing your top?"

"Because nobody's supposed to be up here but me!"

"Who says?"

"What?"

"Who says nobody's supposed to be up there but you? *The Flag-pole-Sitter's Rulebook?*"

"There's a *Rulebook?*"

"Oh, sweet Jesus. No, there's no rulebook. That's my point, genius."

"Oh, so I suppose Saint Simeon had girls up there?"

"If he didn't it wasn't because there's a rulebook for sitters."

"Well, there's morals up here just like there are down there. There's right and wrong. There's good and bad."

"There certainly is. And Carmen says she had a good time."

"Of course *Carmen* says. She has to, to get her money from you. She's a pathological liar. She's got a license to lie. You been had, old timer."

"She says you had a good time too."

"You know what? You disgust me. This is all just so disgustingly beneath you, *champion.* Then you call 4RealNews so they can send the chopper and catch it on video."

"What the hell are you talking about?"

"You must've teamed up with Hoover's ex-boss from Kerridge's cult. God, to think once upon a time you were my *hero.*"

"No heroes up there."

"What do you call Saint Simeon?"

"Brother. No hero. Ancient brother."

"I don't call *you* brother. You spit in the eye of the most basic tenets of flagpole-sitting."

Blake fell into a prolonged coughing fit. Recovering, he said, "You big slow *toddler.* There ain't no basic tenets up there. You want tenets, you want rules, *make* 'em. That's *your* world, king! When I was up, I enjoyed visitations from a *fine* lady."

"You had *sex* with a *woman* up there?"

"I *made divine love* with the woman of my life."

"I don't believe you. What was her name?"

"What do you care what her name was? Her name was Rose. You getting down?"

"What do you care if I'm getting down? I make the rules, remember? I'll get down when I feel like it."

"I ought to tell you—I've seen your 'commercials.' And that morti-fying interview."

"Oh, you did, did you? Oh, *now* I see. *Now* I get it. Shipwreck Blake is *jealous!* Nobody interviewed *you* on TV! Nobody begged you to do commercials in a major media center on your rickety little pole in Bumfuck, North Nowhere. I got eight thousand dollars for that *Times* commercial. And this Blaze toothpaste deal? *Ten* thousand."

"You're getting down."

"Maybe, maybe not. I make the rules."

"You're getting down."

"Listen close, Blake. I wouldn't get down off this pole now if you sent up a mob of sluts from Babylon and a rafter of assassins from Madagascar."

"Joe, did you know that Ferdinand Magellan never made it around the world?"

"That record is as good as mine already. I may *never* get down."

"His ships made it, but he didn't. He died in the Philippines. Think about it."

"You'll *never* get me off this pole! *Ever.* Not with a neutron bomb! Fuck what Magellan did or didn't. You hear me?… Hello?"

When the "Your time has expired" recording came on, feeling profoundly watched, I carefully replaced the phone in its cradle, lay on my back on the platform and stared into the dilated eye of the old, cold, unblinking night.

59

JOE

The previous commercial makers had wanted to get right up there on
the platform with me to work their black magic, but I'd scorned their requests and banished them to the cherry-picker. With Blaze toothpaste, I
insisted they hop right on there with me.

"I thought that was against the rules," said Hoover.

"The sitter makes the rules."

"You clear it with the Guinness boys?"

"The Guinness boys can blow me."

"What about our record?"

"*Our* record?"

"You get disqualified, entire enterprise goes up in smoke."

"Enterprise? You mean money. I have a higher enterprise. Fuck
money."

"Says only he who has plenty."

It was a humid October afternoon in tight, precarious quarters. We
were on the twenty-third take. The sound and camera crew maneuvered
around me on the platform, with Hoover, the director, and the Blaze
rep (staving off vertigo) on a cherry picker alongside the platform.

I had allowed them up, let them lower my belongings to the ground,
combed my hair, shaved, sold my integrity and took their money. I
would continue to smile and say the words they put in my mouth, but I
would also let them know what I thought about them and my corrupted
self and the whole miserable soulless ritual of avarice and deception.

"For a smile that'll light your world, use Blaze!" I said. I squeezed the
tube, it farted a great blob onto my toothbrush, and I began to brush as
if I hated my own teeth.

"Cut!" said the director.

I spat into a paper cup. "Turpentine."

The Blaze rep to the director: "Time to cut our losses."

"Give us five," Hoover said.

"Last chance," said the rep.

Hoover jumped onto the platform from the cherry picker and steered me to a corner. "You're blowing it, chief. You get yourself a temperamental rep, your high-riding spokesman days are over."

"*Spokesman*," I scoffed. "I'm a flagpole-sitter."

"Lemme tell ya, man, I've covered the human condition for two decades and I see it every day—opportunity knocks, fella gets a little change in his pocket, little stardust in his eyes, maybe a little pussy flashed his way—boom—what comes quick, goes quicker. This is a supersonic ticket to the land of your dreams, or a long step out the baggage door at 50,000 feet. Your choice, mon frère."

I'm a happy Reaganite now, chewing my cud of cash & slapping myself on the back. Clover says we have 15 grand in the bank, the Patch is raking in the cash. And the loan is about paid off.

I liked to think I was a man of books, a spiritual man, a man above the common material run. But they drew a buck under my nose & I howled like the Whore of Babylon.

Wow, a blast of fresh bread aroma! Must be a bakery around here. How could I never have noticed it before. Reminds me of the Helms truck in West Covina. That smell turns the city into a village. And now as sudden as it came it's gone.

Shipwreck would have leapt at the chance to do commercials. I may be a whore, but I'm no pimp.

He was right about Magellan never making it around the world. I had Nate check out a book. Magellan died in the Philippines from a poisoned arrow shot by natives who didn't care to be Europeanized. Magellan did not sail around the world! He died failing, and the world remembers him centuries later for a world record he never even achieved!

Dig this diary entry of Magellan's: "124 days out. Scurvy throughout the ships. No food. Eating rats and wood." That's a snack Clover might whip up for her beatnik mob.

It's 1981, not 1521. Modern virtue is not Middle Ages virtue. Magellan ate rats & wood but if somebody'd plunked down a stack of Clover's pancakes in front of him, he would have gobbled those things like I gobble mine.

60

JOE

It was my thirty-sixth birthday. Clover threw a party for me in the shadow of the pole. She baked a cake with a little pole and platform. It was nice. Nate gave me a picture book on clouds. Jinx and Hoover were there, along with a pack of coffeehouse denizens, strangers. Clover led a round of "Happy Birthday." I sat in the trapdoor, looking down on the revelers like the man in the moon, hot with longing and cold with resentment.

I called Clover later to tell her thank you and I love you and I'm so sad and lonely, but she beat me to the punch with the stunning news of a sold painting and an upcoming show.

"Wow. That's wonderful, Clove. You sold it?"

"Five hundred dollars."

"Wow. Amazing. How did all this transpire?"

"Well, this man, Sam Knight, he runs a gallery on Melrose, he came in and said he liked my paintings. I thought, well, you know, men. Then he brought somebody over, and they bought one on the spot, and then he called me later and said he wanted me in a show. It won't be just me, it's two other painters, also, women painters."

"Well, damn, congratulations. Guy wanders in. Wow, what a break."

I'd slaved over *Holder & Biggen* for a decade, rewriting it ten times, casting it out to scores of agents and publishers to no avail, and here overnight, without even trying, by absolute blind luck, thanks to a total stranger, she sells a painting for five hundred dollars and snags a show.

"You're not upset?" she said.

"Upset? Why would I be upset? Upset how?"

"I'm being silly."

Did she mean was I jealous, was I suspicious of some total stranger who would give a show to an attractive woman whose work boasted one remarkable feature—people with no faces? Although weren't gallery owners pretty much gay by definition?

"You think I'd be jealous of this guy?"

"Jealous of *Sam*?"

"Oh, is he gay?"

"How would *I* know?"

"Well, come on."

"Boy, do I feel stupid. I guess I did mean jealous, but I meant jealous of *me*. For selling the painting and getting the show. When, you know, your novel and everything—"

"*What*? No, no, no, no, no. Clover, I couldn't be happier for you. Besides, I've got a project going that puts that moldy old novel to shame."

"Oh, that adventures in pole-sitting thing you're writing for Hoover?"

"How do you know about that?"

"He told me. He eats here now and then."

"I'm not writing it for *him*."

"By the way, Carmen called me last night."

My blood stopped in its tracks. "Who?"

"That little fellow graduate of yours who keeps popping up all over the place."

"Oh, *that* crackpot." I bowed my head as if before the executioner. "What'd *she* want?"

"She wanted to tell me she'd been up on there. On the pole."

"*What*?"

"And that she gave you a, ahem, blowjob."

My blood left my body like a red tablecloth yanked out from under everything left on the table. "She *what*? Well, you know she's a crazy fucking lying psycho bitch, you know that, right?"

"Uh, to put it mildly. But why would she say such a thing?"

"She needs a reason? She's a pathological liar. She's *evil*. So, what'd *you* say?"

"I told her to fry in hell." Clover laughed, heavenly music to my ears. "Did Kerridge cure *any* of you damn people?"

"Kerridge!" I said. "That's it! Of course! Kerridge put her up to this!"

"Why?"

"To get you going, to stir shit, to get me down. Save his reputation, his *enterprise*. Bald-faced psychos, both of 'em. Clove, when I get down, the craziness? It's all gone. Poof! And what remains, it'll be perfect."

"The perfect remains, yeah," she said. "Normal would be enough. Normal would be plenty. Regular average normal would be just right."

61

JOE

Something woke me. I yanked my mask off, pulled my earplugs out. I swore something had poked me. It was darker than usual. A bad smell hit me, a mix of sulfur and feet.

I was not alone. Something crouched in the dark behind the stump of pole. It had a big head, tufts of hair, flat nose, teeth glittering in the moonlight. "I'm dreaming," I whispered. "I'm having a nightmare." I watched the thing. It watched me. It was no nightmare.

My lightning thoughts: I'm dead the escaped gorilla from the zoo found me if I scream it'll snap my neck if I jump the fall kills me might only break a leg it'll chase me down tear me limb from limb rip my throat out can't scream toying with me could my heart burst?

It half-rose, bent forward, knuckles on redwood. It growled, tenderly, as if easing me into the pending horror. A fresh blast of that ghastly stink. "Our Father, who art in Heaven," I whispered. The trapdoor was shut. I leaned for the latch; the creature grunted. I inched a hand toward the phone; it grumbled, slammed one great paw against the platform.

I screamed, "Clover!" but it came out a parrot squawk.

The thing nodded, its lust to brutalize me palpable, patient, building. It growled; out of terror I growled back.

It tilted its head, put a finger to its mouth. What the fuck? Was it hungry? Had it climbed up for food? I grabbed half a stale bagel and offered it. It knocked it out of my hand, thumped its chest rat-a-tat, and stood to its full height, which, to be honest, wasn't that much taller than me. Perhaps it was a youngster, or a female. Maybe I had a chance after all.

It began investigating my possessions. It picked up my boombox, smelled it, shook it angrily, then flung it over the edge to the sidewalk with a crash. Certainly that would wake Clover, she'd look out, call the cops. But what could the cops do before it finished me?

I considered playing dead. It would grow bored and climb down. I fell over and lay still. The beast stood over me. My heart shrank to a dot.

The thing nudged my head with its big hairy stnking knuckle. It lowered its face to mine. I fought not to retch at its fetid odor, the breath of hell, rancid blood, death. I lay insensible with terror.

It left me, picked up the binoculars, listened to them, dropped them over the banister to shatter below. It began fiddling with Jinx's ficus.

Maniacally, I leapt up, reared back, decided that a punch to its monstrous head would only break my hand, and instead delivered a roundhouse right to its midsection, which folded around my fist with a macabre flabbiness.

"Oof!" it said, and crumpled to the platform. "Uhhhhrrr," it groaned, rolling around with its knees up. I moved in and pummeled its head, which gave around my fists. I attacked, squeezing and twisting to snap its neck, but its head popped right off in my hands!

I screamed and dropped it and jumped up, gawking at the face of none other than Shipwreck Blake, sweat-drenched, gasping, grabbing his belly.

"Get me out of this!" he cried. "Get me out! Get me out!"

Shipwreck Blake, World Champion Record-Holding Flagpole-Sitter, my erstwhile idol, lay sprawled on the mummybag in his purple boxers, gathering what remained of his wits, the headless ape duds draped over the pole stump. That black stone shone on its gold chain against his chest.

I paced the platform, grateful we hadn't gone over in the fracas. Now I was in charge. "And what is that hideous stench?"

"Limburger. All I could find. Smeared it on suit. Bad plan. Came in a dream: find ape suit, climb up, give flaming sword speech. Got lost in character, plus your punch. Can't catch my breath. Not man I used to be."

What depths of unhingement had the old champion descended to? Is this what flagpole-sitting did to you? "And that harlot you sent up!" I said. "She called my wife!"

"Oh no." He shook his head. "Not good."

"Not good? Ya think? You didn't direct her to do it?"

"Let me catch my breath."

"Never mind. I don't care. Man, if I had any doubt about your scruples or your sanity…"

Despite being at death's apparent door, Blake looked to be in pretty good shape overall for an old-timer: fit physique, if on the extra-slender side; a sort of Don Quixotieish oblong head; a jaw like a fist; broad Paul Robeson nose; and the teary, blinking eyes of an almost mercury color in that urban twilight up there, the eyes of a child who had just survived a near-calamity instigated by his own ignorant wrongdoing.

"You have the scruples of a billy goat." I meant to mock him but a tenderness in my voice betrayed me. My compassion proved premature.

He managed to prop himself up on one elbow. He shook his head as he surveyed the platform. "Good God," he said. "Telephone. TV. Computer? Refrigerator! Exercise bike. *Banister!* Simeon Stylites chained himself to his pillar. *Chained* himself, son. Have you no scrap of shame?"

"Asks a pimp in purple underpants. Okay, I see you've caught your breath. Now get up, grab your ape suit and your flaming sword, and get the hell off my flagpole."

"Whatever he's up to," he said, as if to himself, "it ain't flagpole-sitting." He tried to stand, then oozed back down. "Give me a minute."

"Is there *any* abomination you wouldn't stoop to to drive me off this pole? Would you shoot me to protect your record? We both could have tumbled off here and broken every damn bone in our bodies."

"I made a mistake."

"A *mistake?*"

"Could you signal my driver down there?" He pointed with the back of his head.

I spied the dark Lincoln up Western, gleaming in streetlight. "A chauffeured limo and you're lecturing me about a telephone? O, ye hypocrite."

Shipwreck bowed his head. "Yes," he whispered. "I've lost my compass. You're right."

"Are you playing another game?"

"The day is terrifying beyond contemplation. The future is bleak, mutant. So we long for the past. It's not greed for money that runs things. It's lust for the past, for innocence lost. We all want to go back."

"Not me."

"Nothing's meaner than a man hunting for his innocence."

"Is this your flaming sword speech? If so, I'm not feeling the heat."

He looked at me with the eyes of a watchdog. "Cynicism is the last refuge of the damned."

"What the fuck are you talking about? Look where I am! I'm no cynic. I'm a fucking dreamer! If there's a cynic up here, it's the one trying to kill the man with the dream. The same dream you once dreamed!"

"And I handed you that dream." He groaned as if to give up the ghost. "But it's a common act, after all. Right this moment eight other sitters are up right now around the world."

"Are you serious? How do you know that?"

"Don't worry, they're all pretenders. But who am I helping? *You.* Wonder why?""

"*Helping?*" He couldn't keep his addled philosophy straight for two thoughts in a row. I hated that I was starting to feel sorry for him. "You must be in some deep despair to pull this crackpot stunt. You know, despair is the only unforgivable sin against the Holy Ghost."

Shipwreck propped himself against the stub of the pole and pulled the ape suit around himself. "It's 'blasphemy,' not 'despair.' *Blasphemy* is the only unforgivable sin against the Holy Ghost."

"*What?* No, it's despair."

"Blasphemy."

"Where do you get *blasphemy?*"

"The Bible. It's all I read for 444 days up there. Plus the *Tao* and *Alice in Wonderland.* It's blasphemy. *Jesus* felt *despair,* for Christ sake. 'Father, why hast thou forsaken me'? How could *despair* be an unforgivable sin?"

"Damn it, that's exactly what I thought! I *told* Clover that. So, it's *blasphemy.* Well, well, well. What *is* blasphemy exactly?"

"Could you sit down?" he said. "You're making me nervous, pacing around there."

I hesitated, then sat in the rocking chair.

"Jesus drove the devil out of a fellow," he said. "Fellow couldn't hear, couldn't speak. Then he could. The Pharisees were jealous. They said Jesus healed the guy by the devil. Jesus said it was by the Holy Spirit, and to say it was the devil was blasphemy, the only unforgivable sin."

"That's blasphemy? Well, that's just as weird as *despair* being unforgivable. You mean to tell me that murder, war, torture, defiling babies, pushing some old woman in front of a train—that's all forgivable? But saying this guy was healed by the devil is unforgivable? Doesn't sound right. I think we might have a mistranslation on our hands."

"To cast out a devil is to heal," said Shipwreck. "To heal is to forgive. The devil doesn't love anything but hatred. So the devil can't forgive or accept forgiveness, because forgiveness kills the hatred. Every human being is a failure, morally, so without forgiveness, the whole spiritual universe collapses on itself in weeping and gnashing. Follow?"

"No. It doesn't answer my question and just brings up more." I couldn't tell if I was arguing with a genius or an idiot. "To heal is to forgive? Okay, okay, I can see that. And the devil can't accept forgiveness because it would end his hatred, and all he *is* is hatred, so to accept forgiveness, he'd disappear. Right? Which is interesting as hell, but I still don't get how to say the devil healed somebody is unforgiveable. I'm not saying the devil *could* heal somebody, but it's simply *stupid* to say it, not an unforgivable sin. It's preposterous."

"What's *not* preposterous? Life and death are preposterous. The *universe* is preposterous, so everything anybody does *in* the universe is preposterous. Why are you up here?"

"Why the hell are *you* up here?"

"To forgive you."

"*Forgive* me? *You*? For *what*?"

"For breaking my record."

"Hey, if I *do* break it—"

"*If*?"

"—*when* I break it—"

"Remember—Simeon sat for thirty *years*."

"So you say. I'll have the *modern* record."

"For a remarkably common act: sitting."

"It's a *calling*."

"Who's calling?"

"You know who."

"God? Why would God call us to do something as preposterous as sit on a flagpole?"

I leaned forward. "Hey, old man? Why don't you just one time in your fucking life say *exactly* what you fucking mean?"

He sat straighter, wrapped himself tighter in his ape suit, and recited: "That I might be more alone with thee, three years I lived upon a pillar, high six cubits, and three years on one of twelve; and twice three years I crouched on one that rose twenty by measure. O Jesus, if thou wilt not save my soul, who may be saved? Who is it may be saved?"

I rocked, nodding. "I ask you to say what you mean; you quote Tennyson again."

"Tennyson mocking Simeon."

"*Mocking*? No. *How*? He's *admiring* Simeon. He's *praising* him. He's holding him in total high regard for his commitment to the ascetic and the spiritual."

"He was laughing at Simeon, or weeping for him, because Simeon believed that sitting on a pillar for such and such years, at such and such a height, would save his soul, and that if *he* wasn't saved, then the riffraff below had no chance at all. What hubris, eh? Fortunately, Tennyson studied Simeon more, experienced more of his own humanity, gave up his cynical judgment, his heart opened like a big flower, and he saw not a deluded would-be saint in Simeon, but a remarkable *human being*. Every sitter is remarkable, Joe, and you are especially remarkable with the flaming sword of your abandoned wife and son hanging over your head."

"Oh, now *you're* gonna start on that? I didn't abandon anybody. They're right down there. We talk every day. They're fine. Nate's reading *Hawthorne*, for God's sakes. And it sure as hell hasn't hurt Clover—she's carved out quite a little enterprise for herself."

"You must be proud."

"I am." I was rocking like a madman in that rocking chair. "Damn proud."

"And her paintings in a show."

"Yeah." I stopped rocking. "How do you know about that?"

"What's her friend's name, Sam, is it?"

"Her *agent*."

"What's his last name again?"

"Knight. Why? How do you even know about him?"

"Wasn't a Knight involved in that art fraud a while back? No, I think that was *Dan* Knight, never mind."

"You're perverse," I said. "*You're* the fucking devil."

He stood on ambivalent legs, holding the ape suit closed with one hand and the balustrade with the other. "Borrow your phone?"

"What for?" I fetched it. "Too bad you didn't throw that over. You owe me a new boom box and binoculars, by the way."

He looked at the phone. "Does this work?" He put it to his ear and knocked it with his knuckles.

"It's not a bongo. Did you push the buttons? Push the buttons."

"I thought I did." He pushed them and waited, nodding at the view. "Picked a heck of a spot."

"It picked me."

Side by side at the banister, my deranged compadre and I drank in the night. He was a mad son-of-a-bitch, Shipwreck, a complete stranger in many ways, but a brother in flagpole-sitting nonetheless, the first I'd met, along with the spirit of Simeon who I could sense behind the sky, and it all felt like nothing I'd felt before. As preposterous, as insane as the situation might have been to anybody else, to me, and I was certain to Shipwreck as well—the two of us standing together in the Los Angeles night, sixty feet in the air—it felt like the most perfectly normal circumstance possible in this world. The lights of the city furnished our vista with comfort and warmth. I caught a whiff of that mystery bakery again. All this under stars, well, a handful of stars, and a snip of moon on the brim of the western sky.

"Saint Cloud," he said, "I had a forest, a billion stars."

"I had that in Utah. Didn't help."

"You went up the orange tree when your father died. I'm trying to see it. You were, what, fifteen?"

I didn't care anymore how he knew what he knew. "Just turned thirteen."

"Tough age. Simeon entered a monastery at thirteen."

I realized he was still holding the phone to his ear. "Is that thing ringing?"

He set it in the cradle on the banister and gazed at it. "I was ten. My father fell from a balcony. Six stories. Drunken fight. Both went over, other fellow landed on my father and lived."

"Jesus. You were ten? Nate's ten now."

"It changes everything. It changes the world."

"Yeah. After that there is no world. He took it with him."

Shipwreck nodded. "You're a tree ripped out of the earth."

"Roots in the air," I said. "Reaching blindly."

He put his hand to his side.

"You okay?"

He nodded. "How long you been up now, Joe?"

I looked at the blackboard. "Two hundred and eighty days."

"Well, from here out, you're on your own. I won't bother you again."

"I highly doubt that." He clutched his abdomen, moaned, and crumbled to the platform. "Come on," I said, "no more. Please."

He pulled his legs to his chest, rolled on his side, and spewed a torrent of black vomit across the platform.

"Jesus Christ! Is that *blood?*" It steamed like a dragon in the night air. I put a hand on his back. "Help," I whispered, like a sleeping man, then stood and shrieked "Help!" to the empty street, "Help!" to the distant limo, "Help!" to the darkened apartment. I thought: Sniper! "Are you *shot?*" I shook him.

"Ulcer," he rasped. "Call my car."

"I'm calling 911," and I did.

He vomited more and went limp. I touched his forehead: cold as a frog. I pulled the ape suit over him. 911 answered.

"I need an ambulance! My friend threw up blood! I'm on Western! Clover's Patch! Oh, Jesus, what's the address? Across the street from— Yes! I *am* the flagpole-sitter! That's where we are, up on the pole. Hurry, in the name of God!" I hung up. "Shipwreck, can you hear me? Ship-wreck!"

"Walter," he whispered.

"Walter? That's your name? Well, they're on their way, Walter."

I had one last paranoid flash: could this ulcer be a hoax? Fake bloody vomit? It would be beyond deranged, demonic. He could have fucked with the phone, so when I called 911, I got his people instead. He would convince me to help him down to the ambulance, clinging to me till I was on the ground with him, then he'd stand up and dance with satanic glee.

But the old sitter's entire body trembled and he looked in my eyes with unfakable suffering. I would do whatever he asked me to do. The siren cried in the distance. He grabbed my hand and stiffened as if electrocuted.

"Shipwreck! Walter! Don't die, man! They're coming! Hang on!"

The torque in his body ratcheted up. He squeezed as if to crush my hand, then, slowly, his grip eased.

"Good," I said, "that's good, it's passing, you're breathing. They'll give you what you need, everything'll settle down, everything's settling down."

He lay there, his eyes shut, his mouth open. I believe he wheezed, "Forgive me," but the ambulance drowned him out.

Once the ambulance guys sized up the situation, which would require the lowering of a man on a stretcher sixty feet straight down a rope ladder, they called for a firetruck, which made short order of the job. Scattered bystanders watched like zombies as Walter was lowered down the truck ladder which was perfectly equipped for such a task. I watched from the open trapdoor. He had not held onto me nor asked me to ac-company him. His chauffeur was in the middle of it, stricken, appearing far more friend than employee as they loaded Blake into the ambulance.

Nate stood in the café door in his pajamas. "What happened?"

"Man had a problem," I said. "He's all right. Go back to bed. Everything's okay."

Blake raised his head and he and Nate saw each other. Nate scratched his neck, closed the door, peeked out the window. How had the commotion happened to wake him but not Clover?

Walter gestured his driver closer, pointed at me, muttered something. The driver called up: "He's going to Cedars."

I gave them a thumbs-up. "Get that ulcer taken care of!"

The chauffeur looked puzzled. "He wants to know if you're coming with him."

Before I could respond Walter gave me the weakest of human smiles and managed to raise an open hand in farewell. I returned the loving gesture.

62

CLOVER

Sam had let me out in the alley so I could go in the back door. I was slipping the key in when out of nowhere a siren and red lights started up in front and tore off up Western. I ran down the driveway and as I reached the sidewalk and saw the ambulance speeding away, one of my heels caught and I went down like a sapling.

"*Clover?*" called Joe through the trapdoor. "What the hell?"

I grabbed my head. "Is it Nate! Is it Nate!"

"No," Joe said.

"Oh, thank you, God! Thank you!"

"It was just some guy. Are you all right?"

I got to my feet, using the corner of the building as a crutch. I removed my shoes and cursed the broken one.

"What are you *doing?*"

He meant what was I doing stumbling around in the middle of the night in heels and a long red coat he had never seen before.

"I went to that pre-thing," I mumbled, and suddenly Sam was standing there beside me! I assumed he'd driven away after dropping me off, but here he was picking up the broken heel, taking my arm, fussing, dusting my coat, asking how I was as I twitched and nudged all the signals in the world to get away from me.

"Joe, this my agent, Mr. Knight." I pointed at Sam and then up at Joe.

"Sam!" Sam called. "Hello!"

Joe gave a slow, knowing head-bob.

"That's my husband, Joe Magellan, flagpole..." I was going to say "flagpole-sitter," but it seemed absurd, so I stopped.

"Good to finally meet you!" said Sam. "Good show up there! Extraordinary! Well, good night!" Sam handed me the broken heel, bowed weirdly, and marched up the driveway.

"Lotsa excitement," I said.

"Are you drunk?" Joe said.

"*What?* No! *Drunk?* I tripped!" He had never seen me drunk, never seen me drink. I wasn't as drunk as I must have appeared, but I was drunk enough to fuck everything up, whether I cared or not. "I'm exhausted down here, going morning to night, doing everything. *Drunk?* That's rich!"

"Where were you?"

"I told you, this pre-get-together thing for the paintings."

"In the middle of the night?"

"You know what? I'm not gonna stand here and get the third degree! Especially from somebody in the air. Not for going to an art business meeting!" I wound up and hurled the broken heel into the street.

63

JOE

I locked the trapdoor to stop myself from climbing down. I paced. I chased dark thoughts that got darker the more I chased. I caught a whiff of Limburger, grabbed the ape suit, and as I hurled it over, a paper fell out of the head onto the platform. It was the Tennyson poem. I resumed pacing, twisting the poem.

There had to be fifty innocent explanations for Clover and Sam, but I couldn't think of one. Shipwreck's blood had soaked in, leaving a black fan-shaped stain in the moonlit redwood. "No cleanin' that," I said. I started to call her. "I'll be damned," I said. I unplugged the phone and slid into the bag like a bayonet in a scabbard. After hours of tossing rage and grinding fear, I drifted into a snowbank of sleep.

By morning light, Clover's betraying me with that braying Sam seemed completely impossible. But if the impossible proved true, I would go down and take care of business, because nothing else would matter.

Somebody had made off with the Limburgered ape suit. I inspected Shipwreck's hideous bloodstain in the daylight. It was still moist. It smelled like rust. I plugged the phone in and called the hospital. I said I was "Walter's son." A nurse informed me he was medicated but in "satisfactory" condition. I asked her to tell him I called.

Two seconds after I hung up, the phone rang. I unplugged it. Clover came out and hollered my name, banged on the pole, went back inside. I sat rocking and brooding. I grabbed my journal. The pencil blazed over the page:

She's fucking that cocksucker. It was written all over them red as sin from the devil's bowels. Only an idiot would doubt it. She's drinking! She was drunk! She's fucking that fucker & she's drinking. God help me!

Man, if I get down for this because of her… But what if nothing IS going on? If I was her that's EXACTLY how I would act. But if I was him that's not anywhere *near* how I would act. He could be one of these narcissists who don't even feel or care enough to show shame & guilt.

I saw it with my own eyes! But what EXACTLY did you see? It didn't LOOK good, but I should listen to her. It's *Clover*, man! She wouldn't do this! Call her!

Clover yelled from the apartment window. I ignored her. I thought about the thing with Carmen and grabbed my harmonica and blew blues in a frenzy till a reed popped.

What about Nate? He's no idiot. If they're that careless with me, how careful are they with him? He must have inklings. He's like a sponge, he soaks up everything. I need to talk to him.

IF YOU DID ANYTHING I WILL SEE TO IT THAT YOU REGRET IT LIKE FIRE TO YOUR LAST DAY YOUR FINAL BREATH ON EARTH!!!

I can hear their phony drunken conversations, him gushing about her paintings, staring into each other's bloodshot eyes, him kissing like some bloodless robot businessman. I must be in shock not to climb down & kick his pansy gallery ass & snatch Nate out of that cesspool of depravity!!

CLOVER O CLOVER, YOU TRAITOR, YOU HARLOT!!!

So, she turns out to be the same lying drunken manslaughtering slut she was when she went to prison, laying in wait for me at that poetry reading, with Camus' *Myth of Sisyphus* sticking out of her purse, her evil innards dormant like a satanic pupa for 12 years now. The way the woman was is the way the woman will be.

She *will* pay. That'll save my sanity up here—knowing I'll have my day. She let that WIMP put his stinking yuppie maggot-gnawed gallery-prancing COCK inside of her! Did he see her TATTOO of MY NAME?! He had to have! O JESUS HELP ME! Help me like you helped the BLIND and MUTE man!!

If she did *this* to me, what wouldn't she do? Would she spend all our money? That'd be *nothing* compared to this. I have NO IDEA what's going on down there. I could be on the moon. They could have a fucking coffeehouse CULT going! What do I really know about her? Are her parents really dead? That was very appealing, both orphans, only children, no families to deal with. How could we lose? But what do I really really know about her? NOTHING! Oh, Nate, what have I done! I *have* abandoned you! Oh, my son, my sweet darling pal! I'm making myself crazy writing this. But I'd be crazier if I stopped. It's the journal of a falling man & if I stop writing I'll hit.

Vengeance be so mine. I will wait. I will not get down. I will exercise the patience of Job. I will groan in righteousness until the day my wrath is worked on those two devils. I will not get down.

❧

The scissors of the sun idly cut a circle in the top of my skull. I crawled under the umbrella and breathed with my mouth open, a sick animal under a bush. It was almost December—how could it be this hot? It was like a pizza oven. I wondered if I would feel better if I vomited. My feet itched. They appeared puffy, swollen. My ears rang. Could something have bitten me? Had Shipwreck picked up beriberi from his travels and given it to me via his bloody vomit?

I plugged the phone in; immediately it rang. I let it scream ten times louder and louder before answering.

"Joe! Oh, honey, thank God you answered. Thank God! Joe? Nothing happened. I swear to you. *Nothing happened.*"

Oh, Jesus, that it were so! "What do you mean?"

"I know what you're thinking. And I don't blame you, the way it looked, but nothing happened. Period." Oh, God, convince me, even if it's a lie! "I went—with Sam, yes—to this little private pre-opening event where the artists meets some people."

"You never said a word about it."

"I was so nervous I couldn't even think about it, much less discuss it."

"It lasted till three a.m.?"

"When we left it was still going. Honey, could you come to the edge so we could see each other? I'm in the window." I came to the banister and sat on the edge with my legs hanging over. "Thank you," she said.

I could barely see her, peering through the louvers of the living room window. I wanted to bawl with gratitude that I'd been wrong as rotten dirty rain about her. I wanted to get every little kink straightened out. "Were you drinking?"

She groaned. "Yes. Please don't get mad."

"God*damn*, Clover."

"I wasn't drunk, I was dizzy. I had like barely half a glass of champagne."

"It sure didn't look like half a glass. Maybe it's been so long your tolerance is way down. But I can't believe you drank *anything.*"

"Imagine how *I* feel." She daubed her eyes. "I was so anxious, and everybody was drinking, I don't know, it was like a panic attack, and I remembered what you said about never panic, so I *had* to have something."

Another memory-twinge of Carmen and me popped up. "Was Sam

drunk?"

"He didn't drink at all. He was driving. I wasn't drinking to get *drunk*. It was like a professional necessity. But I understand if you make it more. I've been worried about the Patch too. It's going good, but trying to paint upstairs, and putting so much pressure on Solana—although she's glad to do it, and she *is* a fast learner—she ran readings and different things at UCLA for a couple years—she's in English *and* business—and taking care of Nate—"

"She's taking care of *Nate*?"

"*I'm* taking care of Nate. Not to mention taking care of you, knucklehead—which I love doing, however tired I might get. You know how insecure I am about my paintings, and here I am meeting a bunch of artsy-fartsy bigwigs. A sip of bubbly didn't seem like a mortal sin."

"What were you doing sneaking in the back way?"

"Did I look like I was *sneaking*, falling down all over the place?"

"You wouldn't have come up the driveway at all if you hadn't heard the siren from Shipwreck's ambulance."

"*Shipwreck*?"

Damn it, damn it! "We're not talking about that now."

But she knew a good thing: "Shipwreck *Blake* was in that ambulance? Oh, my God, what did you do to him?"

"Nothing." I glanced at the stain. "He was visiting and his ulcer started bleeding."

"You said it was some guy."

"The more you change the subject, the more my suspicions rev back up. He's all right. He's in a lot better shape than you were last night sneaking home drunk."

"I wasn't drunk and I wasn't sneaking! We park— Sam stopped to let me out back there because—"

"What was that? '*We park*'? What does that mean?"

"Will you stop picking apart every word I say?" She moved back a little from the window. "All I started to say was 'we parked' and I changed it to 'Sam parked' because he was driving."

"No, you changed it to 'Sam *stopped*,' a lot different than 'parked.' Parked means parked, stopped means stop and then go. And 'we park' means more than once."

"Oh, for Pete's sake. Well, he *whatevered* back there because that way he can go through the alley and be headed in the right direction instead of doing an illegal u-turn on Western." She moved back up to the window. "You have *nothing* in the whole world to worry about. Will you please believe me? Please?"

What was I doing? She did so much for me, for us, carrying such burdens down there. "Is it a good idea to leave Nate alone till three?"

"I left the number of the gallery with him. He's mature for his years. He's growing into a young man while you're up on that pole, mister."

"He's *ten* years old, Clover."

"Actually, he's eleven." She jammed her face right up against the louvers. "Joe, please see how stupid this is, you big dumbbell. I'm happily married to the love of my life."

"Is *he?*"

"Sam? Married? It's never come up. It's a business relationship. We don't discuss personal matters. He's a gentleman and a professional. With fine taste in art, if I do say so myself." I looked at her in the louvers. It was like talking to somebody in jail. "Honey, I'm sorry I had a drink. And got home late. And didn't tell you beforehand about the pre-opening. And left Nate by himself. Although you still haven't asked me how it went. 'How'd it go, Clover?' 'Very well, thank you.' Except for six or seven nervous breakdowns along the way."

"The muck-a-mucks liked your paintings?"

"They said they did."

As she described her experiences at the event, I considered the appeal of her faceless paintings—maybe they captured something of the Weltanschauung of the Reagan era. Which brought me back to Sam and those nagging little unresolved bedevilments. I was horrified to be thinking that she had planned to bring him inside, into our bed, with Nate and me right there.

"Clover, I'm sorry, but if the guy stops to drop you off—"

"I thought we were done with that."

"—he would have been long gone by the time you came running all the way down the driveway and tripped."

"He must have heard the siren before he drove off. How do I know? Call him and ask him yourself. If you want to know all these obscure details. Call him, make a big fool of yourself."

I was about to concede, to drop it, but that "big fool" challenge sounded like bluster. "What's his number?"

"You're being silly. You'll screw up my show. What would you say to him that could possibly make this better?"

"Maybe I don't care about making it better. Maybe I want to know the truth. Your not giving me his number is just making me more suspicious."

"Hold on." She gave me the number. "Any more questions, Sherlock?"

I looked at the number. Carmen crossed my mind again, like a peeping Tom going back and forth past the window of my conscience. If Clover *had* been with Sam, the Carmen thing might save my sanity, give me something to blast her back with. But if there *was* no Sam thing, then the Carmen thing would be sitting there by itself, and if Clover found out, I would roast alone on the spit. The weight of betrayals lowered my forehead to the platform.

Clover purred, "Honey, you're worrying yourself sick about this ridiculous stuff. Nothing could come between us, between you and me. Did you sleep at all last night?"

"Not much." More than sleep I wanted to hold her. The thought of sex repulsed me—ensnarled as it was with the greased pythons of guilt and jealousy. I wanted to lie down and take a warm dry innocent nap with her, like in the Garden of Eden before things went bad.

"Will you tell me about Shipwreck some time," she said, "when you feel better?"

"He swung by to say hello. Pay his propers. Just an old harmless guy, turns out."

"You're taking it mighty calm. What did you talk about?"

"We barely said hello, then he got sick. Oh, the boombox and binos fell over when I was scrambling around calling 911. Maybe we could get me replacements later?"

"Lemme write that down. Binos, boombox."

"Clover? Could you come up?"

"*What?* It's verboten."

"Nothing's verboten, it turns out."

"Since when?"

"As long as I don't get down, everything pretty much goes. Good God, those mobs were up here making commercials."

"I thought that was a special dispensation. A commercial's not the same thing as having your wife up there for sex."

"Who said anything about sex?"

"Well."

"Will you come up?"

"Honey, I've got a business to run."

"I thought Sangria pretty much runs things."

"Solana. She comes in later."

"Come up later, then."

"Well, you spring this on me after ten months. I feel deceived. Why'd we have phone sex if I could go up there? Why didn't you tell me this before?"

"I didn't know before. If you don't want to come up, say so."

"Wait a minute. Did *Shipwreck* tell you it was okay for me to go up?"

"Are you coming up or not?"

"Joe, he's sabotaging you. He's getting you to break the rules so your record won't count."

"Are you coming up? Yes or no. Fuck the rules. Fuck the record. No, you know what? Forget it!" I slammed the phone down.

She called me back. "Don't you want breakfast?" I realized I was famished. "How does buckwheat pancakes with warm boysenberry syrup sound? Fresh-squeezed orange juice, English muffin with real steaming butter?" I was a helpless fucking infant up there! "Lower the basket and I'll put your breakfast in. Don't punish yourself to get back at me for something I didn't do."

Waiting for breakfast, I dialed the number, to see if it was indeed Sam's. It was busy for a couple minutes, during which I suspected she was calling to warn him. When he finally answered, "Knight Gallery, Sam speaking," I hung up. Carmen sprang forth topless in my head, grinning. Which would be most appalling—that I alone had cheated, or only Clover, or both? It was a madman's dilemma, but my preference was to have me be the only cheat. Jealousy was far more excruciating than guilt. Jealousy was a gut-devouring badger compared to the indigestion of guilt. Guilt you could deny, but jealousy was an open gushing wound.

"Honey!" Clover called from below. "Pancakes!"

64

JOE

I called Cedars-Sinai and was informed that my "father" was sleeping and that I could try later. To divert myself, I dipped into "Saint Simeon Stylites," the Tennyson poem Blake had left behind in the ape head:

> Now am I feeble grown; my end draws nigh.
> I hope my end draws nigh; half deaf I am,
> So that I scarce hear the people hum
> About the column's base, and almost blind,
> And scarce can recognize the fields I know;
> And both my thighs are rotted with the dew;
> Yet cease I not to clamor and to cry,
> While my stiff spine can hold my weary head,
> Till all my limbs drop piecemeal from the stone,
> Have mercy, mercy! take away my sin!

I looked out over the city and saw nothing but myself and Carmen in our desperate act, beasts grunting in the middle of the air. That triggered an avalanche, my lifetime of sins, betrayals, deceptions, failings, double dealings. Did I believe, with Simeon, that living on a flagpole in absurd sacrifice could mysteriously right all my wrongs, could green the wasteland of my life?

I called Shipwreck again. Walter. The phone rang ten times, somebody picked it up, dropped it, knocked it all over the table, finally found the handle. "What."

"It's Joe."

"My son." He was doped to the gills.

"By the way, do you have any real living family?"

"Yes, I do. Real son. We lost track. Talked, oh, five years back? It's on me. Bad man, bad father. Selfish as death. Changed some, very little, way too late. *You* got a chance though. Man, I'm just flyin'."

"What do they give you for an ulcer?"

"Spackle and morphine."

Morphine for an ulcer? "Well, after last night, thank God it's only an ulcer."

"Only? I'm eighty-nine years old, Junior."

"Eighty-nine! So, you were...*seventy-five* when you set the record? Jesus Christ. Hey, I hope you didn't want that ape suit back. It fell over the edge in the commotion." He groaned. "I saved the Tennyson poem. I assure you, there's no way he's mocking Simeon in there."

"Look at the damn footnote. First page."

I found it and read aloud: "'Simeon, Stylites of Syria, outdid all his contemporaries in the extremes to which he aspired to mortify the flesh. The poem expresses satirically the poet's distrust of asceticism, with possibly a gibe at his aunt Mary's brand of Calvinism. This is one of the poems Tennyson would read with grotesque grimness, especially such passages as "coughs, aches, stitches," etc., laughing aloud at times.'"

"See?" said Walter.

"Maybe he was laughing nervously. Maybe he was sympathetic to Simeon but feared showing his sympathy for such an extreme character."

"Is this how you teach literature? Make it up as you go? He *mocked* Simeon. Tennyson was an asshole. He may have come around later, but too little too late."

"If you hate the poem, why do you tote it around like a talisman?"

"The bastard at least *wrote* about Simeon, even though he understood nothing." Shipwreck coughed, choked, and took a minute to recover. "Your resistance to the truth is wearing me out."

"They say how long you're gonna be in there?"

"A while, my friend."

I was warmed by the appellation in the midst of his hectoring. "Call you later?"

"Please do. Your simple mind is sweeter than morphine. Adios."

PART V

Grasp the good fortune
that the ground on which you stand
cannot be any bigger
than the two feet planted on it.

—Kafka

65

CLOVER

Sam and I sat in Xampura's, a posh bar overlooking Santa Monica Bay. The place was dark and quiet and we had our backs to the sun and the sea. He watched me stir my Bloody Mary with my finger.

"What's wrong now, Clover?"

"What's wrong *now*? For God's sake, Sam. Are you deaf?"

"You said you don't think he knows."

"I said he's *acting* like he *might* believe *half* of my load of damn *lies*. He's not blind. He's not a moron. We're stumbling around falling down drunk in the middle of the night."

"I don't believe *I* was stumbling around."

"Well, congratulations, Mr. Innocent. Mr. Sober." I sipped my drink and tapped the ash off my cigarette.

"I wish you weren't smoking."

"I wish I wasn't, either. How about drinking? Do you wish I wasn't drinking? Do you wish you hadn't eaten me? Since we're going through the seven sins."

"I wish you wouldn't talk like that."

"Oh, Jesus."

"It was a beautiful act, which I for one don't regret."

"Okay."

"What do you want to do?"

"What do *you* want to do?"

"Well, to be candid—and I dislike hearing myself say this—but considering the circumstances of the situation, and your attitude toward me at the moment, we might, for the time being, perhaps think about backing off a bit, personally."

"I knew it. Boy, it doesn't take much heat to drive you squealing from the kitchen."

"Unfair and false. I have no problem with the heat. But I'm thinking of what's best for you. You're the one who's upset."

"You're not?"

"I'm upset that you're upset. Although I don't understand why. Joe does not know. How could he continue to fiddle up there if he believed Rome was burning below? It sounds to me that you convinced him everything is innocent between you and I."

I watched him through my cigarette smoke, deciding I didn't care enough to correct his pretentious grammar. "But it's *not* innocent, is it?"

"That depends on how one happens to look at it."

"What planet does *one* happen to live on? Cheating on your husband is innocent in your stoical philosophy?"

"I'm hardly a stoic. I'm quite passionate, in fact, as you should have gathered by now. What you're not taking into account, in *your* momentarily *hysterical* philosophy, if I may, is that my *love* for you, in and of itself, is innocent. You may now ridicule my love for you, if you wish. No? In any case, what we were *discussing* is whether Joe knows or not, which I hold that he does not. In some circles what we did is not even considered sex, although I suppose you wouldn't abide such an open-hearted assessment at the moment. In any case, Joe is not my concern. You are my concern. If it didn't threaten your state of mind, I wouldn't care in the least what Joe knew or not."

"Could you do me a favor? Could you stop saying his name every two seconds?"

He breathed through his nose. "All I'm trying to do, Clover, is ease your anxiety."

"It's not anxiety, its fucking guilt."

"Why must you do everything you can to antagonize me when all I want to do is help you?"

"I don't know, I must be a bitch. Is that what you're trying to say?"

"All right. You're wholly intent on being malicious and implacable."

I was. I wanted him to fire back so I could unload and be done with him. Then maybe Joe would never find out, over time it would go dull in my conscience, he would get his record and come down and teach, and I would produce my little paintings and never complain about anything again. I downed my drink and signaled to the waitress for another.

"That won't help," said Sam.

"What will?" I rubbed my face with both hands. "Oh, Jesus, how'd I get myself into this? Everything was perfect, and I fucked it up."

"Oh, stop it. You're making art again. You have me. Your Patch is a wonderful, enjoyable center of creativity and—"

"I hate that fucking Patch. I'd burn it to the ground if I could."

"I refuse to believe you're serious. Darling, that's where we met."

I watched him. To call me "darling" at this point— How could a man so cultured be such a bonehead? I hadn't planned to bring it up, but now I wanted to rub it in: "Joe asked me to go up there."

"Where?"

I laughed. "Where do you think?"

"On the *flagpole*? What for?"

"What do you think for?"

"Well, that's, that's, that's against the rules."

I realized that telling Sam was a new betrayal of Joe. "I don't want to talk about it."

I grabbed my drink from the waitress and took a gulp. "I gotta get away from that goddamn *Patch* before I do some real damage."

"Wherefrom did this sudden antipathy for the coffeehouse arise?"

"Wherefrom *you*. Going crazy over my paintings, selling one, putting me in a show, giving me big ideas."

"Well, I assure you I have no regrets about that."

"That place has served its purpose. I'm sick of it. Thank God for Solana. What would I do without her? To go-getters." I raised my glass and took a drink.

"If that's the way you feel, have you considered selling the place? I could look into it for you."

Sell the place! He could do it. Could he do it right away? I would have to wait until Joe got the record and came down. Although it could tie me tighter to this man, this anchor. "Everything's closing in. Closing in and coming apart at the same time."

"Clover, can you imagine how such talk makes me feel?"

"No, because I'm imagining how *I* feel."

"Are you going up there?"

"I told him it was kind of sudden."

"'Sudden'? He's your husband."

"You *want* me to go up there?"

"To ask me that borders on the malevolent. I know you're upset, Clover, and I do love you, but I'm reaching my limit on the amount of verbal abuse I'm going to tolerate."

"Good." It wasn't this poor bastard's fault, I thought. If I'd used the brains God gave me, I would have stopped it before it started. I could have kept it professional, artistic. It was all on me. I loathed him and I loathed myself for loathing him. I blew smoke at the ceiling. "You're right. I'm sorry."

"Thank you. And I understand."

He smiled and I smiled wanly back, thinking, How can I get rid of him and still have my show? How could I have looked in this handsome, insipid face, let him lose himself down there, let him say he loved me. Joe will never forgive me. And Nate, Nate. All for a little unmitigated appreciation from a new man, a stranger. And art.

"Clover, you're not angry with me. You're angry at Joe."

My lover was a rational, earnest businessman in a 500 dollar suit, no scintillating individual, as I had prettily imagined, not even a flag-pole-sitter. Were we exchanging the show for the sex? Had the bill been paid, or was more due? Was he doing it with the other women in the show? No, he was in love with me, it was all over his face, oozing like mule sweat. I wanted to vomit my bloody brains all over that tasteful white tablecloth.

Sam took my hand in both of his, his smooth, well-meaning, mani-cured alien paws. I pulled free, stood up, downed the rest of my drink. "I have to go."

"You're not going to do anything."

"What, kill myself? I wish."

"Could I have a kiss?"

"Am I going to kill myself, and can you have a kiss. That's a man for you."

"Are you going up there?"

"Don't ask me that."

"You have to tell me."

"I have to go."

66

NATE

I watched Mr. Rogel walking back in forth in front of the class. I saw his mouth moving. I thought how after the ambulance I got a drink of water and heard something and looked out and saw Mom and that Sam in Sam's car in the alley.

I didn't tell anybody. I hated her. I couldn't tell Dad because he would get down. They would get divorced. I couldn't tell anybody because my mom was a whore now and everybody would find out.

I couldn't stop thinking over and over about her and that Sam. I kept watching them. I don't know how I could keep holding on to that glass of water. I didn't really know what they were doing but I knew what it was. Then she got out and I went up to my room. I layed down and got dizzy seeing it over in over.

I could run away. I could never tell nobody and pretend I didn't see it. I could grow up and hate them more and more until I didn't care. Hate her for doing it and hate him for going up there and letting her do it. I could grow up and get strong and rich and not need nobody and nobody could tell me what to do. Then I would tell them what I saw and they could beg me to accept their apology and they'd never do it again. I would look at them and not say nothing. Just watch them like they wasn't even there.

"Nate?" It was Mr. Rogel.

"Huh?" I said. The class laughed.

"You're not listen-ing, Na-than-iel," Mr. Rogel sang. "Shall I repeat the question?"

"Okay," I said.

"What was the name," sang Mr. Rogel, walking down the aisle closer and closer, "of the gentleman, who is credited, as the first explorer, to sail around the world? I think that's one question, you particularly, might find, on the tip of your tongue."

Mr. Rogel was standing over me now. My face muscles were full of Mexican jumping beans. "If you mean who I think you mean," I said, "he didn't sail all around the world." My voice was funny, like it was coming from the future. "He died in the Philippines. His ships went on ahead to Spain. But he didn't go because he was buried in the Philippines. He died by poison darts by a tribe that didn't want to take his crud about things."

One kid squeaked a giggle.

"Did I ask that?" Mr. Rogel said, not sang. "Did I ask any of that?"

"You mean like pretend he *did* sail all around the world?"

"I asked for the man's name. And I deliberately added 'credited with.' Do you think you know more about the history of the world than I do? It's not important whether he or anybody else sailed around the world. What's important is that you listen, carefully, to each question I ask, and then you answer that question. Which you did not. Do you agree?"

I nodded a little like a bob-doll but I didn't look at him.

"I didn't hear you."

I looked right at him. "Yes." It came out like a cat hiss.

Mr. Rogel walked away up the aisle. "Now, who would like to help our little revisionist historian with the question?"

I thought I was going to whisper it but it came out not quite whispery as I thought. "Pompous dickhead."

Somebody gasped. Nobody laughed.

67

JOE

I perused the clouds book Nate had given me for my birthday. It was packed with gobsmacking photographs of every cloud found on earth, many snapped by the astronauts from the space shuttle. I glanced up from the book to the genuine articles gliding above, from towering cumulonimbus dominating the mountains to the north, to icy cirrus streaks straight above. Against a wall as blue as fresh paint, the afternoon voila'd glorious concoctions, a cloud extravaganza.

The phone rang. It was Shipwreck. He sounded sharp as a tuning fork. I couldn't have been happier to hear from the old fellow. I don't know if I wish I would have known that it would be our last conversation or not. After an encouraging update on the ulcer, we two flagpole-sitters shot the leisurely breeze concerning matters large and small.

I was led to inquire how he came by the name Shipwreck. "I was a headstrong little bastard. Didn't get what I wanted, I'd lie on the floor, play dead. Daddy'd say, 'Walter got hisself shipwrecked again.' My brothers picked it up."

I lay on the sleeping bag and adjusted the umbrella to block the sun. The cirrus hung around the canvas like shark ribs. "Did it work?"

"Never. My brothers stuck their toes in my ribs. Daddy'd say, 'He's done for. Who wants his clothes? Call up science, say we got a warm one.' Course, the name clicked when I heard about Kelly."

Some kind of drifting clouds passed like fields of snow from a moving train. "Kelly who?"

"Shipwreck Kelly. You don't know Shipwreck Kelly."

"Should I?"

"Have I put it all on the wrong horse, Joe? A man ignorant of the entire history and tradition. Shipwreck Kelly brought flagpole-sitting into the twentieth century. Never heard of Simeon, never heard of Kelly."

"Maybe I'm a savant. I heard of *you*. So, what'd Kelly do? Sat for *forty* years, I suppose?"

"Forty-nine *days*. But he actually *sat* the entire time on a platform the size of a telephone directory."

"For forty-nine days? Impossible."

"It was. Till he did it."

"How'd he sleep? Where'd he shit and piss?"

"You're as bad as the landlubbers. 'Where'd he shit and piss?' This is a lark for you. A hobby. I ever tell you I put that pole up in Saint Cloud with my bare hands?"

"Did Simeon put his up? Some million-pound stone pillar? Who cares who put it up? Your flagpole looked like drunken monkeys put it up."

"It was hit by lightning. Knocked me out. My flipflops saved me."

I saw a spider in a web in the girding of the umbrella. "The paper didn't say anything about lightning." I wondered how the hell a spider would even get up there.

He snorted. "Paper implied I was a bum."

"You weren't? You looked like a bum in the picture."

"I'd been up 444 days. Seen yourself lately? At least I knew why I was up."

"I know why I'm up."

"It wasn't for no record. They asked me about it. I didn't know there *was* a record. I didn't give a shit."

"Wait a minute. That was your first time up?"

"Had no reason before."

"You go up after?"

"Do it right the first time, you're done."

"You went up one lousy time and dare to lord it over me?"

"I wanted to know more. I climbed down, taught myself the roots of it, the antiquity. Came to honor the chain of sitters through the ages, and my small place in it. But the *record*? Didn't care about that moron's bauble then, care less now."

He'd fired all his guns, I was still up, and the record was slipping through his gnarled fingers. All he could do was pretend not to care. "Why else would you go up?"

"To atone, son. I'd tell you what for, but you'd stick it in that smart-aleck book of yours." At that, he fell into another coughing fit. It went on, wound down to a whinny, started back up.

"Would you please call a damn nurse?"

He set the phone down, then came back on. "I worked for a man," he said. "He slept with my wife. I found out about it. She went with him. I stole his business. It ruined him. He killed himself. In front of my wife."

"Good God. How do you know that's why he killed himself?"

"I know I'm rich. I know how I got that way. I know he's dead. I know how he got that way."

"What was the business?"

"What difference does that make? Construction. I sold it later. I wanted to hurt him bad. I wanted to— Oh, dear, look at this, my machines're goin' loco."

"Call a nurse. Ring the bell, man."

"Change the subject."

"What happened to your wife?"

"You know what 'change the subject' means, Magellan? Tell me about *your* daddy. He left you."

"He didn't *leave* me. He *died*. Your father left you?"

"He fell. I told you. It's in one ear and out the other with you. Like a bird flying through an empty barn. What were his last words to you?"

I shook my head. "I remember a little smile. I think he knew. My mother was taking him to the hospital. I thought he was getting a checkup. I didn't know about his heart. Nobody talked about anything. He went in on Thursday. Friday, I heard her crying. Saturday, it was one of those days with the sky and the wind and the clouds. Like today. She came home from visiting him. I was in the back, way up in our big maple tree. She called me. I climbed down. 'Daddy's gone.' Boom."

"Thank you." He was working for his breath. "Please forgive me for sending Carmen up there."

"Why did you *do* that?"

"Forgive me? And for the blind Frenchman?"

"You said that wasn't you."

"And the gorilla business?"

"I'm glad *you* survived that one."

"Forgive me for what I did to Bill?"

"Bill?"

"My boss. The one who stole my wife."

"Why should *I* forgive you for that? Get him to forgive you."

"Him who killed himself?"

"Oh yeah."

"How do you teach without a memory? Do you remember what happened to Ahab's leg? Is it on the poop deck? Is it in the crow's-nest? Where is it, Professor Magellan?" The course of our conversation was as mysterious as the whale's through the sea.

"You know," I said, "if you were on the pole to atone, how could you let a *woman* up?"

"I didn't let her. I have no idea how she got up there. It's love. There's no contradiction. People are obsessed with contradiction. Ever notice that? Rose was an angel. I knew her name, nothing more."

"She was the 'woman of your life' and all you knew was her name?"

"Joe, please—say, 'I forgive you, Walter, for all you've done to me, but especially for what you did to old Bill.'"

It was absurd, but he sounded shaky and it seemed important to him. "I forgive you, Walter. For what you did to me and old Bill."

"Thank you. You don't mean it now but you will. You were the only one who could forgive me. Because you're the only one I ever told."

"Well—*if* that's true—thank you for trusting me."

"I hope you have the human decency to keep it out of your book. Nobody respects the mystery anymore. No detective will ever solve it. Nobody's simple enough, quiet or still enough to live in the unknowable. Everybody's so smart. So cool and clever. If you could see how beautiful you are up there, the way you rassle and contend with yourself, with petty nothings, with God. My dear spiritual bumpkin."

"Bumpkin!"

"I want you to have my record, Joe. Will you take my record and make it yours?"

"You were just disdaining the hell out of that record."

"Promise me you'll get my record."

I tried to remember—had I decided to stay up or get down? "*Promise* you?"

"What are you gonna do, argue with every single goddamn thing right up to your last second on earth?"

I wouldn't have to keep any promise—it was *my* quest, and my *rules*—but it might soothe his ulcer. "Yeah, all right, I promise."

"Don't let us down. You took an oath from your soul to Simeon's soul to my soul. Do not get down."

"Well, if nuclear war breaks out I'll get down."

"Why? You remind me of the fellow who saw people as walking trees."

"What fellow was that?"

"We have so far to go. It's impossible. But we're going. We're moving. Okay, I'm tired. The stars are coming out."

"What? It's the middle of the afternoon."

"It's been nice chatting with you."

"Okay. Yeah. Well, it's amazing how thing's have worked out, isn't it, old pal?"

"So long, Joe."

"Can I call you later?"

"You can try."

68

CLOVER

I plopped on the couch by the phone. The Patch was jumping downstairs in Solana's able hands. Somebody played a loitering sax that noodled up to me with handclaps and laughter and wafts of linguini. I had a drink and imagined the earth opening and swallowing the whole building. That coffeehouse was gobbling my heart like a warthog.

I was an artist, not an entrepreneur. If I didn't start painting soon, I'd wake up one day hating my life and everything in it. I was trying, but nothing was happening, nothing I didn't immediately despise and destroy.

I wanted to paint and drink. Drinking got me going with the painting. Then I drank more and lost track. I tried painting faces, but they looked like masks, frightened, angry, frightening.

And space. Space was shrinking. I gauged the little living room as if it were an object in my hand. Most of the furniture was Charley's leftovers. It was dingy, no room to spread out, more like an attic than a home. I could buy new things, I could paint, but I didn't. I'd poured all I had into the coffeehouse.

And when would I put Sam out of his misery? Nobody would leave me alone. Sam, Joe, Nate—one after the other. Men clambered at my skirt like sharks.

What I really wanted was to withdraw everything from the bank, rent a car and split. Not tell anybody. Let them take care of themselves for once in their narcissistic mewling infantile bloodsucking lives. I took a drink, grabbed the phone, dialed.

"Hello!" Joe said, peppy as a cheerleader.

"It's me." My voice cracked, but it went right past his big snow globe head.

"Honey! You won't believe this—Shipwreck and I are buddies! Walter his real name is. Incredible! We're talking about all kinds of amazing things. Shipwreck and me, pals! Can you believe it?"

"Hunh. Wow." Couldn't he hear the woe, the floor buckling under my voice? I took a drink. I loved ice, but he'd have heard the tinkling. That he would have heard.

"Come up tonight. It'd top off a wonderful day."

"Nate got in trouble at school."

"Oh no. Not the flagpole again."

"He called his teacher something. Like, oh, pompous dickhead."

"*What?* How could he *possibly*— You-you-you *told* him what I did!"

"It was supposed to be a warning against drugs."

"Oh, brilliant, Clover!"

"Look, the kid's angry. It's coming out one way or another."

"Angry?" Joe said. "About what?" I snorted. "Okay, what happened?"

"Mr. Rogel, the teacher—who *is* a pompous dickhead, by the way— asks Nate a question. Nate thinks Rogel's making fun of him. Nate says what he says. In front of the class. He says he was only telling the truth, 'like Dad did.'"

"Goddamn it, Clover. Put that kid on there."

"He's coming home on the bus. I was supposed to get him, but the car wouldn't start."

"Is there *anything* that's not falling apart down there? What's wrong with the car?"

"Gee, I don't know. Let me put on my overalls and I'll find out." The car was a lie. In my state I couldn't go to that school and face those dead-soul bureaucrats. I took a drink, mourning for ice. It struck me how small and fragile the glass looked, and how gigantic my hands felt.

"If I pulled that as a *kid*," Joe was saying, "my father would've been down there so fast my head would spin."

"Yeah, if only we could find Nate's father to straighten that kid out."

"I'll call the school."

"Thank you." I felt cold, a nice, natural cold, as if I had found the temperature I was born for. I felt like a glacier with tourists on a cruise ship gasping as one whole side of me cracked off in slow motion and collapsed into the sea. "I don't think I can handle anything more right now."

"I thought what's-her-name was running things down there."

"It's *Solana! Solana!* You deliberately forget her name. Like any name-less drone could run this place. It's sexist. It's racist."

"I'll call the principal. What's his name again?"

"Powell."

"Powell. And I'll talk to Nate. Everything'll be all right."

I stared unseeing across the shrinking room. "Her mind's like a shiny new trap."

"What?"

"Solana. She can hold a million details up there, all in a line. Some big thing she does in an hour, it'd take me all day. Sometimes I wonder if she's a witch."

"Okay. Well, I'm gonna call Powell and take care of this thing."

"Thank you."

We waited.

"Are you coming up tonight?"

Sam and Joe appeared in my head together, stunned to see each other.

"Come on, honey, it'll do both of us so much good. We need it. We need a little loving. I know I do. Don't you?"

Oh, God, I thought, what have I done! "Please don't pressure me. I have pressure coming from everywhere. I'm like a rat in a trap. I'll see how I feel later. Just please don't pressure me. I'll let you know."

69

JOE

Baby, you couldn't get up here now with a battering ram. I'll never be one of these wimps who whine for it. I'd sooner give Carmen a call. I'll chop my foot off first.

"Mr. Magellan! Mr. Joseph Magellan!"

I looked over. Below stood a tall, fit, crewcut man in a dark suit and sunglasses. Government was written all over him. "Who wants him?" I said.

The man laughed and took off his sunglassses. "Picture me in a nurse's uniform!"

"*Jinx*? Damn, man! I thought you were FBI!"

"Been to the bank. Performance art." Jinx stepped back and read the blackboard. "Two ninety-three!" I shrugged. "Mr. Nonchalant!" he called.

I had a brainstorm. "You want to come up?" I hollered a lot louder than I had to.

"It's against the rules."

"Sitter makes the rules. Come on up!"

Jinx slid the sunglasses in his pocket and spit on his hands. I dropped the ladder and the safety harness, and he made his not surprisingly deft way up the ladder and through the trapdoor. He stood on the platform, holding onto the pole stub. Turning carefully, he took in the panorama. "Oh, Lord," he said, crouching as sensations took over. "Is this *moving*?"

"Nothing's moving. It's solid. Breathe. It'll pass."

Jinx whispered, "It's high. The world is big."

Watching him drink it in like a child, especially in those FBI duds, I perceived anew the singularity of my realm. Pride warmed my heart. I *was* representing Shipwreck, Simeon, Kelly, all those who sat before. In a sense though, I had transcended them. They had their penance and atonement, their exalted motives, but I knew the best part—the clear, simple, original happiness of it. The joy of just sitting up there, high atop the big world, in but not of it.

Jinx stood, still holding on. I helped him to the chaise under the umbrella and fetched some water. "Let your eyes just drift over the surface of things."

"It's like there's nothing under us. It's like, what's holding us up?"

A change of subject was called for. "You're sure spiffed out. What were you doing at the bank, if I may ask."

"No, you may not. Kidding. Getting a loan. I'm buying another theater. In Torrance."

"Wow. Expanding, eh? You get it?"

He nodded. "And you helped."

"Who, me?"

"You inspire me. I can't believe you *live* up here."

"I guess they don't know you as Jinx at the bank."

He smiled shyly. "Ron."

"Ron!" We laughed. "Hey, you remember Shipwreck Blake?"

"That old fancy Dan son-of-a-gun who tricked you down?"

I described my encounters and entanglements with the aged sitter—minus the Carmen incident. By the end, I found my voice catching on my fondness for the old man.

Jinx was damp-eyed himself. "What a trickster. He's certainly put you through the wringer. I doubt I would have taken it as well as you. He means a lot to you. Wow. We're both doing well now. Clover, too. The Patch is the talk of the town."

"I suspected. She doesn't tell me much."

"Are you getting along better? Or am I butting in again?"

I wanted to talk about it, and Jinx was the one to talk about it with, but he was chums with Clover, and you could not trust a woman (even if she was a man) with sensitive information about another woman. That fear was the reason for the lie of omission about Carmen. And now came one of commission: "We straightened it out."

From his knowing squint, he knew I had lied, and for the rest of the visit, pleasant as it was, our conversation suffered from the exclusion of the one subject I needed to talk about most.

Jinx climbed down and visited Clover. Not thirty seconds after he bounded back across Western, Clover called me to announce, "I'm coming up tonight," and hung up.

Nate came marching home as if going to war. He glanced up at me and down again, knowing what was coming.

"Nate!"

The boy stopped fifty feet from the pole. "What!"

"It's time for a little talk!"

"Go ahead!"

"You want me to yell what I've got to say?"

"Go ahead!"

"Don't tempt me, pal!"

"Go ahead!"

The exchange had already drawn eyes and ears along the boulevard.

"Come up here and we'll talk!"

That stopped him. "I don't want to go up there! You can't make me!"

"Go inside! I'll call you!"

Nate put his head down and strode into the coffeehouse, and I, trembling, dialed. Clover answered. "Did you hear how that little brat was talking to his father in front of the world?"

"I heard his father yelling at the top of his lungs."

"How are you raising that kid down there!"

"Oh, are you asking for it."

"Oh, boy," I said, "that'll straighten him out."

"*What?* I'm talking to *you! Joe! You're* asking for it!"

"Could you put that kid on there?"

"Not if you're gonna yell at him."

"Will you please put him on the goddamn phone? If you want me to take care of this, then let me take care of it."

"Promise me you won't yell at him."

"I won't yell at him!" My voice cracked and set me off on a coughing attack.

"Dad?" Nate was near tears.

I wheezed, "I'm so mad I'm choking to death."

"I'm sorry, Dad! I'm sorry I talked to you like that and I'm sorry I said that to Mr. Rogel. It just came out! I'll never do it again. I'm sorry, Dad!"

My rage took wing. "It's okay. I'll talk to Powell. We'll get through it."

"I'm not in trouble?"

"Oh, you're in trouble, all right. Tell me what happened. Why'd you call your teacher that?"

"Why'd you call *your* teacher that?"

"You're sorry and two seconds later you're playing games again?"

"Should I of *lied?*"

"There's a difference between lying and blurting out whatever's on your freaking mind."

"So, it's all right to *think* it?"

"It'd be best not to even think things like that, but that's a little unrealistic. If you find yourself thinking it, say to yourself, Don't say it!"

"Okay. I'm sorry, Dad."

"You didn't say it to me. You'll have to apologize to your teacher, and the class."

"The class!"

"You *said* it in front of the class. Why'd you say it?"

"Mr. Rogel asked me who sailed around the world, and how I should be the best one to know. He was making fun of our name. I said he *didn't* sail all around the world. And then he says he didn't ask that and do I think I'm smarter than him about history. He says sit there and answer the question. And he called me a visiting historian that needs help. So then before I knew it I called him that."

If this were even a half-way accurate account, Nate had hit the nail on the head. "You can't call your teacher names, pal. Period. Even if he deserves it. It ain't gonna work. You're gonna bring crap down on your head you don't need. You gotta pick your battles."

"Okay. I'll apologize to everybody."

"It won't kill ya."

"I can do it. I'll just do it."

"You'll be a bigger man than I was. Apologizing would have been better than getting thrown out of class and drafted." I let that soak in. "Since we're here, is anything else going on that could use us talking about?"

"Like what?"

"Well, sometimes when people do something they wouldn't normally do, I mean something that's not too cool, it's because they're upset about something else, something *extra* going on that might not have anything to do with the thing that they did. You know?"

"No. Not that I could think of."

"If there *was* something extra, would there be a reason why you wouldn't tell me?"

"Like what reason?"

"Why would you ask what reason if there wasn't anything to not tell me?"

"I don't know."

"If you think of anything, will you call me? We'll talk about it. As far as the apology goes, stand there and be brave. Keep it short and sweet and mean it as much as you can without being corny. In a day or two you won't even remember it."

"I wonder if," Nate said, "if maybe there's something extra going on in *everybody's* life, and that's why they do something not cool that they wouldn't normally of did."

"You picturing anybody in particular?"

"No. Who? No. Well, thanks for talking, Dad. I gotta go. Bye."

70

JOE

"Joe!" Mr. Powell said. "Glad you called."

"Yeah. So, Mr. Powell, uh—"

"Andy."

"Andy. I'm calling about, uh—"

"I know, I know," Powell said. "Can I be honest with you? Man to man? Iconoclast to iconoclast? Rogel *is* a pompous dickhead. I couldn't have said it better myself."

The first time Powell let Nate off the hook—with the flagpole business—it was a surprise, a relief, a delight. But there was something demented about this. Would I descend from the pole to discover that I was the only sane person left on earth?

"I'm beginning to suspect you might be right, Andy, but do we really want Nate to think that he can—"

"No, no, no, no, no, no," said Powell. "Of course not. What do you recommend? An apology? Not sure if it should be to Rogel, or the whole class. Whole class, it could be traumatic for Nate. What do you recommend?"

71

JOE

I wrote on the blackboard: 300. All was calm, all was bright. The hospital informed me that Walter was sleeping peacefully. I decided to tackle the last nagging problem in my happy little universe: my wayward agent. I had made my final decision regarding the pole, and, before implementing that decision, had decided to make one last raid on the nest of the golden goose. I got Hoover's answering machine.

"Listen, Pete, this is it. Call me back in one hour or I start entertaining offers from—"

Hoover grabbed the phone. "I'd like to see my imaginary competitors top the gig I got set up for you! How's Secret sound?"

"*Secret?* The lady deodorant?"

"The candy bar."

"Never heard of it."

"Ever hear of Nestle's? That's who makes it."

"Oh. Okay. That's pretty good."

"Pretty good? We'll need a dumptruck to haul the green from this score, my man. And it's *made* for you. It's a *secret* why you're up there. Get it?"

"How much?"

"Not yet solidified. Tell you this—it's close to more than the others combined."

"Close to more?" I tried to do the figures but got dizzy in dollar signs. "When?"

"Haven't quite nailed that down."

"What *have* you nailed down?"

"Leave it to me. Stay put. Gotta go."

Everybody had to go.

I luxuriated in my blessings. Pals with Shipwreck, 300 days up, Nate's school jam resolved, another lucrative gig, and, the pièce de résistance— Clover was coming up after days of deliberately weak excuses: she had her period; Nate needed homework help; Solana had her period; Nate had a tummy ache; she hurt her back laughing at *Laverne & Shirley*. She had put me to the test, tempted me to revert to my short-tempered caveman ways. Reassured, she would haul her wifely charms up the pole that very evening.

Manna was upon me. I surveyed my kingdom, El Río de Nuestra Señora La Reina de Los Ángeles de Porciúncula, the sweetest little city on the sweetest little planet in the sweetest little galaxy in the sweetest little universe in town.

I'm a flagpole-sitter, I was born to be a flagpole-sitter & now that I've abandoned myself to the mystery & grandeur of the calling, without concern for that vulgar record, my life is finally going the way it was meant to go. I've proved I can stay up as long as I want. So now (after one last soul-rotting commercial for the sake of my family's financial future), I'm going to get down.

I remember a meditation teacher once telling me that you don't have to sit in a full lotus with your eyes closed to meditate, you can meditate anywhere. Well, a flagpole-sitter can flagpole-sit anywhere, in the air or on terra firma. Flagpole-sitting is a state of mind, "sitting on top of the world," a by-product, like happiness, of being true to thyself.

I sat cross-legged in the shadow of the orange umbrella and meditated on a random stanza from Tennyson's Simeon poem:

> Bethink thee, Lord, while thou and all the saints
> Enjoy themselves in Heaven, and men on earth
> House in the shade of comfortable roofs
> Sit with their wives by fires, eat wholesome food,
> And wear warm clothes, and even beasts have stalls,
> I, 'tween the spring and downfall of the light,
> Bow down one thousand and two hundred times—

The phone squealed. I unplugged it and read on:

> Or in the night, after a little sleep,
> I wake; the chill stars sparkle; I am wet
> With drenching dews, or stiff with crackling frost.
> I wear an undress'd goatskin on my back;
> A grazing iron collar grinds my neck;
> And in my weak, lean arms I lift the cross,
> And strive and wrestle with thee till I die.
> O mercy, mercy! wash away my sin!

I sent a great atoning sigh out over the world for all the wrong I had done and all the right I had left undone. I vowed that (after the Secret ad) I would climb down and steadfastly teach, devoutly be friend, father, husband. Love and penance slopped from my heart's bucket and fell upon the unknowing heads of the lost wanderers below.

"Oh, life," I said. I plugged the phone back in, yearning for human connection to transmit my love. "Sweet life," I said, and it rang and I answered.

"Joe? It's Sam."

"Sam? Clover's agent?"

"Yes." He sounded out of breath. "I'm calling to inform you that we're involved."

The most obvious interpretation of "we're involved" leapt to mind, of course, but in my serene and saintly state I sidestepped that meaning as deftly as a matador sidesteps a one-ton bull, for Clover had steadfastly denied my every suspicion and fear.

However, because nature abhors a vacuum, and because the job description of the mind is to provide explanations, however preposterous, for every situation, a second interpretation arose: Sam and Clover were "involved" in that "art fraud" that Shipwreck had deviously dropped into one of our conversations.

"Did you hear me?" Sam asked.

"I hope this isn't about some art fraud you've dragged my wife into."

"*What?* Clover and I are involved with *each other.*"

My heart reared up like a terror-stricken stallion.

"I love Clover," the man spluttered. "Deeply. I'm calling for one reason—to plead with you to set her free. If you love her as well, and I'm confident you do, in your fashion, then you'll release her. Let's not turn this into an even more terribly awkward and painful situation than it unfortunately, but inevitably, already is."

I dropped the phone and sat there, in the middle of the air, alone and alone. I felt myself slipping, perhaps into shock. I believed Sam. He was too transparent a pontificating imbecile to be lying about this. Clover had betrayed me, betrayed Nate, betrayed everything, then lied like the devil about it again and again.

I grabbed the phone and gagged, "What do you mean 'involved'?"

"Joe, I know this must hurt you, and I'm sorry for that, I truly am, but we have to deal with reality and accept it courageously, for all our sakes, and the sooner the better."

I rasped: "What do you mean 'involved'?"

"Romantically. Biologically."

Okay, I thought. Biologically. Romantically. Whatever happens, never panic. My voice came out cool as a snake sliding through the grass. "Does Nate know about this?"

"No. I believe not. However, you're absolutely correct, if I understand your implication—the boy is a high priority."

The urge to violence rose through my shock like sulfuric acid through crushed ice. "I'll tell you what the highest priority is."

"Yes?"

"Turning you into dead meat."

Sam sighed wearily. "I hoped and prayed we wouldn't journey down this particular path. However, let me say this to you—don't do anything you'll regret. I'm quite well-connected."

"Well-connected? What does that mean, the Mafia? You little shithole. The bones of your neck are going to be well-connected to my snapping hands, you punctilious cocksucker."

"Joe, for God sakes. May we please at least *act* like adults?"

I wanted blood, but information first. "You know what? You're absolutely right, Sam. May I ask, does she know you're calling me?"

"As a matter of fact, no, she does not."

"Has she told you she wants me to 'set her free'?"

"To be frank, she doesn't know *what* she wants. Yet. In my studied opinion, she feels a certain loyalty to you, if I may, in large part because you're the father of her son."

"Okay. First, never mention my son again as long as you're lucky to live. Second, are you telling me that you've been fucking my wife, Clover, while I've been up here? Is that what you're saying? Is that the cold hard brutal fact that you're presenting me with?"

Sam sighed a big, sorrowful, condescending sigh. "She and I shared in an act of sexual congress, yes, but it was rooted in a profound, abiding love, I most decidedly assure you."

I wondered how I could be engaged in this conversation and not have wheels flying out of my skull. "How many times?"

"Oh, dear. Well, you have the right to ask, and you have the right to be informed should you ask, which you did. Once, to date."

So, it could have been in a drunken stupor. Did that make it better or worse? "Did she tell you she loves you?"

"To be honest, in so many words, no, she did not. But one knows when another is experiencing love for one. I understand her reluctance to speak her heart, considering the circumstances. I certainly didn't hesitate to tell *her*, because I do. Love her, that is. And I think in your best moments you might dare to admit that you do not, because, if you did, would you be pursuing whatever chimera you're pursuing up there, while she starves below for the love she deserves?"

The full carnal act of him and Clover was too fiendish to envision. "Did you kiss?"

"Joe, don't do this to yourself."

"I asked you a question."

"We did, once, yes, if you refer to lips upon lips."

"How do I know you're telling the truth?"

"Why would I lie about it?"

"To make me blow my top and climb down and find you and beat you to a bloody fucking pulp and drive her away. You could be lying, you could be insane, you could be—"

"She has a small tattoo," Sam said.

I waited, but he was waiting too. I said, "She could've just *told* you about that."

"I saw it."

"What's it of?"

"Your name. In a heart."

Oh, God, no, no. "Where is it?"

"Her abdomen."

The thought of Sam's eyes playing over that tattoo, the thought of Clover letting that happen, brought it home to stay. All right. I died. I turned to stone.

I held down the button on the phone, let it back up, and dialed Clover before Sam could. As the phone rang, for no known reason, I thought of Shipwreck.

"Clover's Patch," my cheating wife said.

"Clover."

"Joe! Honey! Hi!" I heard laughing chatter behind her. "Hold on, I'm gonna take the phone in back." A door closed and it got quiet on Clover's side. "I'm so excited about tonight. I feel like a schoolgirl."

I was in hell, but a certain power, an insane perverse consolation, resided in knowing what I knew, and in knowing that she did not know that I knew, although, once the secret was exposed, that power would vaporize and a voracious doom would devour me and her and our entire world. "Yeah."

"What's wrong?" she said. "You sound funny."

I realized Sam could have called me from right down there, with Clover listening, from the coffeehouse, or the apartment, or Clover's bed! Our bed! "Is Sam down there?"

"*Sam?* No. Why?"

"How's he doing?"

"I don't know. We haven't spoken lately."

My bullshit-detector did not stir. "Why not?"

She took a long breath. "I'm thinking of looking for a new agent."

Again she registered truthful. If she wasn't lying, Sam was, and if Sam was lying, he was a master psychopath. But the tattoo! "Why?" I said.

"He makes me uncomfortable."

I let that go by. "What about your show?"

"I don't know if I'm ready."

"Did you happen to mention your tattoo to him?"

"My *tattoo?* To *Sam? No.*" She was telling the truth. She hadn't *mentioned* it to him. Sam had *seen* it. "*Why?*"

"Because he described it to me. To a T."

"Sam?" All the wind was gone from her sails. "When?"

"When he called me, five seconds before I called you."

"He called you? Oh. Oh, my God. You know what? I think I *did* tell him about it." She was lying. "I was—this is so embarrassing, Joe, please don't get mad, but— It was when I was drunk, had that drink, at the pre-opening thing. Remember?"

"Stop."

"And I was thinking about you, and wishing you were there, and I thought of the tattoo, and must have blurted it like I was talking to myself, with the wine, and it just came out. You can't get mad at me for *that*, can you?"

The lie was hidden in her fairy tale like a bloodclot in the pocket of a white suit. "He told me everything, Clover."

"What do you mean?"

"I want you to let it sink in that I know."

She tried to brush the blood off the white suit: "If that nut twisted around something innocent like the tattoo, that's proof I was right about him. I didn't want to say it before, but I think he's psychotic."

"You picked him. You better hope Nate never finds out about this. Do you want to leave me for him?"

"*What?*"

"My beloved wife is fucking that cocksucking motherfucking jerkoff asshole sissy."

"Where are you getting this? Oh, my God, how amazing this is. That liar girl—Carmen!—she said she was up there and something happened! And she's a sick liar and nothing happened, right? It's happening again! Right here, with Sam! What is this? What is going on?"

I hesitated. Was a trade-off happening? A return to the Garden of Eden? But the Sam and Carmen matters were in no way comparable. A full-blown affair dwarfed an unintentional blowjob. "Apples and oranges," I said.

"*What?* What's *that* supposed to mean? Are you saying something *did* happen between you and her? *Was* Carmen up there?"

"Yeah."

"You lied! Oh, you-you-you-you *lying*— If something *did* happen between him and me, I'll tell you this—it wasn't some disgusting bestial act with a lying little slut on top of a filthy whorehouse of a flagpole!"

"So something *did* happen with you and him. What was it? Just tell me!"

"We didn't fuck. We're not fucking. At least there's that."

"What *did* you do? Did you kiss?"

"I don't know. We might have. If we did, it was nothing. It was like sisters kissing."

"Sisters! Just fucking tell me what you did and get it over with."

"Oral."

"Oral! Oh, Jesus. Who on who?"

"Him on me."

"Oh, Jesus in hell."

"Once. That's all."

"That's *all?*"

"What did you do with *her?* What did *you* do with that lying girl *pig!*... You're not answering. Oh, Jesus!" She burst out weeping. Her cries tore me like the claws of a beast.

Out of nowhere that blue jay Curly landed on the banister and glared at me. I shook my head at him.

"Nothing happened," I said.

"Nothing happened? Why did you let me think it did!"

"I'm hurt, I'm crushed, I wanted to hurt you back."

"Was she even up there?"

"No."

"Oh, God, Joe. What have I done! What have I done!"

"Were you drunk?"

"Yes! Of course! I was wasted. But it'll never happen again. It's over! I swear to God!"

"Does he know it's over?"

"I'll beat it into him till he does. Tell me there's a chance you might forgive me even if it's our next lifetime."

I winced at the memory of Carmen wiping her mouth with the back of her hand. "Anything's possible."

"Oh, thank you, thank you."

"First, we have to agree that Nate never finds out about our—"

"'*Our*'? Goddamn it, Joe, what are you doing to me? Was Carmen up there or not? Tell me, please, in the name of God! I've laid my heart out naked on the table and it's pumping my blood away!"

I felt relief before I even said it: "Okay. Yeah. She was up."

"Oh, thank God. Tell me the *whole* truth. You know what I've done. I'm a sinner, a drunken slut. If you tell me you did *something*, even *thought* of doing something, it *might* keep me from going *berserk* with guilt. If you love me at all, please tell me something happened. *Anything*."

She would dig the mine until I gave up the gold just to stop her pick and shovel. Traffic hissed like a frying pan.

"Okay," I whispered. "Something happened."

"Oh, God, thank you. Did you kiss?"

"No."

"You didn't kiss? Was it…intercourse?"

"No."

"Thank God. Was it…oral, also?"

"Yes." It was out. "It was her, her on me."

Now at last we were both feeling the same hideous things at the same time. My heart fluttered around like a big dumb thumb. I broke down.

"I'm completely nuts right now, Clover. What did we do? My brains are disintegrating! My heart is mush!"

"Mine too."

"How did it happen? I was minding my own business." I refrained from blaming Shipwreck, who deserved to be dragged into the swamp of responsibility with us. "I'm sorry, Clover!"

"Did it happen when she said it happened?"

"Yeah." I was calming down. The worst was over. The truth did indeed set you free.

"So," Clover said, "*before* Sam even *touched* me, you let that little lying *cunt* up there to do her thing with little helpless you and your little helpless cock."

"What?"

"At least I never said I didn't know how it happened."

"You tried to blame it on being drunk!"

"You let that skinny little pig put her lying mouth on your fucking prick!"

"Oh, man, how could I be so *stupid* as to be honest with you."

"You fucked her mouth!"

"You fucked his! Okay, listen, let's stop, this is getting out of hand."

Clover pounded the phone into the cradle. I called her: busy signal. I paced the sun-warmed redwood in my bare feet as if life would ever be sane again. The dark buildings downtown towered against the ugly filthy sky.

Only one thing to do: climb down and save our grievously mangled marriage. Nothing else mattered. The promise to Shipwreck was straw, the quest a vicious hoax. Don't even think about Secret Chocolate Bar.

Opening the trapdoor and swinging my legs in, I caught Clover watching me through the louvered living room window. No rage or heartbreak in her face, but anticipation, lips parted, eyes wide, as if watching numbers in a lottery she had fixed. And then she was gone.

"Oh," I whispered. "You did it to punish me. You got him to do it knowing he would spill the beans and I'd have to get down."

I pulled my legs out of the abyss and dropped the trapdoor.

A horde of barbarians would not drive me off that flagpole now.

Oh, if I had only resisted Carmen! What power I would have wielded, even in agony. My only power now was to stay up on that accursed pole. At that moment, at long last, nothing mattered to me but sitting, just as she had claimed and feared. I was dead now to all but sitting. I fell to my knees and thought, Oh, fill me with flaming arrows from head to toe! Roast me like a swooning saint in my own juices! I would not get down. I would never get down.

72

JOE

"If you think it'll help, I'll get down right now."

"If you did," Clover said, "you'd blame me."

"How can I stay up?"

"Don't get down because you're afraid anything's still going on."

"How would I know?"

"How would I know nothing worse happened up there than what you said?"

"Nate doesn't know anything?"

"If he did, it'd show, I'd see it."

I stayed up, she stayed down.

&

"Apology to your teacher go okay?"

"Yeah. It was pretty okay."

"Well, good. You're growing up, Nate. I'm proud of you."

"Okay. Thanks."

"Can I ask you something? What do you think of that Sam?"

"Why?"

"Just asking."

I could hear him breathing. "I saw something," he said.

"Well, seeing can be tricky. Something can be one thing and look like something else."

"Why didn't you ask what I saw?"

"What did you see?"

"Them kissing."

"Who?"

"*Mom* and *him*! Who do you think!"

"Are you sure?"

"I know what kissing is!"

"Where were they?"

"In the alley. In his car."

Did the whole thing happen in his backseat in the filthy fucking alley?

"Well," I said, "in show business, Hollywood, art—everybody kisses everybody."

"I knew I shouldn't of told you."

"I'm glad you told me."

"*Glad?* Are you gonna get down and beat him up or what?"

"For a kiss? No. This isn't a movie, pal. They got a little carried away because of Mom's paintings. I talked with her about it. Adults can act as silly as kids sometimes."

"You talked to her about them kissing? Why did you pretend you didn't know!"

"I wanted to hear your side. I talked with Sam too. We straightened it out."

"You *talked* to him? Oh, who cares. I'm not gonna run away. I don't want to go to Juvie. I'm gonna get rich and live in a castle by myself."

"Well, that's a crappy goal. Listen, Nate, I love you. And Mom loves you too. Would it really make you happy if I got down and beat Sam up?"

"I hate Mom."

"You don't hate Mom. You're mad. It'll pass. Nobody's perfect, not even Mom."

"She wouldn't have even done it if you lived on Earth like a normal husband."

"So, I should get down."

"Who cares? It's stupid to go up there, it's even stupider to give up and get down now."

"Some things are more important than living on a pole."

"You shoulda thought of that before."

73

JOE

The platform creaked. In a good wind, the redwood liked to complain, but there was no wind now. Certain spots whined or groaned when stepped on, but I was sitting, still as water, meditating on the Tennyson poem. I heard it again, next to me, the hair on my arms jumped, but there was nothing there. An unseen knuckle knocked the stub of the pole, and I jumped away like a cat at a cucumber.

And that was it, nothing more. The monsters of my and Clover's betrayals were gnawing my wires inside. That had been my fear, madness, both from failing to fulfill my calling and from succeeding, breaking the record but losing my mind in the process.

"I'm getting down," I said.

I would tell Shipwreck and only Shipwreck. Let the others be caught unawares when I appeared like Lazarus in the doorway, righting wrongs and cracking the whip. I would stroll between the tables amid yuppie whisperings: "That's Joe Magellan, the flagpole-sitter."

I called the old gentleman in the hospital. I owed him forewarning. I anticipated crypto-mystical gewgaw from him and a reminder of my (coerced) promise to break the record. The phone rang and rang. I hung up. I grabbed the Tennyson poem, hoping Simeon's suffering might make sense of my own:

> O my sons, my sons,
> I, Simeon of the pillar, by surname
> Stylites, among men; I, Simeon,
> The watcher on the pillar till the end;
> I, Simeon, whose brain the sunshine bakes;
> I, whose bald brows in silent hours become
> Unnaturally hoar with rime, do now
> From my high nest of penance here proclaim
> that Pontius and Iscariot by my side
> Show'd like fair seraphs. On the coals I lay,
> A vessel full of sin; all hell beneath

Made me boil over. Devils pluck'd my sleeve,
Abaddon and Asmodeus caught at me.
I smote them with the cross; they swarm'd again.

How could anyone believe Tennyson was *mocking* Simeon? The poem was a full-on homage to his superhuman suffering. He must have been pure spirit by the time he ascended, his body an empty potato sack discarded behind. Thirty years he sat! I hadn't sat one. Nevertheless, brothers of the pillar and pole were we, Simeon and me. He had been a shepherd; I herded students. The medieval holy man and the modern substitute teacher, driven by the same uncanny spiritual summons. Simeon took the lonelier ascetic road, I the way of marriage and family. Much anguish he endured, but could he have marshaled the aplomb with which I ironed out Nate's messes at school? Did he withstand the boiling oil of sexual treachery? The vise of jealousy tightening upon the marital heart? The white-hot urge for revenge? Would he have resisted Carmen's obnoxious charms? Would he have hurled her off the pillar?

I lay back on my chaise and gazed at the distant Hollywood Hills, which could have been Mount Hermon rising over ancient Syria.

I read the next line aloud: "'In bed like monstrous apes they crush'd my chest.'"

What! Unbelievable! There it was in one sentence: the ape incident, the betrayals "in bed," and "crush'd chest" right after I pictured my heart in the vise of jealousy.

I reached for the phone and dialed again. "Cedars-Sinai," the woman said.

"I was calling Walter Blake's room."

"Thank you." She put me on hold. Soothing flute music came on.

How much of this had Shipwreck planned? Was there indeed a thread of wild destiny binding us flagpole-sitters across the centuries? I felt for a moment elevated above my earthly troubles, which seemed trivial leaves rolling along in a trivial wind.

The woman returned. "Are you a relative, sir?"

"Yes, his son. Joe. Joe Blake."

"One moment, please, Mr. Blake."

Could the codger have up and hobbled out of the hospital and they were afraid to tell me, his son?

Someone picked up the phone. "This is Dr. Terry."

"Has that rascal escaped?"

"Have I met you, sir? This is Mr. Blake's son, I understand?"

I bluffed: "Yes, you understand. Didn't I say I was? What the hell's going on?"

"I'm sorry to have to tell you, sir, your father has passed away."

"*What?*"

"I'm very sorry. You were aware of his condition, were you not?"

"Uh, Doc, you got a mix-up on your hands. I want Walter Blake, old slim Black guy, white hair, gray eyes. He has an ulcer."

"No. Is that what he told you? Mr. Blake, Walter suffered from inoperable T4 prostate cancer."

"No, no, no, he has a fucking *ulcer*. He climbed a sixty-foot pole a few days ago. You folks need to get your shit together. This is a dreadful error."

"No. It is he. I made the pronouncement. I signed the death certificate."

"Wait a minute. This is some trickster pal of his! Oh, this is *not* funny. This is going too far, even for him. I'll come down there and kill him myself. He'll *wish* he was dead. Man, you guys had me going. Put him on. I'll smack that son-of-a-bitch from here to Sunday."

The man put the phone down and the woman picked it up. "Mr. Blake?"

"That old bastard pal of ours has *no* scruples. *None.*"

"Listen to me, sir, please. Your father—Walter Blake—has died. I'm sorry."

Shipwreck's bloodstain gazed at me from the redwood. I felt again the midsection of the ape suit crumpling around my fist. My voice sounded far away: "He told me he had an ulcer."

"If so, he was not telling the truth. Did you not know your father was dying?"

I shook my head. "*He* knew?"

"Oh yes. This may be consolation—he told me he would die today."

"How could he climb a flagpole right before he went in the hospital?"

"I'd say it was impossible, but exceedingly strange things have been known to happen toward the end. Your father was an exceptional man."

"Could it have damaged him? Climbing a flagpole?"

"It couldn't have helped."

Punching him in the stomach couldn't have helped either. Loss broke in me like a yolk. "Oh, Walter."

"I'm sorry."

"May I ask your name?"

"Joan Keller, RN."

"Joan, thank you. Did he— Is there a funeral, or—"

"I gather the arrangements are being handled by business associates? Are you in contact with them?"

I shook my head. "Was he alone? At the end?"

She hesitated. "No."

I suspected Joan may have been lying to ease my pain, my guilt for failing to be there for him, and I was grateful to her for that.

74

JOE

I would not only get down, I would get down right then, that second. Anything less would dishonor my grief for Walter Shipwreck Blake. But as I grabbed the handle of the trapdoor, my grudging pledge to the old brigand rattled in my skull like chains in an attic. I still held the Simeon poem, my thumb on the line about the monstrous apes in bed crushing my chest, which I never had the chance to discuss with him. If I got down, his gray-eyed ghost would haunt me to my last breath.

All right, I thought, if *I'm* not getting down, then at least everything that isn't me *is.*

I stood and stuck the poem like a six-gun in the waist of my pants. My eyes went to the two stacks of books. I blinked. I cringed. They were *books.* My horror at the thought of throwing them over told me that was exactly what I needed to do. I would hurl them right into the teeth of death.

I grabbed the first stack, went to the edge, made sure nobody was down there, took the one on top—Camus' *Notebooks*—and dropped it over. Falling, it opened maroon wings and before it hit, I dropped the whole stack over to tumble and flutter and smack the sidewalk like a flock of dead birds. Atop the second stack lay Nate's clouds book, which I set on the pole stump, then cast the remainder over without looking.

Over went the new boombox, which shattered into whirling black shards. One by one, I released my possessions to the concrete six stories below—the new binoculars with a crack!—the umbrella with a smack!—the chaise lounge with a nosedive crash!

Once again cars slowed and pedestrians stopped in their tracks. Clover and Nate and a clot of customers disgorged from the Patch.

"What are you doing!" my wife cried.

I dropped the television over (thinking too late of flying glass) and it struck like a bomb, face-first, thank God, with a little silver eruption which sank back into the chassis.

Drowning out Clover's anguished calls, roars of encouragement rose from bystanders up and down Western as each item plummeted and smashed to earth. I hoisted the mini-fridge onto a banister post and held it there teetering as the mob chanted, "Drop it! Drop it! Drop it!" I took my hand off and the fridge tipped over, spun languidly and hit with a thud that lit my bones.

"Wait! Wait! Wait!" Clover grabbed fallen books while she could, then over went the unused computer and printer, a stack of unread *L.A. Times*, a small globe, an alarm clock, a basket, incense and holder, hairbrush, aspirin, mirror, candle, back scratcher, wild animal calendar, then a varied flurry of accoutrements, my arms a windmill, grabbing and hurling, flinging and tossing, back-handed, fore-handed, sideways, through my legs, over my head—including an old stained cardboard box which was spinning free in flight before the familiar feel and heft of it registered: the only copy of my 999-page epic novel, *Holder & Biggen*.

In the middle of the air the lid flew off and in slow-motion at the top of its arc the box turned upside-down and pages of the epic by the hundreds and hundreds dropped, cascaded, fanned out in the wind like cards in the dealer's hands, a swarm of manic white bats in the sun wheeling down Western, a plague of tumbling scenes, lost characters, motiveless actions, run-on sentences, preposterous relationships, regrettable symbols, endless conversations, shoehorned expositions, ramshackle themes, murky subtexts, and half-baked dreams—all suddenly and utterly as precious as breath, as light, as life itself—going, going, gone.

Clover and Nate chased up the sidewalk, grabbed a page, another, stomping on a third, urging others, customers, shopkeepers, strangers, to join the pursuit, and they did, with no idea what they were chasing.

I grabbed the banister. "Let it go! Clover! Let it go! Let it go! Everybody! Let it all go!"

She stopped and looked up at me. I put my hand on my heart. She slumped. I threw her a sad kiss. She let the pages fall from her hands, called after Nate and he ceased the chase, too, and the rest followed one by one. A man in a Lakers jacket set down his pages as if caught stealing.

"Thank you!" I shouted. "Thank you!" My book had never been so cared for, its mysteries never so passionately pursued. "Thank you! I love you! God bless you! I love you all!"

The phone rang. I ripped it loose, took a look down, dropped it over.

That left me with the clothes on my back, and the bare necessities—sleeping bag, toilet, journal.

I tore off my T-shirt and Levi's and flung them over. I pulled the Tennyson poem from the waist of my shorts, tucked it under the sleeping bag, and sat in the middle of the platform. In my smeared vision the lines stood on the page like an aerial view of burned buildings. Was I going blind? Was I dying? Three long clouds, like ships in mast, passed before the sun. I blinked my vision clear. Curly, the blue jay, stood eyeing me from the banister.

"Shipwreck's dead," I whispered. "Fly away." The bird cocked its head, squawked, and took off to tell the world.

75

CLOVER

Nate and I bagged up Joe's smashed things for the trash. Two disorderly stacks of books huddled against the café, nervous about their fate. I'd shooed lookie-loos away and my customers back inside where they tried not to stare at poor Nate and me in my shame and rage and fear. I squeezed his shoulder. "We need the dolly for the fridge." The fatigue in my voice alarmed me.

"Is he gone crazy?" Nate said. "His mom went crazy." Then, as if alone: "What if he did it because—"

"Because what?"

He blinked. "Because I got in trouble. Then I remembered I got out of it. So, I don't know." He grabbed two black trash bags and dragged them up the driveway. You thought of body parts.

Was there any way Nate knew about Sam and me? I didn't want to think about it. One nightmare at a time. I grabbed a bag myself and lugged it alleyward. That poor, bloated, brilliantly deluded, now desecrated manuscript. I saw it blowing down Western, wet in the gutter, torn by tires, shredded, dissolving, washing out to sea, years of work turned to fish food. If he no longer cared even about that, what might be next to go?

༄

That night he sent me down a scribbled poem called "The Clouds of This World From The Space Shuttle":

Cumulus towers collapse over Western
& over Rhodesia glass wings
of the pileus soar.

Stratus, floccus & castellatus turn
& turn around the Caribbean.

At Cherbourg violet nimbocumulus
from a warm front
halo the climbing moon.

Cirrus billow
in a ring over Wimbledon.

Too terribly lovely to leave out,
some names having something
to do with clouds are

eye wall, glory ring, mountain
wave, cloud street, hub cloud, sun
pillar, soft rime needle, fog bow, ice
fallout, rope cloud, supercooled air
& distrail blob.

Looking down
through the shuttle window now,
it's night—no clouds over Lake Tahoe
where my mother & father honeymooned.

Lights of cabins dot the shore.
I pop the hatch &
one by one drop everything
down into the middle of
black Tahoe far below—

my keys, money, MasterCard, clothes, my
TV, chaise, books, my
past & future, umbrella, car, my
apartment, telephone, binoculars, my
novel, my mother, father, wife, son, hero, friend—
& then I jump out myself
right behind my

keys, money, clothes, TV, books,
past & future, phone, novel,
father, mother, wife, son, hero, friend—
splash splish splash
splish splash
splish splash splish splash
splashsplishsplashsplishsplash—

& everything sinks
but me.

He asked me how I liked it.

"How do I like it? It scares the holy shit out of me."

"What? No, no, no, it's *liberating*."

"Maybe for you. It's not too liberating for me and Nate to get thrown out of a satellite into Lake Tahoe and we sink while you're bobbing liberated on the surface."

"Well, you're not really sinking. It's a poem. It's about a momentary state of mind."

"I don't see how you could even show that to me."

He took to waiting till I was back inside before opening the trapdoor and hauling up his meals, which he returned half-eaten. He stopped shaving and adopted a bird's-nest hair-do. Not to mention living in his underpants in wintertime. He did let me talk him into sending up a bathrobe and wool mukluks.

One morning, along with breakfast and fresh underwear, I placed a new walkie-talkie in the basket and took it as a good sign when it did not immediately come crashing to the sidewalk.

Some chatty cub from the *Times*, photographer in tow, showed up at the coffeehouse. He was "following a tip that the flagpole-sitter cracked up." Luckily, Pete Hoover had been tipped to the tip and called to forewarn me. Pete claimed to have no idea why Joe had blown his top, but assured me that Secret candy would drop Joe "like last week's fish" if his crack-up got around. Apparently an individualist kook was one thing and a madman in his underpants another.

Hoover and I cooked up a story: Joe was "remodeling," which included "the planned dropping of old stuff" over the side. He had simply put gravity to work. The cub bought it, reluctantly, for a lunatic's rampage was a story, a flagpole makeover was not. He asked if Joe was living in his underpants.

"Bathing trunks," I said.

"In winter?"

"L.A. winter. How about lattés and croissants? On the house."

Once again, I held the short end of the marital stick. Joe was free to act out his emotions while I stuffed mine, and babied him besides. Of course nobody had a gun to my head. I yearned to blast him with my fury, but feared driving him over the literal edge. I needed babying myself, which Sam was eager to provide, but I would no more accept his comfort than sleep with him. I continued seeing him, professionally, selfishly, for the sake of my show. That braindead call he made to Joe was the pin in the boil of our mischief. He had told me he "couldn't bear the lies any longer." I said, "*You* can't bear the lies! Men are genetically incapable of thinking about anything in the universe but themselves."

The coffeehouse hadn't opened yet. I called Joe on the walkie-talkie. He answered, a good sign. We engaged in small talk, tiny talk. I tried to talk him into a phone. "You can't call 911 with a walkie-talkie. What if something happened? Think about Shipwreck and his ulcer up there, honey."

"Okay. Phone."

My foot in the door, I convinced him to take the umbrella back up, and the sunblock. I was about to also suggest some sort of trousers.

"Is there some way," he said, "you could rig me up a loincloth?"

"Loincloth."

"Like Gandhi wore. And Jesus."

"Jesus did not wear a loincloth."

"I thought you'd be happy to get me out of these underpants."

"Well, if you put it like that…" Oh, so him in a loincloth was a *gift* to me? "I've never made a loincloth before. There may be a gap or two. Were you planning to wear underpants *under* the loincloth?"

"That kinda defeats the purpose."

The *purpose*? "Honey? Have mercy. Tell me what this is about." He was silent. He sighed. He was close to saying. He wanted to. "Wait a second," I said. I went outside with the walkie-talkie. I needed to see his face. "Could you open the trapdoor?" He did. The orange frame of the platform with the blue sky behind made his dreadful appearance even more disturbing. He did not look good at all, kneeling there in his underpants and robe, swaying and bleary. He had lost weight. His beard resembled mange and his hair stuck up like weeds. My eyes felt glittery with fear. What was to become of us?

"Please tell me what's going on."

He looked down upon me as if from a door in a cloud. All the sounds on Western seemed to cease. "It's Shipwreck," he said.

"Shipwreck?" The name pulsed like an evil star, pumping rancor through me. "What did he do now?"

"He died."

"He *died?*"

"It wasn't any ulcer. It was cancer. They couldn't do anything. So, he just... He died."

The loss, the need, the youth in his voice raked my heart. I prayed it was true, that the son-of-a-bitch was dead.

"I'm so sorry, honey." If it was a hoax he was pulling on Joe, I'd kill him myself. "That's what's been doing this to you." He nodded. "Thank you for telling me."

"We barely got to know each other," he said, and wept in the sky.

"I need to come up. Can I come up?"

"I hit him. In the stomach. He vomited blood. There's a stain in the redwood."

"Oh, Joe. Let me come up."

"If you came up, I'd get down when you went down."

"You could."

"I promised him I'd stay up," he said. I gritted my teeth so he could see. "I'm sorry, Clove. It must be awful to be married to me."

The way he said it—so matter-of-fact, as if he had no hope of ever changing—somehow gave me hope.

"I'm sorry you're going through this. Missing Shipwreck."

"Thank you."

"I know how much he meant to you."

"Thank you," he said.

He closed the trapdoor gently, and I closed the café door without a sound, as if the room of a sleeping child lay between.

76

JOE

It rained for three days. Whole time I had a cold. I was on a ghost ship. I vanished in the rain & snot. Sat in the storm like Simeon must have. A couple streets over a little girl rushed out of her house & ran around in it. L.A. in the rain is an immense sigh. I hoped for the worst. How about pneumonia. They'd have to come up and drag me down; I'd put up a convincing fight. I blew my nose so much it started bleeding for the first time since I spotted with Dostoevsky. I let it bleed down me, mixing with the rain. It was justifying.

Then it stopped—the rain, the cold, snot, blood. The sun, that baker, charged out jolly in his big white hat, smacking his hands together, flour flying. I was still alive, still up.

I woke at 3 a.m. to the humming of the streetsweeper. Lonely, thoughtful job. Long thoughts, long as the streets. Humming of the streetsweeper like the humming of a soul.

I remember going into my father's closet after he died. I found his comb in a pocket of his suit. I smelled it. He was gone, but the smell of his hair on his comb remained. The molecules of the smell of his hair became a part of me.

CLOVER

My morning duties completed and the coffeehouse reins handed to
Solana, I climbed upstairs to putter about the musty little apartment, to
think about painting, and to drink.

I had let that dreamy talk with Joe about Shipwreck's dying soften my
resentful heart. Knowing there had been a kindred flagpole-sitting soul
in Joe's life, I accepted, with a measure of peace, my inability to pierce
the bamboozling mystery of that goddamn quest.

But days of rain had eroded my compassion, as if that virtue had
been makeup slapped over the ugly truth. Over and over like a man o'
war the rejection stung me, his rebuff of my offer to climb up and ease
his grief. No matter who had died or betrayed or got died on or got
betrayed, I had laid myself on a platter for him, and he had said thanks
but no thanks. Meanwhile he was doing everything he could to die in
the rain and cold.

"Fuck him," I said.

Again the ruckus of laughter, jabber, clanking kitchenware, and jazz
slopped up the stairs after me. The Patch was a ship's hold, packed with
self-satisfied hedonists oblivious to the seawater climbing their little
crossed legs. The ship of fools was going down and I was drinking in
the captain's tower. I finished one and fixed another. Give me a reef, I
imagined, to smash head-on my shitcan of a life.

Joe should have just married that mad old goat. Maybe he *had*
married him in some mystical goddamn way. Him on his Russian pole
while I below pushed a giant muckball up Clover Mountain. I sounded
deranged to myself and didn't care. Not too deranged to hold the lid on
the gurgling Magellan vat. My darkest wish was that everything would
come to a glorious head and detonate, covering everyone with globs of
stinking truth. Then let the bastards clean it up themselves for the first
time in their spoon-fed, drooling lives. I stirred my Bloody Mary with a
pretzel. "Thar she blows," I whispered, and took a long drink.

JOE

I sat on the platform in my loincloth, holding up a Secret Chocolate Bar in its red, white, and blue wrapper. I had washed, shaved, tidied the platform, but I insisted on the loincloth, on principle. Take it or leave it, I told them, and they took it. It was one of those bracing January days where the sun hid in the sky like a white cat in milk. My balls churned with the thrill of fearless indifference.

"Secret," I said to the camera. "I have one. Guard it with your life." I took a bite and chewed slowly with my eyes closed as I had been instructed.

"Goddamn it!" the director said from a corner of the platform.

I spat the bite into a paper cup full of the things.

"They can't guard it with their goddamn life if it's your secret! It's 'Secret, I have one, have one yourself, and guard it with your life!'"

"He'll get it, he'll get it," said Pete Hoover from the cherry-picker. He called for a break and huddled with the rep and the director as the camera and sound guys retired for a smoke in a corner of the platform.

The ad-makers had had to endure barking horns from my fans, a low-flying news copter, caterwauling sirens, weak sunlight, even my imp bluebird pal Curly swooping in and out of the shot. But the primary snafu was my perverse, hostile self, deliberately fouling up one of dozens of little details, doodling a razor along the neckline of the golden goose. I felt Shipwreck's spirit hovering, nodding, smiling. I closed my eyes and meditated on a line from Tennyson's Simeon poem: "What is it I could have done to merit this?"

The rep stared at me. "Freak in a diaper."

"Loincloth," Hoover corrected. "Gandhi wore one."

"Not in a candy commercial."

79

JOE

One year up. Clover threw a party. Set up speakers outside for me. Patch was packed. Woman sang a folksong about outlaws. Guy wrote a poem about the pole as a sunflower with 445 petals. Clover made a cake, sent up a piece with one big orange candle.

Where is Shipwreck buried? I'll find out & go, when I get down.

If I had to do this for 30 years I'd eat myself alive. I see why Simeon obsessed on God—there's nobody else up here!

It was Shipwreck walking around, invisible, across the poem, tapping on the pole. Happened right after he died but before I knew it. Was that his farewell? Blessing? Curse?

Nate's pulling straight As to show us how mad he is. I kidded about some dumb thing. "I don't feel like goofing around," he says. I farted into the walkie. "That's stupid," he said.

Clover says Sam is still giving her the show. I pretend I don't want to kill him. Or her. Or both. I won't ask her not to do the show. She would still do it, and hate me for asking. Our marriage is like that monstrous unstable expansion bridge in the old newsreel, twisting in the wind with the jalopy of our love bouncing wildly in the middle.

Something's on fire in the middle of Hollywood. I can't see what it is. Red flames wave & black smoke clambers through the gray sky.

How can I get down with only months to go? Getting down frightens me now as much as going up once did.

Clover admits drinking but swears it's nothing like the old days. Says she never drinks & drives. "Beer or two after a hard day."

80

Joe's Secret commercial proved to be a masterpiece of serendipity that produced a sales spike and seized the imagination of viewers across the Southland: What is the secret of the flagpole-sitter? What did he know that the rest of the city, the world, humanity did not?

Providentially, Dr. Malcolm Kerridge filed for bankruptcy the day the Secret spot debuted. Every story on the collapse of Kerridge's Obsessions Seminar empire included mention of the flagpole-sitter whose success had played a central role in Kerridge's fall, along with the seminar master's previously hidden gambling obsession.

Newsworthy once more, Joe was invited by 4RealNews to do a taped interview with the brash, beautiful, up-and-coming Sylky Snyder, Hoover's replacement on what was now *Confessions With Sylky*. The ambitious young reporter had been assigned the interview by Kerridge's disciple at the station.

Hoover knew an ambush when he saw one; he warned Joe, but some bitter defiance drew the flagpole-sitter like a moth to Sylky. He needed to bang foreheads with fate, to break the logjam of his life, to usher in disaster or conquest, he didn't particularly care which.

"It's just a conversation," he told Hoover. "Two human beings having a chat. Nothing simpler, nothing more natural in the world."

PART VI

"Life is the childhood of our immortality."

—Goethe

81

JOE

"What do we *really* know about the man on the pole?" Sylky asked the camera. "Let's peel this enigma hidden in a riddle wrapped in a loincloth, and see what we find."

Sylky leaned forward on the chair (which Clover had sent up for the occasion) as if to query a lost child; I sat serene as a bull's-eye.

"How long have you been up here, Joe?"

"Three hundred and seventy days."

"Let's bottom-line this: Are you a mad, desperate, anti-hero for our mad, desperate, anti-hero times? Or a two-bit con-man manipulating the good-hearted American public?"

I scratched my whiskers. "Two-bit flagpole-sitter minding my own business."

"Why have you resisted all efforts to help you overcome this anti-social self-destructive obsession of yours?"

"You mean the efforts of that bankrupt, *toupée*-topped, rageaholic, gambling addict, so-called Doctor Malcolm Kerridge?"

"Cut!" the suit barked from the cherry picker. He gestured Sylky over. The two turned their backs to me and Hoover and the sound/camera guy. They whispered briefly; Sylky returned and resumed:

"Joe, is it true you've become a very wealthy man as the result of your stunt?"

"I wouldn't say wealthy. Money's a by-product of following your dream."

"No law against turning the dream into a commodity."

"Money's not why I'm up here."

"Of course not, you're up to snatch your hero Shipwreck Blake's world record. A most worthy quest, I think we'd all agree." She winked at the camera. "Joe, you're a teacher, albeit a substitute. How can you ask parents to let you educate their children when you have essentially abandoned your *own* child and wife to live on a flagpole?"

"I regret that in order to follow my heart I've had to not be the absolutely best father and husband I might have otherwise been, yes."

"An excellent deflection. Let's get back to your hero, the man whose record you seek to break, your mentor, poor old Walter Shipwreck Blake. How much truth is there to the rumor that you played some role in his untimely death?"

"He died of cancer."

"Cancer accelerated by a climb up a certain flagpole? Cancer accelerated by an altercation with a certain disciple?"

How the hell? "No idea what you're talking about, but if I were you, I'd watch it."

"Oh? Now, your lovely entrepreneur/artist wife, Clover, works herself to the bone running a coffeehouse below, while you lounge up here in your loincloth. She's having a show of her paintings at a local gallery owned by her agent. Will you be attending?"

"I'd love to go to that opening more than anything in the world."

"But you have more important things to do. I hear your son has found himself in a pinch of trouble at school. Could that be related to your stunt?"

"It was nothing. It's been ironed out."

Was there anything she didn't know? The lights seared, the sun screamed. Had Clover spilled the beans to Sylky in some drunken late-night call? Or Nate, cornered on his way home from school, dazzled by her evil celebrity charisma? Would her coup de grâce be exposing Clover's and my infidelities?

"Need a break, Joe?" called Hoover.

Sylky waved the agent hush. "Is it true that twenty-five years ago your father failed to deliver on his promise to build you a treehouse?"

"Treehouse?" I laughed. "Somebody fed you some bad info, madam."

"Why would your uncle Wayne feed me bad info?"

"Uncle Wayne?" Where'd she dig *him* up?

"Was there a giant maple tree in your backyard in West Covina?"

"There was. So?"

"And a pile of redwood lumber at the foot of that tree?"

I looked at her, over her shoulder, eastward twenty miles, to West Covina, to that November afternoon twenty-five years gone. My mother called me, I climbed down, she told me. But no lumber, no redwood at the foot of the tree. While I was there I looked around, focused, peering, not at the foot of the tree but against the fence, half-hidden by foliage. *Was* there something there?

"You're remembering," Sylky said.

Was that it, hidden by the overgrown Boston ivy? As if peering back at me—2 by 4s and 4 by 4s and planks, I could see it. It had lain there till we moved, a sullen undergrowth, lurking, dark green heart-shaped leaves swirling over it all, black widow spiders, shadows.

"Break-time," Hoover said.

Uncle Wayne had been there for my father's funeral, helping his sister, my mother. He was a quiet man, a good man, level-headed, conservative, smoked a pipe. Not brilliant, or even articulate, but thoughtful in his way, observant, naturally kind. He wouldn't lie, but he may have lost a few marbles through the years. He had to have gotten the treehouse business from my mother, whose own mind had been beginning to go already by then.

"In a world where war, poverty, and injustice rage unchecked," Sylky intoned into the camera, "a grown man, a substitute teacher, lives on a flagpole. Joe Magellan. Anti-hero? Pretender? Symbol of our desperate times? Or selfish child on high, brooding his life away, scolding the world for a broken promise from the buried past? You decide. This is Sylky Snyder, *Confessions With Sylky*... Pack it up, boys." She gave my cheek a little pat. "It was good for me, Joe, hope it was good for you."

82

4RealNews edited the interview to highlight Joe's most helpless moments in close-ups, freeze frames and slo-mo. Clover stood like a live
nerve in the back of the packed coffeehouse, enduring the spectacle
as long as she could. When the inquisition moved to the subject of
child abandonment, she stole upstairs and rapid-fired Bloody Marys.
She could hear her loyal patrons booing and hissing Sylky throughout,
which only intensified her rage and mortification.

Nate came bounding upstairs. She didn't bother to hide her drink.
"I hate that Sylky Snyder!" he said, pacing, poking the air. "I hate her!
I hate her! How could you make fun of somebody that their dad didn't
build them their treehouse because he was dead! I wish he would of
picked her up and threw her over! She's the b-word!"

"What b-word is that?"

"The bitch b-word! I hate her!"

Nate's rage anticipated the fury of the entire city. Callers swamped
the station denouncing Sylky's cruel ambush. Her merciless onslaught
transformed Joe from selfish bum to sympathetic underdog. The
"good-hearted American public" brushed aside the abandonment issue,
the fast buck charge, and the wicked implication that Joe was involved
in some other flagpole-sitter's demise. The treehouse story, meant to
toxify and trivialize the quest, had instead proved a simple and moving
explanation for it, refreshing public intrigue with the valiant, heartbroken sitter.

Rival stations were happy to stoke the anti-Sylky uproar. Forced to
make an on-air apology, Sylky was unable to mask her natural insincer-
ity, which ignited another round of howling callers and resulted in her
reassignment as roving agriculture reporter at a sister station in Fresno.

83

JOE

A monstrous sting ray flapped ever-so-slowly around the platform in my dream, regarding me with gentle eyes.

I called information. Uncle Wayne has the same number he had twenty-five years ago. He didn't believe it was me. He'd gotten crank calls since the interview. He "hadn't no clue 'bout the hubbub." He asked what was I doing up a flagpole. For the world record, I said, to keep it simple. Everybody understands a world record. He reminisced about what a wonderful man my father had been, how smart, how successful. "Likely a good thing he can't see this."

I asked him if it was true, what Sylky said, the redwood & the treehouse. "I shouldn't talk about that," he said. I said, "You talked to Sylky about it." "Not fond of the past. Bygones be bygones." I told him it wasn't his past I was asking about. He said, "You always were a self-centered boy." I told him he was the only one alive who knew about it & it was real important to me. Yes, he said yes, it was true, except for the promise, which "maybe she made it up." "Vic planned to build you a treehouse. Ordered the wood, died, lumber got delivered. Marge said play it for a toolshed. So long now, need to take my heart stuff."

Somehow my number got out. Besieged by fans about the interview. One said I reminded her of her fisherman son. She claimed she'd sent me a letter with quotes on perseverance. I never got it. I asked Clover. She said no, no letters, postcards, nothing. Could she be dumping my fan letters? After what's happened, I wouldn't put it past her. Nor blame her.

Most callers are surprised I answer. Must think I have a secretary up here. A lot ask about the treehouse. The treehouse that wasn't. And Dad. One guy couldn't say why he called, just had the urge. One woman knew why: phone sex. Sounded Swedish. I thought about it. Won't be a visit from Clover anytime soon. Who would know? Low warm voice in the darkness. Don't know how I hung up on her. Coulda been another set-up.

Visits from "old friends"—from high school, the army, college, and a former student who remembered something he said I said—about the boat in *Heart of Darkness* being the human heart driving upstream through hell on a journey to God. Wonderful to be remembered, but for some flamboyant image I can't recall saying? Maybe I was a livelier teacher than I thought.

One oddball dropped by, insisted he brought me popsicles when I sat up in the orange tree in West Covina. I asked him what flavor & he screamed at me & stomped off.

A woman called and swore that watching my interview had cured her gout.

A fast talker called, claiming to be a local political wheeler dealer who had some association with the Revitalization Committee (whatever happened to that?). He wanted to know if I'd be interested in running for councilman. I tell him I don't even know what council district I'm in. So what, he says. He says, Think about it. I think about it. Politics, changing things, punishing evildoers. Power, wealth, prestige. Hero to the downtrodden. I see myself as mayor, senator, president. The guy was probably calling from an insane asylum.

I believe my fans are drawn to me for some deeper meaning, beauty even, something transcendentally sincere, earnest, in this devious & ironic world. Simply sitting up here, I'm helping them, encouraging each in his or her own mystery.

In the wake of the new publicity, other commercial interests want me. Hoover's pushing me to sign long-term with Secret. I'm not averse, just serenely indifferent.

Clover & I have so much to talk about & go on & on talking about nothing.

Nate's anger at me diminished in the hammering I got from Sylky. I invited him up. He thought about it. "No." "Why not?" "I don't want to." He's the age I was when my father died. Even before my father died, I remember trying to toughen myself up, not grin so much, get tough in my eyes & mouth. Lifting weights, Dad teaching me how to turn your left jab as you threw it so it'd meet the guy's jaw flush & you wouldn't break your little finger knuckle.

84

JOE

I emerged from the Sylky tsunami a simpler man, more determined, healthier, ascetic. I meditated, did hundreds of push-ups, sit-ups, jumping jacks, ran in place. One evening, I sat on the edge, arms on the banister, chin on arms, legs a-dangle, attending the subsumption of day into night, layer-of-light by layer-of-light leaving. The phone rang.

"You heartless bastard!" Malcolm screeched. "You have driven me into the ditch of bankruptcy! Do you imagine in your wildest dreams that you've *won*?"

"Pull yourself together, man."

"I tried to save you from yourself, and you hate me for it!"

"I don't hate you. I don't have any hard feelings for you whatsoever."

"*You* don't have any hard whatsoever feelings against *me*!"

"I didn't do anything to you. You gambled everything away."

"Incorrect! Incorrect! You know *nothing*! You vicious simpleton! Who *wouldn't* fly to Vegas to let off steam after herding you self-obsessed lunatics all weekend."

I was astonished to feel unabashed compassion and pity for the abusive loon. Or pity, at least. "Malcolm, my being up here has nothing to do with you. I was a flagpole-sitter long before I ever heard of you."

"How fascinating! Did I request your autobiography? I have some news for you, Mr. Flagpole. Keep your eye on the horizon tomorrow."

"What's that supposed to mean?"

"It means keep your beady eyes peeled to the southeast. You may observe a speed-bump in your satanic highway."

"Malcolm, I urge you to get on with your life. Let your obsession with me go."

"Don't tell me about obsessions. I'm the King of Obsessions! You're my *patient*. Get your wife to send up a straitjacket to go with that dimwit diaper. I beat you at my game, and now I'll beat you at yours! Eyes to the southeast, you smug hobo!" He slammed the phone down.

❧

The next day, Curly stood on the banister, hopping back and forth, murmuring blue jay nothings in exchange for unsalted peanuts in the shell. The rascal snatched a nut, took off, disappeared in a tree, behind a building, around a corner, down an alley, hid said nut, sailed back for another.

The southeast called to me like a tell-tale heart. Nothing different stood out but a small mustard-colored construction crane, as common and benign in the city as a giraffe in the savanna. I saw no man in camo on it, no sun glinting off no rifle.

The little blue gentleman returned. He had one bent tailfeather. "Curly Whirly," I said. I'd taught him a few tricks. I put a peanut in my ear, he hopped onto my shoulder, claws a-gouge, glared at me with shameless paranoia, beak-plucked the nut from my ear and pushed off. I watched him fly, as if on a rolling wave, up and down, up and down, where, a speck, he lighted on the precise crane in question.

I grabbed my replacement binos: the crane held a red pole, a slash against the white sky, and atop the pole a platform which resembled my own, with much added mass.

"No," I said.

The dot that was Curly shot in the air as the crane lowered the red pole and platform. Kerridge wasn't going to shoot me. He was going to put that pole in the earth, climb up, sit on that platform, and, from morning to night, torment me with his simple presence aloft. I watched the activity in the distance as if observing preparation for major surgery on a vital organ of my body.

"He's going up," I said. "He's going to sit."

If Malcolm Kerridge could sit on a flagpole, then anybody could. And if anybody could, then flagpole-sitting meant nothing. This was worse than if he took a shot at me.

"What am I thinking?" I said. It wasn't the going up, it was the staying up. I knew what it took to persevere up there. His urge for vengeance would not sustain him against that relentless army of urges to Get Down Now!

All you had was time, time the devourer, gnawing away any safeguard that stood between you and your fears, between you and yourself. Did Kerridge meditate? Was he capable of slowing his madhouse mind? Could he himself practice the psycho-mishmash he taught? Could he sit and watch the city for hours on end like a lizard watched the desert? Could he endure the heat, wind, rain, cold, smog, temblors, and,

worst—the unblinking monotony? With no devotées around, his tyran-
nous personality would turn on itself. He might not last a day, that bitter
little man to the southeast. I imagined him over there right that moment
yammering commands to the workers as the terror of ascending grew
within.

I wondered how, if he were indeed bankrupt, he had come up with
the funds required to pull this stunt.

"Oh yes, please go up, Malcolm," I said. "Climb that flagpole, Doctor. Give her a go. Show me how it's done."

All morning and deep into the afternoon I witnessed the implanting
of the red pole (at least a story higher than my own) and platform
(wider by half). My eyeballs bulged as I recognized the ones in charge
of Kerridge's project as none other than of Lu and Duc. I cursed those
turncoats.

Unfortunately a dark two-story office building blocked my view of
the lower section of the pole and all ground-level activity. I hadn't *seen*
the deranged charlatan himself, but it had to be him.

Through that day and the next, wielding their tools like Van Gogh
his brushes, Lu and Duc brought Kerridge's new home into creation,
a great red sunflower of iron and wood. They stocked it with enough
supplies and conveniences to fill a living room, highlighted by what
looked to be at least a 40-inch TV. "There's your blasphemy," I whispered.

Late on the third day, the one and only Dr. Malcolm Kerridge, in
what appeared to be a lemon-colored sweatsuit, made his precarious
way up an attached aluminum ladder through the trapdoor and onto the
platform. He stood and began to bounce around like Rocky with his
arms in the air. He grabbed a pair of binoculars, located me, and waved.
Peering through my own binos, I grinned and nodded and waved back.
He must have believed I was faking my joy, for he mouthed profanities
and gave me a pair of middle fingers. Rage would fuel him for a while,
but emotions, like exotic birds, come and go. I was in fact giddy with the
promise of entertainment, as well as the good doctor's simple company,
for my own sake and that of the spirits of those who had sat through
the centuries, for I was certain they were also watching. Malcolm's stay
would not last long; his inevitable failure would bring me a pure and
quiet thrill, whatever it might do for Simeon, Shipwreck, and the others.

As evening came, I watched him putter around in the ghostly light. He turned his big TV on and plopped down on a La-Z-Boy. He kept glancing over the edge as if to make sure the earth was still there. He put his hands over his face, pulled them away, looked in my direction and back at the TV. I knew precisely what he was going through, and, for that moment, I felt for him, a trembling neophyte, a scared child. I, now the seasoned veteran in flagpole living, felt naught but kinship and compassion.

85

JOE

Having endured unthinkable mutual infidelities, Clover and I were still talking, even flirting with hope and all its perils. Nate and I seemed to be reconnecting as well. Time was eroding his resentments. "I'm glad you didn't get down," he said.

I had come up fearing I would climb down flat broke, in debt, but with seventy days to go, we had accumulated a dreamload of cash, along, of course, with an expanded spiritual consciousness—by-products of doing what I loved to do and had been long called to do. And now I had a little companionship besides, and I would help him any way I could. I had learned from Shipwreck how *not* to mentor.

The phone rang. "Guess who!"

I looked to the southeast. My compadre waved across the gulf and I waved back. It felt good, truly, having someone up there with me, even him. Especially him. "Malcolm!"

"Bastards finally got my phone in."

"Welcome to the world of flagpole-sitting."

"Oh, by the way—guess how high mine is. Give up? Seventy feet. Loc and Du said that's ten feet higher than somebody else's. And I have eighty more square feet. You catch the lights, camera, action this morning?"

"I noticed some kind of ruckus."

"That was the crew from 4RealNews. Gonna be a little story about me tonight. Me and my new aerial enterprise. Guess what I'm going to do up here, Joe. Not sit on my ass and twiddle my thumbs like you, I'll tell you that. Give up? Psychotherapy."

"On yourself?"

He laughed. "Still the same droll hillbilly. No, I'm going to take your lamebrain self-obsession and squeeze a socially redeeming and lucrative enterprise out of it. I'm starting a revolutionary therapeutic regimen on high. Deviants like you will flock up here and make me rich all over again. I'll beat you at your own game. To hell with those seminars.

One-on-one on a flagpole—that's the future. I envision franchises. Fifty minutes—thousand dollars. I'll rake it in."

I'd been willing to mentor a newbie, but he was already rubbing me the wrong way. "Therapy, for a grand an hour, seventy feet in the air on a flagpole, with a bankrupt con-man in the midst of a complete mental breakdown. Sounds good to me."

"Do I look like I'm having a breakdown? Can you see me dancing over here? I'm at the top of my game! Besides, a man *has* to be crazy to deal with you lunatics."

"Well, I hope your stay is fruitful in every way."

"There's nothing to it! It's like lying on the beach at Waikiki!"

"Okay, well, looks like you got things under control over there. Have a good evening."

"What? Wait. Don't you want to talk about…things?"

"What things?"

"Well, flagpole-sitting things."

"Maybe some other time. I'm busy with my autobiography. It's the chapter on your seminar. But ring me if you get lonely and scared. I'm here for you."

I asked Clover to watch the news. Sure enough, 4Real did an interview with Kerridge, who touted his "innovative return to the world of healing—private therapy on top of a seventy-foot flagpole." He did not mention me, and neither did the interviewer, obviously a plant from Kerridge's disciple at the station. Malcolm claimed to have been inspired by "the pillar-sitters of ancient times who cured the sick and lame." He insisted that "questions" about his "financial and legal circumstances" had been "put to bed." He said, "I look forward to reclaiming my rightful place as the humble beacon of the therapeutic community."

86

Joe

On the advice of his attorney, Malcolm shut down Kerridge's Flagpole Counseling after a grand total of one patient, who simultaneously christened and buried the enterprise by vomiting all over the platform and suing the next day for ten million dollars.

The seminar master commenced calling me non-stop, spewing outrage at his fate and predicament. I listened. He jabbered and ranted and slammed the phone down, paced a while, then called back and picked up his mad rant where he'd left off.

"These slobs and their goddamn demons. I don't care anymore. Did I ever? The hell with it." He sniffed. "Still stinks like puke up here. But how can I get down? Had to shoot my mouth off, what a snap this pole shit is. Can't get down." His voice had a thousand-yard stare. "Losing my license, motley slander, idiot technicalities. And *you*! You're why I'm up here! You need to take responsibility for the consequences of your actions, man! Help me! I helped you! You are not helping me!"

This was how it was meant to be, I saw, from the beginning, how it was laid out and waiting from the beginning of time. I also saw I would do the impossible. I would love my enemy, Dr. Malcolm Kerridge.

"Malcolm, listen to me."

"I've heard it all."

"Will you listen to me?"

"Tell me one goddamn thing I don't know."

"I've been exactly where you are right now, Malcolm, and if you want to stay, you better learn fast."

"Tell me. Go, man, go."

"Acrophobia, claustrophobia, pure dread, existential nothingness, that's what awaits. Screaming vertigo, the agony of boredom, suicidal temptation."

"Jesus Christ, is this the helping part?"

"It can be a lonely living hell up here, Malcolm, but it can also be a

Heaven in the serenity it delivers. It's all part of the wondrous mystery of flagpole-sitting."

I proceeded to give him a panoramic mini-course in the arcane art and craft of sitting. I drew on every nook and cranny of my own experience, plus the wealth of knowledge instilled in me by Shipwreck. With a tenderness I did not know I had, I guided the piteous seminar master through the fears of the moment and the reefs to come, that he might begin to understand the forces at work aloft since the first caveman climbed the first tree. I described the techniques and tricks of resilience and endurance, the general maintenance of daily sanity in that little square pressure cooker on high. I marveled at the splendid array of learning I had accumulated up there, on the other poles as well, the so-called flops. I realized I had been busier, more industrious and productive than I had ever dreamed. I had been gathering spiritual sheaves, even when I felt like a deluded lummox in suspended animation. I was passing to Malcolm all I had just as Shipwreck had passed it to me. I said things that stirred myself, though I had no idea where they came from: "You have to *true* yourself to the pole. And let the sitting true you to yourself." In a strangely familiar and tender cadence and tone, an almost new voice, I articulated the insights I had gathered, about sitting, about temptation and survival, about love and death and grief.

"Do you ever get used to shitting in this chemical box?" he said.

"Did you hear anything I said?"

"Just tell me I'm having a nightmare."

I had an intuition. "Malcolm, I beseech thee—grab this opportunity to change, give up your ambition for control and power. Yield without guile to this transformative experience, and one day you will emerge lean in spirit, mental flab hewn away, and all that remains in the sun and the rain will be at last the true inner Malcolm."

I braced for a blast of cynical mockery, but instead I heard a noise that took me a moment to recognize as muffled weeping. In the binoculars he sat in the middle of the platform, his arms and legs wrapped around the top of the pole like a child.

"You know," I said, "all that scary stuff about me and my father that you blabbed on and on about so obnoxiously and sadistically at your seminar?"

He sniffled. "Yeah?"

"I've thought about all that quite often."

"You have? All my father was close to was his pigeons. He was close to the roof and the cages and the birdfeed and the tarpaper and the filthy sky over Newark. He'd come home and go straight up there. Then come down for dinner and go back up. And that was that." He was quiet again.

"I'm sorry about that, Malcolm."

"Well, everybody needs a hobby. He worked hard. He never beat me. He didn't die on me. He didn't abandon us. Hey, he certainly didn't go live on a flagpole for a year." Suddenly he howled: "Oh, somebody! Help me! Have mercy on me! Am I bound to end my days on this totem pole to human idiocy!"

I couldn't leave well enough alone. I babbled anew on the development of the sitter's consciousness, the mundane and the mystical, meditation, the sun and moon and stars, sirens, the Santa Anas, screams in the night, gunshots, car alarms, birds, the silence behind everything, dreams, my theory of flagpole communications, food, smells, distances, traffic, ants—

"Magellan, if you don't shut up, I'll jump!"

"Okay. Maybe I can't help you after all. But you're on a flagpole, Malcolm, and I'm the only one who *can* help you, if anybody can. And if I can, I'm here. Okay?"

I heard him breathing. "So, *that's* how you plan to drive me off here. By loving me." He pulled himself to his feet and shook his fist. "You'll never get me off this pole! I'll be up here long after you're gone and forgotten. Go ahead and get that record, Magellan, and then I'll pulverize it and cast it to the wind!"

He resumed the same vicious call/hang up/rant/call back cycle, desperate, then manic, then sullen. I had overestimated my determination to be there for my comrade. I hung up on him again and again, then unplugged the phone entirely. Trapped on that shrinking platform, and deprived of a target for his ranting, he watched endless television, paced, yapped to whoever he could get and keep on the phone, paced, devoured a mountain of junk food he had delivered by the hour, paced, flipped through magazines as if in a doctor's waiting room, paced, and, when he tried to sleep, flipped and flopped like a fish on a dock. I knew he was coming to know the most exquisite of the many flagpole bedevilments, the constant freedom to pop that trapdoor, climb down that ladder to the merry old ground, and end your flagpole misery in a blink.

Malcolm's despair served to heighten my serenity, as the abyss behind the moon amplifies its luminance. I felt guilty for such peace of mind, but what could I do? I was a creature who had learned to breathe in a strange new medium, and Malcolm was a fellow creature who had not, who would drown in paranoid defiance rather than learn and change and grow.

He crouched in the center of the platform and began to rub the top of his head with both hands. For twelve weekends he had tortured me, because he could, because I had to be there to save my marriage and my sanity, then he rubbed salt in my wounds at the graduation. But I could not deny my kinship with the desolate little fraud, for we were now fellow warriors on a shared quest.

In fact, by choosing to stay up and suffer, Kerridge inspired me to simplify and purify my own stay. On the fifth night of his wretched sit, I resolved to terminate my mercenary pursuits. I called Hoover and left a message: "Got some breaking news. No more commercials, no more interviews, no more sucking Mammon's rotten, maggot-ridden tit. Thanks for everything. God bless you. Farewell."

That night I snapped awake, fully alert. I looked over at Kerridge. Through the binos, in the blinding moonlight, he sat on the edge of his red platform, calmer than I'd ever seen him, his arms crossed on the banister, his chin resting on his hands, watching me.

87

CLOVER

I sat on the bed with my Bloody Mary. It was opening night of the show. Joe didn't know. He made it easy not to tell him. The more I drank, the louder the wolves of my self-doubt howled. My paintings were jokes, like he always said, abortions, faceless crap. Not that he had the balls to put it so blatantly, but I knew that's what he felt. In fact, he'd been trying to placate me lately, but his contempt for my art leaked out like black juice from a rotten potato.

Again I flirted with the fear that Sam had taken on my paintings for one reason and one reason only—to get in my pants. Well, he'd sure as fuck gotten in, hadn't he? And now I was ready to go to the show that would expose me to the world in all my deluded slut-doodling glory.

I peeked in Nate's room. He sat at his desk, absorbed in his spelling homework. He spelled aloud "brain," "cocoa," and "dynamite." I wanted to go give him a squeeze to within an inch of his life, but he'd smell the vodka. Not that he didn't know already. Not that it wasn't another item on his little unspoken list of resentments around there. I knocked on the door and stuck my head in. "I'm late, honey, bye. Wish me luck?"

He looked at me, the tip of his tongue sticking out the side of his mouth, as if he had no idea what I was talking about, which would have been the last arrow through my heart, but he remembered and his face lit a front porch. "Oh yeah, good luck, Mom. I hope it goes real good. Everybody will love your paintings. You'll sell out!"

Sam had offered to pick me up, but I drove myself. I wanted to be able to escape when the night began falling to pieces as I couldn't imagine it not.

At the show, despite Sam's noblest efforts, I began knocking back glasses of champagne, which roiled and churned with the Bloody Marys and had me on a queasy sea by the time the first swanked-up visitors sauntered through the gallery door.

88

JOE

I woke early and plugged the phone in. Kerridge was watching TV and pacing. He had cut back on his calls to me, and I wondered if Hoover might be trying to reach me to talk me out of chucking the commercials. In fact, I felt I might have been hasty in shooing the golden goose. A minute later, the phone rang. I would play hard to get, then yield. I cleared my morning throat and answered. It was Nate.

"Mom's not home."

"What do you mean?"

"From the *show*."

"What show?"

"The *painting* show!"

"When?"

"Last night!"

Oh no—she must have told me and I forgot. It hit me that Sam could be involved in this. "Did she leave a babysitter with you?"

"No."

"God damn. What time is it?"

"Six forty-two a.m."

"Is the car in the back?"

"No."

Left the kid by himself while she spent the night with a bunch of rich gallery yuppies and that fancy phony. All right, then. She had crossed the bridge of no return. I would climb down, grab the boy, go to a hotel, call a divorce lawyer, boom, she'd never know what hit her.

However, first things first, namely, lie to Nate. "Oh, wait, I remember now. She told me she was gonna spend the night at a friend's place after the show."

"Who?"

"Betty."

"Betty? I never heard of any Betty."

"Pretty sure it was Betty."

"Why didn't she tell *me* that?"

"Maybe she did and you forgot."

"She's not at any Betty's. I know where she is. Sam's."

"*Sam's*? No, no, no, no, no."

"How do you know? You don't know anything!" He hung up and didn't answer when I called back and left more slapdash lies on the machine.

Across the gulf I gazed at Kerridge, as if focusing on his frenzy might give me the relative serenity I needed to handle this fresh crisis. It did not work. His giant TV flickered and flashed as he paced and clicked through the channels. I pictured Clover in Sam's effete arms, sleeping off their debauched celebration of her show. Maybe the whole smug galleryful of in-crowders had themselves an all-night orgy, their fancy clothes strewn everywhere as they snored the morning away. Nothing in the world was stopping me from climbing down, going over to that prick's estate, marching in and standing there while those two human rats cooked in my glare. Terrified, Sam would quiver like a hare. She'd jump up, a sheet around her, rush to me, her face twisted in the agony of guilt. Instead of strangling them, I'd turn and walk out, at a measured pace. She'd stumble after me, begging, bawling. I'd be steel, ice, stone, petrified wood, concrete. She'd throw herself down in the street and I'd drive around her. I wouldn't even look at her in court. I would win Nate and return to teaching, with all my heart, with new techniques, and live a life of sorrow and wisdom, with women wanting me when I went shopping for groceries for myself and Nate, but I would be too sad for love, which would make me even more desirable. Meanwhile, Clover would send Sam packing and spend her life trying to make it up to me, maybe enter a nunnery. I would forgive her on my death bed, with my last breath, and she would soak my face and pillow with bittersweet tears of gratitude and grief.

I fumbled through the jumble for Sam's number. He answered, groggy.

"Sam," I croaked.

"Who is this?"

"Joe."

"Joe? What's wrong? What time is it? What happened? Is Clover all right?"

"How would I know?"

"She's not there? She's not home?"

"How could she be home and there at the same time?"

"*Here?* No, no, no. I followed her home after the show. Are you *certain* she's not there?"

"Why the hell would I call you if she was here? The car's not here either."

"She must be in there. I watched her walk in. Go see."

"What?"

"Stop being petulant! Get off that damnable pole and go in and see if she's there! This is serious! Go, go, go!"

Sam's words produced in me a sequence of emotional implosions from fury to mortification to dread. I began to hope she *was* at his place. "You better hope I *don't* get down, you asshole, because the first thing I'm gonna do is crack your motherfucking neck!"

"Let's back up," Sam said. "Let's catch our breath. Okay. I followed her home. She *had* been drinking."

"Drinking? Why'd you let her drive, you halfwit!"

"Unfair. You know how she behaves when she's been drinking." No, I didn't. "I imagine I could have stopped her with physical force, but violence against women, even if unruly, is not in my repertoire."

"When did she leave?"

"About...ten."

"Ten! Jesus Christ, man! We gotta call the hospitals. I am getting down."

"Hold on—it's my other line." He clicked over.

"Oh, please, God," I said, "let it be her. I beg you. Let her be all right. I'll forgive everything! *I'll* join a nunnery!" Life without her reached for me from the abyss.

"Joe," Sam said. "It's Clover. She's okay. I'll call you back."

89

CLOVER

I woke to the crash of an iron door. I sat up on a sagging bunk and the room swam, a big room full of women and bunks. It was a jail.

I was in jail! How did I get in jail!

My head rocked, pain jabbed my ribs. I thought I smelled shit, it was my breath.

My last memory: throwing up on a woman who had purchased one of my paintings. After that, nothing. My heart thrashed like a cat in a breadbox. I touched my face, found scratches, dried blood, sore spots, on my arms as well. I stood to see if I could, I could, I sat right back down.

Shards of the night clawed through my hangover: vomiting, a fuss, driving home, Sam followed me, I went in, I went back out for more booze, went off a road, hit something, glass broke, darkness, lights, voices, arms, hands, sirens, black out.

I got to my feet like an old woman. One leg jerked out wildly and I stumbled. Somebody cackled. I remembered how to will myself not to vomit. A cop sat at a desk outside the bars. "Sir? Could you tell me what happened to me? Magellan? Clover?"

He shuffled papers. "DUI. Reckless driving. Destruction of property."

I closed and opened my eyes. "Did I hurt anybody?"

He shook his head. "Killed a fence."

"Was anybody with me?"

"All alone."

I leaned against the cold, greasy bars and thanked Jesus for that one unrepayable mercy. I thought of Nate, but I had one call, and Nate couldn't bail me out. If I called Joe and he got down to bail me out, he'd hate me. And if I called him and he *didn't* get down, *I'd* hate *him*. He'd freak out if I called Sam, but who else could I call who wouldn't have to break the bank to get the bail. And God knew what the bail was.

90

JOE

Sam called me back with a rundown of Clover's night. I burned with gratitude that she wasn't dead or worse, and burned with gall that she had called Sam.

"She had one call and I was the only reasonable choice," my wife's lover informed me. "How could she call you? If you climbed down early for her, she'd never forgive herself. Frankly, that record at this moment of crisis, its absurdity cannot be measured. Now, I feel rather uncomfortable with this next item, but I'm conveying it to you at her command. She wants you to tell Nate that she spent the night at Laura's. Laura was another artist in the show. She asks that you tell Nate she was too tired to drive home after the stress and excitement of the opening."

"Laura's," I said.

"I'm merely relaying her request. It's up to you."

"What about the car?"

"'Totaled' was the term she employed. In any case, I'm going down now to bail her out."

I hung up and called Nate and told him the lie.

"Now it's Laura's? You said Betty's."

"Well, she wasn't at Sam's."

"Who said?"

"Sam."

"How do you know he's telling the truth?"

"How does anybody know anything?"

"Oh, sheesh."

Sam pulled up in a black BMW, Clover struggled out like a ninety-year-old woman, tottered inside, and Sam took off.

I called, she wouldn't answer. I paced like a beast in a clearing. Kerridge sat in his La-Z-Boy with his binos aimed my way.

She called. "I'm glad you're all right," I said. "It was nice to hear it from *him*."

"I had one call. Were *you* gonna come down and bail me out?"

"I was insane with worry up here, Clover."

"I'm sorry. I sold five paintings at the show."

"Jesus. Congratulations."

"Of course it'll all go to a lawyer."

"I told Nate you were at Laura's, by the way."

"I told him the truth."

"*What?*"

"He'd find out anyway."

"Did you tell him it was your goddamn idea that I lie to him?"

"It didn't come up. What's more important, the mess that happened to me, or your stupid little lie?"

"It's *your* stupid little lie. And the mess didn't *happen* to you. You happened to *it.*"

"Jesus Christ, you think I *tried* to have an accident?"

"I'm just saying that for somebody who just got out of jail for drunk driving, especially considering what you did years ago that cost a human being their life, you might consider not being such a self-centered rationalizing nasty *bitch.*"

She slammed the phone down.

❧

Nate called me after school.

"Are you getting a divorce?" he said.

"No. Why, did she say something?"

"Just how she's not gonna take it anymore."

"Take what? Drunk driving laws?"

"She said you called her bitch. She said don't ever call a woman bitch."

I ground my teeth. "That's good advice."

"I wish you were down here."

"You want me to get down?"

"Quit asking me that. Just 'cause I wish you were down here doesn't mean I want you to get down. Dad? Is Mom gonna be okay?"

A lie poised to leap like a toad from my tongue, like all the lies people told me when my mother commenced her madward slide. "If I *have* to get down," I said, "I will."

"Dad?" Jesus, *every* question was terrifying now. "Can you see a long ways up there?"

My entire being sagged with relief. "Yes. You can. In every direction."

"How far?"

"Well, the platform's so small, and you can't see what's holding you up, so it feels like you're higher than you are, and that you're seeing a lot farther than you're seeing."

"Can you see five miles?"

"Lot farther than that. You forget things like miles. Your mind grows different ways of seeing up here. Sometimes everything is so far away it's like nothing is there at all. Sometimes everything's so close you could grab the snow on Mount Baldy and make a snowball."

"Make a snowball. I bet I'd like to see it some time. See what it's like up there."

Was he tempting me to ask him to come up again? So he could turn me down again? Maybe it was his way of paying me back for my fatherly failings. I couldn't handle another rejection right then. If he wanted to come up, he'd have to ask.

"Do you want to come up?" I said.

"I don't think it would be a good time right now," he said.

91

JOE

Hoover finally called me back. "I'm ready to sign long-term with Secret," I said. "Show me the dotted line."

"Uh, yeah, unfortunately, amigo," Hoover said, clearing his throat, "I'm picturing the dotted line Clover had to sign to get out of jail for driving drunk into a ditch."

"What? Where'd you hear that?"

"*Times* guy tracked it down, called me. Story in 'Metro' tomorrow."

"Oh, my God. Oh, Clover. And those goddamn kids'll eat Nate alive."

"Yeah. Yeah. Far as Secret goes, my friend, I did my best, but... you're horsemeat."

"*Why*? What the hell does Secret care what somebody's wife is up to?"

"Well, they don't want folks reaching for their candy bar thinking, 'Drunk driving, automobile accidents, broken bones, marital problems.' Those are *not* candy thoughts."

"Broken bones? What broken bones?"

"Didn't she break a couple ribs? That's what I heard. In any case, pard, believe me, I played every string on my violin. Nothing doing. In fact, they pulled the one you did. Hey, my other line's blinking, bud."

"Well, wait a minute—what-what-what else can you get me? What about my book?"

"What book?"

"*Adventures of a Damn American Pole-Sitter* or whatever."

"I'll have to get back to you on that, chief. Keep your chin up."

And thus the miracle of making money flagpole-sitting came to a screeching halt. Our lives and livelihood had fallen back into the drunken clammy hands of a woman swinging by a fraying thread.

Before I could begin to digest this skyburst of bad news, a man in a dark blue suit called to me from below. He carried an attaché case and a fancy red shopping bag. I lowered him a walkie-talkie and discovered him to be John Tipton, the executor for the estate of the late Walter Shipwreck Blake. Mr. Tipton claimed to have sent me a letter, which I informed him I had not received.

"You're a beneficiary of Mr. Blake's estate," Mr. Tipton informed me.

This piece of information detonated in my consciousness like a sun of molten gold. Tipton rattled on but my heart raced into the future at the speed of greed. God knew how loaded Shipwreck had been, and as central a spot as I occupied in his life, the entire estate might have been headed my way. I was in for a killing. I would never have to work again. I might start my own school and teach for free, for the sheer thrill of it. I would be my technique, me, unleashed. My life for the first time, the Magellans' life for the first time, would be nothing but freedom to do and be as we pleased.

Tipton placed the bag in the basket. "Mr. Blake has included an explanation with each item. I do need to secure your signature, sir." He included in the basket some papers and a pen from his attaché case.

I hauled it up like a treasure chest from the bottom of the sea. I glanced in the bag— one big box and one small one—skimmed the paper, signed it, and lowered it back to Tipton.

"Please read and honor Mr. Blake's instructions. Thank you and have a good day." Tipton dropped the walkie-talkie in the basket and went on his gentlemanly way.

I closed the trapdoor and sat in the rocking chair, the red shopping bag on my lap. I watched Tipton climb in a Mercedes up Western and pull away. I would buy a humble new VW Beetle with my inheritance. I would be filthy rich, but nobody would know it, and when I died and they found out, they would admire me for my remarkable modesty.

The smaller item in the bag was white, the size of a ring box, with a red ribbon. I supposed there could be a check in it, if the check were folded up, which was exactly the kind of posthumous Zen clowning around Shipwreck would go for. Or a deed to a house, a mansion, a chateau in France. I would quietly sell it and we would acquire a more humble abode.

The big box was wrapped in heavy brown shipping paper, the size of a toaster. It had not only physical heft, but gravitas. It would more likely be the one with deeds, keys, jewelry, gold.

I took a breath and tore open the small box. Inside, sitting on a square of cotton, was the little polished piece of dark gray stone that Shipwreck had worn around his neck, attached to its gold chain.

I sat there and looked at the measly pebble, turned it over, rolled it around in my fingers. I gave it a sniff. It smelled like an old brass doorknob. God knew where it had been. The chain could be worth something, if it *was* gold. I looked under the cotton—a piece of folded-up paper sat there! I unfolded it—not a check, nor a deed—but a brief note from Shipwreck:

Dear Joe,
This is a chip of Simeon's pillar in Turkey. Yes, the pillar he sat on for thirty years. Yes, the pillar Tennyson was writing about. Don't worry how I came by it. It's a long story and I have no time.
Fondly,
Walter

"This is from the fourteenth century?" I said. "From Simeon's actual pillar?"

I closed my hand around it. I tried to feel something through the centuries. It had no authenticating paperwork with it; whatever it was worth would be in the mind of the beholder. I slipped it back in the little box and replaced the lid.

That left the big box. I pulled it out of the bag and held it in my lap. It had to weigh ten pounds. More than a pebble awaited in there. I broke the tape on the shipping paper and unwrapped it. It was a simple mahogany box, with a hook-latch in front, and a small envelope taped to the top with "For Joe" on it in elaborate scroll. I opened the envelope and read the hand-written card inside:

Dear Joe,
God bless you. You're holding my ashes. Spread them from up there after you break my record.
Thanks,
Walter

92

JOE

Clover walked so slowly out of the Patch she could have been underwater. She could have been ready to walk off the edge of the world. I lowered the walkie-talkie. She removed it from the basket and placed my breakfast inside.

"Was it in the paper?" I said.

She nodded. She didn't look up.

"Do you want me to get down?"

She looked up Western to the hills over which the shadows of clouds swept. "The thought of you getting down now scares me more than anything. Isn't that crazy? You being up there is the only thing holding everything together. Isn't that funny?"

93

Nate

I got off the bus but I didn't go into school. I went across the street down to Newberry's. I made a beeline for the sunglass rack. I put on a pair with the price tag hanging down and walked right out. It was the "Crazy Days Sale" week. A man had on a hobo costume that stopped me outside. He grabbed my elbow and pulled me back in. I let him do it. All the sales workers were dressed up like other type of dickheads. Muscle men and nurses and a joke man in the colors suit that the king gets mad at. It made it like a nightmare you couldn't get up out of.

The cops took me to the station and called Mom. They took it easy because I was choking and crying. Mom had on sunglasses and a black scarf when she got there. She lied. She told the cops when Dad got hold of me I will have wished they'd locked me up and thrown away the key. I said Dad didn't have that long of arms, and I laughed through my nose. The cops looked at each other, and Mom grabbed my hand and dragged me out.

94

CLOVER

I'd taken enough psychology to know that adolescent shoplifting was rooted in anger, and that anger masked pain and shame. But my trouncing hangover deprived me of the desire or ability to apply that knowledge to the real world. The last thing I wanted was to explore the cause of Nate's anger, pain, and shame. It was all I could do to drive him home without vomiting out the window.

"This is a one-shot deal, right?" I said. Nate nodded. "Have you done it before?" He waited, then shook his head. "Will you do it again?" Another wait, another shake. "Well, then, we don't have to tell Daddy."

He sat there, peering ahead, his jaw like a bear trap.

95

JOE

I meditated, expecting nothing. I had not yet been informed that my son was a thief, but with other predicaments dropping like bowling pins on the tin roof of my mind, it would have been an achievement to simply sit still for five minutes.

I was dumbfounded, then, when the meditation advanced effortlessly from breath one. My troubles offered no resistance, scattering like leaves. Time slowed, worries crumbled, my chi rose through my chakras, bliss shimmered like a forehead ruby. A man with no hope of inner peace had lulled the gates of serenity off their hinges.

When I opened my eyes, the city presented herself to me as a bride, her beguiling wares laid forth for my perusal. The green sea of the Hollywood Hills leapt and dropped along the northern line, littered with mansions, and litter in the long gutters of Western sparkled like patches of snow. Miracles of freeways, speeding machines, wires, streetlights, billboards—all forms of longing, of reaching, under a sky as pale as Venus's belly as she stepped from the sea. Every human activity and drive, even greed and violence, I saw, were nothing but attempts to connect, to lose one's dreadful self, however perverse, insane, or barbaric.

Malcolm was jumping up and down and waving his arms in the corner of my eye.

"More people have died than are alive," I said.

In some sort of mad serenity, I turned to my fellow sitter, across the great divide, my brother Malcolm, still waving and hopping. I plugged the phone in. It rang.

"Seen the *Times*?" said Malcolm. "Big story on your wife's drunken scandal. Be all over TV tonight. Ain't life a bitch?"

"Malcolm, reveling in an event that brings agony to an innocent child does not put you on the side of the angels."

"What, your kid? I didn't bring your kid a *dime* of agony. Not a *nickel*. Look to the flagpole-sitter on that score."

"You might summon a little compassion for a fellow sitter."

"I'm no fellow anything. I'm up here to show the world there's nothing to it. To laugh in your arrogant face. And I'm loving every minute. And now your drunken artiste wife crashes that orange tincan through a fence." He released the laughter of demons.

"Remember, Malcolm, and I hate to say it, but things happen on a pole."

"What *things?*"

"Like it or not, you're one of us now, Malcolm."

"I'm not one of nobody!"

"Talk to you later, my brother."

96

JOE

I'd be damned if I'd let Sam find Clover a lawyer. I had to stand up and reclaim my own wife, even if she was no damn good. I called Jinx. With his shady business entanglements, he had to have a tough lawyer in the wings. What was the world coming to when the only human being you could trust, the only person with principles you knew, was a transvestite pornographer named Jinx?

He was glad to give a recommendation. "She ain't cheap."

"She?"

"You have something against women lawyers?" I had to stop to remember what gender Jinx was. He gave me the number. "Is Clover still not drinking?"

"So she says. Who knows? I'm on Neptune up here. Maybe you could talk to her?"

"Sure."

"Then maybe call me after?"

He ignored that last. That's the problem with people who put principles over loyalty.

"How's little Nate handling all this?"

The hook of those words "little Nate" tore across my heart. "The kids are riding him, but he's toughening up."

"Yeah?"

"Oh, man, how can I stay up here, for God's sake?"

"How can you get down, for God's sake?"

"I can just climb down!"

"This late in the game? You'd derail the whole space-time continuum."

"What a father I am."

"I wish mine had lived his whole life on a friggin' flagpole."

"Thanks." In turn I thought to show some interest in him. "How are *you* doing?"

"Don't ask."

"Business trouble?"

"Business is tops. It's a man, sweetheart."

"Oh. Do you tell people right away what your deal is?"

"If I suspect they don't know."

"*I* didn't know. You didn't tell *me*."

He laughed. "I knew nothing would happen. Despite your flirting."

"I wasn't flirting with you, but if you thought I was, then obviously I didn't know you weren't a woman, so you should have told me."

"Well, I knew you were just a married man stretching his wings. Seeing if he still had it. And he does. But I won't tell."

This was going pretty well. "So, you have relationship trouble."

"Yes. I have a wanderer on my hands."

"Cheater? Dump him."

"Short and sweet!"

We laughed.

"Stay up there!" Jinx said. "The rest will come out in the wash."

97

Jinx

Clover was always out or busy or said she'd call me back and didn't. So I slipped in in the middle of a poetry reading and stood in the back. It was packed, smoky, candle-lit. I looked around for Clover while a young man in black with a shaved head rumbled into the microphone:

"I slammed on the brakes and her forehead slammed the windshield. I fucked her cousin. I lived off her babysitting a blind boy. I drank and hit her after she slapped me after I pushed her after she called me a lazy freeloader. I sort of raped her in the old days. I masturbated in the bathroom while she practiced her cello. I fantasized killing myself if she died. I ran a red light. I heard her going crazy in her voice and tried to joke as the blood started down her face. I didn't try to joke. I judged her for letting her forehead go into the windshield. I judged her for letting her forehead go into the windshield. I judged her for letting her forehead go into the windshield. Thank you."

The place went nuts. What the bloody frigging fruck. My drunken lunatic father could have written that poem, if he knew how to write. Lucky for me, that was the last poem of the night.

Clover lurked in a corner, lighting a cigarette with the butt of the last one. She appeared delighted to see me. "Jinx!" She grabbed my hand and dragged me upstairs. It was not the first time I had seen this phenomenon—a person who at first shunned me like pond scum later glommed onto me like long-lost kin.

"It's hopping down there," I said.

"It's a loony bin." Clover headed for the kitchen. "Want a drink?"

"Tea'd be nice."

"Yuck. I need the real deal after that bilge."

The apartment wasn't much. She had put a lot more into the coffee-house than the living quarters. I watched her open and close cabinets and drawers.

"Well, you're doing good business."

"Oh yeah, we're rolling in the green. Solana started charging for the readings and music, instead of passing the hat. Come on, don't make me drink alone. Let's have fun!"

"I'll pass. Have to drive to the valley early."

She stopped. "We'll have tea." She grabbed the teabags, then paused. "Oh, hell." She dropped a teabag in a cup and grabbed the vodka bottle. "Why is everybody making a big deal out of this?"

"Out of what?"

She poured a hefty glass of vodka and opened the fridge. "All I did was bump a fence with a crappy little car that belonged on the junk heap years ago. Nobody cares I sold five paintings. Seven, now."

"I care. I told you it was wonderful."

"I know, you did, I know." She topped the vodka with orange juice and held her hand sideways to her mouth. "I'm buying a car."

"Well, you need one."

"A *new* one, which I know I can trust you not to tell Mr. You-know-who Skinflint." She pulled her cigarettes out, lit one up, and started to take a drink with the cigarette still in her mouth.

"Girl, you're gonna spin off into outer space."

"Big relief for everybody if I did." She took another swig of her screwdriver and a hefty intake of death smoke. I got up, grabbed her by the shoulders, steered her to a seat at the kitchen table, took her drink and set it down, then her cigarette and crushed it out. "Hey!" she said. "Hey!"

I sat beside her. "Clover. I know what you're going through."

"How could you possibly know what I'm going through?"

"The drinking. Believe me, I know."

"I don't have a drinking problem! I didn't drink for fourteen years!"

"And why didn't you drink for fourteen years?"

She looked off to one side, into the past, wept, and let me hold her.

98

JOE

Clover and I were discussing the lawyer Jinx found for her. Clover says, "Oh, she said don't worry about the shoplifting." I said, "You're shoplifting?" "Oops," she said.

She said not telling me about Nate's arrest was tit-for-tat for me not telling her about Nate's flagpole-climbing. No charges, no record, he swore he'd never do it again. I believe him. After my father died, I shoplifted (a Duncan Super Tournament Top), got caught & never did it again.

She sold all ten paintings in the show, plus five she had stuffed in her closet & hadn't framed yet. Notoriety from the drunk driving fiasco proved a boon to her art. The vultures snatched every faceless masterpiece like flapjacks off the grill. With all the bitterness about, it hurts to be happy for her, which hurts worse. She's not that excited herself—a sign of conscience?

It's a minefield between Nate & me. Like spies communicating in Morse code. Man code we make up as we go. We talked about the shoplifting. He was properly rueful & I properly dished out the warnings & wisdoms. But of the dark lurking shapes of things under it all, we steered clear.

She bought a car. A big fat fucking shiny black Buick. BRAND NEW! "I see you got a rental." "I bought it." "No." "Yes." "You're kidding." "Why would I kid about something like that?" "How much was it?" "A lot." My head's still spinning.

WHAT CAN I DO ABOUT IT? For all I know, we could be dead broke, she could be conjoining nightly covens, planning to sacrifice Nate on one of the picnic tables. Jinx could be in on it, along with everybody up & down revitalized Western.

Who can you trust? Besides Curly my wild little blue jay colleague. I don't trust him to be there for me, but when he is there, I trust him to be 100% himself. Or herself. Cold truth in blue feathers. Terror shines in his beady eyes. All he wants is that peanut & never pretends otherwise. One human action out of ten trillion *might* be so free of subterfuge.

99

JOE

Clover's Buick sat in the driveway in a glaze of dew, shiny as a fresh plum. Good for her. After all, what was money for? I was sick and tired of worrying about crap I couldn't do a damn thing about. She emerged with my breakfast in hand. I beheld her. She was still giving me my daily bread, after all I'd done and left undone. It was powerful circumstantial evidence that Creation in at least one particular was indeed good, as God was said to have proclaimed. I called her name. She looked up, guileless and ardent at once, sleek red hair, blue eyes, and lime-spring dress, solid little body with a mind of its own, bright face shining my way like the light at the end of the tunnel.

 I had barely two months left up there. On my little desk a hot cup of Clover's strong black coffee steamed away, filling my nostrils with the aroma of earth and caffeine and hope.

A man, woman, and child holding hands on Western stopped in the shade of an awning to look in the window of World of Candy. Perhaps it was the most wonderful moment in their lives.

I had been opening to books again through some mysteriously evolving conversion. Dipping into a story here, a chapter there, a random verbal string I found myself lingering upon. Kafka, Hawthorne, Flannery O'Connor, Heraclitus, Jung, Dickinson, Hugo, Singer, Cervantes, Shirley Jackson. I took in an image or phrase or entire sentence and a little bell would go off and I'd look up and cast my imagination into the city like a fishing line. That was all I could handle, all I needed for the moment. It was good to have that happening, perfect, to have that fine little development playing in me.

Malcolm, astoundingly, remained aloft, if by a thread. At the moment he was pacing in red underwear and a Ramar of the Jungle pith helmet. The underpants were no doubt meant to mock my loincloth, which I had recently replaced with my trusty old Levis. I was Joe, not Mahatma.

The air was warm, rich, close, a greenhouse. Curly sat atop a lamp-post one street over, flitting like a pilot light. Traffic surged through the artery of Western, muted to a rustle in the heavy air. Mashed potatoey clouds tumbled before an aluminum sky. Some kind of middle distance construction to the south, in the direction opposite from Malcolm, barely registered. On a side street a young man rode a bicycle up on a lawn and fell over. The air stood musky as compost. Not a single leaf moved.

I had the feeling I had forgotten some momentous appointment and now it was too late. I lifted my binoculars to Kerridge, moved them southward until the hurly burly of crane and men and material to the south jumped into view. Zooming in, I saw the crane hoisting a flagpole with platform attached. My heart thumped in my head like noises from a closet. I recognized the man running the crane—Lu—and the man riding the platform—Duc.

Somebody else was going up.

There would be three.

I swooned; my stomach grabbed itself. Then I thought, If my quest is defileable, Malcolm has already defiled it. I was up and would stay up, regardless. What did one more fool matter?

But what if this fresh sitter was no fool? What if—? No. I had set a singular goal for myself, I would soon accomplish it, and even if some interloper climbed forth and topped it, it would remain an essential and wonderful fact in my life. Did Simeon care about the Guinness Book? The record had never been anything but a worm on a hook. It got me up, it kept me going. Not that it was mine to give, but if this new entity wanted the record and had what it took, welcome to it, sir or madam, welcome to it.

Accordingly, the event-in-progress filled me with a Christmas-morning-like thrill. All was enlivened. I thought of Shipwreck. I thought of Simeon. I needed to talk with somebody who understood. I dialed and watched through the binos as Malcolm grabbed the phone like a mongoose grabbing a rattlesnake.

"We got company, brother. Look to my left."

"Your left, which would be my right. What am I looking for? Oh. What are they doing? That's those Vietnamese! They're putting a pole up! They're putting a pole up." He looked across the gulf at me. "We can't let them! We have to do something! They'll ruin everything."

I laughed at his innocence. "What'll they ruin?"

"Are you playing dumb? We can't just let any asshole up here! It's the beginning of the end!" He looked through the binos at the third pole. "Oh," he said. "I see. It all makes sense now."

"What makes sense now? Malcolm? What makes sense now.?"

"It's fine," he said. "I need sleep. Good night, Joe."

100

JOE

Yodeling sirens woke me. You get used to them up there. I turned over, poked my earplugs deeper. The squalling converged in the near distance and stopped. I remembered Malcolm's "It all makes sense now." I sat up. Flashing red and blue lights under his pole illuminated the overcast. A circling helicopter poured its spotlight upon his platform.

I grabbed the binos just as Malcolm, bright naked, shoved his La-Z-Boy right through the balustrade. I reached for my phone as he lifted and flung his big-screen over the edge. "Don't jump, Malcolm," I whispered. "Please don't jump."

Through the mishmash of emergency lights from above and below, a fire ladder rose to the platform. Two figures in yellow raced up with a stretcher and leapt onto the platform. Malcolm hurled what looked like a full-length mirror, the two interlopers ducked, the mirror shattered in an instant of red, white, and blue shards. They wrestled Malcolm to the platform, fastened him to the stretcher, and had him down the ladder, into the rescue truck and away in what couldn't have been more than three minutes.

Astonished, stricken, I knelt to pray for my fallen comrade:

"Please protect Malcolm. He's lost his mind getting revenge for something I believe you want me to do. He couldn't help it any more than I can. I'm grateful for his brief company. Please give the poor wretch solace and loving care, if you will. I miss him already. Amen."

101

The third sitter, it turned out, was no spiritual brother, no companion of the mystical quest, but rather Eliot Menlo, a member of the sales staff of Stan Anderson Cadillac. Anderson, a local millionaire car dealer, had followed the adventures of both Joe and Malcolm, and envisioned the flagpole-sitting as a brilliant unmined marketing treasure. He had a pole and platform installed in front of his lot on La Brea, and, amid fanfare, balloons and searchlights, sent Eliot up to stay until one thousand Cadillacs were sold by his ten franchises sprinkled through the Southwest. Anderson's plan: one thousand customers would be inspired to purchase a thirty-thousand-dollar automobile so that a salesman might get down from a flagpole.

Eliot threw in the towel on day two, quit his job, stole one of Anderson's Caddies, got drunk and drove it into the ocean off Malibu.

Anderson had the pole torn down the next morning and Joe, once more, sat alone.

102

JOE

Jinx's lawyer wanted five grand up front, and in return guaranteed Clover traffic school, probation, and a handful of AA meetings, which was precisely what she received. Her night out cost us twenty grand, including the fifteen thou that Clover finally revealed as the price tag on the Buick. These expenditures brought a three-day tic to my eyelid. Agonizing over the money the ordeal had drained from our savings eased some of my shame for not being there for her. She assured me she had been fine in court alone. In fact, she had turned down an offer from Jinx to keep her company. The plea had been set and signed beforehand, she explained, and she had passed the time in court reading a book.

I hoped she *had* been alone. I could see Sam's arm around her, whispering little courtroom nothings, maybe peddling a painting to some bailiff during a break.

"What were you reading?"

"The Big Book. *Alcoholics Anonymous*. Recommended by my lawyer."

"Been to any meetings yet?"

"You don't really have to go. You can sign the court card yourself, scribble some name in there. A woman told me in court."

"What woman?"

"She'd been through it before."

"Oh, legal advice from another drunk driver. If the judge tells you to go to the meetings, Clover, I think it might be a good idea to go to the meetings."

"It was bad enough pretending to read the book."

"Would you rather go to jail or go to the meetings? ...Clover?"

"I'm thinking, I'm thinking."

103

JOE

Nate called me to announce, "I'm getting a PhD."

"Good for you. In what?"

"Anything that you make whole lots of money in to buy a mansion with a moat and armed guards and pit bulls and an electric fence."

"That's how you want to live?"

"You tell me think for myself."

"How is armed guards and pit bulls thinking for yourself?"

"Everybody wants a big house nobody can get in. Anyway, I don't care what you think."

"I didn't say how I think. I just asked you a question."

"I don't care what anybody thinks."

"You know, people who say they don't care what anybody thinks are just trying to get people to think they're great for not caring what people think."

"Huh? Do *you* care what people think?"

"Some people. You. Mom."

"Ha. Me and Mom didn't want you to even go up there."

"Well, a person can care what people think, but that doesn't mean he's going to live his life based on what they think."

"Then why care what people think if you're gonna do what you want anyway?"

"Because what somebody thinks might help you decide what you think yourself. No man is an island. You ever hear of that?"

"Can I come up?"

"What?"

"Can I come up?"

"Up *here*? When?"

"Now. You asked me to before."

The platform shrank around me. He'd had his chance to come up, him and Clover both.

"Hmm," I said. I picked up the little white box, took the stone out and held it in my palm. I closed my eyes and squeezed the stone. I could feel all of time in it, as if it had come from a star.

"Sure," I said. "Come on up."

He hardly said a word. He moved slowly around the edge, one hand on the banister. He drank it in. It was a day you could see clear to China. I watched him and tried to see it as he saw it, all brand new.

He went all the way around and stopped where he had started. He turned and ran his eyes slowly, meticulously, over each of my meager pole belongings. I blushed. Then he turned back and worked around the banister the other way, gazing into the distances, stopping to study several things or areas in particular, without a word.

Done, he looked at me and blinked, winced, as if I'd intruded on his experience. "Thanks, Dad." He stared at my bare feet. "What?" I said. "You're on the thing." I was standing on the closed trapdoor. "That's it?" I said. He nodded.

I called him afterward. "You didn't say if you liked it." "It was different." "Different than what?" "Than what I thought it would be." "How did you think it would be?" "I don't remember, now I was up there. It's so open. You're all by yourself. Well, you were there." "Not much longer." "It was like a wood cloud. So *open.*"

104

CLOVER

I felt better driving to my first AA meeting in a new Buick than I would have in the old Bug. I practiced sneers in the rearview mirror. I smirked. I glared. My mask for these twenty stupid, degrading, court-ordered meetings would be so thick with contempt that when I walked in the room those do-gooders would not dare look me in the eye, much less come at me with that twelve-step claptrap.

The power of rushing along in that sparkling black Buick, Rod Stewart's "Young Turks" blasting on the radio, put me in a mood to take no shit from nobody. Oh, I hoped those squares would try something, those brainwashed zombies. I would go to their meetings, and after that, sayonara. I remembered those AAers waltzing into prison to sow their humble-smug platitudes, and an hour later sauntering out free, back to their cozy little hillside homes.

I parked and moved up the walk toward the open door out of which light poured from a little room jammed with a laughing, jabbering mob. God, if I ever needed a drink. I would have come loaded but feared they'd give me a breathalyzer.

I stopped outside, pretending to look for something in my purse. Actually I was looking for something—that mask of contempt. Okay, try casual, I thought, but there was no casual in there, either. Nothing but naked jackrabbit terror.

I stepped into the room as if into an alternate dimension. The AAers welcomed me with Stepford grins. Woozy, sweaty, breathless, mumbling, a spy in the house of sobriety, I managed to pour myself a styrofoam cup of black coffee. They had me penned in next to the refreshment table. Their giddy gibberish swarmed in my head like insect static. I opened my mouth to gulp the thinning air. The lights stung my eyeballs. Oh, Floor, I prayed, open up, swallow me! Better yet, Let the whole world end right now!

I had manslaughtered my boyfriend, survived a year in prison, buried my parents, and endured childbirth, marriage to Joe and his damn poles, and cheating on each other. What harm could a bunch of simple-minded boozers do me?

I spotted an empty seat in the back corner against the wall but some smiling doofus sauntered across the room and cut me off at the pass. He looked like he knew me.

"I'm Roy," he said, offering his hand.

"Hi, I'm Clover." Damn! I'd planned to lie about everything.

"Clover," he repeated, "Clover," nodding. "We better get seats." He guided me to two chairs in the middle of the room and sat next to me. "First meeting?" he asked.

"It shows?"

"Little bit. We were all there once," said the zombie to the human being.

I surveyed the hive of happy chatterers. "Hard to believe."

Roy laughed easily. "It takes a little time, a little work. It's worth it. You'll see. If you stick around. I hope you do. I hope we all do." He was a pleasant babbler. Anything beat sitting alone in that hotbox of crusaders.

Some other nerd moseyed up, Roy introduced us, and the two men talked quietly. Roy kept turning to me so I wouldn't feel left out. I drank my coffee and studied the side of his face, his eyelashes, his smile, how he tipped his head and nodded as he listened, the easy swirl of his earnestness and humor. I let myself imagine I knew him, and liked him, trusted him. I thought about how it would feel to fall in love with him. I idly compared him to Joe, to Joe and Sam. In fact, he seemed a nice mix of the best of both, more serene than Joe, more natural than Sam, with Sam's ability to focus on me, without the glomming, and Joe's presence, without the intensity.

So, not only had Plan A—utter contempt—gone down the drain, here I was swooning at the first hint of male human decency.

The other man left and here came barging up a large woman in a fisherman's hat. Roy slipped me his card.

"Roy, what are you up to?" the woman said. She got him up and took his seat. "The women stick with the women," she whispered to me. "I'm Emmylou." For some reason I was unrattled by big loud Emmylou. She took Roy's card, crossed his number out, not heavily enough for me to not make it out, and wrote hers on the back. Over her shoulder I watched Roy gladhand his way around the room, glancing back at me a couple times. Maybe my brief detour through AA wouldn't be so dreadful after all. I could play the game for twenty of these silly socials. Emmylou chattered on, patting my arm now and then.

A bigger surprise, the meeting itself proved rather entertaining. It was a spirited event, full of funny, poignant stories about both boozing and sobriety. Who knew how much of it was true, but it was certainly more involving than *Love Boat* or *Three's Company*, which I would have been otherwise watching, drunk.

Afterward, Emmylou invited me out for coffee with some other AAers, but Roy was not among the gathering cluster and I declined, lying about a sick son. I drove home in a pink cloud, distracted myself puttering around the Patch, chatted absent-mindedly with some regulars, and got in everybody's way until Solana shooed me upstairs.

Still bent over his homework, Nate barely looked up. We said hi. I should talk to him, I thought, ask him about his life, connect. But how bad could things be, as industriously as he was applying himself in school, and he had that new friend Freddy, Teddy, a little too sure of himself, but a bright, charming lad.

I sat on the bed by the phone and studied Roy's card. It said he installed aquariums. I considered where an aquarium might go in the coffeehouse. Maybe he'd heard of Clover's Patch and would be impressed that I owned it. There were good, healthy, innocent reasons to call—questions about AA, how the meeting was, getting a sponsor, etc. Nothing was going to happen. I waited a while, not so long as to start thinking about a drink, and picked up the phone.

105

Joe

I was mostly happy without a TV. You get the urge, and the pain of not having the urge satisfied, but they pass. Gratefully, I had begun to reconnect with my old friends, namely, books. I was presently reading the inimitable Thomas Hardy's *Jude the Obscure* ("Perhaps there was no great sin in a woman adding to her hair, and he resolved to think no more of it.").

However, my curiosity led me to borrow a little TV from Clover, for one hour, to watch back-to-back interviews with Malcolm Kerridge and Eliot Menlo on 4RealNews, concerning their brief adventures in the flagpole-sitting trade.

Malcolm was interviewed in a blue bathrobe on the grounds of Vistaview Psychiatric Hospital; Eliot from a cell in county jail.

Malcolm described his stay on the pole as a time of "unmitigated joy," except for the descent. And of that tumultuous descent: "A bee stung me, I'm allergic."

A nurse reached over to fix his bathrobe, which had parted on his ivory beachball of a paunch. "Stop that!" Kerridge snapped. "Let them see!" His eyes went wet and crazy. He spoke into the camera, defiantly holding forth his naked belly. "This is the toll a lifetime of curing you has cost me! Yes, I'm pregnant! Pregnant with your twins, Neglect and Cruelty!" He turned back to the interviewer. "When I recover from my allergic reaction, I'm going back up that flagpole and stay as long as I can endure the bliss. It's absolutely the easiest mindless fun a man can have in a world where imbeciles run free. Anybody can live on a pole. There's nothing easier, nothing more fun!"

After a commercial for Forest Lawn, they brought on Eliot Menlo, the former Cadillac salesman.

"One night I was drunk," Eliot said. "I laid there looking at a big fat moon. I had a girl up there, to be honest. We was flying high. The moon had one of those weird rings around it. I was tripping on it, and all of a sudden, the man in the moon turned into the Reverend Jerry Falwell.

The reverend was wigwagging his finger at me and a voice rumbled in my head, 'Stop selling cars, trying to be a big shot!' It was God, if you ask me, speaking through Jerry from the moon. 'Go be a preacher!' God told me. 'Get a Bible and be a traveling preacher! Save souls and make up for all the bad you done!'"

Eliot explained that his stoned flight to Phoenix with a pair of prostitutes in the stolen El Dorado was a vain attempt to defy his calling. However, "behind bars, like Jesus was, I surrendered to the will of God. I read the Good Book and pray like it's no tomorrow, 'cause it isn't. I already got a little preaching in—to my cellmate Ralph, who weren't quite ready for it, to tell you the truth." Eliot narrowed his eyes at the camera. "How about you, my friend, how's *your* soul runnin' these days? Better hop to it!"

Lowering the TV in the basket afterward, I struck up a conversation with Clover. She had grown talkative lately, mostly about her AA meetings. Her rapid and ardent attachment to that organization suggested cultish behavior, but I couldn't fault the effect it had had on her. She was unremittingly warm, gentle, congenial, and contented. I thanked God for her transformation, even if it proved temporary, even if the source was a brainwashing cult.

I ran those interviews around in my head, particularly the vision claim of Eliot, the Cadillac salesman. His tale stank of the same self-serving rot as Kerridge's. He was a bald-faced con-man angling to cut his jail time. Nevertheless, his so-called vision irked the hell out of me. Though no doubt fabricated in its entirety, it bugged me that he had had the intuition and gall to bring it up, to recognize that such a phenomenon would be an expected, even integral part of sitting on a flagpole for any length of time. It lit the feeling in me that there was something missing from my own quest, from my now nearly accomplished victory. Isn't that exactly what Simeon's poem had been all about—visions? Eliot had been up an hour or two and understood that visions went with flagpole-sitting like ice cream with apple pie, and here I was, about to become world champion, and I'd never had a single one.

Requests poured in for interviews about the interviews. I declined. Did I not wish to gloat over my vanquished adversaries? No, I did not wish. Did I feel no urge to update the city on my adventures, my insights on current events large or small, life in general? Yes, I felt no urge. I was a flagpole-sitter, that was all, and there was nothing more to say.

PART VII

"You can withdraw from the sufferings of the world—
that possibility is open to you and accords with your nature—
but perhaps that withdrawal is the only suffering
you might be able to avoid."

—Franz Kafka

106

Moving along the banister, Joe beheld the astounding proliferation of flagpoles and flagpole-sitters across the city, from the Pacific to the mountains and beyond. He counted those he could see: "...twenty-three, twenty-four, twenty-five..."

"Flagpole Fever," the media called it.

When the first of the mob ascended—"Number 4"—Joe had laughed it off: "One more fool going where no fool should." Number 4 was a college fratboy, inspired, according to 4RealNews, not by Joe's success but by the interviews with the failed Kerridge and Menlo. Kerridge had declared it a blast up there and Menlo proclaimed it the airborne path to a spectacular spiritual awakening. That was exactly what everyone wanted: 1. fun; and 2. a life-changing personal message from God.

Joe was certain the youngster, when he discovered it to be neither, would crack like a nut and be the last of his raggedy competition.

Two weeks later, not only was the college boy still up, but over a dozen other sitters had joined him on poles and platforms that sprouted like a virus, like alien weeds across the city. Joe referred to them as "visitors," and they included three women, a newlywed couple in Hawthorne who intended to create their own little Eden in the air (they lasted two days), and a nuclear family of four who had decided to spend their two-week vacation on a flagpole (they lasted two hours). The various eccentrics who were able to endure a while established a communications network amongst themselves, lending one another the strength and resilience that alone they could never have mustered. They ignored Joe, or chose not to invite him to join their precious network. "Fine by me," he said to himself.

The field of flagpoles continued to grow, fifty, sixty, seventy. News reports no longer even mentioned Joe as the inspiration for the craze, crediting instead the scoundrels Kerridge and Menlo. They had proved to be the Johnny Appleseeds of flagpole-sitting, their ludicrous accounts enticing normal human beings to abandon their normal lives for flagpoles in front yards, backyards, parking lots, vacant lots, alleys, hillsides and cul de sacs, and, finally, from Long Beach to Simi Valley to Riverside, one hundred and eighteen flagpoles had been erected or commandeered for the practice, however dimly, however brazenly, of the ancient art and craft.

Each day Joe woke to the strange sight, the eerie sight, yet obscurely familiar, as if the vision had emerged from the shadows of his own subconscious, or his soul, and radiated out across the Southland.

Though Lu and Duc had put up the fratboy's structure, the propagation of poles quickly outgrew the capacity of the father-son duo. Competing construction firms entered the arena. Soon, a standard, bare-bones pole and platform, installed, could be had for $1500. If an adequate pole was already in the ground and available, the price came down accordingly. Offered as well was a range of custom poles in an array of materials with ladder, trapdoor, accessory, and color options. One pole was striped like a barber's, another checked like the finishing flag at an auto race, another a psychedelic pattern. The structures stood from twenty to almost ninety feet, and the platforms came in a host of shapes—round, hexagonal, kidney-shaped, etc., like backyard swimming pools.

Joe prayed the builders knew what they were doing. He didn't want anybody hurt or, God forbid, killed by a fall or the collapse of a shoddy structure some fly-by-nighter had stuck up there. He wanted every one of those deluded souls gone, gone now, gone yesterday, but not by disaster. They might believe Kerridge or Eliot had inspired them, but Joe knew they were his own flagpole-sitting children, and if calamity struck even one of those naifs, he would be responsible in the court of his heart.

The nearest interloper to Joe was three-quarters of a mile away, farther than Kerridge had been, but what if someone went up right across Western, or next door? What a nightmare to have one of these turistas that close—calling, waving, disco and sitcoms blaring.

Worse, with a mob of other sitters up, how could he climb down as planned? His descent would mean nothing, a leaf falling in a forest. What if he climbed down and a slew of them, challenging and encouraging one another, broke his record en masse? It would be as if he had never been up at all.

To be sure, Joe had long realized that the record was a trivial facet of the quest, a wiggling worm on the spiritual hook, but did that mean he was supposed to lie back and allow a collection of mountebanks to saunter up and grab that record for their own? He was haunted by the paradox, by the connection between the nonsense of the record and the glory of the quest. Simeon had dwelt upon his pillar for thirty years— he was aware of time passing, days, months, years, decades. He wasn't in a trance. He was counting. Even a saint has an ego. Joe knew that's what Tennyson was writing about—Simeon's struggle to overcome his miserable ego, to shed it and crawl away and fly free.

Of course, knowing what Joe now knew about the rigors of long-distance sitting, it was daft of him to fear that any of those duffers would come near his record, his record-to-be. Would even one have what it took to stay and sit and *be* amidst the stampede of inner urgencies, without going mad before such dreadful, lonely, prolonged self-confrontation?

Joe's refusal to do more interviews drove the media deeper into the arms of the new generation of "blabbermouth dilettantes," as Joe called them. In fact, everybody *but* Joe seemed to be talking about Flagpole Fever.

"This is good for the whole calling," Clover said. "You should be proud. You're the new Wright Brothers, honey. Do you think they were unhappy that other people built airplanes? Like it or not, it's bigger than just you now."

In this last stage of the quest Joe ought to have been emptying his mind that God might fill him with some measure of wisdom, grace, enlightenment, ecstasy, or plain simple peace. Instead, he was bedeviled by indignation at those marauders. Lean, weathered, and whiskered, he was Billy Budd facing an unfathomable provocation. He was Van Gogh at his easel, surrounded by a pack of finger-painting barbarians as he completed the revelation of the crows in the wheatfield. He was Henry Ford watching the arteries of the city thickening with automobiles built by pretenders. He was Kafka's hunger artist forgotten for the pacing leopard. Joe gazed at what he had created and what he had created taunted him without mercy. What had once been his mysterious obsession alone now flourished like devil weed. The quest had been ripped from his depths and franchised.

Yet there were moments when Joe went giddy and gushed with wonder: "Look at this! What a splendorous vision! Look out there, Walter! Could you imagine? Flagpoles and sitters galore!"

Was he not vindicated, his life, his obsession? If he were indeed

deranged, all those others were as well, and they were surely not deranged—a plumber, veterinarian, stockbroker, chiropractor, dancer,
astronomer, for God's sake.

On the surface, the craze was a happy public event. Underneath, for
the individual sitters, a shakier reality prevailed. For many, after taking in
the sights, chattering to gawkers on the ground and calling friends, cro-
cheting, watching TV, the honeymoon quickly wore thin. They began
to stagger like amnesiacs in unfamiliar rooms, pummeled by vertigo,
exposure, loneliness, by their own relentless thoughts. They reached for
the banister like the blind, the platform shrinking, the distance from the
earth expanding under their feet.

Joe knew the battles they were fighting, driving themselves to go
one more day, another hour, pacing like prisoners, their delirious minds
chanting get down, get down, get down now, now, now, now!

And why shouldn't they simply pop the trapdoor, climb down and be
done with it, this absurdity of absurdities? Under the stars, they tossed
and turned and snapped awake from nightmares of falling or being
pecked to madness by wild birds reclaiming the air. Joe was certain that
one night the nearest fellow in his sleep cried out for his mother.

He empathized, but they had made their bed. Through the binoculars he witnessed the deterioration of the ones in range, and knew the
rest would soon endure the same collapse of sensory realities. They had
ascended on a lark and now found themselves on a spiritual Everest for
which they had neglected to prepare.

God bless them all, he thought. They were family, for a spell, brothers and sisters. Many had already outlasted his own earlier efforts. How
innocent each looked on the palms of their platforms, a newborn on a
leaf, dear, dizzy, doomed. Each a gift offered in sacrifice to the city, to
the sky, to God.

He wanted to call, visit, whisper to each, I'm here, I see, I know,
I feel, I understand. He pulled Simeon's pillar stone from his pocket
and held the smooth warm object to his chest. He loved them and
their glorious ignorance. He yearned not to soothe, but to save them.
Because of him they had come to a place they did not know, did not
belong. It would be easier if they gave up and climbed down before
they began to really care about what they were doing. That was the
worst part—caring beyond the point of no return, beyond the point of
wondering what the meaning of it was. He had been sinking in the same
wonder for a decade. They were children who had picked up a piece

of the incomprehensible, thinking it a toy, and now they ailed from the enigma that had corrupted their reason. Expecting fun or an easy thrilling God, they found themselves in a raging sea, masked by silence and the stillness of time. He felt the weight of that responsibility, as Shipwreck had felt responsible for him.

"They could have called," Joe said. "They could have said hello." He sat and picked up the poem about his medieval brother:

> But yield not me the praise;
> God only thro' his bounty hath thought fit,
> Among the powers and princes of this world,
> To make me an example to mankind,
> Which few can reach to. Yet I do not say
> But that a time may come—yea, even now,
> Now, now, his footsteps smite the threshold stairs
> Of life—I say, that time is at the doors
> When you may worship me without reproach;
> For I will leave my relics in your land,
> And you may carve a shrine about my dust,
> And burn a fragrant lamp before my bones,
> When I am gather'd to the glorious saints.

107

JOE

In the fifth week the college boy, the putative leader of the lot, dismounted under cover of darkness. His capitulation had a snowball effect, the floodgates gave, and the others came down like lemmings.

The fever had not run its course, however, for many of the vacated poles were re-occupied within a day or two by fresh tenderfoots.

"They're renting the poles now," Clover informed me. "By the hour, day, and week. They have waiting lists."

"This has devolved into total desecration," I said.

"Yesterday you said you loved them like your very own children. Oh, by the way, they're popping up in other states now. There's one in—"

"No, no, no. Change of subject, please."

"Well, I had a real good meeting this morning. It was what they call a step study. And they were on—*we* were on step eleven."

As she embarked on another of her epic AA adventure tales, I grabbed my binoculars and squinted across the city at the imps in the rafters, defiling the temple. The nearest wore a blue jumpsuit on a yellow pole a quarter mile away, the farthest was tucked into the hills by the Hollywood sign. A loose necklace of others serpentined from LAX around to the Coliseum and over near the golden statue of the Mormon Temple on Santa Monica Boulevard. They went about their business anxious as pigeons, without a grain of knowledge of the history of the endeavor, of Simeon with his boils in medieval Turkey, or Shipwreck on his ramshackle pole in Minnesota, or, for that matter, little forgotten me on Western. Somebody had finally gone up on Kerridge's former pole, a woman of a certain age. I thought, If only I could have talked with him about all this, my dear Shipwreck.

"So, when you're down," Clover was saying, "maybe we could meditate together. I'm feeling a little better about things. Well, you know, a day at a time."

"I'm proud of you, honey. I'm glad for you."

"Should we talk about it when you get down? I'm afraid, too, you know. Are you getting down the exact day you break the record?"

108

CLOVER

I hoped Roy wouldn't call back. I needed a drink. Joe wouldn't commit to when he was coming down. What if he stayed up? I'll do what I want, I thought, Nate'll get older and stronger, and Joe will, what, grow wings up there and fly away? Maybe everybody would be happier if he did stay up. How will it ever be good for us again anyway, with the bleeding scars. Sometimes I don't care, sometimes I want to kill him, or march into the desert to repent. I know I've learned, changed, grown. I fear he's the same old Joe. If I did leave him, could Roy be the one? Nothing's happened, but I'd miss him if we broke up. "Broke up," that's not the right term. I'd have to find all new meetings, if Roy and I got involved and things went bad. Or the hell with AA, just do it on my own. I've picked up enough handy hints to get by without those well-meaning squares intruding into my life. If I could only have just one lousy little drink to relax and not worry about everything for a while. Or two.

109

JOE

No TV, no radio, no papers. How peaceful without these "necessities." The town crier should come back: "There is a woman on 4th Street in a dirty black sweater & torn plaid pants! She is hungry & cold! Talk to her! Give her some of your food! Give her your coat! You have a bunch of coats at home! You have a home! There is a man on a flagpole on Western! Leave him alone!"

I observe the world, I write down a thought if it insists, silly or mysterious ("The city is the subconscious of some big thing." "There is a crick in China's neck."). I'm officially reading again. *The Castle*. Kafka. It's as if I never read it before. *The Cloud of Unknowing* again as well. It's by an unknown monk, from around Simeon's time. They are very different in their takes on the mystery, Kafka and the monk, but both are humble, child-like books. I'd like to read and teach only books I love.

Kafka: "It was late in the evening when K. arrived. The village was deep in snow. The castle hill was hidden, veiled in mist & darkness, nor was there even a glimmer of light to show that a castle was there. On the wooden bridge leading from the main road to the village, K. stood for a long time gazing into the illusory emptiness before him."

Cloud: "I speak half playfully now, but try to temper the loud, crude sighing of your spirit & pretend to hide your heart's longing from the Lord."

Fewer sitters every day. God bless each & every one, especially as they're climbing down.

I watched a hawk being kind of attacked by a bunch of crows. The whole ten minutes I watched the hawk, silver against the white sky, he did only one thing—slowly ascended higher & higher in a wide spiral, without even moving his wings. There were six crows at first. They never dared touch the hawk, but squawked & swooped & pulled away several feet short every time. As the hawk sailed higher, one by one the flustered crows peeled away, until the last lumbered off, stoned on the elevation. The hawk remained, a lonesome speck, rising until you could not see him.

Nate is becoming more himself, a familiar stranger full of surprises. Today he said, "I love you for being a weird father."

One abiding sitter intrigues me. A woman, on the elderly side, happens to have gone up on Kerridge's ex-pole. She's only been up a little while. Calm from the beginning. She's sitting in an armchair in a flowing all red get-up under an umbrella, reading a book, staring into the distance. Her platform contains the minimum, no TV. She appeared settled in from the beginning, as if she'd been up before. I've never caught her looking my way once. The others at least had the idle curiosity to gawk now & then at the one who started it all.

110

CLOVER

I climbed in bed in the middle of the day, pulled the covers over my head, and gave way to an exquisite sorrow for myself. I burst out crying, for myself first, then for Joe, who once again had no idea what was going on in my head, and for Nate, growing into a young man with a secret thought life of his own, and back to me, and when I ran out of gas, I savored having a drink to top off so satisfying an emotional out-flooding, but remembered I wasn't drinking anymore, which brought another little after-wave of weeping.

I had showed Solana the picture of the big aquarium I picked out for the Patch from Roy's catalog. She looked around. Space was tight. "Where would it *go?*"

I didn't care about the aquarium, only about Roy, about getting him over there, seeing him, talking with him. Solana's question smacked me with the idiot absurdity of my crush. I so much admired her incapacity for subterfuge. That straight-shooting go-getter. I was dependent on her, trusted her so implicitly, it felt like love. Roy's suggestion that I minimize my stress for the sake of my sobriety made it easier to let her take charge of the coffeehouse. From the books to the bookings to supplies to the menu to the help, Solana was at the wheel. I slipped happily into the back seat, humble and grateful and sober.

In fact, now that I'd gotten a little sobriety under my belt, my most daring dream was to sell the Patch. I spent barely any time down there, hiding out upstairs in between meetings, reading, painting, thinking about painting, and not drinking. All I had to do was walk in that place and the oxygen felt like it was being pumped out of my blood. I remind-ed myself of Charley choking on a meatball. The better the place did, the more money we made, the more oh-so-cool people crowded in, the more I felt like a trapped fly in a pretty web.

At the same time, I felt increasingly comfortable at meetings with Roy and those *earnest* AA hayseeds. I'd always thought earnestness a most annoying human trait, a Hallmark card trait, but lately it had been growing on me. In fact, I liked thinking of myself as earnest now. I got earnest just thinking about it. Solana was too earnest. I didn't want to be that earnest, not earnest all the time. I would have liked somebody calling me "naturally earnest." "Clover has an organic earnestness about her," I said aloud.

So, that was my dream: sell the place, flee the city, commit to my art, maybe go back to school, perhaps complete my degree. But the thought of leaving Joe, losing Nate—no. If only I could go off, do what I wanted, and have Joe and Nate at the homestead waiting when I needed a break from doing what I wanted.

First things first, as they were trying to teach me in AA. Take the next indicated action. Which meant sell the place. Oh, God, the very thought—Emancipation! I would leap with joy up and over Joe's plat-form. I kidded with Solana about selling it to her since she as much as ran it already.

"I'd like that," she said, straight-faced as ever. "I'll talk to my par-ents." I knew they had money.

"Just like that?"

"Just like that."

It was too much to hope for, a dream, I didn't dare dwell on it, but oh, imagine getting that transaction in the books before Joe came down.

In the meantime, she was right, Solana—that aquarium was too grand for the coffeehouse. I got Roy's catalog and found a more mod-est one. A blue fish and an orange fish stared at me from the cover. Beautiful little gentle fish swimming in rectangles their whole lives in a glass box to give human beings a moment of serenity. What would I do if I were a little blue or orange fish with big black eyes and angelic fins, stuck in a glass box, living on crumbs? I remembered reading that when an aquarium fish is released into open water, it continued to swim in a little space the very size of its bowl.

I shivered at the thought, relaxed, slid off toward sleep. Sleep was as good as a drink. I wished Roy were there, not to do anything, only to talk, to tell me wise, soothing things about life and sobriety while I fell asleep. There was no chance of us sleeping together. Very, very, very little. I believe he was as attracted to me as I was to him, but I had learned my lesson, and he had made it clear that although he was single he was "*assiduous*" about not getting involved with other men's women. As soon as he said it, I assiduously started thinking about what it would be like to sleep with him. I felt safe to think about it, because I trusted him to assiduously not let it happen. Assiduous, I thought dreamily, with Roy's aquarium catalog and all the little fishes inside wrapped in my arms. It was one of those words that you knew for sure what it meant—assiduous—until you started thinking about it.

111

Norman squinted in the restroom mirror. Beside him, Nate compared his own bird's nest with the taller boy's meticulous coif. He wet his fingers and tried to mash down a flap of hair that stuck out above one ear like a toy flag.

Some boy tried to squeeze in front of Norman to get to the sink. Norman barked, "Hey, dork!" and the boy saw who it was and ducked back. "Watch it or I'll sic my best friend Nathaniel here on ya!"

Nate looked around. Nobody might be afraid of Nate but they were all wary of Norman. He had come in in the middle of the term, a year older and taller than everybody else, held back and transferred around for fights and general troublemaking, including a sports gambling ring he had started at his previous school. Nobody liked Norman, including Nate, but Nate admired him, and liked that Norman liked *him*, or at least acted like he did. Nate couldn't think of any reason why Norman would pretend to like him, no way it could pay off for Norman, so he thought maybe he really did like him for some unknown reason. Maybe there was a hidden rebel in Nate that only Norman could see. Some kids didn't like Nate for no good reason to start with, so, he figured, why not be friends with Norman and give them a *real* good reason.

Plucking a hair out of his nose, Norman said to Nate, "I bet you never even had a best friend before."

Nate frowned. "Yes, I did."

Norman laughed. He brushed off the shoulders of his adult-like kind of golfing shirt. If it had been anybody but Norman wearing those fancy, old-man sports clothes, somebody would have branded him a fag, but nobody was about to mess with Norman. He wasn't scared of anybody and he didn't care what anybody thought. He was the crazy guy in a teenage movie who everybody watches because something big and messy was going to happen any second around him. Being friends with Norman made Nate feel like there was finally something in his life that was really *his*. Norman was something special and it was rubbing off on Nate.

Also, his friendship with Norman agreed with his decision to get rich and be able to do whatever he wanted, because Norman was rich and did whatever *he* wanted. If he was friends with Norman, richness might rub off too. Even though Norman's parents never let him have any money. They said it was because he wasn't responsible, but he said it was really because "they have a hold of their money like two monkeys fucking a basketball."

Norman finished fiddling with his hair and nodded at himself. "Come on," he said. Nate followed him out and they headed for the tables. It was lunch hour.

"Name one best friend you ever had," Norman said.

"Not you, that's for sure."

Norman laughed. "Boo hoo," he said.

They were alone now and Nate felt like being honest. That was one good thing about his obnoxious classmate—you could be honest with him. In fact, you *had* to be honest. It took your breath away how Norman blurted crazy stuff out and wouldn't let you say normal things. "My parents moved around too much for me to have a best friend before."

The moving around thing was only part honest. Nate had always pretended to be shyer than he was because any kid who got to know him would have found out about the flagpoles, which everybody knew about anyhow now, and anyway those other people all went up there and found out it wasn't so easy, was it. The only problem was that he had pretended to be more shy than he was for so long that he had gotten stuck in it.

"Fuck parents," Norman said. He spat like a gunslinger. "Parents are born stupid." He put one foot up on a bench and surveyed the lunch yard. "Damn! Look it that one in the blue with the monster jugs."

"Paula," Nate said. He put a foot up on the bench too. They watched a group of boys horseplaying with the laughing Paula and another girl. One of the boys saw Norman and Nate watching and said something to the others. They all glanced over and another boy said something and they laughed.

"Hey, you fags got a problem?" Norman shouted. Nate winced at "fags." "Look it those retards," Norman said. Nate wondered if "retards" was worse than "fags," as far as calling somebody it. Paula said something to the other girl and the two stared over. "Hey, Paula, want some?" Norman said. Paula gave him the finger. Norman said, "What's that, your IQ or your bra size?" Paula stuck her chest out and turned away. "Ever try to get in her pants?" he asked Nate.

"Maybe I did," Nate said. Norman laughed. Nate took his foot down.

He wanted to say something about Norman saying retards and fags. Clover told him to never just stand there if somebody said something like that or else it looked like you agreed with them.

"Got any smokes?" Norman said.

Nate shook his head. "You can't smoke here."

"If I had one, watch me. Boy, this place is a valley of walking dead. So you moved around, big deal. You don't have to move around like a bunch of stinking gypsies to be stupid."

"Who's stinking gypsies? Do you have to call everybody a buncha names? Fags and retards and gypsies and everything."

"Whoa, Jesus, jump down my throat. My parents only been in one house since I was born and they're stupid as glaze donuts." Norman sat up on the table with his feet on the bench.

"Mine aren't stupid," Nate said.

"Oh yeah? Is driving around drunk smart? Is painting people without no faces smart?"

That stung because Nate had made fun of the paintings himself when he told Norman about them when he was mad at her. "People bought all her paintings. You don't know anything about paintings."

"Oh yeah, sorry, man. I shouldn't of said that. Sorry. Really."

That surprised Nate. "Okay," he said.

"Is it freakin' stupid to live on a freakin' flagpole?" Norman said. "Or is that freakin' smart?"

"Okay, why don't you shut up." The sorry was a trick. "If he's so stupid, how come you want to make money off him?"

"Oh, you *don't* now all of the sudden? Stupid people is exactly what you make money off of. He made a few bucks off his stupid self, in case you forgot."

"Just quit calling him stupid."

"Okay, he's a genius. He's Alfred Frickin' Flagpole Einstein."

"Do you have to make fun of *everybody*?"

"I don't have to, but I like to."

"Well, then, you're the one that's stupid."

"Yeah, but I'm your best friend, so what's that make you?"

"Who said you're my best friend?"

"Boo-hoo. You don't like me now?"

"Not when you act like a, a, a retard!"

Norman laughed. "You're just like me, Nate. We're thinking men. That's why I picked you to be my best friend in this stinking pinatentiary.

We're the kind that gets ahead. We rise to the top, like cream dee la cream. We dive down where the pearls are, while the other morons float around like turds in a bowl."

"I thought you said we rise to the top."

"We swim to the bottom, grab the pearls, rise to the top, and then the turds sink when they see how special we are."

"Can't you rise to the top with the pearls and still be nice to the turds?"

"Nope. Make lotsa cash, or be nice. It's the rule of life. One or the other."

"I'm gonna do both."

"You'll be the first, except for Jesus, and he wasn't too nice all the time."

"Did he make lotsa cash?"

"He could of, but he messed up. Went legit." Norman looked out over the schoolyard. "Paula, mm-mm. Look at them bazooms. She could float a battleship. Imagine gettin' your mouth wrapped around one of those, slurpin' away." He slugged Nate's arm a little harder than playfully. Before Nate knew it, he hit Norman back, harder than he meant to.

"Ow! Goddamn! You got a punch for a little fuck, man. Your fist's all bones." He turned toward Nate and looked at him. Nate thought he was going to really hit him. "Listen, Nate. I never really had a friend before, either. Thanks for being my friend, bud." He rubbed his arm. "Now, how we gonna make some cash off your brilliant old man and his orange-ass flagpole? When's he getting down?"

"Like, about, a month?"

"A *month*? Damn nation! We gotsa beat feet, little bro!"

112

JOE

27 days to go, and what have I got to show?

Even with Clover's legal bills & new car, we're more loaded than anybody could have imagined. But am I wiser? Spiritualer? A better man? Or a bigger idiot than ever? The American people deserve to know if their flagpole-sitter is an idiot. Who but an idiot would declare that he's not an idiot?

Was the blowjob spiritual? It did save my sanity to have gotten it before finding out about Clover & Sam. Forgive me, Clover, for I forgive you. Oh, lie! Whale lie! Well, I *want* to forgive you. My insides are a ghost ship on the sea of what we've done.

"They endured," Faulkner said. Endurance is 95% of wisdom. Endure long enough and you're bound to discover something small (because everything big is in ruins), something simple, hiding in plain sight, something you've known forever and keep forgetting, because it's small & strong & hiding in so immense & ruined a world.

I shoulda coulda written a book while I was up. Instead of thousands of silly, pompous, sullen little chicken scratchings.

I do feel sometimes like a monk on a snowy mountain. I look down, nothing is near; look up, all is hidden, look around and see only myself.

I see Nate, Clover & me sitting in a nice living room in the future—sunshine streaming in, reading the paper, feet up, windows open wide, enjoying the view, a veil playing like jazz over everything, woven of mystery & sorrow. God, help us learn to love in the midst of the storms that tear us limb from limb.

Only 3 other sitters still up, says Clover. Only one in sight is the old woman where Kerridge sat. The rest stand empty. Ghost platforms to go with the ghost ship inside.

The numbers had dwindled to 20 or so, then an itty bitty earthquake hit in the middle of the night. There've been plenty little shakers, you get used to 'em, ride 'em out, but this one was bad enough for Clover and I to call and see if we were okay. The pretenders freaked & scurried down.

I suspected the old woman was Kerridge himself in a wig and dress, or some psycho he'd hired. But he doesn't have two nickels to rub together, and—I called—he's still in Vistaview.

I wish I could make out the titles of the books the old woman reads. Wonder if she wonders what I'm reading. The "Kafka" on the cover is pretty big, but if she's got binos I've never seen them. Neither have I seen her on a phone. She meditates, does yoga and that slow-motion karate. Up there in years, she sometimes appears younger, which could be the way the light keeps changing the details of everything all the time up here.

I was wondering if maybe she could be an actual nun or monkess, on sabbatical.

She has three outfits—big capes or bathrobes—one black, one white, one red. And big stylish hats to match, which, in my opinion, subvert her austerity. Sometimes she lugs around a picnic basket. It tipped over one time, I swear she had *chains* in there, *big* chains, *anchor* chains. Which would mean she's simply crazy. That would make sense & settle everything.

She has yet to acknowledge my presence. At this distance, she could be slyly eyeing me all day & night. She may not realize I'm here, that I'm the one responsible for her being up.

I've never seen her eat, much less ablutions, etc. I'm not watching her 24 hours a day, and she's got that umbrella & there are ways to do things up here that defy perception. One thing irks—Curly deserted me for her. He drops in here, spends five seconds, flies straight to her and hangs out. If she has better peanuts, I've never seen her feed him.

Clover said she hadn't heard anything about the woman. The media's dropped the craze like a dirty sock.

There's a crisis in the Middle East.

Nate's acquired ambition, studies, gets As, thinks for himself, even found a friend, some sort of entrepreneurial type, I gather from Clover.

She's getting it together. We talk every day.

I've got a few more gray hairs. White. I like it. It allows me to suspect I must be old enough to have acquired some measure of wisdom which has simply not yet made itself known to me.

113

CLOVER

"So," I said, "shouldn't I get going on those steps pretty soon?"

Roy stirred his coffee. "You sure should." We sat in a booth at Armstrong's, a post-meeting fellowship hangout. The place was riddled with sober alcoholics guzzling coffee and wolfing pie and merrily yammering away. "You get a sponsor yet?"

I groaned. "I don't know anybody but you."

"The steps get complicated. Emotional. Especially four and five. You need a woman."

"You keep saying that." I held my cup with both hands. "What if I'm a lesbian?"

That stopped him. "*Are* you?"

"But you *could* help me through step three?"

"Better to do them all with one person. You get momentum. Rapport."

"What if I *hate* women?"

He laughed. "What about Melinda? What about Lorna?"

"Melinda's stuck up. Lorna hates me. I just don't trust women."

"You'll come to trust. You'll learn to trust. Trusting feels good."

"You know, if women should stick with women, why did you come up to me and pour on your charm at my very first meeting?"

He shrugged. "You got me," he said. "We are not saints." That was a quote from the Big Book. "You know what," he said, "maybe it wouldn't hurt to get you started, since you just seem to be hanging around doing nothing anyway."

And right there and then, we did the first three steps lickety-split. I was one giant nerve. My stomach spun. I felt like I was walking the plank. I thought, My God, I'm doing the steps. I admitted I was powerless over alcohol and not exactly managing my life. I said I loved the idea of my freaking sanity being restored, and I was willing to but had no idea how to turn my life over to that Higher Power. He said that was what the rest of the steps were for. He said the third step was where many newcomers stopped, choosing to drink rather than do the dreaded fourth and fifth.

I said, "Can you just tell me how you start it, with a newcomer, the fourth step?"

He laughed. "I see what you're doing, you know. Well, I do what my sponsor did. He just said start with the most horrible thing that I would never tell anybody in the whole world ever."

"Oh, God, I know what that would be for me." And before he could stop me, I spilled every single thing I could remember about the argument with Bobby in the bar, the cops pounding on the door the next morning, the red sleeve on the bumper, the handcuffs, and on to court, the sentencing, being banned from Bobby's funeral, the year in Frontera. I never looked at him once. I was like a fire hose until I was empty. Then we sat there a while in the murmur of the coffee shop.

"Did you love him?" he said. "Bobby."

I whispered, "I barely knew him."

He nodded. He said he wasn't a therapist or a priest or anything like that, just another sober drunk. He said what a terrible thing I'd gone through, and put others through, and he hoped I'd stay sober and never have to go through anything like that again, or bring others such suffering. He told me there were ways to make amends to people who were gone.

"He had a family?" he said. I nodded. "Not now," he said, "but you might consider making some kind of amends there at some point down the line."

I thought about it for the millionth time. "I could never do that."

"I know. I wouldn't want to do it. But things change. Maybe never say never?"

"I don't know." I shook my head. "So...is that it?"

He laughed a little. "Does it feel like that's it?"

I thought about it. "No."

"It's a good beginning. You notice I didn't run screaming from the room? Now get a woman sponsor."

114

JOE

Fog is here, low and drifting. Halos shimmer around every light. Squint, they're sparklers. O, Enchanted Town. Enchanted World.

The old woman, in all black against the bright mist, is doing her slo-mo flamingo karate, both arms up like wings, one leg out, her neck & head & long white hair just so. I have to blink to be sure she's moving at all. She's the only one left. Me & her.

A herd of white buffaloes glides between us.

Fog gets me in a Heaven frame of mind. Everything is hidden in itself. Heaven is drifting away from my opinions, like an astronaut drifting away from the spaceship. Hell is opinions. Have you an opinion, Monsieur Fog?

I had a girlfriend—a Catholic. Her brother had some sort of severe mental retardation. He was about 15. His skin was like freckled china. She brought him for a visit from the home where he lived. He was round, plump, no muscles. We were sitting on the floor and he was holding my hand. I could tell he liked me. It made me feel that he could see my soul and that he loved me. I kind of got nervous and started to pull my hand away and he kept hold of it. It was the strongest grip I ever felt. He was smiling. It was otherworldly, like the grip of a god. He wasn't even trying to squeeze. The happy expression on his face had no strain in it. He had the strength of an angel, because he had no opinion that could get between him & the power of what he was doing, so nothing existed but his desire to do what he was doing.

The fog is leaving like a billion brides, revealing the old woman in black, sitting on the far edge of her platform, her back to me, swinging her legs like a child.

115

Nate and Norman's big day arrived. Riding to school on the bus, decked out in his suit and whale tie, Nate twitched thinking of all the things that could go wrong. If even just one little part went bad, the whole gigantic plan would crumble like the Tower of Babel in the Bible. He would be suspended from school, have to run away to avoid juvenile hall, die a horrible death in a train boxcar or a raft on some river, and not only would he be dead but everybody would laugh at him.

Norman is the one who came up with the scheme after the school's recent Fathers and Sons Day, which featured talks from the fathers about their jobs. Norman's father rhapsodized about his wonderful holding company, named after himself. Nate's father was, of course, indisposed, which served to inspire Norman's delinquent mind. It took five seconds for the entire scheme to hatch in his perverse imagination and stand on wet and shaky legs. Nate expressed grave doubts at first but found himself sold on Norman's pitch step by seductive step.

The plan: to get Mr. Rogel to set up a field trip for the class to go to the flagpole so that Joe, unable to attend Fathers and Sons Day, might share about his work, such as it was. The students would be able to see and question the barely acknowledged mastermind behind the recent flagpole craze.

Both Mr. Rogel and the principal, Mr. Powell, came to see the boys' ambitious project, and the rebel Norman's enthusiastic participation in it, as something of a miracle, and Nate as the miracle worker. It didn't hurt that Powell so heartily admired Joe and his quest.

Joe, however, rejected the notion wholesale.

"He just wants to hog the spotlight," Norman said.

"He doesn't care about any spotlight. He could be on TV every day if he wanted."

"Dream on. That pole crap is kaput. Look, you gotta talk him into it. Cry or something. Bang your head against the pole. Say you'll kill yourself."

∾

As Nate pleaded his case to Joe, a tiny screaming Norman in a devil suit

jumped up and down on his shoulder. Nate told Joe all the kids expected him to do it, and if he refused, Nate would be too embarrassed to
ever show his face at school again.

Joe thought it over. It would be a big step in winning Nate's heart,
and it might even be fun, all those kids squealing with delight below. He
relented.

One part of the plan that only Norman knew about: the students
would climb the ladder *onto* the platform—for ten dollars each, under
the table. When Nate heard of that addendum, he put up a proper stink.
"My dad'll never let a bunch of kids run around up there!"

"He let *you* up."

"I'm his son!"

"Look, he won't want to hurt their feelings. And he won't want everybody to hate you for lying. If it makes you happy, we just won't tell
him. We'll show up with the kids and say your mom was supposed to
tell him. And she forgot. We'll blame it on her."

"She'll be right there and say we're lying! And even if he let anybody
go up, Mr. Rogel won't let kids climb up any sixty-foot ladder!"

"Your pop's got that harness. Look, I got it planned out to the tiny
detail. Those kids are going up that pole. I'll be in total charge. All you
have to do is think of that two hundred bucks, man," which was the
take Norman had projected for each of them.

The students balked at the price tag. One threatened to tell Mr. Rogel
that they were charging for the field trip. Norman lowered the fee to five
bucks, and in the end let everybody give whatever they could scrounge
or steal from their parents. He sweetened the pot with a money-back
guarantee, as long as they didn't talk. The two hundred bucks turned out
to be sixty and change.

"What if something goes wrong?" Nate said.

"What if the Russian Army lived in your underpants? It'll go like
clockwork, and we'll grab thirty bucks apiece. It's foolproof. It's not the
celebrities and entertainers that makes the big bucks, it's the people that
pull the strings, the onteperners—namely, us."

To reassure him, Norman insisted that Nate keep the money in his
own locker. Sixty bucks wasn't looking like that much to Nate anymore,
with all the risks involved. However, they had crawled too far out on the
plank of supply and demand to turn back now.

Headed for school on the big morning, Nate contracted yellowbelly
fever. Some blabbermouth would spill the beans. He couldn't stand the

pressure. If the police weren't waiting with handcuffs, he would run straight to his locker, grab the sixty dollars, hand it over to Mr. Rogel and beg for mercy. He would blame the whole mess on Norman. He would say he only went along to keep from letting everybody down after they told him how great he was for making a new man out of Norman.

With nary an authority figure in sight as he entered the school, Nate broke into an anxious trot for his locker, opened it and grabbed the lunch sack the money was in, but it wasn't. He reached around in there and came out with a scrawled note:

Hey Nate I got to beat feet for grenner pasteures. You coud blame it all on me everybody will anyways. Your best freind Norman.

116

JOE

The fog had moved back in, its shoulders nudging the underside of my platform. The sky above remained clear, a dizzying blue. Palm trees, lightposts, rooftops bobbed out of the fog and sank back in. The old woman stood on her platform, a phantom in the fog, her ample body poised in a loose white robe. Her long hair swaying, she hopped back and forth, foot to foot, in some way that made her body appear to pause in the air. My platform creaked and lurched as it began to grind through the fog toward the old woman. I threw myself to the redwood. The whole structure shuddered as it inextricably tore through obstacles toward her, like an icebreaker cleaving through asphalt, cement, shrouded buildings. Fog muffled the clamor of destruction. I listened for screams below. Looking behind, I saw the coffeehouse and apartment safe, all the lights on, nobody in sight. Suddenly close now, the old woman stood, her face strong and old and calm, shining in the blue light of the night and the fog. In a far corner of the sky lightning struck like a dagger. I braced for thunder but only a clicking came, behind me. It was Shipwreck! On my platform! Alive! He held a bouquet of spoons in each hand, playing them against themselves and against the redwood, right on his bloodstain, clicks and clacks like tap dancing. He looked up, brow knit with creative focus, nodding in time to his playing. I turned and the old woman was right there now, a leap away. She danced from foot to foot, solemn and buoyant at once, large and light, her bright old face and long white hair. The platforms bumped gently, like boats. I could have jumped from one to the other. Shipwreck played and the woman danced. She had a wispy white chin beard that looked beautiful, spiritual, meant to be. The platforms jostled and parted. Shipwreck played, clickety clackety, and she reached to me to join her, her face shining like an old book, her eyes crazy with stories, and I did, leapt across, free of effort or fear.

117

Riding the bus to the flagpole with his and Norman's rambunctious victims, Nate rolled his whale tie up and let it unroll down his chest over and over. Fear filled him like a load of wet cement poured into a hole in the top of his head. It was a field trip to the end of life as he knew it. Neither Joe nor Mr. Powell had any idea about twenty-eight kids actually climbing up the ladder and onto the platform. Powell had finagled his way in as chaperone to meet Joe. Nate had prayed that somebody would stop the whole thing, God, Mr. Powell, or maybe one of the kids would spill the beans to a grown-up. But, no, the horrible plan was moving like a grinder, pulling Nate and everybody else into it inch by inch. Joe would never let any kids up there, and Mr. Powell, forget it. Worst of all, this was the exact time Norman swore he would be there with big ideas to save them in case the plan went south, but he and his big ideas were nowhere to be found. Norman had gone missing, word was, and the authorities were after him. On top of that, nobody even knew about the missing sixty dollars yet. Nate pictured himself sharing leg irons with his "best friend" as they escaped from Juvie through a swamp.

Joe and Clover were ready and waiting when the bus pulled up and disgorged the gaggle of manic children. To facilitate communication, Clover held a little bullhorn, and in the open mouth of the trapdoor Joe held another. The students clamored around the pole like hound dogs around a treed opossum. Woozy, Nate meandered over and leaned against the Patch.

"I'm first!" Alba shouted, setting off a chorus of competing claims.

"Silence!" Mr. Powell demanded, and the pack clammed up.

Clover handed Powell her bullhorn and leaned with Nate against the building. "Fun, huh?" she said. "You okay?"

"First," Powell said in the bullhorn, "let's all thank Nate's father, Mr. Magellan, for allowing us to visit him today and ask questions about his uncommon vocation."

"Thank you, Mr. Magellan!" the children bellowed.

"You're quite welcome!" Joe called.

"Okay, Melissa," Powell said. He handed the girl the bullhorn. "You go first."

Melissa looked at the instrument. "He has to lower the ladder."

"What for?" Powell said. "Ask a question. Push the button."

"What would you like to know, Melissa?" Joe bullhorned.

"No," Melissa said. "We're supposed to climb up there."

"Well, that's not happening," said Powell. "Ask a question or lose your turn."

"We're supposed to go up there."

Powell laughed. "No, you're not."

"Yes, we are," Manny said, and others agreed.

Powell got serious. "Who told you that?"

"Norman," Peggy said. "Nate and Norman."

"Is that true?" Nate heard Clover ask him. Everybody looked at him. His head felt like a basketball.

"We paid them to climb up," Melissa said.

"Paid?" Mr. Rogel said.

Students yelped out various dollar amounts with which they had parted.

Joe, unable to decipher the discussion, used the bullhorn: "What's the question?"

Powell said, "Nathaniel, is this true?"

The flagpole-sitter's son swallowed, clapped the whale tie to his mouth, took an absurd step forward, as if off a plank, and vomited.

118

JOE

I wanted to climb down and hold him. Clover took him inside, Powell herded the kids on the bus and off they went. That little hood Norman got nailed with the bulk of the blame. Nate is using his allowance to pay the kids back. We talked. He's learned a lesson, about deceiving & letting yourself be deceived. I love him and can't wait till I'm 60 and he's 35 & we can look back at this & laugh our socks off. Maybe he'll get a story out of it.

Did I say this is my last day up? The first thing I'm doing down there, after a drop-in at the party Clover's throwing, is stretch my legs, go for a nice long walk. Maybe go see

Right then something slammed into the platform—THUNK!—up under among the braces. I lay down with my head through the trapdoor and peered and poked around.

There *was* something there: a small damaged area in the crook of one of the braces. The wood had been splintered. There was a hole. My mind offered up the deranged explanation that there were termites in the wood and a pocket of them, or the queen, had gotten heated up by the sun and exploded.

I could just reach the area. Flicking the splintered part away, I stuck the tip of my little finger in there and yanked my hand away—something alive was in there! Or at least warm. I got a pencil and stuck it in and tapped. It was hard.

"That's a bullet," I said. I lay on my back, flat, still. "Somebody shot at me."

Maybe it was a stray, like the one that hit *Crime and Punishment*. Some drunk firing a random round.

It's my last day up, I thought, somebody doesn't want me to get that record. Not even Shipwreck would go that far. And he's dead! Did you see him dead? Stop it, man, he's dead! Then who? Kerridge? He's at Vistaview. Whoever it is, are they eyeing me through a scope?

I crawled to the edge. Nobody down there appeared to have heard a shot.

Should I call the police? Why would somebody shoot just once? I thought, I could be in their sights this very second and they could be pulling the trigger and this could be my last thought. Who would even know until somebody found me dead?

The old woman! The mystery sitter!

I slowly reached for the binos. She was looking at me, for the first time, as far as I had seen. Standing and looking right at me. Had she seen? Seen what? Had she heard the shot? I dared to wave. She didn't do anything for a long moment, then gave one slow windshield wiper of a wave. At least one person would see if they tried it again and hit me.

The phone rang. I picked it up. "Hello?" Silence. "Are you the fucker who shot at me?" I heard breathing. "You gutless coward!" In a fit of bravado, I stood up. "You see me, you chicken shit? Take your best shot, asshole!" I braced, gritted my teeth for the bullet. "Come on, you yellow dog! You don't scare me! That record is mine! Nobody drives me off this flagpole! It's my home! My San Simeon, my castle! Come on! Take your best shot, yellowbelly!"

Whoever it was hung up.

I looked at the old woman, who watched, leaning forward on the banister now. I dropped the phone and danced around with my arms up, because she was watching me. I was hours from the championship, and if this was it for me, I wanted to dance, and have somebody see me dancing, and she was there.

119

CLOVER

I hadn't been to an AA meeting since telling Roy off. He hadn't even called to see if I was alive. Going to a meeting now would be lonelier than sitting home feeling sorry for myself, or puttering around in what might as well be *Solana's* Patch anymore. Painting would have been like pulling my own teeth. The little apartment shrank and the chatter and clicking plates from the coffeehouse were as ghosts and debris knocking around in the hold of a haunted ship.

And Joe was getting down the next day! God have mercy!

The thought crossed my mind that it would be easier to go buy a bottle and get it out of my system, start fresh again tomorrow, or the next day. Who would know? Tell Nate I was going to bed early, drink myself stupid one last time, start going to different meetings where nobody knew me and I could raise my hand as a newcomer again with a minimum of nausea and shame.

I heard all those AA squares in my head chattering about call somebody before you drank, or get down on your knees. I hadn't anybody to call, now that Roy had abandoned me, and hadn't I already been praying?

Okay, I would pray, damn it, God knew for what. To keep it interesting I went to the liquor store and came home and told Nate I wasn't feeling well and was turning in early. I knelt by the side of the bed. If I prayed before I drank, God would know my heart was in the right place. I got to "Forgive us our trespasses as we forgive those who trespass against us" when the phone rang. I waited until the machine picked up. It was Jinx. "Oh, Jesus," I said, "that's all I need."

120

JOE

I'm sorry, Clover darling, for every jab of pain I ever brought you. Don't let my self-obsessed idiocy weigh you down one more second with not forgiving me as I forgive you for any residual suffering in us from what we've done. Soon I'll vanish again into your dazzling green-brown-gray-with-glints-of-gold eyes, hold your rebellious warmth against me, meet your ardent mouth, smell your pale neck and your furnace red hair, love you with complete abandon as if for the first time. We survived the heartcracking, the nauseating, the unthinkable. We'll work it out. We have to. We want to. Don't we? I do. We'll talk about it. We'll talk about everything. We'll forgive and let the broken parts heal as they will and begin afresh.

I dreamed of my father & mother. They were up here with me. They were exactly the same as they had been. They walked around the perimeter, holding hands & admiring the view. I never remember them holding hands. In the dream I tried to remember things about them, but I couldn't even remember their names. All I could remember was that I loved them and that I wanted to tell them and I wanted them to know.

They came & knelt before me. They took my hands & looked up into my eyes. They were looking for something. They were looking for me. Their whole faces were so careful & kind. My mother said, "I forgive you, Joe." She must have meant when she was sick. I wasn't as good a son as I could have been. I was locked inside, afraid & selfish. My father said, "I miss you, pal." I had missed him a million times but never once thought about him missing me. They reached up & I closed my eyes & they tenderly ran their hands over my face.

Soon I will have one thing I don't have to prove anymore. You prove something why? So you don't have to prove it anymore. Then you relax until the next thing you have to prove comes along. Ah, to get to a place where there is nothing left to prove. Is it possible?

Why was I called, why did I answer? I feel like I'll always have a secret in me that's so much a part of me I can't see it, that every time I start to tell it to myself, the words refuse to form.

121

JOE

A fine April rain fell on my last morning up. I had planned to beat the sun up, set Shipwreck's ashes free before anybody was about, then quietly climb down for an aimless solo stroll around the city, and the hell with the party Clover was obligatorily throwing for me.

Instead, I slept like a bandit and woke to a mist settling on my face. Morning rush hour sizzled below on black shiny Western. Rain was not conducive to the dumping of a box of ashes from seventy feet up. I imagined the contents clumping mid-air and plopping on pedestrians' heads and cars slipping and sliding around on it, on him. So there I was, worrying about Shipwreck Blake one more time, instead of wallowing in my victory over him. I could hear the old coot chuckling at me succumbing to his final demented trick.

I wrote "445" on the wet blackboard.

I knelt and hooked the chain of Simeon's stone on the stump of the pole so that the relic hung at eye level. I meditated on it, its ancient heritage, its austere beauty, the light it took and held, the light it refused, the souls who had touched it from Simeon to Shipwreck to me. It had been part of the pillar that held the saint high for thirty years. The drops of rain on it, running down, may have contained some of the same molecules that ran down it when it was part of his tower fifteen centuries before. I closed my eyes.

It was a simple meditation, brief, no expectations, no frills. I wrapped it up with the words of gratitude I used, no matter how the experience went: "Thank you, God, for a perfect meditation."

As if on cue, the rain ceased, the sun gnawed through, and a brisk northward breeze came up to discreetly disperse the ashes. I peeked in the box: it was minute material, like white sand, no bone bits. A passerby might be whisked with a few grains, but that was life in the big city. To be scattered from the pole was what Walter had wanted, and to be scattered from the pole was what Walter would get.

I stood and stretched. Out of nowhere a storm rose in my heart. In a minute I'd be down. I picked up the mahogany container, moved to the edge, felt an encouraging surge in the breeze, and opened the box to heave the ashes forth—when I caught a milling of people around the pole below, at the same instant they spotted me at the edge.

It was the party crowd Clover had invited to celebrate my descent. I had agreed to a few folks, and would have been disappointed had nobody showed, but there had to be thirty people down there, and more inside. I had told her I would climb down later in the afternoon, planning all along to get down early, but she had out-planned me. Seeing me, the mob chittered with nervous delight.

I stepped back from the edge. Should I betray Shipwreck's last wish, or dump it and have it swirl back and cover the partygoers? I hoped he was choking on his laughter.

I would take it with me, dump it where I dumped it, and if he didn't like it he could come on back and do something about it. I looked around for something inconspicuous to put the box in. My eyes happened to settle on the loincloth. It was clean. It would do. Walter would frown, he would not approve, which made it even better.

I popped the trapdoor. The crowd hooted and clapped and hoisted beer bottles and champagne glasses. There had to have been a hundred of them down there. Who were they? Clover stood in the middle of the swarm, sheepish.

"Goodbye, old home," I said. I would mosey up tomorrow or the next day and haul down my motley gatherings. I would have to dismantle the platform at some point too.

I remembered to pay my regards to the old woman on the other pole. She happened to be standing on her head at that moment. She had been a good neighbor while she was there, respectful, minding her own business, a lovely silent companion. I waved. "Keep the hearth warm," I said.

I imagined her watching me as I climbed through the trapdoor. Standing on her head, she would see me climbing up onto the earth.

The crowd squealed as I descended. I had no idea who most of them were. On the last rung, I regarded the remarkable faces of my wife and son. "You're huge," I said. "Are we sure it's 445 days?"

Clover nodded hurriedly. Her face said her heart was full of tears she would not let go of until the perfect moment. I steeled myself and stepped onto terra firma. It was over.

"One small step for Joe Magellan!" Jinx hollered. Clover and Nate threw their arms around me.

"Welcome home, Dad," said Nate. It sounded a little rehearsed. I put my hand on his face, he put his hand on my hand, Clover got in there, and we held each other like a family drowning in happiness, or at least relief. People cheered and our tears streamed, hot and free. I glanced at the platform, its trapdoor like a shocked mouth.

The crowd was a motley band, black and white and brown, teenaged to elderly, richly dressed to casual as myself, but there was something of awe in each face, admiration, recognition, proximity to some small puzzling greatness. It made me feel powerful with the secret, powerful and defenseless. "Who *are* they?" I whispered to Clover.

"Regulars, neighbors. They followed your quest. They feel like they know you." She blew her nose, then made a face at the loincloth-wrapped object in my arms. "What's that?"

"Stuff."

She raised the bullhorn: "All right, everybody! We're going inside now! Head 'em up! Move 'em out! Raw-hide!"

Familiar faces popped from the amorphous horde as we oozed like an amoeba toward the door. There was Jinx waving from the outskirts in a purple suit, Pete Hoover raising a beer, Alp from Mike's Shoes, and Lu and Duc the master builders peering as if they'd never seen me before. And was that the German woman from the hardware store who had warned me the platform would collapse and kill somebody? She was gnawing on some treat at a buffet in the back.

Solana stood placidly in the middle of the coffeehouse, watching and wiping her hands surgeon-like. She too looked different than she had from the pole—younger, and, oddly, smaller. I smiled awkwardly and she smiled awkwardly back.

"Hi, hi, hi," I said to everybody's greetings. "Thank you, thanks for coming, good to see ya." Good God, I thought, not down a minute and I'm right back faking it in my old grinning mask. Such, I thought, is the human curse. And who did I spot against a wall under one of Clover's paintings? Malcolm Kerridge! His black dye-job was growing out, an inch of stark white sprouting underneath. He looked like a glaring skunk.

"I thought Kerridge was in an insane asylum!" I said to Clover.

"Oh, they let him out a few days ago. He called and begged me to come. He wants to make amends. Try and be nice. He's been through hell. Everybody deserves a second chance."

Kerridge's demented scowl did not signify amends. Was it the scowl of an assassin? Now he was barging toward me as if to finish me with his bare hands. Instead, almost knocking the box out of my arms, he wrapped his after-shave-soaked self around me and wept. "I'm sorry, Joseph Galileo Magellan!" he blubbered. "I was a deranged craven asshole. Forgive me!"

I patted him on the back. "Forget it, Malcolm." He wouldn't let me go. His stinking bittersweet aftershave had the coffeehouse spinning. Something was happening with the lights. I held the box tighter. Clover appeared and turned me by the shoulders, a phalanx of guests parted, and there on a picnic table sprawled a huge orange cake in the shape of the pole and platform, with countless candles on top a-blazing.

"I wanted 445 candles," Clover said, "but settled for a hundred. You need any help?"

"Uh, yeah."

They watched me like a wall of mooncalves. "Well, help me," I said. They crowded around and we blew out the bonfire. Smoke billowed up and everybody coughed and laughed, swatting it away. Pete Hoover got a round of "For Joe's a Jolly Good Fellow" going and upon its merciful conclusion, Clover whispered, "I'm drinking 7-Up, by the way."

Solana cut the cake and passed out slices. "Come and get it!" As the throng closed in I looked around for Nate to tell him I was going for a walk. He'd been standing right there beside me. I put my hand on his shoulder. "How you doin', pal?"

"Okay!"

"Kinda crowded."

"Yeah, noisy!"

"Look, I gotta get out of here for a little bit, go for a walk, find my legs, decompress."

He looked stricken. "Are you going back up?"

I laughed. "No! That's finished!"

A hand landed on my shoulder. "Jinx!" We had us a hug.

"Guess what?" said Clover. "Jinx is my sponsor. And, oh—this is Solana." We shook hands. "Solana is the new owner of Clover's Patch," Clover said.

I said, "The new what?"

"We sold her the coffeehouse," Clover said, not even pretending to worry about my reaction. "Her parents are helping her. We did quite well. We can live upstairs until we get another place. Although I think

I've found us a nice duplex in Silverlake, with room for my studio. I'm gonna paint again—with faces! *And*—I might go back to school to get my degree."

"Wow." All this startling news left me utterly and inexplicably calm.

"Officer Merton!" Clover said, looking behind me. In the doorway stood our old friend, that world-weary cop. Was he the only cop in the city? He loitered over and stuck out his hand and we shook, taking each other's measure up close for the first time. He was chubbier and wore a wry little smile that I hadn't discerned from the platform.

"How about some cake?" Clover said.

"Can't stay," Merton said. "So, you're the man on the pole."

"Was."

"Step outside for a sec?"

"Something official?"

Merton led me out where he had double-parked. He leaned back against the car, removed his sunglasses, but didn't look at me. "When all those copycats went up," he said, "I thought about it. Like to get away. Really get away. Damn world. Drive a man nuts." He slapped the car door. "Can't now, but maybe I'll drop in sometime, off duty. Get some tips, case I go up. Not here. Maybe the woods. Maybe Duluth. You know, I talk to Charley. Keeps telling me about Duluth." He put his hand out, I shook it. "Just wanted to say. I get it." He nodded. His radio crackled gibberish. He got in, saluted me, and tore off down Western as if after the devil himself.

122

JOE

I peered back inside. They all seemed fine without me, talking, laughing, drinking, eating my cake. Nate watched me. He smiled and waved, like a little man, one hand up, like an Indian, a Native American, like I wave. We regarded each other a moment, he looked away as if somebody had called him, and I set off up Western.

Everything looked different from the ground. I could have been in a hole, or underground, in a cavern. Wobbling along the sidewalk as if on baby's legs, I looked back over my shoulder. The platform was a deserted island in the air. I might have hacked it out of a jungle, a patch of civilization the wilderness would now recall. I imagined green twigs sprouting from the redwood, rust eating the orange paint, the ink of every impression in my journal fading already in the sun.

I happened to look into the distance at the old woman's red pole. She was hidden, at that ground angle, from my view.

I began my jaunt, surprised that not a soul recognized me. I was again just another member of the lost, anonymous tribe pretending it knew where it was wandering, and it felt good, it felt right, easy, giddy-making. I imagined we were all in some big outdoor play, actors who felt like giggling, but it wasn't in the script so we were holding it in.

My legs jittered as I made my way up Western. My body strained to re-establish its relationship with the planet. I deemed to take it slow, let my senses sip, dab like a dragonfly at the brimming cityscape. I had the sensation of being underwater, ambling along the ocean floor. My eyes felt huge, breath short, face flushed.

To steady myself I focused on a yellow building with balconies and a For Rent sign, a Coke billboard full of grinning blond youths, a shaggy palm tree. The jumbled sights, sounds, and smells of the neighbor-hood rolled over me—bawling horns, foods frying, tangling languages, dreamy self-absorbed faces, structures towering with shadows and

power. Everything was close, big, loud, fast—a doorway altercation between a shouting couple, a long-haired skateboarder coming right at me
and swerving at the last second, a mattress propped askew in an alley, a
middle-aged woman in a short green skirt stopping to let her German
shepherd piss on a sad tree, a siren seeming to come from everywhere
at once, meat, sweat, wine, french fries, exhaust—but I kept moving
through the sensory deluge, meditating on how it wasn't personal. It
was *good* to be out and about, down and about. I was champ now, even
if these roaming souls knew nothing about it. I had done what I set out
to do. It was a victory lap, shaky, overwhelming and anonymous, but
sweet.

At Western and Morada, on the opposite corner, a Chicano boy no
older than Nate hawked bags of oranges. I had an instant, almost manic
craving and started into the street against the light. Horns barked me
back to the curb. There had been no red lights on the platform. I acted
normal, whistling, cradling the box of ashes in its loincloth. The green
light came and I crossed and bought a bag. The oranges were big and
bright, ten for two dollars.

I turned off Western up Carmelina, less busy, more trees, quieter.
After half a block the shops and stores gave way to houses and apartment buildings. I found myself in a large shadow and stopped to eat
an orange. I looked up. I stood under a flagpole and platform. The red
flagpole and platform that Kerridge had put up and that the old woman
had moved onto in his wake.

The great red edifice of the pole and platform was situated on a
corner, twenty feet or so off the street, in the middle of a bright green
lawn, with a small house set way back behind a dark unruly hedge. Eerily,
the ladder, a mighty aluminum contraption with extensions and notches
for fitting over posts on the pole, reached clear to the ground, and the
trapdoor stood open. It wasn't safe, especially for an old woman—anybody could climb up there. Or what if a child tried to take advantage
of such a dangerous opportunity? The sun shone through the trapdoor
and lay a square of light in the middle of the platform's shadow.

The neighborhood was neat and clean. A mailman made his rounds.
A gardener mowed a lawn. Unloading groceries from the trunk of her
car, a woman glanced at me, a stranger standing on the sidewalk.

I waited for the old woman to pass by the trapdoor, to look down
and see me and be surprised, delighted.

"Ma'am?" I called up. Perhaps she was meditating. "Hello? Ma'am?" Did she speak English? "Ma'am?" I started up the ladder, calling every few rungs. It was a cumbersome climb, as I still toted the sack of oranges and the box of ashes. Nearing the trapdoor, my heart slammed hard from the effort and the unknown. "Ma'am?" I croaked. I poked my head through the hole.

There was nobody there. The platform was empty but for a pair of binoculars and a white hat. I had never seen her using binoculars. The hat lay upside-down, flamboyant, tipsy. She must have packed her few accoutrements when I was at the party. She must have waited for me to climb down, then climbed down herself.

"Ma'am?" I called, absurdly, as if she might have been hanging over the side. I wanted her to know I was not up to anything nefarious. I shoved the oranges and ashes away from the trapdoor and lifted myself up. Standing and turning slowly, I took the city in from a fresh and disorienting perspective. It was like reaching into your right pocket with your left hand. Everything was cockeyed, cubist. It was like looking into your living room from a window that hadn't been there before.

I knelt and fingered the hat. The binoculars were the very brand I had. "I wonder why she left them," I said, just to hear a voice. I felt as if she could be listening. I honestly had the thought, before I could dismiss it, that she was there, that she was invisible. I had never spoken with her, never looked her in the eyes, didn't know her name or anything about her, but I missed her.

I stood with the binos and scanned the city. I went right past my orange flagpole, backed up and found it.

I blinked. Somebody was on my platform! My hands shook, I felt woozy, I couldn't hold the focus. They were crouched, their back to me, looking down, as if praying. They looked up.

"Nate! What are you doing! Get off there! Get down!"

My son stood and walked around, sixty feet in the air. He lifted something from the top of the pole: Saint Simeon's stone. He went to the edge. My brains dropped into my stomach. He looked over. Clover, on the sidewalk, jumped up and down and waved her arms. Partygoers spilled out of the coffeehouse. Nate hauled the rope ladder up; Clover made a grab for it, too late. Deftly, he hooked it and closed the trapdoor. He must have watched how I did it. Clover crazily tried to climb the pole itself, then began to bang her head against it until the party people stopped her and shepherded her inside.

Nate sat on the platform, against the pole, his back to me, reading one of my books. I should have raced home and gotten him off there. Instead, I sat, stuck a finger of my free hand in an airhole of the plastic bag of oranges and widened it, pulled one out, pressed it against the platform and began to peel its thick fresh skin with one hand, studying Nate all the while through the old woman's binoculars. I pried an orange wedge loose, popped it in my mouth and bit down. Sweetness flooded me. Nate looked back over his shoulder in my direction. I gave an enthusiastic wave across the divide. I don't know if he saw me, but he turned away.

Something like the missed swat of a hand brushed the back of my head.

I squawked in terror, but it was Curly, landing on the banister. He eyed the orange. I broke off a bit and held it in my palm. He hopped over, grabbed the morsel in his beak, hopped back, and flung it over the edge. He trilled and looked behind me.

The old woman stood in the hole at the top of the ladder, watching me.

"Jesus Christ!" I yelped. I blundered to my feet, fumbled the binos one way and the orange the other, and both flew over the edge.

She climbed up slowly onto the platform. I awkwardly tried to help but she grunted me away. She was old as the hills. She wore a blanket-like coat with big red, blue, and yellow squares. Her arms were inside the thing. She looked over and made a low sound at Curly on the banister; the bird burbled back.

"I thought you were gone," I said.

She picked up the hat and put it on. Her long white hair hung down like tangled light. There was no shyness in her dark eyes. Stouter and darker up close, she looked like an American Indian, maybe part Eskimo, or Peruvian, an ancient Peruvian farmer, far from her green mountain, her arms inside her coat. Maybe she had cocaine in there. Maybe she was on cocaine.

She stared at me, her face wider at the jaw than the temples. I thought she could be a hundred. She'd stood on her head! Climbed that ladder! Her face was plowed with wrinkles. It looked like fresh brown clay.

I looked at the other pole in the distance. Nate was still there, sitting and reading. A few people over there milled on the sidewalk below.

I pointed with my thumb. "My son's up there now."

The old woman nodded and seemed to smile or wince.

I said, "Do you want an orange?"

She brought her arm out, I dug an orange out of the bag, plunked it in her hand, and her arm and the orange disappeared inside the cloak. She irkingly failed to thank me.

She said something in Spanish, low and soft, and gestured with her chin at the cloth-covered box of ashes.

"What?" I said.

She made a nodding sideways gesture with her head as if to signify a flying bird.

"You know what's in there?" She nodded. "How do you know?" She shrugged.

I thought, why not? I knelt and lifted the box from the loincloth, unhooked the latch and popped the lid. I looked over. There was a guy in a baseball cap sitting on some steps a couple houses up poking at a carburetor or something, and playing kids yelling somewhere. There was some wind, but not much.

"You wouldn't be Rose, by any chance, would you?" I said. She stared at me with her head tilted to the side, like Curly, like the bird. "Are you the one who was up there with Shipwreck Blake?"

She gave that same wincing smile and spoke in Spanish, then in English: "You need to know everything."

I watched her. "Is that it?" I moved to the edge, thought a moment, whispered, "So long, Shipwreck. Walter. I love you, my friend. God bless your soul." I heaved the ashes over. They flew up, burst, we watched them, white, like flour. They went out and drifted a while against the blue sky.

123

Joe

Walking back home, down Western, cradling the sack of oranges, minus two, I watched Nate. When he saw me, he scooted to the other side of the platform, his back to me.

I was relieved to find the sidewalk empty under the pole. The trapdoor was shut and the rope ladder hooked at the top. I looked back at the old woman's platform. I couldn't see her. I peered inside the coffeehouse. The party was over.

A little bell rang on the door as I walked in. The handful of folks turned to me. Clover was not among them.

"Congratulations, Mr. Magellan," a young man said.

I thanked him. Recorded fusion jazz played politely in the background. Solana, behind the counter, smiled. The others returned to reading, chatting, eating. I stood there holding my oranges, appreciating the considerate ambience. Clover had done a good job.

Solana said, "She's upstairs."

I thanked her. As I wended my way through the tables I became aware of the oranges. "Hey," I said, holding up the bag. I passed them out. There weren't enough to go around, but a few declined and it came out pretty near perfect.

The door to the apartment was unlocked. I poked my head in. The shades were drawn. Clover was asleep on the couch, on her side, facing me, a green shawl half-covering her. She had on a yellow summer dress. A soft little lamp in the corner gave just enough light to the whole room. Her hands lay tucked between her thighs. She looked like a painting. Whatever had gone on with us while I was up there, I could have stared at her there in that moment until I turned old and fell over.

She stirred. I thought of scooping her up and carrying her to bed—maybe she was waiting for just that—but if not it could be a mess, get everything off to a terrible start.

I sat on the floor beside her. I looked at her, her hair, her face, her lips, her neck. I touched the back of a finger to her cheek. She brushed at it and scratched there, then opened her eyes.

"Hi," she said, as if I'd never been gone. She puckered and I leaned in and gave her a kiss, brief, gentle, perfect. Everything was perfect so far. She said, "How was the walk?"

"Good." It wasn't the time to bring up the old woman. It wasn't the time to bring up anything.

"Guess what," she said.

"I know. I had nothing to do with it."

She eyed me. "Please get him down. Then come back."

The boy let the phone ring many rings. "Hello?"

"Get down. Now."

"Okay. I can't stay up just like an hour?"

"What are you doing?"

"Nothing. Thinking about life."

"I saw you reading."

"No."

"One of the books up there."

"Yeah. Yeah."

He was lying. Why would he lie? My journal. "Did you find a big black and white notebook?"

"Uh-uh."

Everything was in there. Everything. "Nate, tell me you haven't been reading it."

"It was pretty personal, so I didn't read very much of it."

What if I, at eleven, had read such a journal written by my father, his whole array of inner workings laid out defenseless before my eyes? I wished I had, although I was a man of thirty-six wishing it. Was it better to know too much than not enough? There was no perfect amount. It was always either too much or not enough.

"Sorry, Dad."

"Well, whatever it was, you can't unread it. We ought to probably talk about it, at some point. I would prefer, strongly, that you don't read anymore."

"I won't. I promise."

"You got one hour."

"Okay. Thanks."

"You're welcome."

"Dad?"

"Yeah?"

"What if I didn't climb down?"

"What if you what?"

"How would you come get me?"

"I wouldn't come get you. But there's a crazy woman down here, and I'm pretty sure she would be out looking for a box of dynamite."

"Oh, okay."

"You got your watch on?"

"I like it up here, Dad."

"One hour, pal."

৯

ACKNOWLEDGMENTS

Thanks from my heart to all those who helped me with *Oranges for Magellan*—my dear first reader and always encouraging wife, Paris; Emily Uhry, the first stranger to connect with Joe and Clover; Howard Cole, a friend who read and appreciated an early (and much longer!) version of the book; my friends at the late great ABNA; Bill W. and my Old Higher Power; to my blessed first blurbers, Joanna Higgins, Jim Nichols, Brendan McKennedy, and Olivia Dresher; to my sisters Barbara, Jeanne, and Kathy, and my mother and father, who together gave me the foundation to love life and words and to think for myself; and thanks especially to Jaynie Royal and Pam Van Dyk at Regal House. Thank you all.